OUTMOVE

OUTMOVE

Brandt Legg

LAUGHING RAIN

Outmove (Book Three of the Inner Movement)
Published in the United States of America by Laughing Rain

Cataloging-in-Publication data for this book is available from the Library of Congress.
ISBN-13: 978-1-935070-22-1
ISBN-10: 1-935070-22-3

Original poems attributed to Lihn written by Roanne Lewis
Cover designed by: Stephanie Parcus
Title page illustration by: Amber Mayes
Original song attributed to Flannery written by Roanne Lewis

BrandtLegg.com

For Teakki and Ro

Time's a funny thing, I thought, as I woke Amber and Linh. In the year-and-a-half since Rose returned with Clastier, the world had become a distorted, tortured version of the one where I'd grown up. Hiding and learning were all we ever seemed to do and I was tired of both.

We rushed into the portal. Omnia's agents couldn't be far, the heat warning had my body temperature soaring. Our habit of sleeping within sight of a portal, for a fast escape, had kept us alive this long, but didn't necessarily provide protection. Omnia Agents could pursue us inside and often had.

"Aunt Rose was supposed to meet us today," Linh said. "I guess we'll catch up with her in Yellowstone." We never stayed in the same place for more than a night or two.

It had been a long time since we found out that Aunt Rose's death, betrayal, and cooperation with Lightyear had all been staged, and yet it still bothered me. Shockingly, Rose was also a mystic, a scholarly one at that. Her methods, unconventional even by the standards of the whacked-out crew of ten mystics I'd been learning from, commanded respect among the others. Yangchen and Rose had manipulated portals in a way still unclear in order to bring Clastier into our current lifetime. He and I shared a soul but we were very different. His wisdom and selflessness had become my greatest inspiration. Circumstances kept us apart most of the time, but our chance would come. They had brought him back, not to help me defeat Omnia, but to prepare me for the time after. As it turned out, that proved to be a frivolously optimistic plan.

"If we make it to Yellowstone," I said, "this portal goes to Mt. Shasta and you know that's a military base now." In the twenty-one months since we discovered Kyle's body at the Outin lodge, the Movement had grown into a worldwide revolution. And although I was the symbolic leader, it had cost more than I could tally. The mall attack, which preceded Kyle's brutal murder, received all the attention, but it was my mom's death that nearly ended the Movement. Inner Force, or IF, the violent faction within the Movement, was responsible for her killing, but no one could find them . . . or stop them.

"IF is just escalating things," Amber said. "Why can't they see that their violence is strengthening Omnia, not weakening them?"

Linh shot Amber a look I wasn't supposed to see. For months after IF murdered my mother, I shut down and although there were others who ran the day-to-day affairs, the Movement seemed to lose its impetus because of my lack of involvement.

Mom and I had failed each other in many tragic ways. My difficulty in handling the guilt made me useless to the Movement until she twice appeared in my dreams and brought me back from a desperate place.

In both dreams I wore a silver shirt, shiny and heavy. My pants were a glowing blue liquid. Mom was in a dress woven from living flowers of every color. She handed me a plate of cake and ice cream. Each bite contained scenes from my childhood. In them I could see that she always knew of my destiny, and that of my brother, Dustin. The knowledge wasn't conscious. It came from a soul level and she denied it for the same reason we all do – fear. But in each bite of the sweet desserts, for which she was famous, I tasted love and forgiveness.

Prior to her murder, I naively thought the Movement was on the verge of victory. Lightyear had been publicly humiliated, its evil leader, Luther Storch, silenced by an assassin. Even Linh's parents and Amber's sister were released, as public opinion momentarily swung away from the Department of Homeland Security when their Stalinist tactics were revealed. And most importantly, Linh and Amber remained alive.

We'd been regrouping after the raids had shut down three-quarters of the Movement's centers, and we had discovered a new way to avoid the remote viewers. Rose gave the Movement great advantages with her knowledge of the inner workings of Lightyear. Clastier's papers were being readied for mass distribution . . . it seemed we were so close. But that was before the sleeping tiger awoke. Lightyear had just been a tiny division in an organization old with power, deep with connections and stunning in its coldness and greed - Omnia. They had such a grip on the world that the Inner Movement's dreams of change seemed to be a mere whisper in a hurricane.

"IF has to be stopped or the Movement will become just another casualty of this crazy war," I said. They'd both heard it before. "Our powers have expanded, the Movement is huge, but at the same time, Omnia's strength is out of control."

"You need to be leading the Movement," Amber said, as we pushed farther into the portal, unsure where it would take us. "And not just as a figurehead."

"Spencer and Yangchen think I'm still too young and inexperienced to assume leadership," I replied.

"They're just waiting for you. You have to know that you've grown beyond those limitations," Linh said. "Then you will lead."

No one was actually stopping me from making decisions. They usually consulted or at least informed me. Still, that didn't change the fact that I was king, bishop, knight and pawn in a multi-dimensional chess game that would decide the fate of humanity. The battles were played out in both the physical and non-physical planes across a grid of past, present and future.

ooooo

Inside the portal, the heat warning would usually subside, but it hadn't. We'd come to the camp a different way. Yangchen had told us on the astral that this portal led to Shasta.

"We've been in here a long time," Amber said.

My temperature rose higher. "Something's wrong!"

2

Just ahead, six Omnia agents emerged from the portal's distant swirl. We spun around, retraced our steps and tumbled out of the portal. Linh and I grabbed Amber's arms since she still couldn't Skyclimb. We reached the treetops and propelled ourselves toward the portal we'd come from the day before. The laser bullets shattered branches and leaves below.

Omnia's advanced weapons cut lines through the trees ahead and to our south. They didn't know our exact location, but we were known to travel in the trees. Now that they were out of the portal they could obtain their location from GPS and call in the helicopters. The black gunships haunted me in real life and even more in my nightmares.

I reached Spencer on the astral to warn him that we were being pursued and our only escape was the portal that led straight to where he, Yangchen, and several others were hiding. Spencer, who had collapsed after Rose and Clastier showed up in Taos, was doing better now.

That same day, the first of a series of horrific school shootings had taken place - hundreds of kids and teachers died - and what came to be known as "the great division" had begun. After the child massacres, each increasingly worse than the one before, mall attacks happened on each coast, and the U.S. quickly became more divided than at any time since the American Civil War. The "conservatives versus liberals" drama exploded off cable news and talk radio into violent demonstrations. In the beginning the argument concerned only gun control, but soon, as the rhetoric and rage ratcheted up, abortion, immigration, racism, economic reform, housing and even food labeling became battlegrounds. Demonstrators clashed, violence increased, and martial law was declared for a six-day period. National Guard troops aided by elite Department of Homeland Security units were deployed to more than seventy cities. Troops remained permanently in Washington, D.C., New York City, Los Angeles, Chicago, Miami, Houston and San Francisco enforcing curfews, quelling demonstrations and manning military checkpoints.

"Nate!" Amber screamed above a vibrating roar, as the first two choppers came into sight. We dropped into the canopy, making us easier to spot from the ground. We were still too far from the portal.

"Nate," Spencer said on the astral, "Yangchen is coming."

"It's too dangerous," I said.

"That's why she's coming. We can see it. More than a hundred agents just poured out of the portal from Shasta."

The trees behind us exploded as one of the gunships fired large caliber rounds into them.

"Drop thirty feet, there's an opening you can Skyclimb through for almost two hundred yards. Do it now!" Spencer said, as he continued to guide us through a torrent of bullets and missiles. "There's six more choppers, fifty more agents. They know it's you."

Terrifying flames engulfed a large section of forest. Missiles and lasers hit closer every second. "We're not going to make it!" Linh yelled.

Then, suddenly it stopped. Chips of wood, flying branches, bullets and even smoke suspended as if the video we were in had just been paused. Yangchen appeared.

"Hurry!"

We followed her Skyclimbing back above the trees and saw the helicopters frozen in midair. It all started again as we slipped into the portal.

"How did you do that?" Amber asked before I could.

"There is a vortex between the two portals; it's just a

matter of aligning an energy core to connect them and it's possible to stop time for a few moments," she said wearily.

"But what about us? Why didn't we stop?" Linh asked.

"That's the tricky part, isn't it?" Yangchen said. "We'll talk about it later."

ooooo

A van picked us up on the other side of the portal. As we sped down the highway on the way to our next "safe" house, I reflected on the irony of what we'd just escaped. All guns had been banned in the U.S. except in certain rural areas where hunting rifles were allowed, effectively disarming the population, leaving little hope of resistance. For those who didn't like it, it didn't matter – free speech, free press, and the right to assemble were severely limited. Across the country, surveillance drones regularly crisscrossed the sky. Arrests occurred constantly but it was difficult to say just how many were incarcerated since reporting on them was also a crime.

Booker, the Movement's billionaire benefactor, said, "Due process needs a new name because it is no longer either." More shocking than all the restrictions were how rapidly they occurred and how many citizens supported them. By the time they realized the cost it was too late. We'd become a dystopian society. Booker was still wealthy and powerful but many of his U.S. assets had been seized. Fortunately, he'd been long preparing for these times and a large portion of his holdings were untraceable or held in foreign nations.

During all the time we'd been on the move, both the IM and IF factions of the Movement continued to grow. The great division had unintended consequences for Omnia. It had driven tens of thousands of diverse people into the Movement and because Omnia also led an international crackdown, resistance was building globally. The countries most accustomed to freedom, the U.S., Australia, Canada and Great Britain, had the best-organized undergrounds. But Omnia had centuries of experience using fear tactics to pit people against one another. They were expert at creating distractions and stopping unrest with economic cycles and subduing uprisings with wars. But as Spencer was so fond of saying, "This is a different kind of revolution."

3

Our new "home" for a few days was a remote property in Colorado that Booker had recently acquired.

Amber and I woke early and went for a walk. She held my hand as we walked the high trail above the river. "You seem distant this morning." She was twenty now, I almost nineteen.

"We let Fitts hunt me and then it was Storch . . . hell, even the Catholic Church sent a posse after me during my life as Clastier. People have been coming for the Jadeo for centuries. No more." I turned to face her. "Starting today, I'm going on the offensive. I'm going to find the man running Omnia and end this."

"How do you end it?"

"By winning."

Amber let go of my hand as Linh ran toward us. "Spencer and Yangchen are waiting for us. They can't stay much longer." Although the girls and I, at our insistence, remained together, Booker, Rose, Clastier, the mystics and other Movement hierarchy all traveled separately. We would go weeks at a time without seeing them.

When we reached the yurts, Yangchen and Spencer looked distraught. Both mystics had become our family over the past two years. They were often opposed to each other, but their knowledge was unrivaled by all but the elusive Dark Mystic, whom I'd been trying to find since learning of his existence. Yangchen had once promised to help me, but both she and

Spencer agreed that now was not the time. One day my knowledge would surpass theirs and I would seek him on my own.

"You're worried," I said to Spencer.

"Yes. It's risky to go on the attack against Omnia." Spencer almost died the day I was killed at Outin. And when depression and gloom closed in on me, he suffered too. It had taken him more than a year to recover physically from what those in the Movement called "the Outin incident." We were the two most important people in the Movement, but the incident in which we almost died resulted in one of our greatest coups. The one hundred and four soldiers who had witnessed my resurrection became ardent supporters of IM and proved invaluable as the Movement worked to infiltrate the military industrial complex that supported Omnia.

"You know my plan? But I just decided. Of course you know," I said.

"This day has been a long time coming. We've debated it many times in the parallels." The parallels were the confusing, colliding, coexisting half-dimensions all around us.

"It's a past future thing, too," Yangchen added. Between Outin and various portals used during the past couple of years, occasionally things happened more than once and at times in reverse order; still others never occurred at all. It was difficult to keep it all straight, until I let go of my preconceived notions of . . . well, just about everything. Our physical world is extremely limited.

"Great. If we've had this conversation before, then you must know all my arguments and we don't need to waste time discussing it." I smiled.

"Much has changed. We're here in the now. Tell us your thoughts, your plan," Spencer said.

"What are we even talking about?" Linh asked.

"I want to hunt down the leader of Omnia and stop him by all reasonable peaceful means," I said, smiling at Yangchen. Before we left Taos, well over a year ago, Yangchen had won the violence-non-violence debate. Spencer was resigned to using soul powers peacefully and letting love guide our strategy. Still, I expected him to embrace my new plan to pursue rather than run. It was closer to his nature. The U.S. was heavily involved in three wars and, covertly, in dozens of other conflicts. Blood and brutality needed no more support.

"How do you know Omnia's leader is a man?" Linh asked.

"No woman could be that cruel. Not to sound sexist, but how many wars have been started by women, how many mass murderers were women?"

"Let's stick to the matter at hand," Spencer said.

"We're already winning," Yangchen began. "Omnia wants two things above all else. Nate dead and the Jadeo. As long as Nate lives and the Jadeo remains in his hands, Omnia cannot ultimately succeed."

"Define succeed," Spencer said. "How much wealth and power determines success, if –"

Yangchen cut him off. "Spencer, you know what I mean. Omnia may appear to have won, but not really, as long as the people are able to see that these material things hold no real power."

"There's a long way to go before people really believe that we can reach our souls through love and reclaim our power," I said.

"Nate, once they see what you are capable of, they will believe. That's why every generation has seven who can so easily tap their soul powers. It gives everyone a chance to remember who they *really* are," Yangchen said.

"But then why do the seven always land in mental institutions, become drug addicts, alcoholics . . . or wind up getting killed?" Linh asked. "And do you know how many people don't even believe the soul exists? We haven't been able to figure out a way to get Baca, Kirby and Amparo released and they're mystics."

"Linh, I know it's been a long difficult time in hiding," Spencer began. "But we are making progress. The Movement is growing in numbers and influence. We will soon –"

"We simply have to find and contain Inner Force," Yangchen interrupted. "They threaten all that we have worked for."

"I don't understand how you can't stop IF with all the powers at your disposal." Amber eyed Spencer suspiciously.

"Amber, it's complicated," I said.

"Now you sound just like Spencer." I could hear her frustration. Every time the Movement seemed to make progress, IF members would resist a raid or attempt to interfere with Omnia-sponsored CIA operations. And since IF was using soul powers to fight back, the denials from the Movement as to IM involvement were used to further discredit us.

"Our non-violence stance makes it very difficult to rescue the missing mystics," Spencer said. "We can't just send a band of mercenaries to break them out. And, Amber, you know we don't even have their present location. The two times we've managed to find out where they were being held, our attempts were met by Omnia forces nearly capturing Nate and me."

"They must be freed," Yangchen said.

"Damn it, they will," Spencer retorted.

Before I could respond, a sudden Outview pulled me in and I was gone. They'd grown in both length and frequency since the Outin days. Omnia was no longer combating us just in the present, and with the blurring of times it was hard to know if they ever had limited themselves to a modern fight.

I looked up and saw him, a familiar yet unknown adversary.

4

I was no longer the fifteen- or sixteen-year-old terrorized by Outviews. I could navigate my way inside one as if I was running around my old hometown. The couple of years since the first Outviews had brought extraordinary new abilities and given me a glimpse of powers so great that I finally understood why Omnia might fear me. There he was, the one I called Dunaway, a man, although the last two times "he" was female. He knew I recognized him and smiled at my presence as if he'd been waiting for a long time.

"Whatever I would say to you right now would sound rather clichéd. So instead, I'll simply ask a question; do you have full-forward-memory?" Dunaway asked. We were seated across from each other at a small table in the corner of a drab coffee house. I glanced away from his bearded face trying to gather my thoughts, trying to answer his question . . . and mine. Adjusting to Outviews was easier than it used to be, but not instant. Still I could quickly pinpoint dates and facts from the life I was visiting.

It was snowing outside. We were in pre-revolutionary Moscow, January 1917. Yes. I realized there was full-forward-memory but not beyond memory. That is to say I could recall all my lifetimes up to and including Nate's but not lifetimes beyond Nate's.

I nodded. "You don't belong here."

He shrugged. Dunaway was a "walkin," meaning this was not his incarnation; his soul had simply occupied another body. This was an impressive feat and something I was unable to do. I was not even sure if the soul that normally occupied the body I was staring at was aware of what Dunaway had done or needed to give permission, or was even still active in this life. I'd ask Yangchen when I got back, if I got back . . . there was always a doubt about where I would land next as the Outviews had become massive and complex compared to my earlier episodes.

"Are you going to kill me?" I asked calmly, while surveying the room. Dunaway had caused my death in at least five earlier lifetimes and I believed there was a strong possibility that he was either the person who ran Omnia or someone who worked for them.

"Perhaps."

"Why?"

"You are a great problem," he whined.

"Will ending my life in this incarnation make me less of a problem?"

"I do not know."

"Then maybe I should kill you," I said, glaring.

Dunaway smiled at my suggestion, his teeth stained from tobacco and tea. "I thought you had pledged to use only peace for your cause."

"I won't make that pledge for a hundred years."

"Yes, but your forward-memory –"

"Shut up, tell me who you are!" Two old men looked up from their plates and stared.

"You wouldn't believe me if I told you, old friend."

"You are no friend of mine."

"Victor, or should I call you Nate? You must know by now that there is no difference between friends and enemies. They each teach different things but in the end you learn the same."

The front door burst open, a bullet hit Dunaway, his face covered in blood as he collapsed onto the table, dead. The man who fired the shot grabbed me. "We must go, Victor, now!"

I recognized Dustin, his soul.

"He would have killed you." Dustin had saved my life. His grim expression transformed into a smile. "It works both ways, brother."

"What difference would it make if he'd succeeded? I'd still come back as Nate. Dunaway has done this before."

"Yes, you'd come back as Nate but it would be an entirely different world you'd come back to, had you died here today." His breath hung in the icy air.

This was my first physical encounter with Dustin since I found out he shared a soul with Luther Storch, the head of Lightyear. Of course the husky Russian who'd just saved me wasn't really Dustin, but it was his soul. We darted down back alleys and narrow streets, fighting against the blowing snow. Dustin pointed to a door across the street. "That one. Four quick raps."

"Aren't you coming?"

"I'm late for a meeting. You know the Bolshevik revolution comes soon?"

"Yes . . . always revolutions."

"Omnia is involved in this one, too." He embraced me quickly, firmly. "Hurry, go now." He pushed me and jogged into the frigid wind.

"Which side is Omnia on?" I yelled.

He laughed. "What do you think? Both!"

ooooo

The door opened. An old woman, her bright white hair pulled back severely, stared at me. I feared she might turn me back out into the storm.

"Come, Dosen, come," she said in a voice stronger than her frail frame.

"I am not Dosen," I said, as the warmth of the house made me shiver.

"Not yet." She winked. "But you will be . . . many lifetimes from now."

"Good. Then I can stay? I like your fireplace."

"Oh, Dosen, I could not make you go. I've been waiting a very long time." She stood on her toes and pulled off my hat while brushing the snow from my shoulders. "Do you have news of Clastier?"

"Yes." The question should have surprised me but it didn't. "I do. But who are you? What am I doing here?"

She smiled. "Come, sit. Nicholas will bring tea." Her wrinkled hand absently traced my face. "You know me, but, of course, this is before all of that. I am Tesa."

"It's strange being in an Outview and not recognizing someone."

"We have met many times but they are all in lives beyond your time as Nate."

"Then the world survives my lifetime." I exhaled. "Maybe I didn't mess things up too badly."

She laughed but quickly turned serious. "It depends, Dosen; that is why I am meeting you here this day. In your life as Nate there is the greatest crisis. You know this." Nicholas, a man almost as old as Tesa, set down a tray of tea between us. "Dosen, a crisis brings danger but also opportunity. Yet opportunity can be quite treacherous." Her thumbs were rubbing the inside of her fingers. "Now tell me of Clastier."

"He is in my time."

"Yes, I know this, but has he been freed."

"From whom?" A wave of panic went through me.

"Dosen, would you be a gentleman and pour the tea?"

"Oh, yes, of course." It wasn't until much later that I realized she had changed the subject.

"There is much we can do. There is some we cannot." She moved her hands in the air six inches from my face. "Do you see?" A scene opened, as if a frameless, twenty-inch television had been turned on.

"You're a mystic."

"Quite so," she squinted. " Now back to the view."

"It's Hibbs," I said.

"It's you."

"I know, I mean me as Hibbs."

"We're looking at 1912. There were ten people alive who could stop Omnia. Hibbs was one of them."

"With the roll of documents from his safe?"

She nodded.

"Who were the others?" I asked.

"I'll give you a list. Hibbs knows them all. But Omnia will murder seven of them along with 1500 others."

"The Titanic?" I asked, remembering my history. "You're not saying Omnia sank the Titanic in order to silence its critics?"

"Yes. Nine of the ten were on board. Two narrowly escaped but were killed three years later."

"But the Titanic hit an iceberg. So they . . ." I stuttered.

"Do you know how simple it is to move ice in water?"

I stared in disbelief.

"As with all things of this nature, when there is a need, a convenient event is found. There were reasons the Titanic needed to sink which had nothing to do with its passengers. But what a neat and tidy package for J.P. Morgan. He owned the ship, and was able to get nearly all of his opponents on board."

"They were opposing the creation of the Federal Reserve?"

"Yes." She smiled, impressed, as I put the pieces together. "Omnia's most powerful tool. And the creation of the federal income tax, and the coming war in Europe. All these things made Morgan and the other members of Omnia astonishingly wealthy, and more than that, they insured Omnia's absolute power for the next hundred years."

"And we can stop it?"

"You can try, Dosen . . . but they will attempt to thwart you with their enormous resources. Like you, Omnia has people who understand the flexibility of time and they have learned to communicate across lifetimes."

"Let me see the list of Omnia's opponents."

"Hibbs knows them all. Can you recall them?"

I thought hard, as if remembering playmates from kindergarten. Then, all at once, my lifetime as Hibbs came through. "William Thomas Stead, John Jacob Astor, Alfred Vanderbilt, Benjamin Guggenheim, Archibald Butt, Francis Millet, Oliver Smith, Harry Widener, and my/Hibbs' business partner, Clarence Moore."

"These were extremely prominent people they needed out

of the way. Only something catastrophic with many deaths would cover up their deed." She picked up her cup of tea. "This is how they have always done things."

"But how did they get everyone to sail on the ship?"

"Chance and a variety of methods were used to make certain all would be on board. It was the maiden voyage of the most magnificent ship ever built. You as Hibbs, with your knowledge of the scheme, could not be swayed, so they planned to deal with you later."

"It's unbelievable."

"It shouldn't be. Morgan's associate, Henry Clay Frick, as well as dozens of other 'connected parties' cancelled their passages at the last moment."

"They'd been warned?" My mouth went dry.

"Yes, Morgan himself failed to board even though he had reserved the finest stateroom and had assured many he'd be along. Are you all right, Dosen?"

"I'm just stunned that one of history's great disasters was pre-planned."

"Are you? Dear Dosen, you should have learned by now that things are seldom as they appear. History is always a fictionalized version of the truth. How can it be otherwise unless you are there?"

"But how many other world events were staged to manipulate people?"

"Whenever the result of a major incident is war, you can be sure it was manufactured. This is *always* the case. It's the events like the Titanic that are more difficult to trace but it's about the money. War is always about money . . . issues cited as the causes are only excuses used by the profiteers. This is why only peace can lead to the truth. It's impossible for people to return to their souls through war."

Tesa could not give me much instruction, only that I must make every effort to convince these men not to travel on the Titanic. Obviously, I couldn't just telegraph these important people and tell them I had knowledge from the future that the 'unsinkable' ship was going to sink. The only one who was more than a business associate was Clarence and that was a complicated relationship. Clarence was going to England to purchase fifty pairs of foxhounds for the Loudon Hunt not far from my/Hibbs' estate. I didn't approve of fox hunting and we'd had several arguments over it. We were also in disagreement over the use of some property we owned together for the same reason. But the real difficulty between us came because his wife, who was a close confidant of my wife, had recently discovered I had a mistress. She had pressured him to persuade me to end the affair. I would not. Still, my plan was to be somewhat straight with him.

My power to enter a lifetime through Outviews didn't always work but this time it was perfect. As Hibbs, I became aware of Nate and my forward-memory when waking from an Outview dream. The initial confusion Hibbs felt quickly turned to a satisfied smile. "I knew it," Hibbs whispered.

His personality was fascinated with the experiences and knowledge of our soul and he cancelled his meetings for the day to think about them. Those hours were also used to devise a plan for stopping the Omnia opponents from sailing on the

Titanic. There wasn't much time; although I had arrived seven weeks before the Titanic would depart Southampton, all the opponents were readying to leave for Europe on the trips that would allow them to return on the ill-fated liner. Once they were abroad the opportunity for easy conversation would be gone. I started with my partner.

"Clarence, this may be difficult for you to believe but I have it on good authority that there's a plot afoot to sink the Titanic. I beg you to return on another ship."

"Good God, man, is this one of your jokes? I hardly -"

"No, Clarence, I am certain of this information and that the conspirators will succeed."

"Where is your proof? You must take it to the authorities."

"I have no concrete evidence to present. Only my word. You know me to be an honorable man."

He raised his eyebrows and regarded me with fresh skepticism. "Billy, I'm sure I would have to ask your wife about that."

"You'll not survive the journey. You must listen to me."

"I don't know what this is about. How could such a thing be planned and undertaken in secret and to what end? Billy, who in the world would want to sink such a magnificent ship?"

"It's Morgan and his cronies. Nine of the ten most influential opponents to the creation of the central bank and the federal income tax will be on board."

"This is preposterous. Morgan is certainly an egomaniacal ass but a mass murderer? No one would kill so many people over profits."

"Don't be naïve, Clarence. Death for profits is a daily occurrence for companies. And this is not just about the central bank or taxes. They mean to entangle us in the coming war in Europe. Death for profits, that's all war is."

"There may never be a war in Europe and even if it comes, America wouldn't join in. Damn it, Billy, your politics have clouded your good sense."

"What harm would it be to take another ship?"

"The Titanic is the best."

"You're wrong."

"It is you who are wrong. Excuse me, I'll take my leave from you now."

Clarence avoided me until the day he left for England, when he dropped by my office. "No hard feelings, Billy, we'll have drinks when I return and talk more about stopping these disastrous fiscal policies. Oh, and by the way, J.P. Morgan, himself will be sailing on the Titanic."

"He'll never board that ship, it'll never make it to New York, and Clarence, if you get on the Titanic, you'll die in the icy waters of the North Atlantic."

"Damn you, Billy, and your curses. That's an awful way to send a friend off." He slammed my door and I never saw him again.

I tried less direct approaches with the others, going so far as to invent business deals, land speculations and schemes that would have cost me substantial sums. Changing history is possible but very difficult and I was not experienced enough for the task. Vanderbilt and Milton Hershey, a personal friend, listened.

There was a chance a few others might not be on the Titanic but mostly my efforts were in vain.

On the evening after the last opponent left for Europe, I poured myself a drink and reflected upon what had been lost. My mistress joined me.

"Nate, you did all you could."

"You have forward-memory?"

"Yes." She was speaking to me as Spencer.

"Why would the Movement risk so much on my abilities?"

"We aren't relying solely on your abilities. There have been hundreds of attempts to change 1912. We'll continue to attack these events and maybe something you did will help. But you have to remember that Omnia has people in 1912 too."

"It's a damn complicated mess," I said, setting my drink down hard causing an ice cube to escape my glass and slide across the table. "The horrendous death and terror that ice will soon inflict, and I have failed to stop it."

Spencer/Hibbs' mistress nodded.

6

I returned from the Outview into a far stranger world than I'd left. Linh was lying next to me trying to keep me warm as I shook uncontrollably.

"Where's Amber?" I sensed something was wrong.

"She left . . . with Yangchen."

"Why? Where?"

Spencer entered. "You've been busy."

"Why would she leave while I was out?"

"She had an Outview at the same time but came through much sooner than you –"

Spencer interrupted Linh. "Yangchen and I were arguing. She is convinced I know who the members of IF are."

"Do you?"

"Do you need to ask?"

I studied him for a moment. "No."

"Amber wouldn't say what she saw in the Outview but when Yangchen decided to leave, Amber went with her," Linh said.

"Did she say anything?"

"She said to tell you she'd see you on the astral and . . . maybe around campus," Linh said, "whatever that means."

"Where did they go?"

"I don't know. Just like us, they aren't traceable."

"You were out for two days," Linh said. "Where were you?"

"Trying to change history." I looked at Spencer. He shook

his head. "Did I do any good at all?"

"It was a long shot to begin with."

"I'll try again."

"Maybe later. Right now we have to play the hand we've been dealt."

"You went back into other incarnations, didn't you?" I asked.

"Both sides have used every available method to work that period from 1912 to 1915. It was the turning point; it created the modern world. Yes, I've cycled through many incarnations of that time."

"Nate, could you include me?" Linh asked.

"The Titanic sank."

"I know."

"I tried to stop people from getting on it. I did save Vanderbilt and Smith."

"They got Vanderbilt a few years later. He died when Omnia had the Lusitania sunk."

"That's why the United States got into World War I, and you're saying Omnia was responsible?" Linh asked.

"One way or another, Omnia has started every war for more than a hundred years."

"What about Smith?"

"He was dead within weeks . . . killed at his home when he allegedly walked in on burglars. The assailants were never found."

"Damn. So only Hibbs survived?"

Spencer nodded.

"How?" Linh asked.

"The documents," I said. "The ones I found in his safe."

Spencer nodded again.

"But why didn't he go public with them?" Linh asked.

"Because his mistress stopped him," I said, staring at Spencer who had been Hibbs' mistress in that incarnation. "Why?"

"It would not have altered the overall history. Only yours."

"Meaning?"

"You would not have been one of this generation's seven.

If Hibbs had died prior to 1937 your incarnation patterns would have shifted enough to eliminate Nate's entire existence."

Linh gasped.

"And you're sure if Hibbs had gone public, Omnia would have survived?" I asked.

"Hibbs would have been killed. The documents insured he was left alone but he was constantly watched and they were ready to pounce at any time. Without the big three we lost on the Titanic, Major Butts, Astor and Guggenheim, Hibbs didn't have enough to stop Omnia. He could have only embarrassed them like we did with the Lightyear-Storch Roosevelt Island video release."

"So how are we going to stop them now?"

"Our numbers have grown, our soul powers increased a thousand fold, and we are not constrained by working within Outviews."

"Then why did I go back?"

"This wasn't so much about winning, it was our last chance to prevent the suffering of the last hundred years. There have been more than a hundred wars resulting in a hundred and fifty million deaths," Spencer said. "When Luther Storch told you that he believed people were expendable, he was quoting from Omnia's manifesto."

"This can't go on, Spencer. We have to wake people up."

"I know."

"What do we do?" Linh asked.

"We can't do it alone," he said.

"The Old Man of the Lake told me I would meet fifteen mystics. I've met eleven so far, counting Tesa when I was in Russia. I need the knowledge of the other four, don't I?"

"Yes."

"And one of them is the Dark Mystic, right?"

Spencer nodded.

"Where is he?"

"I don't know."

"Let's go find him," Linh said.

"I cannot go with you," Spencer said. "We don't get

along."

"How will we find him?"

"He'll find you when you're ready."

"I'm ready."

"You don't get to decide."

"I've got the Jadeo. Wouldn't he want it?"

"The Dark Mystic is the only person on this planet who wouldn't want the Jadeo . . . he doesn't need it."

"Isn't it time you tell me what the Jadeo is?" Linh asked.

Spencer looked at me.

"Not yet," I answered.

"I think I deserve to know what we're risking our lives for, what Kyle died for." Linh's eyes filled with tears but her face remained hard.

"Knowing what the Jadeo is puts you in too much danger."

"More danger than I'm already in now? How dare you!"

I looked at Spencer. He shook his head. "Let's take a walk," I said to Linh.

"Nate, it's not a good idea," Spencer said firmly.

"You're probably right, but if I can't trust Linh, I'd rather not live in this world."

"It's not about trust. It's for her protection."

"You mean the Jadeo's protection," I said harshly. "Besides, she knows I have it and Omnia already has her on their kill list. What difference would it make if she actually understands what this is all about?"

"We took an oath."

"A thousand years ago."

"We're still bound," his voice trembled.

Linh grabbed my hand. "Forget it. I don't want you to break an oath."

"I have an oath to you, too."

"What is that oath?" she asked.

I looked at her and back at Spencer.

"Nate, please," Spencer began. "The wisest course is seldom the easiest and rarely the one our emotions would choose."

Linh wept for several minutes after I told her what the Jadeo was.

"I'm sorry," she finally said. "I never imagined that's what it was. How could I even dream such a thing existed?"

"I know."

"What do we do? Omnia must never –"

"The original nine-entrusted to protect the Jadeo all came back for this lifetime. This is no coincidence. If the Movement is successful then the Jadeo will be opened and we'll enter the light of the post-Jadeo era. If we lose the Jadeo or the Movement collapses, we will continue to exist in darkness."

"But you said one of the nine entrusted is a traitor."

"Lifetime after lifetime we have fought these battles but we will find him this time."

"How can you be so sure?"

"I feel it."

ooooo

Nothing seemed right without Amber but there was little I could do. We were preparing to leave; we moved so often that arriving and leaving were more natural than actually staying at a place. Our destinations were always secluded spots, as far removed from civilization as possible – open mesas, mountaintops, dense forests, remote islands – so our next stop,

Prague, was exciting. I'd been to many populated areas during the eighteen months that Linh called our "lost time" but only in Outviews, never as Nate. And Linh, now almost eighteen, had hardly seen more than a handful of people in all that time.

"Your decision to go on the offensive against Omnia, your agreement to non-violence and Yangchen's accusations of my knowledge of IF have all directly caused the need for us to travel to Prague," Spencer said, as we lifted off in one of Booker's jets from an airfield almost too primitive for modern aircraft. We were in South America so the flight would be long – fifteen hours counting a refueling stop.

"Prague is the believed headquarters of IF leaders," Spencer explained. "We need to find them, meet and come to some kind of arrangement. To succeed against Omnia, there can be no division in the Movement."

"But aren't there dozens of factions?" Linh asked.

"Yes, but they differ only on what the 'real' spiritual truths are . . . and in the end, there is really no difference among spiritual truths, there is only what is. IF is the single faction within IM that believes the ends justify the means."

"Why will IF listen to us?"

"Because you are one of the seven, your awakened powers have no equal."

"Do you mean I should physically restrain them?"

"I think you and I will be able to reason with them."

"If you find them," Linh added.

"I think that will be possible once Nate makes another Outview journey," Spencer said.

"Spencer, you told us in Taos that in order to participate in an Outview rather than just observe it, a time transcendence portal was required. How is Nate doing this?"

"Nate can answer better than I."

"Ever since my death in Outin, whenever I've fallen into an Outview, I see these holographic seams around the edges of the scene I'm viewing. Recently, I pulled one open and suddenly I was participating in the Outview-life but with full memory of Nate and all my lives before Nate."

"Wow. So instead of just watching, you could do stuff?"

"Yes. I've done it in the last three Outviews." As I was explaining this to Linh, I realized I might be able to find Amber through an Outview.

"First," Spencer said, reading my mind, "you need to find Tesa again. She will tell you the way to locate IF."

ooooo

During the flight, I entered an Outview and found Tesa again, still in Russia. Tesa smiled as she answered the door. "I've been expecting you."

"How did you know?"

"I did not know, only suspected."

"I failed."

She waved her hands off dismissively. "We will try again, in other ways."

"All the horrible things happened because I couldn't stop them. So many dead . . ."

"These things are not your fault, Dosen . . . we have all created this reality. Even those of us who know the truth of the illusion have participated in perpetrating it."

"I could try again right now."

"You are not here for that. There are so many times to attempt change, like raindrops making a river, one day we will reach the sea."

"There are some people I must find in my life as one of the seven. They are on our side but their methods of force and violence are undermining the cause."

"Yes, yes, I've seen that trouble ahead. It is more dangerous than you imagine. These matters that seem simple in your life are accompanied by enormous complexities with the perspective of many lifetimes and intertwined souls."

"That's not what I wanted to hear. I was hoping you would teach me another soul power I could use to find them."

"You already possess the way to find the person you seek."

I thought of Amber.

"It is not a love I speak of," she said sternly.

"Sorry."

"Do not apologize for love, Dosen. Finding love takes no special power; love is the power. You are seeking someone who is opposed to love. This person is confused. He thinks he is working to bring an awakening but the ends do not justify the means. His methods are pulling the shift farther away."

"Did he kill my mother?"

"This is a difficult question to answer. For as I said, we all have allowed what is to become what it is. He no more killed your mother than I did, or she killed herself, or you doing it. We all killed her; we have all murdered and saved everyone."

"But he is responsible?"

"Listen to what I said."

"Tesa, I understand that ultimately, we all play our part, and I know that before she entered the incarnation, my mother's soul knew she would die that way. But an action is required and a choice was made and someone decided to have her killed. Was it him, the man leading IF?"

"Yes, Dosen."

I groaned. Another challenge. I knew vengeance was wrong, that it would cloud my judgment when trying to negotiate with this person. But he killed my mom! And he was hurting the Movement. And my pledge against violence was suddenly heavier than ever.

"Life is not easy, this is why it must be *lived*," she said.

"How do I find him?"

"This will not be hard for you. One of the seven always recognizes another one of the seven."

"Spencer, we have to turn the plane around," I said, returning from the Outview.

"What is it?" Linh asked.

"The leader of IF is one of the seven," I said, breathlessly.

Spencer appeared stunned.

Linh gasped.

"You told me that as one of the seven, my awakened powers have no equal. But there's another one of the seven out there."

"I don't understand how this could be. I've accounted for all of you."

"Apparently not!"

"How could you not know that another one of the seven was running IF from within the Movement?" Linh asked.

"Hold on a minute. This is potentially good news. If he's one of the seven then he'll be able to see so much easier. He's like a brother, Nate, you two can understand each other – communicate on the same level," Spencer said.

"I can't even communicate well with Dustin, and this guy is no friend of mine. He killed my mother."

ooooo

I felt like vomiting as the plane's wheels hit the runway in Prague. For two hours Linh had held my clammy hand and repeated Kyle's words, those of Thich Nhat Hahn and even the Old Man of the Lake, trying to calm me. Meditation was impossible. For the first time since learning I was one of the seven, I was going to face an adversary of equal power and Spencer's assurances weren't helping.

"He's not with Omnia," Linh reminded me again.

"He killed my mother," I repeated.

"It's not that simple," Spencer said. "A few years ago you couldn't understand that, but now you do."

"Maybe, but suppressing emotions has always been a weakness."

"Yes, I've noticed." He tried to stifle a smile. "It's not about suppressing, it's deciding. If you are aware enough, you can make a decision based upon your understanding, experience and feelings. You decide how you wish to react to a situation."

"Spencer, are you saying that every murder is preordained by the victim's soul prior to the lifetime in which it occurs?" Linh asked. "So free will has nothing to do with anything?"

"Free will has everything to do with it. The soul has conceived an infinite number of possibilities for each aspect of our lives, including death. If you strangled me right now, I would have agreed to this outcome prior to my birth; if you did not, I would have also accepted that bargain. The ultimate power lies within the soul."

"I don't care about any of that right now. I need to know how I'm going to convince someone who is clearly committed to violence that our way is better. He's not going to be the least bit intimidated or awed by my powers."

"Could he be more powerful than Nate?" Linh asked Spencer.

"It's possible."

"Could he be working with the Dark Mystic?" I asked.

"I suppose."

My head dropped into my hands.

ooooo

Our driver left us in the nearly seven-hundred-year-old Charles Square, one of the largest plazas in the world. Stately buildings lined the roads around what was mostly a grassy park with tree-lined walks. Linh began pointing out buildings she'd read about, including Faust House. She told us that the baroque mansion had been inhabited by many well-known alchemists beginning in the 13th century and several people had disappeared within its walls, including a student of magic who made himself vanish. A more recent dweller had, for years prior to his death, slept in a coffin. The storied building was not open to the public, but there were rumors that a philosopher's stone belonging to the famed 16th century occultist, Eduard Kelley, was still hidden inside. Many mysterious break-ins and fires had occurred there in the four hundred years since his death. "You wouldn't believe the legends about that place. This whole area is filled with mysteries."

"Then it seems appropriate that we should begin the search for IF here," Spencer said.

"I don't need any more mysteries to solve," I said.

A large explosion suddenly sent us running for cover. Smoke and after-flashes kept me pinned to a wall. I called to Linh and Spencer. Then a heavy pressure hit my shoulders and a sack came down over my head. My arms were wrapped roughly with duct tape behind my back, my legs bound. I lost consciousness.

9

I woke up unbound in a cavernous room, which may have been a grand ballroom hundreds of years earlier. The many windows had long been bricked in and plastered. Exposed lath, cobwebs and layers of peeling paint, along with stained and missing floor tiles, gave the dimly-lit space a depressing bombed-out feel. Oddly, none of my powers could open any of the sixteen doors. I Skyclimbed around the thirty-foot-high ceilings avoiding the dusty, and mostly bulbless, chandeliers but could find no escape.

I sat on one of the antique threadbare couches and attempted to reach Linh and Spencer on the astral. Something or someone blocked my efforts. I'd obviously been grabbed by IF. Their leader, the other surviving one of the seven, was likely nearby. And if that was the case, his powers seemed more advanced than mine.

One of the doors flew open setting off a dazzling transformation. The scene was as if it might have been three centuries ago. The chandeliers blazed brightly, magnificent paintings adorned the walls between great windows, outside the setting sun shown over rural pastures. The furnishings, floor and everything else, were renewed and glorious. And there were hundreds of fully costumed dancers filling the space. In the seconds required to take it all in, the man who had opened the door was standing before me.

He smiled at my shocked expression.

"You're Dunaway," I choked, believing he was about to

kill me.

"Who else would I have been?"

"Are you the leader of IF?"

"Of course."

"But you've killed me in so many lives."

"I'm going to do it again."

"Why? If you're one of the seven?"

"No, Nate. I'm *The One*, you're just one of the six wannabes." The dancers were oblivious to us. Waltzing all around as a loud band played.

"What happened to make you this way?"

He scoffed. "Just because someone doesn't agree with you, doesn't mean they're wrong."

"What makes you think violence is the way to defeat Omnia?"

"Why don't you think it is? Some mystic sold you a bill of goods. Omnia is the most powerful entity in human history. Force is the only way to stop them and the only force powerful enough to do it is the Inner Force."

"Violence begets violence. We've got to end the cycle."

"Listen to yourself. You're a pansy. The cycle will end once we've wiped the floor with Omnia."

"Then what? You're going to teach the world about love?"

"Hey, Mr. Savior," his words dripped with sarcasm. "Just because I believe in violence doesn't mean I'm evil. Peace and love, the awakening, are my goal, too. The difference between you and me, aside from me being better looking, is that I'm going to succeed with my goals and you're not."

"I suppose you want me to join you, endorse IF over IM?"

He smiled. "No, Nate. You're wrong. Everything about you is wrong – your philosophy, your methods, the fact that you're the most wanted person on the planet. You've done everything wrong. Coming to Prague was another one of your many mistakes. You're so naïve. I'm frankly amazed you've managed to live this long."

"Really, then why haven't you killed me yet?"

"The timing isn't right. Spencer isn't the only one who can view the myriad of ways the future can play out."

"You know Spencer?"

"Everyone in the Movement knows Spencer." His face appeared disgusted. I wasn't sure if it was because he disliked Spencer or he just thought my question was foolish.

"Does he know you're one of the seven?"

"Oh, he didn't tell you?" Dunaway laughed. "Poor, poor Nate. This is all too much for you, isn't it? They threw you into the deep end a little too young, huh? Don't know who to trust, don't know where to turn. Fight or hide, run or cry." He laughed harder. "Spencer and I are old friends, Nate. You're just a pawn in his game. What a joke. I must say killing you in the past wasn't that enjoyable but when I do it in this life it's going to be very satisfying. I'll be happy to rid the world of such an embarrassment. You're giving the Movement a bad name. Next time you're in an Outview, you should just stay there. Don't bother with this lifetime; you're not ready."

"How did you get to be one of the seven? And how did you manage to retain soul powers when you're such a jerk?"

"I keep trying to tell you, Nate. Your interpretation of things isn't always right. In your case 'hardly ever' is probably closer to the mark."

A dancer twirled within an inch of my face. I recognized him. Although he was white, I knew him as a slave in my lifetime as a slave trader. His presence shook me. This amused Dunaway who stepped back several feet and swept his arm out to the room. As each couple spun past, I realized they'd been with me in prior lives. And one way or another, I'd been responsible for their deaths or caused them great suffering. It was an overwhelming spectacle as hundreds of people danced around taunting me by their presence.

"Welcome, Nate, welcome to your Karmic Ball!" He laughed, then vanished into the throngs of haunting souls. My search for Dunaway was interrupted by a woman sweeping me into a Polka. We relived the horror of what I'd done to her in another life as the music dictated our movements. I begged forgiveness. She nodded and passed me to another partner. Hours later, after dancing with sixty or seventy people, I discovered the crowd was slowly diminishing. It seemed that once I'd completed a dance with one of them, my partner would leave. Sometime the next day, in complete physical and mental exhaustion, I came upon the last dancer. With all the irony flowing, it came as almost no surprise that it was my mother's soul.

She curtseyed as the music began again. I bowed slightly. The lifetime of my crime swirled around as we gracefully glided around the glittering but now empty ballroom.

In the karmic exploration, I learned that she'd been raised on the streets and in various hard orphanages. At ten "he" began working eighteen-hour shifts in the mills, saving every penny, until finally around age thirty he had enough to homestead a patch of land in the wilderness. Two more years of hard work turned the desolate land into a thriving farm. He married and soon hired me, a drifter, to help harvest when his wife was pregnant. In a routine drunk, I caused a fire which killed his wife and unborn child. The fire also destroyed his crop and ruined him. The next day he found me and held a pistol inches from my head, his red, swollen eyes glaring in confused rage. Before I could react he turned the gun on himself. Parts of his face spattered on mine. Without water or cloth I smeared his blood off and walked until I found one of the stray horses and rode away never knowing, until the ballroom, that I had also been the one who killed his parents during a bank robbery.

"Can you forgive me?" I asked my mother's soul, dry-mouthed and weak.

"You are asking for more than the farmer's life."

"Yes," I nodded. "For much more."

She touched my forehead softly like my mother always did when she wanted me to know everything was all right, then faded away.

It was some minutes before I realized I was sitting in the middle of the abandoned ballroom, now back in the dingy state I'd first seen, windows bricked over, musty smell, as if no one had been there for years. Only one door remained open, the one Dunaway had come through. It seemed the natural choice.

I walked out into Charles Square. Confused, I spun around to see the door slam and found the lock beyond the powers of Gogen, then discovered I was at the front entrance to the Faust House. It took a few minutes to find Linh and Spencer in the crowd.

"Oh my God, Nate, where were you?"

"I don't know."

It turned out that the "bomb" was just flash and smoke. I'd been gone less than ten minutes. The police had only just arrived.

"Time's a funny thing," Spencer said.

"Nothing seems very funny to me right now," I said. "Tell me what you know about Dunaway."

Spencer read me. "Oh no."

"What?" Linh asked. No one answered as I stared at Spencer. She scanned the energy between Spencer and me. This was a power she'd developed over the past year. It was one that was still difficult for me. We don't find our powers at the same time.

"Do you still have the Jadeo?" Spencer asked.

I felt my pocket, then the other, a sick feeling overtook me. "He's got it."

"Where'd he take you? He can't be far." Linh said.

"I came out of the Faust House but was somewhere else. The view from the windows was the countryside." I crouched to the ground, closing my eyes. "I haven't seen him for twenty-four hours."

"Nate, I had no idea he was one of the seven." Spencer kneeled on one knee next to me.

"How could you have missed that little detail? Seems pretty important."

"He must have some extraordinary powers blocking parts of himself. I'm not a wizard, you know. I can't see everything."

"You're a hard man to believe, but easy to trust."

"What are we going to do about the Jadeo?" Linh interrupted.

"We have to get it back."

"What if he's already opened it?" I asked.

"We'd know." Spencer's look was desperate. "We do have one hope."

"What?" Linh asked.

"It can only be opened by one of the original nine entrusted," Spencer said.

"But there are still two names on the list that we don't know."

"Yes, he could be one of them. But it's also possible he's an incarnation of one of the names we already know."

"What are the odds he's one of the nine entrusted and one of the seven?" I asked.

"You tell me," Spencer said.

"Maybe we can find him through an Outview. I could try to reach the lifetime with the original nine entrusted."

"No, he has it now. The Jadeo needs to be dealt with in this time. We've handed him the power to destroy the Movement and end any hope for the awakening . . . possibly forever."

Spencer waved his arms in a downward spiral above his head. Everything in the square stopped.

"What did you do?" Linh asked.

"It's a Timefreeze, a variation of a Timefold. Follow me."

We Skyclimbed across the square back to Faust House.

"Are you sure you're not a wizard?" Linh asked Spencer as we landed.

In his concentration, I don't even think he heard her. I was about to tell him that Gogen and nothing else I tried worked on the door, but then I saw it begin to disintegrate. It was as if the door was rapidly aging - hundreds of years in a matter of seconds. Spencer was sweating and turning pale. He pushed through the remaining splinters and dust. We followed.

"This isn't how it looked before."

Spencer scanned the hall. He tapped my chest. "Do you see that?"

"The shadow is wrong," Linh said.

Then I saw it. There was a shadow cast by some unseen light source.

"It's a dimensional crease. Come on."

"How come you haven't taught me all this yet?"

"It doesn't all come from me."

"It's kind of frightening that Dunaway knows all this stuff that I don't."

"Clearly he's a mystic; perhaps he's supposed to teach you."

"Why would he teach Nate when he wants him dead?" Linh asked, as we slipped through the shadow and were once again in the dilapidated ballroom.

Spencer scanned the massive space and Skyclimbed so fast we didn't catch him until he was through a door on the far end. Heavy wrought iron hinges fell among wood shreds and sawdust as we went through. Incredible - he must have destroyed the door in the two seconds it took to cross the room. Once through that opening, we were as far away from Prague as was possible, as if we'd been on a spaceship for years. It reminded me of the ground at Outin, only it was 360 degrees. We were Skyclimbing through space. The scent of honeysuckle and citrus, along with the faint sound of children laughing, were also reminiscent of Outin.

"Where are we?" I asked.

"We're in a dimensional void."

"Where's it lead?"

"No way to know. I've never been in one before."

I looked back and there was no trace of the entrance back to Faust House.

"I can't tell which direction is which," Linh yelled.

"Nate, take Linh's hand. Follow the energy of the Jadeo, it's strong. He can conceal it only if he's one of the original nine."

"So we still have a chance?"

"Too soon to tell."

In the apparent vacuum of "space" it was impossible to know how fast we were traveling but the pressure and weight against my body implied it was a crazy speed. Spencer told me later that time could be shifted within the external fringe of a dimensional crease which was what we were traveling through. He'd been hoping to cut into Dunaway's lead but when we tumbled into a narrow alley in the middle of the night, all trace of the Jadeo's energy was gone. All I knew for sure was that this was not the world we'd left.

Spencer was bleeding but it could have been worse based on how fast we crashed into the stone wall. He'd absorbed Linh's and my impact.

"Do you feel it?" Spencer asked.

"The calmness?" It wasn't the right word but the first that came.

"Yes. Yangchen told me this existed."

"This is a good place, isn't it?" Linh asked.

"Yes, a very good place."

"Then why did Dunaway come here?"

"Dunaway isn't bad because he wants to be. He's bad because he's confused," Spencer said. "We need to keep moving. He may not intend on destroying all hope of the awakening but that doesn't mean he won't do it." He began walking.

"How do you know where to go?"

"If we are indeed in the dimension that Yangchen described, then there is only one place to go . . . Ashland, Oregon."

"Doesn't Omnia have Ashland pretty well secured?" Linh asked.

"Omnia doesn't even exist in this dimension. Can't you feel their absence?"

It was the feeling of childhood. When everything was taken care of. When the pursuit of joy and play were the priorities. When we could eat whatever we liked and sing silly songs. It was all that and much more. The air itself carried a different vibration.

"It's like floating," Linh said.

"What's in Ashland?" I asked.

"People we need to see."

"Am I there?" I asked.

"It's possible, but I don't think so."

We were lucky to be only a few blocks from a bus station; a baker on his way to work gave us directions. The bus to the airport was idling.

"How'd you pay?" I asked when Spencer returned from the ticket counter.

"You won't believe me . . . there is no money here. Everyone works for the good of everyone."

"Like communism is supposed to be?" I asked.

"No, more like soulism or maybe wholism."

It was the same at the very modern airport.

"Free air travel. Wow. Let's stay in this dimension," Linh said.

Everything looked more modern, cleaner, sleeker but according to Spencer we were in the same time as our dimension.

"We were always taught that capitalism was the only way to drive innovation, that individuals needed the incentive of profits in order to work hard."

"Well, whatever they're doing here seems to be working fine, and there is no money, no airport security, no one has even asked for ID. There's time before our flight, let's eat."

There was no meat on the menu. I didn't know if this was true for the whole dimension or if this was just a vegan restaurant. It didn't matter, we were hungry and the food was perfection.

In our dimension the trip would have taken seventeen hours, but in less than eight, we were in Medford choosing a car. The free "rental" car was a combination of solar-, wind- and hydro-powered.

Ashland looked much the same except that many of the orchards north of town had been replaced by modern, gleaming buildings belonging to, according to the SOU signs, Southern Oregon University.

"Are my parents here?" Linh asked.

"I'm not sure, Linh, but I believe so."

"And Kyle!" she added excitedly.

Spencer returned with a rare smile on his face. "Nate, let's go see your dad."

"He's alive?" As a kid, part of me had always believed he was alive somewhere and would just walk in our front door one day. I knew this was another dimension but still, I'd been right.

Linh looked back at me. "Are you okay?"

I nodded but my quivering lip and sweating palms said otherwise.

"Will we meet the Linh and Nate from this dimension?" Linh asked Spencer.

"I hope so. Please remember that happy reunions aren't our purpose here. We need to track Dunaway, retrieve the Jadeo and figure out how to return to our own dimension."

"How are we going to do that?" I asked.

"I'm hoping your dad will have an idea," Spencer said, eyeing me from the rearview mirror.

It wasn't long before we reached the building where my father worked. It turned out he taught Dimensional Studies. SOU was one of the leading universities in the field. We found out later that universities were the largest employers in this dimension, and most specialized in one or another of the countless disciplines of the soul. The University of Virginia was the top U.S. school to study reincarnation; USC focused on Karma, UNM, time travel. ASU was another top reincarnation school, Duke was the lead psychic research school, Texas State University focused on soul powers, Penn State did portals, etc.

My dad, Professor Ryder, had finished classes and was in his office ready to leave for the day. He recognized Spencer immediately. I stood speechless at seeing him after so many years. It felt like an Outview, even some distorted old home movie.

"When did you get into town?" he asked Spencer, hardly glancing my way. "Why didn't you tell me you were coming?"

Spencer shook his head. "Monte, I'm from a different plane."

At first Dad laughed, but then turned serious. He looked from Spencer to me, then back to Spencer. "And who is this?" he asked Spencer, hesitantly, turning back to me. He stared at my face. I couldn't figure out why he recognized Spencer but not me. "Spencer?" Dad repeated, pleading in an almost desperate tone.

"Monte," Spencer said quietly, "this is Nate."

My dad looked into my eyes a second longer, then flung his arms around me. His sobs were, at first, loud wails I'd never heard before. I was crying too. He kissed my forehead and cheeks. The smell of him, sharpened pencils, coffee and lime-scented speed stick, sent me back to my childhood. I wanted to be hiking in the woods with him, talking about all the craziness we'd been through, hoping he could explain it all to me. Did he know about the tin of matches? But the origins of our relationship took precedence – the Jadeo was in jeopardy. I didn't know how much time we had.

Spencer's hands were on Dad's shoulders, coaxing him back. He felt the pressure more than I, for he knew how grave things would be if Dunaway was able to open the Jadeo.

"There's so much to talk about. How did all this happen?" Dad sniffed.

"Why don't you tell us when Nate died?" Spencer's words shocked me but it quickly made sense. No wonder Dad had been so upset. I'd already died in this dimension.

"We lost you when you were just eight, I'm afraid." He fought a new round of tears. "Dusty didn't know what he was doing; it was an accident."

Oh my God, I thought, Dustin had been responsible for my death. They might need a university just to study my relationship with my brother across all the lifetimes and dimensions we'd shared.

"He was trying to teach himself to drive, he was ten at the time, he never even saw you."

I looked into the puffy eyes of my father and asked the question I already knew the answer to but wanted so badly not to hear. "What happened to Dustin?"

"He had a rough year in a psychiatric hospital, tried to kill himself, but he's okay now. He didn't go to college. Lives down in Shasta. He's a writer. I think it would do him good to see you."

"Monte, I'm sorry, I don't wish to seem insensitive, but we have a matter of extreme urgency to address," Spencer said.

My dad turned toward his old friend. "Of course. What is it? What could have brought you all this way?"

"The Jadeo . . . it's been lost."

"My God, how?"

"A powerful young man from our dimension named Frank Muller, but we call him Dunaway."

"Is he one of the original nine entrusted?"

"We're not sure but he is one of the seven."

"You realize this could shatter our dimension."

"I do."

"We could open the Jadeo," Dad said.

"You still have it in this dimension?" I asked.

"Yes. And if we open it we could possibly save this dimension."

"It won't help us in ours. We're walking on a razor's edge as it is."

"Look, Spencer, I need to do what's best for this dimension –"

"No, Monte," Spencer said sharply. "It's the Jadeo. You need to do what's best for the Jadeo."

"With all due respect, Spencer, I've got *my* Jadeo. I've fulfilled my oath."

"Monte, you can't isolate yourself in this perfect little dimension. You know it's all connected. You don't only exist here. The Jadeo is more than a gold box you've hidden somewhere. It's a part of every dimension; you should know that." Spencer slapped his hand down on the desk next to Dad.

It startled me. This was all stranger than an Outview, so

immediate and intimate. Seeing my dad, as I remembered him but from my older perspective, left me in a fog.

"Then why did you come here?" Dad asked.

"Tell him," Linh nudged me.

"Dad, it was me that lost it."

He sighed.

"In our world," I told him, "you were killed when I was twelve and I've been running from the people who did it for more than two years."

"Oh my God, Nate. I'm sorry," Dad palmed my forehead like he used to. "What is this about, Spencer?"

"Our dimension is different. Greed and fear dominate. But we didn't come for your advice," Spencer said, "although we welcome it. We came because Dunaway came."

"The man who stole the Jadeo is here?"

"Yes."

"Where?"

"I'm not sure but in our world, he's from San Francisco. That's where we're heading next. It's the only lead we have."

"I hope this trip works out better than the last time I was in San Francisco," I muttered to myself. I introduced Linh to my dad. He didn't recognize her and didn't know Kyle or Amber. There'd be no reason he would have without me around.

We soon found out online that Amber attended USC-Berkeley studying alternate realities, Linh was two years older in this dimension and was attending the University of Florida, majoring in polybio, or the study of simultaneous multiple incarnations within the same time period. Kyle was studying advanced quantum physics, specializing in wormholes, at MIT, which made both Linh and I smile. There were entire colleges that studied meditation and many around the world devoted to Outviews. Interplanetary contact was a popular major. We were fortunate that they were all home on break. But Spencer said we didn't have time to see them while Dunaway still had the Jadeo.

On the way to his house, Dad explained that several people from this dimension had found access points or portals to other dimensions but few had made it back. Lee Duncan was actually a Portalogist there.

"Nate, your mother and I argued for almost a year. I wanted to look for you in another dimension but she was afraid to lose me, said it wouldn't be the same son we'd known, and then with Dusty's problems . . . I just gave up on the idea, but I never stopped thinking about it. I talked to several colleagues about time travel, to see if we could go back and change something about that day, but no one has ever been successful," his voice trailed off.

"Dad, it was just our destiny in this dimension to wind up this way." I put my hand on his shoulder. "Don't worry, our souls are never far from each other."

12

Dad had called to tell my mother he was going to San Francisco and told her about our visit. She insisted we stop by. He said she was nervous. Me too. Spencer wasn't happy but Dad assured him we'd be quick. Dad was a leading expert on dimensions so Spencer needed his help.

She stood and stared.

I spoke first and couldn't help myself, "Mom, I'm sorry I let you die in my world."

Her eyes closed, a tear escaped down her cheek. "Oh, sweetie, I'm sorry I let you die in this one."

I ran into her arms.

"The universe can be beautiful," Dad said.

Ten minutes later we were pulling out of the driveway. It wasn't the same place where I'd grown up; it was a smaller house six blocks away. I wanted to stop to see Dustin but Spencer won that debate. Nothing mattered but recovering the Jadeo. I didn't need much convincing.

Linh and I fell asleep in the backseat while Spencer and Dad were discussing dimensional theory. Linh's head was in my lap when I woke. Absently, my hand stroked her soft hair. She'd changed so much since the whole odyssey began. Her silent resolve had brought me through many times when my own strength had faltered. There hadn't been enough time to pursue our feelings but somewhere we both realized that our life as Nate and Linh was less important than what our souls knew together.

According to Dad, most schools had soulmate programs, which had developed into a complex science. If we got back to Ashland, I wanted to use Vising to read all the books in his library. It was good to see that, as advanced as this dimension was, physical books still existed, although they were printed on hemp paper, and ebooks were more popular.

In those first moments of awakening, I wondered if I was in a dream. For years after Dad died, I dreamt of us doing stuff together. But this wasn't a dream; he was really driving us to San Francisco. Still, I knew that as soon as we got the Jadeo back, we'd return to our dimension and Dad would be dead again. And if we didn't get the Jadeo back, we could all be dead. For the past few years my life had seemed like one long dream, or really more like a nightmare. But as Wandus would say, "Life is a dream, created by the illusion of who you think you are."

"Nate, good you're awake," Spencer said. "We have a plan of sorts. You and Dunaway have several bonds. You are both members of your generation's seven, both displaced from the same dimension, have each held the Jadeo, are members of the same Movement and practiced many of the same soul powers, some known only to the two of you."

"We can use all that to locate him?" I asked, while Linh sleepily rubbed her eyes and sat up.

"Right."

"Spencer," Dad began, "is it possible Dunaway doesn't know what he's got in the Jadeo?"

"It is possible. The only way he would know is if he read Nate, and reading a mystic is extremely difficult as well as dangerous."

Spencer may have thought that through but it hadn't occurred to me. At least there was hope.

"There's always hope," Linh said.

I smiled. She's been able to read more of my passing thoughts lately. I could block her but that took energy and effort. Now that she knew what the Jadeo was, I had no real secrets from Linh.

"Nate, we need you to concentrate on the Jadeo. You can lead us to Dunaway if you home in on it."

It was no longer difficult for me to put myself into a trance-like state. I meditated several times a day, could induce Outviews and wield awesome soul powers. Within seconds I was back at the beginning of the Jadeo. It was forged by artisans during an age of wonder and mystics. Influence and trade from the stars could still be seen in civilizations unequaled in their advanced knowledge. But there were those who saw trouble ahead. People's desire for comfort began to overtake their pursuits of creativity and spiritual understanding. It's said that input for the Jadeo's design came from many dimensions and times. Then it sat ready, yet incomplete, for many centuries; no one is sure exactly how many. During all that time, life became a paradox, civilizations were said to be advancing as material wealth and conquests grew, while at the same time the advanced ancient ways were forgotten. At the last possible moment the Jadeo was completed and nine people were entrusted by an oath of their souls to hide and protect it.

"I can see the building where he is. I'll go there on the astral and find the address. It's on Baker Street."

We were fifteen minutes away. Now that I had the Jadeo within my energy, its pull was strong. We arrived at the three-story white stucco building. Spencer and I jumped out of the car and were about to Gogen the door when I realized Dunaway was no longer inside.

"We just missed him. He must have known we were coming," I said.

"Where is he now?"

I could see his blurry energy trail. He'd run down Baker Street minutes before. "This way," I said.

Dad and Linh turned the car around and followed. Spencer and I jogged down the street as I traced Dunaway's path. We rounded the corner almost knocking into a woman walking two dogs. Suddenly before us was an ancient ruin and, for an instant, I believed we might have slipped into an Outview.

"There he is!" Spencer shouted. "On top of the Palace of

Fine Arts."

We launched into Skyclimbs and were over the lagoon when Dunaway leapt into a portal above the domed building.

"Damn it," Spencer said, as we landed on the roof.

"Let's go! We can catch him," I said, leaping into the air.

"No, Nate, come back. He could be anywhere, look at the edges, it's a Crossing-portal." I'd learned there were many kinds of portals and a Crossing-portal meant it had numerous exit points, possibly tens of thousands. If it had been a Line-portal, with only one exit, we would have followed. I dropped back down next to Spencer.

"He's from San Francisco," Spencer said, squinting in the sun. "I'm sure he's used this portal many times. It's no accident they built the Palace of Fine Arts under it. Somebody found this one a long time ago and was trying to protect it." The building had been constructed to appear as ruins based on Greek and Roman architecture for the 1915 Panama-Pacific Exposition. It was built to last only through the Expo but was saved by conservationists. Then in the mid-sixties it had to be completely rebuilt. Spencer believed that whoever chose the original location knew of the portal's existence and that the person in charge of rebuilding it must also have been aware of the portal.

"Then let's get back to our own dimension. That's where he is most likely going," I said.

"I agree, but not from here, we could get lost in there. Let's go to Crater Lake."

We spotted Linh and Dad parked on Lyon Street. I told Linh over the astral where we were. It seemed no one had spotted our flight although it wouldn't be shocking to people in this dimension where soul powers were studied in universities. Still we didn't want any attention and were careful about our route to the ground. Walking briskly through the columns, I tripped over a homeless guy in the shadows. I hit the hard ground but rolled up quickly, fearing an attack.

"Got you this time, didn't I, Nate?" the grungy man stood laughing.

"Crowd?"

"You look good, Nate."

"So do you considering you're dead!" I hugged him. He smelled like some small rodent had recently died in his thick, tangled beard.

"No, alive and well, in this dimension anyway, but I guess now that you're here that could change quickly."

"Sorry, Crowd."

"Forget it, Little Ryder. Hey, have you seen Dusty yet? I know he'd love a visit."

"No, we're in kind of a hurry."

"You only think you are. It'll be days before Dunaway reaches your dimension."

"What? How do you know Dunaway?" Spencer asked.

"And how do you recognize me from another dimension when my own dad didn't?"

"I've traveled a bit. Dimensions are a kind of hobby."

"What about Dunaway?" Spencer asked again.

"I'm one of his mystics, and his guide . . . in this dimension."

"Where is Dunaway?"

"He's out there too," Crowd waved up toward the portal.

"Doing what?"

"Same as you, trying to advance the awakening."

"This dimension seems pretty awake," I said.

"You'd be surprised," Crowd said with a laugh.

"Never mind. Dunaway has something that belongs to us," Spencer said.

Crowd raised an eyebrow. "Is that so? Hmmm. Well, he did suggest a barter. Thought he might be willing to give you what you want if you give him what he wants."

"What does he want?"

"He'd like Nate to leave the Movement to him. By either entering another dimension permanently or dying, it makes no difference to him."

"As if we're going to let that happen," Spencer said.

"Where are we supposed to meet him?" I asked.

"Two days from now, at midnight, at Kilauea."

"The volcano?"

Crowd winked and nodded. "It's a stunning sight at night."

"Okay, we'll be there," I said, momentarily silencing any objections from Spencer with my tone. "Crowd, I have to ask, whose side are you on?"

"There's only one side, my brother, and we're all on it." He looked at me, smiling. "Don't worry so much, Nate. You've got to drive the car whatever way you think is right and Dunaway's got to drive it his way. In the end, the only thing that matters . . . is what does."

Once we were back in the car with Linh and Dad, Spencer asked what the plan was. "I don't know yet but we have to get to the Jadeo and the meeting seems the easiest way. Unless you want to chase him across the universe through every wormhole and portal he knows about."

Spencer remained noncommittal but filled the others in on the meeting with Crowd. "I just don't know why guides can't give a straight answer or clear message," I said.

Ever since Linh had the wrong dream about Rose's death, she had studied guides, so I wasn't surprised at her answer.

"Nate, you should know intuition, signs, dreams, and other messages from guides are perfectly clear. We're the ones who muddle them up when they push all that pure information into our human filters. We get confused by the enormity of the data."

"I do know, but thanks for the reminder. It's frustrating being human."

Linh laughed. "Beautifully frustrating."

"Crowd told me that in the end the only thing that matters is what does. Sounds to me like he was endorsing Dunaway's the ends justify the means."

"Not necessarily," Linh said. "You said Crowd said that he travels around many dimensions. He's likely seen the scenario play out so many ways that his statement is true."

"At least to him," Dad said.

Just outside Mt. Shasta, Spencer suggested that, because there was time before we had to meet Dunaway and this dimension was as good a place to hide as any, he'd like to show my dad Outin. "It's not exactly a sightseeing venture. If I show it to him, he can show it to the me from this dimension."

"Can I come?" Linh asked me.

I looked at her, surprised.

"I think it's better if you see Dustin alone."

"Okay, I guess," I said.

"Don't worry," Dad said. "No one is after you in this dimension. We'll meet you back at Dustin's place."

"Practically before you get there," Spencer said. "Reverse time, remember?"

ooooo

I left them at the trailhead closest to Outin's main entrance and followed Dad's directions to Dustin's cabin. It was probably no coincidence that he lived less than two miles from the entrance.

I knocked tentatively on the door; no answer. I was about to check the car for something to write a note on but then thought, what would I write? "Sorry I missed you, signed, your dead brother." There was time to wait.

A few minutes later, I heard his voice. "Can I help you?"

When I turned around, he dropped the firewood he was carrying, then tripped over it as he grabbed me in a bear hug. "Are you real, brother, are you real?"

"If you don't suffocate me."

He let me go and looked at me again. "I've known for a long time we would meet again in this life."

"So, it doesn't surprise you?"

"Hell yes, it shocks me, but I knew, you know? I knew it."

I nodded. A lump filled my throat, as I stared into my brother's strained, tear-filled eyes.

"How did you get here? Where are you from?"

"Another dimension."

"Did you come through Outin?"

"You know about Outin?"

"Yeah, whadaya think I'm doing here?"

"Have you been there?"

"Only in my dreams, I have incredible dreams . . . but I look for it every day."

"Want me to show you?"

He stared at me with desperate, disbelieving eyes. "Nate, I . . . if you could do that, you'd save me. And I know you don't owe me nothing, I mean, I should be trying to make it up to you for taking your life. You were so young, and I just . . ." His words turned to tears. I put my arm around him.

"Dustin, it's okay, man. Stop torturing yourself. You did what you were supposed to do. There was an agreement. That's how these things work."

He looked up at me as if I'd just read the ingredients from a candy bar to him in French. "No, Nate. You don't understand . . . on some tripped-out soul level that may be true, but we're just people here and you died when I ran you over and I had to go on living . . . I had to go on living with it. Do you know how everyone looks at me? Do you know what Mom and Dad think of me? I killed their baby." He choked on more words.

"Come on, Dustin. Let's go to Outin. You'll see things differently."

"Give me a minute. Is that okay? Can we wait just a minute?" He sat on the wooden step and lit a cigarette. I was surprised a dimension like this even had cigarettes and considered suggesting he put it out. Instead, I waited in silence until he finished.

"Okay, I think I'm ready. Sorry about falling apart there."

"Don't worry about it."

He nodded once. "Hey, have you seen Mom and Dad?"

"Yeah."

"Geez, what was that like?"

"Emotional."

The entrance was harder to find than I expected. I was beginning to notice slight variations between my dimension and this one. But Outin was exactly the same. Our roles were reversed since my first visit there. It was some time before Dustin could speak and when he did, I wasn't surprised by his words. "I'm never leaving this place."

"In my dimension you also stayed. We might run into you anytime."

"Is that possible? Does that mean I can't stay?" His voice trembled like a four-year-old worried about not getting dessert.

"It doesn't matter at all. Stay as long as you want." I showed him the lodge, and whispered an apology to Kyle. Then we visited each lake; I carefully explained what they did. "There's a fifth lake called Clarity. You'll like it there."

"I've seen all this in my dreams. I know Clarity Lake, it's small and deep, surrounded by rocks, in the middle of a forest of white trees."

"I think you've been traveling in your dreams."

"You have no idea."

"Actually . . .," but I let it go.

Dustin was consumed by Outin, so much so that I wondered if my whole reason for being was to cross into his dimension just to show him how to get to Outin. But the circles were infinite and I knew he might have needed to be there in order to help me once again in the future. Fate is explosively intricate.

On the far shore of Rainbow Lake we caught up with Linh, Spencer and Dad. Spencer was eager to get back. Dad was happy that Dustin was staying. He had lost me as a kid but watched as his first-born struggled as a wounded bird, trying impossibly to overcome something that was not his fault.

"Change is good," Dad said.

"I belong here," Dustin said, hugging him. No one doubted it.

ooooo

Spencer told us that in this dimension Yangchen was a famous professor at Berkeley. I'd find out later that Amber was one of her best students. Spencer himself was well-known and traveled the world lecturing on numerous topics. We left Spencer and Dad back at his office while Linh and I went off in search of Amber, Kyle and the other Linh.

"Are you excited about seeing Amber?" Linh asked.

"I'm mostly looking forward to seeing Kyle but it won't be like Dustin. None of them are going to know us."

We arrived at Amber's house, which was the same as in our dimension. She answered the door. It took her longer than it should have to take her eyes off of me. There was a definite recognition but she couldn't place it. Linh broke the awkwardness.

"Amber, you don't know us but –"

"Sure I do, aren't you Kyle's older sister, um, Linda?"

"No, I'm actually his cousin, Linh."

"Oh right, sorry. You were a couple of years ahead of us."

"Yeah. But Amber, we're from another dimension." I waited to see how "New Age Mayes" was going to handle that whacky little statement. She didn't even flinch but then things were different in her dimension.

"Which one?"

"You mean you believe us?" Linh asked.

"You're not making it up, are you?"

"No." Linh laughed. "But I have no idea which dimension."

Amber looked at me.

"The United States dropped an atomic bomb on Japan in 1945. We landed on the moon in 1969 and we're dependent on fossil fuels."

"Oh, that's 92426. Scary place. It's the closest dimension to Pasius, ours. Your society is defined by television, the Internet and fast food. No wonder you left."

"We're actually going back," Linh said.

"Why?" Amber asked, as if we'd told her we were willingly returning to hell.

"Trying to save it," I said.

"How can I help?" She was so relaxed and confident. In this dimension, Amber had grown up studying how to reach her soul. Her life was safe and happy here.

"What's your mother do?" Linh asked. In our dimension Amber's mother was a TV star.

"Mom's a singer, semi-famous." Amber kept looking at me. Linh kept looking at Amber. We all felt the familiarity and a pull to each other, but there was a funhouse-mirror element to it. "Do you all want to come in?"

For the next few hours Amber taught us all the big stuff she knew about alternate realities, dimensions and soul powers. We did the same. She had never been through a portal or into another dimension and like most people in her world believed, soul powers were mostly theory, other than the most basic bits of mind reading. Her sister Bridgette had never dated Dustin so she didn't know him, but I promised her if we came back again we'd take her to Outin.

ooooo

Linh and Kyle also lived in the same restored Victorian house. As soon as they saw the Linh with me they invited us up to Kyle's loft. The two Linhs, about two years apart in age, couldn't stop looking at each other. Kyle pummeled me with questions. They, like Amber, had no trouble accepting that we were from another dimension. Being with Kyle and Linh back in the loft, safe from Lightyear and Omnia, made me feel young and free. We joked and giggled for the first time since discovering my dad had been murdered, years earlier. Eventually, we returned to the serious topic of what was going on in our dimension.

"What can we do?" Kyle asked. They were so open and giving, I mean the Linh and Kyle from my dimension were great too but everyone we'd encountered here was lighter and clearly more evolved spiritually.

"Like I said, if we can catch the guy who stole the artifact, we'll be okay. We're going to try to make our dimension more like this one."

"Let me come with you, Nate. I've got to see it," Kyle said.

"It's not a good idea. You've died back there once, I don't want it to happen again." But Kyle couldn't understand the kind of violence, hate and greed that existed in our world. All he saw was excitement and adventure.

"It's a dark, dangerous place," my Linh said.

"Then you two should stay here," the other Linh suggested.

I took a deep breath. "It's calm and peaceful here, like it should be, and I wish we could stay but there's too much at stake."

Spencer reached me on the astral. He wanted to get to Crater Lake. Linh and Kyle walked us to our car. Kyle made another plea.

"I promise when all this is over, I'll come back here and take you for a visit. Please stay here where it's safe. I can't see you die twice."

He leaned in to hug me goodbye and collapsed in my arms. We were both soaked in blood. "Get down!" I yelled, as Kyle and I sank to the ground.

15

The car shielded us from the shooter. The large caliber bullets pierced the cheap steel. Blap, blap, blap.

I knew Kyle was dead even before I got him on his back and checked his pulse.

"Come on, Nate!" My Linh pulled me up while the other Linh screamed. "We can't die, too."

Blap, blap.

I don't remember doing it but somehow we Skyclimbed behind the house and were soon in the trees of Lithia Park.

"We have to go back and check on the other Linh," I said, trying to catch my breath. "We never should have visited them."

"It's too late. We've gotta get to Crater Lake. If Omnia finds us –"

"Where the hell was my heat warning?"

"Nate, warn Spencer. It won't take them long to find your dad."

Spencer didn't respond. I kept trying as we continued to Skyclimb into the steep hills above Ashland. Exhausted, we landed and found a car; Gogen "hot-wired" it. Linh drove. Spencer finally answered. Both he and my dad had been shot. They were heading to the hospital in Medford. Spencer had killed the attackers but didn't know how many more were in the dimension. Then I lost contact.

The entire hospital was under Spencer's influence, but I couldn't figure out what he was doing. He could have been protecting the building from Omnia's forces or trying to prevent the staff from calling authorities or interfering with his own healing efforts.

Dad had taken two shots, one in his left arm, the other just above the abdomen on the same side. But the bullets passed through. Spencer's wounds were something from a combat zone. No one stopped me from approaching his gurney as they wheeled him into surgery. I placed several Lusans on him and opened a healing channel through me.

His voice was weak inside my head.

"Nate, I came here for your father; he needed medical attention. But don't let these people operate on me." I quickly used my powers to clear the room. "If I die, find the me from this dimension and take me back to ours. Take him to Yangchen. She'll know what to do."

"How will I find her?"

"Go to Outin, to Dustin, the one from our dimension. He'll be able to find her."

"We can heal you."

"Yes. I think we can unless Omnia gets here first."

I talked to Linh over the astral. She was still out in the ER. "Linh, you've got to keep an eye out for Omnia and do whatever it takes to stop them."

"Violence?"

"Let's hope not."

"Does it count since we're not in our dimension?"

"I have no idea, but let's hope we don't need to find out."

"Nate," Spencer broke in, "you cannot go to that meeting with Dunaway."

"It's the Jadeo, nothing is more important."

"Being one of the seven is more important than being one of the nine entrusted," he said. His voice was strengthening.

"How can that be? Every generation has seven but there has only ever been one group of nine entrusted."

"Numbers are not everything. Nothing is that simple. The times we are in dictate the importance."

"But aren't they intertwined?" His bleeding had stopped.

"Yes, of course, everything is, even separate dimensions."

"Aren't we messing things up here?"

"It doesn't matter because this dimension is not real unless we are in it. The only reality that is true is the one we are in. So our `whole' world is the dimension we just left."

"So if we fix that, we fix this?"

"Yes. And the ultimate victory is far more complex than you can imagine."

"I understand that every dimension must be lined up, they all must become identical, but won't that take forever?" I could feel the healing surging through me.

"Forever is a definition of time . . . and time's a funny thing." He was sounding better. "For the purposes of our understanding, it's already happened, we just have to find it."

"I think I understand."

"Omnia is here," he said out loud. I smelled smoke just as the alarms began to whine.

Spencer winced in pain as I used Gogen to fling him on my back. Thick, black smoke was filling the corridor, as I raced toward the ER. "No," Spencer said hoarsely.

"I won't leave Dad and Linh."

"Nate. Hurry, turn around. You know you won't survive if you go there."

Choking on the noxious fumes, I closed my eyes, and found myself running away from the ER. My soul made the decision over my personality. I knew it was the right thing to do even as my heart broke.

"You are not abandoning them. We must each follow our own path and not be swayed by suffering. The only way is to let go," Spencer said in my head. "It is what had to happen." I let go with an exhale and thought only of surviving.

We crashed into a wall. There was no visibility and the impossible choice I'd had to make distracted me. Spencer stood up and with strength found somewhere deep within, and a combination of powers I still didn't understand, blasted a large hole through the wall. We crawled through to the outside and rolled onto the sidewalk, coughing and gulping fresh air. I pulled him up onto my back and Skyclimbed away from the building. At the edge of a parking lot, I turned to see the hospital engulfed in flames. Fire trucks started to arrive, sirens wailed and too few survivors trailed out of the building.

"There's nothing we can do," Spencer said.

"That's not true," I said, through gritted teeth.

I dumped him into a car, took one last look, did another Gogen hotwire and then sped out into traffic.

ooooo

We reached Crater Lake near sunset. I'd hoped to see the Old Man but if he existed in this dimension he wasn't showing himself. Spencer was well enough to get across the water on his own. At the top of the Wizard Island caldron Linh and the Old Man sat in deep discussion.

"Linh, you're alive!"

She ran to me. "I was sure you made it but I was worried you were hurt. And look how much better you are," she said, turning to Spencer.

"Everything is so confused within these two dimensions, I couldn't tell. I mean I couldn't feel the change. What about Dad?"

"No." She took my hands. "It happened quickly. I was looking for you. A huge explosion destroyed the ER. I'm sorry."

"Jesus, Spencer. We show up in this Shangri-La dimension and turned it into our screwed-up world. Dad and Kyle are dead, men are running around with guns, a hospital full of innocent people is bombed! We're cursed."

"It's true, our reality is where we are."

"Oh my God, what about Amber? They will have gone for her, too."

"If they did, it's way too late," Linh said.

Her answer shocked me.

"Don't look at me like that, don't you dare," Linh cried. "I lost Kyle again and left myself to die back there."

"We're a disaster, all we do is spread misery. Is this what non-violence is about?" I looked at Spencer.

"We can contemplate all of this later. It won't take Omnia long to find us. Let's go," Spencer said, motioning toward the portal.

"Linh, I'm sorry. What can I say? I'm fighting for my sanity and you're the best reflection of reality I could imagine.

Mostly, I get it wrong and don't act like I know, but I do."

"What, Nate, what do you know?"

I looked at Spencer and then the Old Man, suddenly shy.

Linh wiped her face. "Let me know when you figure it out." She dove into the portal.

"Next time, don't blow it, boy," the Old Man said, pushing me in after her.

We were in the portal for what seemed like hours, but there would be no way to know how long it actually was. The exit was terrifying as we emerged from the portal deep below the surface of churning white water. I caught only a glimpse of Linh and tried to reach her hand before the water separated us. Everything else was about struggling to find air. Which way was up? The force of the water pushing me down was the only way I could tell but it took every bit of strength and several soul powers to get me through the crushing pressure. With no breath remaining, I broke through and was pushed to the edge of a dark pool. Dizzy and weak, I desperately clung to wet leaves and vines to avoid being sucked back out into the eddy. Linh bobbed up, but not close enough to reach. She got to a thin tree trunk. There was hardly enough light to see and the water was thundering. No sign of Spencer. Linh worked her way over to me as I pushed toward her. We finally met and worked our hands into some slippery green rocks. Dawn's light revealed a rushing razor-thread of a waterfall plunging hundreds of feet into our pool from above.

"Lousy place for a portal," I said, but she didn't hear.

"Where. Is. Spencer?" Linh shouted above the water.

I shook my head and scanned the pool.

"Maybe he got lost in the portal. I thought it would never end." But Linh still didn't hear.

She started pointing wildly and nearly got sucked in again. Spencer was floating face down. I took a deep breath and ran across the top of the water. He was heavier than I expected and I fell in. It was impossible to get back into a Skyclimb with him on my back and us bobbing in the water. I looked back toward Linh who was already on the way to help. She Skyclimbed up the lowest bank, opposite the falls, and I was able to follow. We collapsed on a steep slope gripping a protruding branch. Spencer didn't appear to be breathing. Linh and I nodded at each other and together leaped up to a crudely paved observation area for tourists to photograph the falls. I channeled healing through my hands, but Linh pushed me out of the way and did mouth-to-mouth. Soon Spencer coughed water and I resumed my healing while Linh made a Lusan. As he improved, I used Lusans to dry the three of us. Even though the air was humid and warm, we were all shivering.

After twenty minutes Spencer was able to talk.

"How are you feeling?" Linh asked.

"Been a rough day," Spencer said, coughing.

"Linh saved you with CPR," I said.

He smiled at her. "Thanks. Some things work better than soul powers."

"Any idea where we are?"

"Hopefully, Akaka Falls."

"Where's that?" Linh asked.

"Hawaii, the Big Island."

"Did you know the portal is under water?"

"No, never been."

"Uh-oh," Linh said, pointing to a heavyset man walking toward us in khaki shorts and a bright green tank top.

"I hope that's just an early tourist," I said.

"I hope it's Butterscotch," Spencer strained to get up. Linh and I helped.

"Who?" Linh asked.

"Spencer, my old friend," the man called out. "Are you okay?"

"Been better," Spencer answered. "Nate,Linh, Butterscotch."

"Pleasure," the native Hawaiian smiled and held out his hand. "Nathan Ryder, kind of amazing you're still alive. Good things, good things."

ooooo

Butterscotch was not a mystic as I first thought, but a longtime student of Spencer's and an early member of the Movement. The cracked vinyl seats in his old station wagon smelled of pineapples. It wasn't long before we arrived at a delicate cottage constructed of bamboo and teak somewhere outside the little village of Homomu. The dense vegetation around his home in the trees was the kind that comes only with one hundred and forty inches of annual rainfall. It was so deeply green, it mesmerized me. It gave the home a protective feeling similar to Kyle's loft in the other dimension. I was hoping this one would turn out differently.

Spencer's recovery was surprisingly slow, but his health had been fragile for a long time. He and Linh were not convinced I should meet Dunaway at the volcano but neither had a convincing solution on how to stop Dunaway from undermining the Movement or getting him to surrender the Jadeo. Between our problems and the heaviness of our dimension, nobody was in an amicable mood; only Butterscotch's jovial attitude kept us from sinking. In the end, I won the debate. Linh and Spencer would stay at the cottage while I went to meet Dunaway.

Linh handed me a poem just before my departure.

TEARS ARE MADE OF WATER
Tears are made of water and salt,
crusty little cups of strength,
emotions of rain, signs of love,
wet warm, then cold and absent.
Empty they, dissolve, into silence
and melt icy words so often upon my lips.
I see light and shadow, impulse
punctuates indifference and I am left
with salt cracked in my hand,
it disintegrates impatiently.
I stumble through trees,
fists squeezing and releasing,
colors melt, and ache

I drop in easy pieces
crumpled, ashamed
surrounded by sky, the past creeps and burns.
Let ambiguity be planted
to grow into decisiveness.
Let me watch you, like a dove, whose forever
mission of peace can only be forgiven
and understood through flight itself.
I cannot uphold such honesty, calmly
without rival or equanimity.
And you, must know this, too.
Oh but why such uneven step
in this world, this passage?
Oh but why such reticence to be
in this moment. We are children
under no influence. It is this stance
I play, hard and long, and my eyes
steady, challenge, now.
Now! I say.
It is the fabric, the resistance I wish to step into –
all else pales and unravels like insecurity.
Drop too and grow into disclosure. Let tears
cleanse and nourish their sensitivity and waste
upon the ruins of our minds, this landscape,
beautiful and lonely:
dazzling and rich,
we thread its forest into purity.
Tears are made of water, dear friend,
they flow unwillingly down my arm,
into my hand, where dust and salt and
words resign.
I kneel, and touch the earth,
its cool damp – pain memory –
connects identity, and I am born.
Are you with me?

Her poetry had a way of touching me and triggering emotions as if she wrote with the power of her soul.

Spencer brought me back from the deep place Lihn's words had taken me. "Nate, remember you're more important than the Jadeo," he said.

"That goes against the last thousand years of my soul's existence."

"That's why I'm reminding you. The oath you made as one of the entrusted nine to protect the Jadeo across time was a human oath and you've honored it lifetime after lifetime. But being one of the seven comes straight from your soul and even more, it is a consensus of the collective consciousness. You are doing that for all of us."

"I know."

"No, Nate, I see in your eyes that you do not. If you must choose, then you sacrifice the Jadeo. Swear it to me."

"I am not going to enter into another oath without fully understanding the consequences. You'll just have to trust me. Trust my soul."

He stared at me.

"If that moment of choosing comes I will let go and leave the decision to my soul."

Spencer continued to stare long into my eyes. "I can ask no more," he said silently.

"Be well, Spencer. I'll see you soon." I leaned down and kissed his warm forehead.

Linh walked me outside. "I may never see you again," she said, as we stood under the porch light.

"Come on, you know by now that's not possible."

"You know what I mean. Outviews, other dimensions, different times, none of that counts. I want to be with you in our own screwed up world."

"I know. Trust the universe." We shared a whispering, lingering kiss.

I got in the car. "Please, Butterscotch, let's go," I said, quietly.

I couldn't look back. She was right, we might not see each other again.

We drove through the darkness for a long time before reaching the entrance to the National Park. From there, I would have to Skyclimb, but I had a good sense of where to go, having studied maps of the area. It wasn't clear where the meeting with Dunaway would take place, but it seemed a safe bet he would find me. The closer I got to the glowing lava flow, the stronger I felt the pull of the Jadeo. And just at the point where the heat was too great to continue, Dunaway was waiting.

"Good, I appreciate your being on time. This isn't the most comfortable place to wait," he said.

"You chose it, Dunaway."

"I'm not surprised you came. I have not underestimated your naiveté. Are you prepared to make the trade?"

"I'd like to talk first."

"Oh yes, sure. How rude of me. Small talk, yes. Did you enjoy your visit with your friends? How's your dad? Can I get you some milk and cookies? We don't have anything to talk about."

"Why are you so angry?"

"Why aren't you? Haven't we played this game before? If the dimension we just left exists, then what is all the fuss about here? What are we doing this for? Have you ever asked yourself? Or does Spencer spoon-feed you all the answers?"

"We want the same thing, Dunaway. Together, you and I can destroy Omnia without violence. Can you imagine if the world could see what is possible?"

"It's all an illusion, you fool, so the violence isn't real either. It's all about forcing the awakening. Aren't you tired, Nate? Tired of waiting for everyone to wake up?"

"Don't you agree that a soul is a peaceful impulse of love energy?"

"Yes," he said.

"Then we cannot return to our souls through violence."

"Yes, we can. We're talking about the human world, not the spiritual one. We can do anything within this world in order to succeed. In fact, we must do anything. The ends do justify the means, Nate. If we get the world to enlightenment, then it doesn't matter how we got there."

"But we can't get there your way. All violence does is keep us chained to our personalities and that's what Omnia wants. If we act and express ourselves from our souls instead, they cannot win."

"Wrong again."

"You know what seems wrong to me, Dunaway? If you're going to kill me, then why are you trying so hard to convince me you're right?"

"Nate, I don't give a damn what you believe. And I'm not going to kill you."

"You said you'd trade the Jadeo for my life."

"Yes, but you're going to kill yourself."

I knew from Spencer that there was a portal-of-no-return at Kilauea. He'd explained that if someone entered the portal they would never be able to return to this dimension. We assumed that's why Dunaway chose this spot. And I assumed that's what he meant when he said I was going to kill myself.

"You're going to give me the Jadeo and then expect me to go through the portal?"

"Oh, the Jadeo, pretty name for a pretty box. And you know about the portal? Of course you do. Excellent. Well, yes, that is one option. But I rather like the other choice where you leap into the volcano and kill yourself."

Then it dawned on me. "Because you can't kill me yourself."

"Ah ha! You clever boy. Yes, yes it's true. So help me out, will you?"

"But you've killed me in other lives." We both moved back from the heat.

"Look, Nate, one of the seven cannot kill another one of the seven or they revert to being a 'normal' person. I have no intention of doing that. I've tried to go through Outviews to see if killing you in other lifetimes would change things, but as you see, here we still are. So if you'd be so kind to do it for me, I'll give you this precious gold box you seem so concerned with."

A chorus of whispers from ancient guides rattled inside

my head. "And if one of us is threatened, the other must save him, unless the threat is from ourselves," I said, repeating the words I could decipher.

"Oh well, damn . . . good, now you're finally up to speed."

The inner voices were now shouting in whisper, "Ask him, ask him, ask about the seven."

"No, I'm not," I said. "Why don't you tell me what else you know about being one of the seven?"

Dunaway gave me a frustrated look.

I smiled because he had to answer. It seemed one of the seven had to help another one of the seven understand.

"The seven of each generation who are born with an open channel to the universe are connected to one another as are the seven chakras, the seven directions. We each correspond to a chakra, to a direction."

"Which are you?" I asked.

"I am the root chakra, you are the crown – opposite ends of the spectrum, you and I."

"Yet neither could exist without the other."

"But we are the only surviving of the seven." His face was red and tight.

"Maybe, but they all lived within this time, this dimension. Our lives were intertwined and we each played a part."

"Yes, but only one of us is required to create great change."

"That doesn't mean two of us can't do it. Imagine the power if two of us tried . . . together."

"Enough of this, Nate. Do you choose the portal-of-no-return or death by lava?"

"Both are appealing choices but what you haven't told me, which of the directions we are."

"Can't you figure that out by yourself?"

"Let's see, you are not likely north, east, south or west, too ordinary for you. I'm certain you are not within, or even above . . . Are you below?"

"Of course I am, you –"

The ground below opened as a lava tube collapsed and I plunged into a narrow, steamy shaft. Searing, blinding agony overtook me even before my foot hit the lava beneath.

18

In my next moment of consciousness, I found myself partially submerged in a clear pool surrounded by thick ferns. Dunaway was pouring cool water over me.

"Where are we?"

"In the rainforest, not far from Kilauea."

"You saved me?"

"Afraid I had to."

"Then it's true, the seven must help each other."

"Don't think anything's changed. As soon as I get you healed, you're still going to kill yourself. There's nothing to stop me from tossing your gold box into the volcano."

"I'm not going anywhere."

"Fine then. You go on living and screwing things up for me. I'll hang onto your box."

"Why are you so against working together?"

"Because without force there can be no victory against Omnia."

"How do you know? And even if you're right, you must know that a victory that comes from violence will never be lasting."

"Can you stand yet? Because if you're healed, I'd like to get back to Prague. I'm tired of your pacifistic talk. The Movement is no closer to defeating Omnia than it was the day you were born."

"Go whenever you want. But I need your help with one last thing."

"What?" Dunaway asked.

"I need the gold box."

"You can't trick me like that." He laughed. "You're pathetic. And sooner or later I'll find a way to –"

My heat warning rose in my body. I looked at Dunaway. He was already searching the trees. He looked back at me. We both Skyclimbed. It wasn't easy, my feet and legs still ached from the burns, and the vegetation was so dense, there was hardly room between the branches and leaves. Once we were on top, the pool was no longer visible through the foliage. Then Dunaway, who apparently had the power to see through "solid" objects, told me there were several dozen soldiers on the ground where we'd just been. Two helicopters hovered nearby. We were concealed from their view and I was looking for an escape when both choppers crashed into the nearby lava fields and exploded.

"What did you do?" I yelled at Dunaway.

"Killed them before they killed us. You're welcome!"

Military jets appeared and sent missiles into the forest. Everything erupted in flames. We sprinted across the treetops just ahead of the spreading inferno. The soldiers who'd been pursuing us were certainly burned alive. Another wave of missiles narrowed our escape route and I have to admit that I was relieved when Dunaway brought the planes down. We got to a road and hijacked a bus full of tourists. Dunaway drove and after listening to their screams, I put them all to sleep.

"Where are we going?" I shouted.

"Off this island."

"They must be tracking you."

"No, I use the same techniques you do."

"Maybe they figured them out." I was standing in the aisle doing my best to hang on.

"They're using time travel, Outviews and dimensional crossings to locate us. We're running out of time, Nate. We must unite the Movement to destroy Omnia before it's too late."

"We need to pick up Spencer and Linh."

"Jump off anywhere, I'm heading to the airport," Dunaway yelled.

"Spencer will know what to do about the Movement."

"I know what to do about the Movement. I don't need Spencer to tell me. And neither do you."

"Damn it, Dunaway. There is a way we can work together. I know that's how it's meant to be. And maybe you're right, I'm too stupid to figure it out. At least I'm mature enough to admit that. You're like a playground bully." He took a curve too fast and knocked me off my feet. "Jesus, did you do that on purpose?"

He was laughing. "No, but I wish I had."

I got into the seat across the aisle and tried unsuccessfully to reach Spencer and Linh.

"We're going to be less than three miles from where they're staying soon."

"Fine, you got it. If we're alive when we get close, we'll go get your girlfriend and the puppet master."

I looked back and saw that many of the passengers had been thrown into the aisle. It took several minutes using Gogen to get them all securely back into seats. A few had minor injuries so I did some healing.

"How did you see through the trees?" I asked.

"Screw you. I'm not one your mystics."

Two black SUVs came up fast. Remarkably, Dunaway continued to drive the narrow winding road doing a steady ninety miles per hour, and, at the same time, used the rearview mirror to make one of the chase vehicles crash. I almost cheered before I caught myself and decided to come up with a nonviolent way to help. Before I could, the remaining SUV smashed into the side of the bus as we were rounding a curve. Our bus left the road and soared through the air until the wheels tangled in treetops. The bus dropped through the branches, hit another ravine and became a rolling ball of mangled metal. Six of seven rotations later we were three hundred feet down when the bus slammed to a stop. I released the passengers from sleep and Gogen and forced the roof off so they could escape, but most were dead. Dunaway and I crawled out and were already in the steep forest when the terrifying sound of a helicopter filled the air. It was an Apache; fast, agile and lethal. Missiles blew chunks out of the landscape as a constant wall of machine gun fire cut closer. I grabbed Dunaway into a Timefold. We watched as everything around us was destroyed.

"Amazing. Are we suspended in time?" Dunaway asked.

"Yes."

"Can you show me?"

"I need to concentrate or I'll lose it."

Once the area was reduced to blackened burning trees and scorched earth, we left the Timefold and moved toward Butterscotch's cottage. It took an hour to reach it.

The place was deserted. I read the walls and found that Spencer and Linh had just managed to get away but Butterscotch was in custody. Where would they go? They'd been unreachable on the astral.

We saw Butterscotch's station wagon.

"I'm going to the airport," Dunaway said. "Are you coming?"

"This time I'm driving."

"I'll teach you how to do a Timefold if you teach me how to see through things," I said.

"Hey, Nate, we're not a couple of college buddies, okay?"

"Then what are you still doing with me?"

"I could ask you the same thing."

"Because, Dunaway, you know that the two of us, working together, have the best chance."

"You're delusional. Do me a favor; stop attempting to convert me. I'm trying to concentrate. One of us needs to come up with a way off this island. And I doubt you'll be any use."

We didn't talk again until we arrived at Kona International Airport forty minutes later. There were soldiers everywhere but we slipped through as I followed Dunaway to a corporate jet.

"Can you fly that thing?" I asked.

He shot me an insulted look. "Do you know how powerful the soul is? How did you get this job?"

Without authorization from the tower, we taxied to the runway.

"Hey, watch out!" I yelled. Dunaway used some trick to avoid a landing commuter plane. Two airport security trucks raced toward us but we were airborne before they could do anything.

"Nice to be off that damn island," Dunaway said.

"There's no way this thing has the range to make it to the

mainland," I said.

"Oh no, I didn't think of that. Now what will we do?" he whimpered, sarcastically. "Worry not, little one, we're less than two hundred miles from a gorgeous portal."

"Then where?"

"Damn it."

Two fighter jets flew by so close that our plane rattled.

"They're looping back around," I said.

"They're going to try to escort us back to Hawaii. If we don't cooperate they'll blow us out of the sky."

"Gulfstream G550 fugitive aircraft, this is the United States Navy ordering you to return to Hawaii Kona International Airport immediately. Acknowledge," a voice cracked over the radio.

"How far is the portal?" I asked.

"Too far."

"Gulfstream G550 fugitive aircraft, you will immediately return to Hawaii Kona International Airport or be fired upon."

"I guess they know it's us," Dunaway said.

"I think I can put the plane in a Timefold but can you use Solteer to make them see us crash into the ocean?"

"Hmmm, clever." He smiled. "Maybe I don't completely dislike you after all."

"Can you do it?" I shouted.

"Of course I can. I'm a Solteer master."

"Gulfstream G550 fugitive aircraft, you have sixty seconds to turn around or you will be fired upon."

"It's going to be close. I need almost thirty for the Timefold and you have to stage the crash after that."

"Shut up and do it!" Dunaway yelled.

It was possible that it was impossible. Fifteen seconds later my head was throbbing, ten seconds more and my hands were shaking, but we slipped into a Timefold. Nauseous and covered in sweat, I fought to hold the Timefold but after twelve minutes it collapsed when I did.

"You all right?" Dunaway's voice sounded like a distant echo.

I grunted something.

"You're being a little overly dramatic, don't you think? I might remind you that I did my part while flying a jet at the same time."

He tossed a Lusan into my lap. We'd flown at top speed while in the Timefold and continued for another ten minutes while I recovered slowly.

"Damn them!" Dunaway growled.

The jets zoomed past.

"I don't think I can do it again," I said weakly.

"I don't think they'll give us the chance."

Seconds later a missile was heading directly toward us. My brain scrambled for a soul power that could save us. The missile was closing at lightning speed.

"Gogen!" Dunaway shouted.

I focused my dwindling energy onto the missile. It was coming too fast. I managed to nudge it just enough as Dunaway forced our plane into a dangerous descent. We headed straight into the ocean. He pulled up at the last minute and a second later we rocketed into the safety of the portal. The plane became immediately still.

Dunaway was right; it was different from any other I'd seen . . . or even imagined.

"Like the inside of a rainbow, huh?" he asked. The sun shone through sparkling water vapors, completely surrounding us in rainbows.

We stepped out of the plane. "Where does it go?"

"New Zealand." Dunaway said, "But there is a side shoot to Crater Lake, of course."

"Seriously?"

"You don't know much, do you? Most portals connect at the lake." We were moving involuntarily away from the plane.

"Hopefully I can find Linh and Spencer from there."

"Yeah, we wouldn't want you to be all alone."

"What happens to the plane?" I asked, ignoring his sarcasm.

"No idea. Nate, this has been fun and everything, but I'd still like to see you dead."

"We're meant to work together."

"No."

"You're wrong." The colored walls were blurring past faster.

"I can see inside your little box and it's empty, did you know that? Why is an empty antique box so important to you?"

"It belonged to my father."

He studied me. "No, it's more than that. As long as you remain alive, annoying me, I think I'll hang onto it. Might even nose around in some of your past lives and dig up the real reason."

"I could just take it from you."

"You don't know how."

He was right. "I'm a fast learner." I unleashed everything I knew, beginning with Solteer to put him to sleep and Gogen to pull at the Jadeo, but nothing worked. Before I finished, we stood on a cliff overlooking Crater Lake. He went into a Skyclimb freefall over the lake and reached the Wizard Island portal less than half a minute before me, enough of a lead for an escape.

The Old Man stopped me from jumping in after him. "Hey, boy, slow down. You'll never find him in that maze. He could be anywhere in the world now, anywhere in time, another dimension . . . You go in there and, before I can dream of doughnuts, you'll be lost forever."

"Ohhhh," I threw my arms down. "How did I screw that up?"

"He's a slippery one. Don't worry, you'll see him again." He patted my back. "In the meantime, Spencer and that pretty girl aren't far away."

20

Following the directions the Old Man gave me, I took the portal-to-anywhere and arrived at Booker's place a few seconds later - an 11,000-square-foot house overlooking Klamath Lake, with a glorious view of Mt. McLoughlin. Detailed stonework, round rooms and towers carved out of the rugged landscape reminiscent of an English palace. A large tropical conservatory stood near the house, where mangos, papayas, plumeria, bananas, and orange trees grew. But what really made me know it was Booker's, aside from the four-wheel-drive golf carts, were the runway, heliport, two hangars, and FAA-approved fueling center. The entire fourteen-hundred-acre estate was also solar- and wind-powered. Even with no return portal, getting back to Crater Lake would be an easy fifty-minute drive or about fifteen minutes, as the crow flies, Skyclimbing.

Security awaited at the stone entryway, but they waved me by as one spoke into a mic concealed in his clothing. Inside, a gorgeous three–story atrium, crowned by an octagon skylight, towered over smooth mica-flecked, clay walls, and the same octagon pattern repeated itself on the inlaid tile floor. Spencer walked in from one of seven halls, which opened from each wall. He smiled when he saw me. "I'm happy to see you alive."

"Likewise."

"You don't have the Jadeo."

"No."

He nodded. "We'll worry about that later."

"Where's Linh?"

"Sleeping upstairs."

"Are we safe here?"

"Are we anywhere?"

"How did Omnia find us in Hawaii?"

"They were onto Dunaway somehow. I'm sure we're fine."

"Rose is here also." It had been a long time since we'd been in the same place. I was eager to see my aunt. "But before you talk with her, I'd like us to take a few minutes."

"Sure." I followed him down one of the halls, which led to a grand dining room, past a commercial kitchen and eventually out to a deck of stunning blonde wood with posts and railings carved in animal totems. In the near distance a man-made waterfall cascaded two hundred feet over rocks that appeared to have been there forever. The only thing interrupting the view of Klamath Lake was a three hundred foot, lavender labyrinth in the middle of a perfect lawn.

"It's good to see Booker still has some of his money," I said.

"Oh, don't worry about Booker," Spencer said.

"Is he here?"

"No, too risky to blow the cover of this place. They watch him very closely. But we'll catch up with him somewhere in the future."

"Ah, the future. What do we do with that?"

"Things are about to get rocky, I'm sorry to say."

I couldn't help but laugh. "Are you serious? They haven't *been* rocky?"

"People are being tortured, killed, whole communities locked up; tens of thousands within the Movement have disappeared; millions of others are in prisons."

"Are you trying to cheer me up? I know all this."

"I'm trying to say it's time." Spencer coughed.

"Are you okay?"

"You need to step up. You're not a boy any longer," he said, ignoring my question. "Don't allow confusion to run your life. This is your time."

"But I don't know what to do."

"And I can't tell you. Most people let their lives go by, never taking control. They watch it instead of living it. You are not most people, yours is not an ordinary life. Find the answers you need, discover the way. It's time." He seemed gaunt, aged.

"Then I want to see the Dark Mystic."

"I'm not stopping you."

"But you are unless you tell me where to find him."

"You're not listening. There comes a time when external learning reaches a point of diminishing returns. Everything you need is within."

I stared out at the lake, suddenly noisy with Canada geese. He was asking a lot of me. But Spencer was also telling me that he believed in me, that I was ready, and that made me feel good. His opinion meant more than any other.

"Thank you," I said, turning to face him. "I'll try to live up to your expectations."

"You've already exceeded them. All you need to do now is live up to everything you are. Do that and you'll not only amaze yourself, you'll change the world."

ooooo

Later, Aunt Rose found me sitting in Booker's rose garden, thick with award-winning flowers, many in colors I'd never seen before nor imagined.

"You're here, right in the middle of my favorite spot." Chiffon and silk scarves trailed behind her, competing with the palette of hues before me. "Can you believe the varieties of roses this man grows?" Rose hugged me tight. "Ooooh," she purred, "just look at you. You're so grown up. You make your poor aunt feel old."

"You are old, Rose," I joked.

"Hmm, I guess you're right."

"But you're wise, too."

"Ha, I don't know about that."

Even after all this time, my relationship with Rose was somehow unsettling. She had gone from banished aunt, to psychic savior, to dead, to a traitor and now to a wise mystic. I often wondered who Rose really was.

"Seriously, I want your advice," I began. "The Movement is in trouble and Omnia is more powerful than ever. I'm supposed to be here to help change things, remind people to wake up. But Rose, I don't know what I'm doing."

"Remember something, honey. It's always darkest before the dawn. Omnia only seems more powerful because they are *showing* more of their power. And if you know anything about Omnia, they don't like to show their power. They are doing it only because they're scared. They know their power is not endless, that's why they are desperately seeking more."

"So what do I do?"

"Come see the labyrinth," she pulled my arm. "You've never seen anything like it." We ran across the manicured lawn. "No Skyclimbing allowed."

"It's gorgeous," I said.

"Sure is. Wouldn't you love some popcorn right now? We could just sit here and watch the lavender in the breeze like a movie."

I laughed.

"Now ask your question, silently to yourself and then walk the labyrinth, concentrate on nothing other than the path you are on. When you come out, ask your question again."

I stepped into the purple and green maze. The plants came up just below my waist and I was lost in a sea of color and intoxicating scent. My steps became slow, small and deliberate. It was silent except for the hush of a gentle breeze. An hour must have passed.

"The only answers that came were Outviews and Clastier," I said to Rose, as she joined me on a bench at the end of the labyrinth.

"Nate, honey, that's it. The Outviews are where you must begin. You need to find the understanding in them. And remember Clastier's teachings, they are within you because you were him. Without those two ingredients, you'll find it impossible to lead."

"Lead, I won't be able to do anything if we don't win."

"Honey, you have to know you've already won. If you don't believe this, then you'll never win. If you aren't prepared for the day when you receive everything you ever wanted, it will never come."

"Rose," I wanted to argue. "What do you want me to do?"

"I want you to consciously create the circumstances you desire. But first you must find understanding and now you know how to do that."

"Prepare a list of my Outviews?"

"Yes."

"All of them? I can't remember all –"

"Of course you can. They cannot be forgotten. Once your list is complete, search each one for the meaning. This is a roadmap for the lessons you'll pass on."

"But I haven't even mastered all the soul powers."

"Who has?" She laughed. "That won't happen in a single lifetime. Lives are far too short; that's why we keep coming back."

"It'll be easier when everyone remembers who they are, what their souls really are . . ."

"Can you see that? Because you need to see it, Nate."

I nodded.

"Work on that." She smiled. "Now, we're trying to hook you up with Clastier so you two can recreate the missing papers. So much to do, wish we had more time."

"Rose, do you realize I almost died today . . . three times?"

"Died? Whatever that means." She rolled her hand dismissively. "Now go study your Outviews before Omnia blows this pretty house up." She handed me paper and pen from her rainbow-colored, sequined bag and left me alone.

I walked over to the pond at the base of the waterfall. Gnarled, knotty, twisted trees like the ones in the Japanese garden at Lithia Park and snow-capped Mt. McLoughlin in the distance gave the impression of being in the foothills near Mt. Fuji.

For hours I assigned names to Outviews and scribbled a

brief description of each. I read the list over and over, reliving the horrors and remembering when, in this lifetime, they almost destroyed me. It was Wandus who originally had told me the Outviews were the key. I silently wished he were here to help. Maybe I could go to him. I looked up to see if Spencer was still on the deck; he would know how to find Wandus. My gaze swept over the waterfall as Wandus somersaulted in slow-motion down from the top.

"Old and young Nate, it is happiness to see you here." His eyes reflected all the colors of the yard, light flickering from somewhere else.

"How did you get here? I mean, how long?"

A yellow smile stretched across his thin leathery face. "You know, I wonder this myself, often. How did I get here? How long have I been here? I will continue to dwell on these questions. When I find the answer I will tell you."

"Are you here to help me?"

"That is one possibility. Let us see." He floated closer. "Why aren't you levitating? You should never get too used to the ground."

I levitated next to him, and we moved slowly with the breeze. "What story do the Outviews tell?" I asked.

"I've told to you this each time we've met, Outviews tell the story of you. What has your soul been through? Did it learn? What happened because of that lesson? This is the tale to tell."

"But I need to understand it first."

"Yes, or not. It would be like me explaining how to rebuild a jet engine."

"Right, you don't know anything about engines. Well –"

"But I do know all about automobile engines, and diesel engines, even small engines such as lawnmowers, but jet engines are an entirely different bird."

I laughed, even though he was serious, or as serious as

Wandus could ever be. We floated across the pond and were caught in the mist of the waterfall.

"Happy, happy, this is fun, fun, fun," he squealed.

I handed him my list. The letters on the pages all arranged themselves into a different order. "What happened to the list?"

He looked at the papers as if they might be on fire. "Oh, I don't understand English so I changed it to my language."

"But you speak it so well."

"No, I don't speak English at all, but you do hear it well." He handed the pages back. "Yes, it is in them. Do you see it?"

"No. Can't you just tell me, please?"

"The greatest treasures are not given, they are discovered."

ooooo

For the rest of the day I toiled alone on the deck seeking understanding in the Outviews. They seemed more like scary ghost stories than life lessons.

I looked up from my Outview papers to see Linh coming toward me.

"I'm glad you made it," she said.

"Even though you're mad at me?"

"I'd never be that mad. But don't leave me again, okay?"

"I can't promise."

"You could, you can do whatever you want, you just won't."

"Please don't be mad."

She shook her head. "Nate, I don't want to die alone and I don't want to live without you. If we stay together then we can die together."

"Let's concentrate on living."

"These are dangerous times."

"I know."

"Outviews?" She motioned to the pages.

"Yeah, trying to find the meaning in them."

"Look for us in them. Then maybe you'll understand me."

I nodded. We were quiet for a while, lost in the scent of lavender and roses.

"Any word on Amber and Yangchen?"

"You miss her, don't you?"

"Don't you?"

"Yeah." Linh left the deck. I put my papers down and watched her walk the labyrinth.

As she went around and around, I suddenly saw my answer. Each life is a circle, and all our lives are a bigger circle of our one true soul life. I scanned my list of Outviews. The Mayan runner pushed into the Cenote by the conquistadors reflected the countless lives I'd spent dying to protect secrets; the time as a Union soldier, when I sacrificed my life to let Kyle go free, was loyalty; Wesley digging his own grave represented karma; even the future Outview where I'd run from drones in the face of an advanced society, although it hadn't happened yet, showed the challenge of the Movement, my ultimate destiny. It went on and on; Amber and I as sisters; Fitts killing me along the river in a prior life; the time I was chased by a slave trader and then *was* the slave trader.

There are no original ideas. Everything has happened before; it will continue to repeat until we, every last one of us, find enlightenment. The betrayals of Amparo, incarnations as Clastier, Dad at Chichen Itza in 1904, and hundreds of other lifetimes . . . each of us play every role, see each emotion, understand all the intricacies and nothing at all. Each life left many great lessons. They were what I would teach and how I could lead people to the soul powers.

But even more important, they showed me the door to enlightenment. My hands pulsed with energy at the realization that I had discovered the key to that door - that every life we have ever lived, ever will live, and all the simultaneous lives we are experiencing in the present, are always here - a cosmic imprint on the fabric of our soul. It's all one life, and because time is a very different thing than we've been led to believe, that one life, the one of our soul, has no beginning or ending, and we may visit any part of it at any moment.

"Nate is only the face I'm wearing for a brief time. It is not who I am," I whispered to Linh, even though she couldn't hear. “I am everything you are.”

22

For days, I journeyed back through Outviews searching for Dunaway. He was untraceable but it was all worth it when, at an antiwar rally in New York during August 1914, I spotted Amber and Yangchen. Instead of being incarnated as someone else as part of the Outview, they were their current selves. I was a thirty-two year old police officer with full memory. I worked my way through the crowd of more than a thousand and told Amber if she didn't return to her own time she would be arrested.

"How did you find us, Nate?" she asked.

Yangchen looked over. "He's smarter than he looks, Amber, but it did take him longer than I thought."

"How did you both get here?"

Amber looked at Yangchen and then back at me.

"Calyndra," I said. "I should have guessed. But why?"

"It takes time to change things. We've been here a year and will stay several more trying to stop the war," Yangchen said.

"But you've only been gone a few weeks."

"Time's a funny thing, isn't it, Nate? Even so, you could not be away from the Movement that long."

"Amber, do you really think being here is more important than what's going on in our lifetime?"

"You two should take a walk. I'm speaking next. I'll be here when you get back," Yangchen said and shooed us away.

We strolled down a side street. "Why did you leave?"

"I'm trying to make a difference."

"Yangchen can do this if she wants but I need your help where we have a chance for real change."

"Stopping World War I would be a real change that could change everything you're trying to change before it even happens."

"It won't work. Come back with me."

"You need time to be with Linh."

"What? Is that what this is about? You're jealous?"

"I am not jealous but of course this is what this is about. You and Linh belong together and it doesn't matter what I want."

"Does it matter what I want?"

Amber smiled. "No."

"Well, I think it does."

"Then tell me, Nate, what do you want?"

I stuttered. "I . . ., Amber . . ., I . . ."

"I know you do." She kissed me. "You're kind of cute, for a cop."

"I love you," I whispered.

"I love you, too, but it doesn't matter."

"What? No. Hell, yes, it matters!"

"You know destiny is a powerful thing."

"Yeah, we're powerful, too." I pulled her into an abandoned doorway. "And what's more powerful, love or destiny?"

"Sometimes, love and destiny can't be separated and sometimes they can't be joined."

"Watch me."

"Nate, the universe is infinite. We'll be together again. We've been together before. In a dimension somewhere we're together right now. We get so much . . . but we don't always get it all."

"Come back, Amber, please."

"I'll be back soon, we still have things to do here."

"Don't you realize nothing will change? The Espionage Act of 1917 and the Sedition Act of 1918 will still pass giving the U.S. government the right to shut down newspapers and imprison people with antiwar beliefs. Eugene Debs will still be arrested while giving a peace speech and he'll be sentenced to ten years in prison and nine million people are going to die in this war."

"No," she stared angrily. "Things can change!" Amber turned away and walked back to the demonstration. I hesitated a moment and was caught on the opposite side of the street as fifteen hundred women, all dressed in black, marched down Fifth Avenue in complete silence. No bands played, no signs or banners, they carried only the peace flag. Crowds of onlookers watched in silent, sympathetic approval. It was a powerful demonstration.

ooooo

That evening Yangchen, Amber and I met in the lobby of the Biltmore Hotel. They had attended a series of meetings, talks, then a banquet and were tired. We headed up to their suite.

"Nate, what if I told you that us spending a few years here might stop the war?" Yangchen asked. "And even if we fail, we may save millions of lives. How do you know that the war you studied in school wasn't changed by our actions here? Maybe WWI originally lasted three more years resulting in fifteen million deaths. Maybe there was a world war one and a half that killed millions more. Amber and I are working with the advantage of knowing the future and knowing ways to change it."

"Okay, I'll grant you that. Maybe you will save millions of lives but I have a different mission in my time, in Amber's time and this has nothing to do with that."

"It has everything to do with that. Everything is connected."

"Do you really need Amber? Can't you do this alone?"

"That's not up to me."

"Nate," Amber began, "go home, I'll be there sooner than you think. Don't get too caught up in the various definitions of time."

"Time? I'm still trying to understand the definition of home."

"You'll be okay," Yangchen said.

"If the time doesn't matter, then why don't I stay and help you, and we'll all go back together," I said.

"Don't be silly, Nate," Yangchen began. "You have much to do, the Jadeo is in dangerous hands, the missing Clastier papers are needed, the Movement is in turmoil, mystics are in prison, should I go on? The list is long . . . and someone has to keep an eye on Spencer Copeland."

"You make it sound so appealing, how can I resist?" I flashed a defeated smile. "Will you give us a minute?"

Yangchen bowed slightly and walked into one of the bedrooms, closing the door behind her.

"Amber, I'm sorry for earlier."

"Me too, and if you promise not to ask me to come back with you again, I'll tell you a secret."

"Okay."

"Every moment away from you feels like a punishment, like I can hardly breathe." Our eyes locked. "If you were in Nate's body instead of the cute cop's, I'd attack you now."

"Tell me where Calyndra is and I'll be back in a flash."

She laughed. "No way, you've been away too long already. Stop letting me distract you." She cocked her head and stared at me. "Nate, your life isn't your own. Sometimes I worry that you think just because all this is happening to you it isn't important. It's everything." Her hand reached for mine. "But know this, if I could have anything I wanted, it would be for you and me to live a quiet life on some tropical island doing spiritual readings for tourists."

We kissed and held each other until we were both trembling with tears.

"You have to go," she whispered between sighs.

"I don't want to."

"I don't want you to." But before I could savor her words, Yangchen barged into the room.

"Nate, there's trouble in the future. Clastier's been taken. You must leave this instant."

A last desperate look at Amber.

"Go!" she shouted.

23

Spencer waited on the deck at the lake house. Clastier had been on his way to meet me there when Omnia agents discovered him in California. We could communicate with him on the astral but were unable to get his exact location.

"Why the hell can't we find him when Omnia managed to?" I blasted as soon as Spencer finished updating me.

"We're working on it but Omnia has developed a way to find your past incarnations and has begun rounding them up through Outviews. Imagine their surprise when they got one in the present."

"Are they going to get Hibbs?"

"Eventually, it's likely. The good news is that apparently it's a tedious, time-consuming process. We've got Yangchen and Tesa working on understanding exactly how they're doing it."

"I just left Yangchen."

"Yes, I know, but she has a way of multitasking."

"Multitasking."

"Yangchen is better at bi-location than anyone other than perhaps the Dark Mystic."

"She can bi-locate across time and dimension, can't she?"

"Yes, she's a remarkable mystic."

"If they can find all my incarnations, what about the current ones?"

"We don't think they are able to use their method on

incarnations that are still not completed. You'd have to be dead for them to find you."

"How comforting," I said, sarcastically.

"We believe Omnia has discovered how to indentify a soul's code - its DNA, if you will. Each soul is, of course, unique, and it has long been thought, among mystics, that a soul carries a marker that once unlocked could reveal every life ever lived by that soul. There may even be a way to detect all the current and future lives as well. Imagine Omnia with information like that."

"I'd rather not. How are they making these breakthroughs?"

"Omnia has their own mystics."

"Yeah, but how are the mystics being convinced to work for such an evil organization?"

"That's the power of Omnia's leader. He and his top lieutenants are masters at manipulation and propaganda."

"I'm having real doubts that we can win this."

"I know you are. But that's a waste of your energy. Here's a lesson for you that's as great as any soul power. Instead of using all your energy and brainpower for worrying, use it to solve the problem and you'll find anything can be overcome."

Linh joined us on the deck. "Oh, nice to see you back in the present."

"Sorry," I said, as if she knew where I'd been.

"Did you find Dunaway?"

"No."

"Anything else interesting?"

"Nate," Spencer interrupted, "you should stay out of Outviews for a while. It's too dangerous. Not only are you left in a vulnerable trance in the present but even more troublesome is that Omnia's agents could pick you up anywhere in the past. We have no idea how many people they now have in how many lives." We told Linh about Omnia's latest advantage.

"You're not thinking of going after him?" Linh asked.

"Clastier is not an ordinary prisoner. He has forward-memory of my lives. If they figure out a way to read him, it's over," I said.

"Then get Rose and Yangchen to send him back. They brought him here, way too soon in my opinion, and they need to fix it."

"They can't do that without getting him to the right portal," Spencer said. "We have to get him quickly."

"Send someone else," Linh said.

"I'm sorry, but as soon as we find where they have him, we're going to have to go," Spencer said.

Linh looked at me. I nodded. "Oh," she huffed and ran off.

"Go ahead." Spencer waved me off. "I'll call you when we get word."

I caught up to Linh in the lavender labyrinth. "Wait."

She turned, glaring, crying. "Why do you want to die? There must be someone else who can go?"

"Linh, it's Clastier."

"I know."

"He's me. His writings are critical to the Movement."

"I know."

"If I don't go, they'll use him to get me. No one has a better chance to rescue him."

"I know."

"Then what?"

"I'm afraid of losing you." She pulled me into a ragged embrace. "I love you."

"I know . . . I love you too."

"Nate, Nate," Spencer yelled from the deck. "Come now! We know where they're holding Clastier."

Before I reached the deck, the swirl of an Outview swept through. I tried to resist but it had me. The last thing I remember was falling face first into the grass as I slipped painfully into an Outview, bound by claustrophobic spirally mist until the lifetime fully enveloped me.

My life as a farmer in Afghanistan during the early 13th century had been difficult but not desperate, until Omnia's men showed up among invading Mongols. The entire village along with my farm and anything else of value for hundreds of miles was ravaged or burning. The only escape route forced me along a cliff high above a deep, wild river. Screams echoed off the canyon walls as I ran. A small party of men on horseback were raping and killing stragglers. Suddenly, less than fifty feet away, I saw a neighbor thrown over the cliff. I was helpless as he flailed. I couldn't hear him land above the Mongols' raucous laughter. It brought back a memory of the lifetime when I secretly carried the Jadeo as the Conquistadors taunted, gutted, then tossed me off a cliff. Throughout the history of our species there always seemed to be men who enjoyed killing. Were these agents working with Full-Memory or was Omnia able to twist some soul power in order to manipulate them?

Only a cluster of boulders shielded me as three men dismounted.

"Root out the vermin," one still on horseback shouted.

From my hiding place, I counted three still in their saddles. One was scanning the area frantically. His face was visible and I recognized his soul immediately. As soon as the shock passed, complete certainty flooded my consciousness: there would be no mercy. It shouldn't have been surprising that Sanford Fitts was among Genghis Khan's raiders. He could finish what he started in San Francisco. Fitts would finally kill me. What would it mean for the Movement, the future? Would Nate ever exist at all? I went dizzy with the possibilities. Then I heard his scream.

"Nate!" Fitts was staring right at me. He and another mounted Mongol charged. Their curved swords raised at their sides. I involuntarily closed my eyes, ready to die. But the next screams I heard were not my own. Had there been other peasants hiding nearby? My eyes flew open. Fitts and his companion had killed the other four Mongols. In my confusion I tried to scurry over a boulder but fell back, scraping my leg.

"Nate, I'm not here to harm you," Fitts said.

"What?" I waited for his bloodied blade to come down on me.

"I've come to save you."

"I don't believe you." I looked for a rock.

"Nate, I would have killed you by now. Did you not just see me murder four of my own men? Don't be foolish, there's not much time."

"You have full memory?"

"Yes."

"But your life as Fitts?"

"Sadly, I will not have my memory in that life."

Making eye contact with the other soldier, I realized that one was Amber and gasped.

"*My friend there* doesn't have Full-Memory therefore has no idea about his future life as Amber," Fitts said, realizing my recognition.

"But he's helping you help me. Why?"

"The web of our lifetimes and the resulting karma is such an extraordinary thing that the word extraordinary should be reserved exclusively for the description of it."

We didn't see the arrow until it pierced the other soldier's/Amber's neck. Fitts spun and shot, killing the archer, who must have thought he was saving me.

"Come, we must go, now," Fitts shouted, impatiently.

I ran to the fallen body of the man who had been Amber, desperately searching for a trace of her soul.

"Nate, he was not Amber. She is alive and well in your future life. We're not concerned with that incarnation at the moment. If we don't get you out of here, your life as Nate will not occur," Fitts said.

I was lost. The personality of my Afghan incarnation was confused. The clarity of my soul to influence his life was fading.

"Do you understand?" Fitts asked. He must have known he was losing me. Quickly, he tied my wrists and lifted me onto Amber's horse. We rode in silence for hours, my saddle tethered to his. When we made camp for the night, he untied me and calmly explained that his soul was coming from a future incarnation years beyond that of Fitts or Ren and, through a technique I taught him in that future life, he was able to enter his Mongol life and act to change it. "Remember," he said, while moving rock slabs to conceal our fire, "time is not from beginning to end, it is all now. Everything that has ever happened or ever will is contained in a single instant."

"It's hard to comprehend," I said.

"You taught me that."

ooooo

The next morning we set out before dawn and rode deep into the night. That rigorous routine continued for five long days until the sea came into sight. Along the way he had tried to teach me various soul powers but the Afghan-me couldn't do any of them. We talked about many of our future lives together. I hoped his version of the future was the one that actually would happened, many things could go wrong between now and then. There were secrets to keep, mystics to find and people to help.

"You'll be safe here," he said. "Get work as a fisherman, practice your soul powers, you'll be fine."

"How can I ever thank you, Fitts?"

"It's not about thanking, it's about forgiveness."

"Didn't I tell you to avoid Outviews?" Spencer asked, kneeling next to me in the warm grass.

"I don't always have control over them," I said.

"I know. I'm assuming since you're still here that you didn't encounter Omnia."

"No harm done. How long was I gone?"

"Only a minute or two. They've got Clastier with the mystics. It's our best chance. But if we're going, we need to go right away."

Afghanistan and Fitts/Ren taught me that some things are more important than a cause or even saving the world. Loyalty and forgiveness were two of them. Monumental things can be built on them and this was the reason Clastier and the mystics needed to be saved. One of the last things Fitts said to me was, "We'll meet again and before again." It was a nice way to put it. I looked forward to seeing him next, whenever that might be.

It was true Spencer and I almost died the last two times we went for the mystics, but I could no longer tolerate their imprisonment. We had failed on the earlier attempts to free Amparo, Baca and Kirby because we were doing it for the wrong reasons. Instead of strategy, now it was for loyalty. Rather than trying to hurt Omnia, this was about helping our friends.

They'd been moved from Nevada into a network of secret

CIA prisons in North Africa and Eastern Europe. For more than a year, since our last try, the mystics had been held at three different locations and we could never identify more than one at a time. Now, suddenly, they were all in the same place again, and Clastier was with them.

"It's gotta be a trap," Linh said.

"Yes, it is," Spencer said.

"Then you can't go."

"Tell that to him." Spencer pointed at me.

"Linh, I'm sorry but they are only there because of me. Almost two years in prison, subjected to who knows what, for trying to help me. Baca saved me from capture or death. I have to do this."

"You sound like the hero in one of those dumb B-movies you used to watch. You don't have to do this."

"Nate, I know I said this before the other missions," Spencer began, "but I must repeat it. These mystics did all those things for you because you are so important to the Movement. They knew the risks and made their choices. They do not want you to put yourself in jeopardy by coming for them. We're in contact with Clastier, he is willing to end his life, he only awaits our word."

"I know and I get that. But I've let enough people down. I'm not going to abandon them. What good is a leader or even the Movement if we abandon people and principles along the way? My powers are their best hope."

"Your powers aren't much good against elite combat units when you've pledged non-violence," Spencer said.

"Have you forgotten the hundred and four soldiers I converted at Outin?"

"That was a different dimension," Spencer said.

"Our whole existence is a different dimension from somewhere," I said.

"Yeah, and that helps you how?" Linh asked.

"Linh, don't worry. This time will be different . . . we have help. Lots of help."

"Nate is referring to six of the personnel deployed at the prison who are sympathetic to the Movement," Spencer told

Linh.

"Why?"

"Those six were at Outin; they're members of the hundred and four," I said.

"Part of the trap. Why would Lightyear put them there?"

"The mystics are in a special class of prisoners. Those six have experience with special people because of their time at Outin," I said, "and there is no evidence that any of them have broken their oath to me."

"How can you be so sure?"

"I monitor them."

"Really?" Linh asked.

"It's not difficult . . . the astral." I smiled.

"Nate, if you really want to go through with this, we need to go now," Spencer said.

"We're going."

"I'm going, too," Linh said.

"Too dangerous."

"That's my point."

"Linh, you can't come."

"Then, I won't be here when you get back."

"Don't say that."

"Nate, I'm not some schoolgirl chasing you around. I'm part of this Movement. Do you forget that I've been through almost all of it with you?"

"I know, that's why you're too important to come."

"Nice try. You and Spencer are the most important people in the Movement and you're going."

"I'm sorry, Linh."

"Nate, our window is closing," Spencer said.

"Good luck, Nate, and goodbye."

26

Booker's helicopter dropped us in a meadow above Crater Lake. After making our way to the Wizard Island portal, we quickly emerged in the jungles of Thailand.

The compound was half a mile away. This was as close as we dared to be since it was likely that the jungle was filled with traps, cameras and guards.

"What's the plan?" Spencer asked.

"Skyclimb to the treetops until we get close and . . ."

"Try shapeshifting," a familiar voice said from somewhere in the thick undergrowth.

"Dunaway?" I asked.

A tiger lunged and knocked me down hard. It was a blur of fangs and claws as I wrestled with the massive cat. With some help from Spencer and Gogen I got free and levitated above its reach. The tiger morphed into Dunaway.

"You were terrified, Nate." Dunaway laughed. "You shouldn't let fear control you so easily. I mean, come on, a tiger against your powers? Don't be such a wimp."

"What the hell are you doing here?" I asked, failing to control my anger.

"Kirby is one of my mystics."

"How nice of you to come and save her," I said, sarcastically.

"I can't let you two peace-loving hippie freaks get her killed."

"We can use the help," Spencer said.

"As long as he doesn't use violence," I added.

"What makes you think you get to make the rules, Nate?" Dunaway asked. "Omnia isn't some pushover. They have mystics and magic, too. Why do you think Kirby isn't able to just shapeshift her way out of this? Omnia has powerful people keeping watch over these mystics and they know you're coming."

"We know they know."

"So Skyclimbing is your big plan? Let me just move out of your way. I'm too impressed."

"Unlike you, Dunaway, I think the universe is based on love and I trust the universe."

"Then trust that I'll do the right thing."

"But I don't trust *you*."

"You two are like a couple of children. Grow up," Spencer said. "We have serious work to do."

"Hey, Spencer, I don't work for you, okay?" Dunaway jeered.

The three of us Skyclimbed to the top of the trees.

I communicated with Spencer directly over the astral so Dunaway wouldn't hear. "I've told our six friends from the one hundred and four that we're here. Clastier and the mystics know, too."

"Nate, I want the Jadeo from Dunaway before we leave here."

"I know you do. But let's not get distracted from our mission. There'll be time for Dunaway and the Jadeo later."

An invisible force hit us so hard we were knocked from the trees and sent tumbling through the tangle of branches. Before I could even right myself, I realized the jungle was burning beneath me. It was an inferno that could have been caused only by soul powers. The sky, lit from bright flames, suddenly filled with choppers. I had no idea where Spencer and Dunaway were. I brought a torrential rainstorm down, which doused the flames and caused the helicopters to retreat. Spencer appeared from out of the smoldering ashes and smoke.

"This way, Nate. Hurry!"

I soared down and followed him into a long tunnel that the flames had formed through the trees. A rushing river of blackened water and debris filled much of the space. We floated toward the compound.

"There's no longer an element of surprise on our side," I yelled to Spencer.

"There never was."

"Our six friends have been instructed to use non-lethal force against their comrades. If we get out of this, we'll have to bring them with us."

The downpour suddenly ceased. Dunaway was Skyclimbing next to us. "You overdid it with the rain, I'd say."

I ignored him.

We broke into a clearing and spotted the building that housed the prisoners. That's when things got very strange. Blue twilight changed to a pink and yellow glow. Everything was pulsating; the sound evolved into a high-pitched hiss. Slow motion blurring of colors and scenery rippled around us. Trees and buildings appeared and disappeared in a collage of time and dimension. There was no way to be sure what was real. Four helicopters fired at us. I caught Dunaway waving his arm in a circular motion above his head apparently causing the choppers to crash into each other. Fire and shrapnel enveloped us. Spencer was hit. I rushed toward him. Dunaway tumbled past in a glowing orb, and, in one fluid motion, left the orb on Spencer as he continued flying. I followed Dunaway through a darkened spiral into the building.

There were soldiers down all over the place - alive but unconscious. The six had been helpful. Once we got through the exterior doors I expected the surreal vortex-world we'd been in to recede but instead it became psychedelic. The corridor flexed and bent, grew and shrank - movement was extremely difficult.

"What powers are they using on us?" I shouted to Dunaway.

He shook his head and pointed forward.

The drugged bodies of seven or eight soldiers rolled into

us as the hall tilted severely until we were dropping down a dark round shaft of red and blue lights. It was a nightmare version of Alice in Wonderland. The unconscious soldiers came down on top of us as we dropped what felt like a mile. Death seemed certain and I fought mightily against fear. We ended in a pile, smothered by the bodies. I used Gogen to free myself. Incredible pain came and went.

Someone pulled me to my feet. It was one of the Outin one hundred and four.

"What is all this distortion?" I shouted, above what was now a groaning siren.

"We don't know, it just started. Thought you were doing it."

"No. Where are my friends?" I asked.

"Follow me," he said. Dunaway was already ahead of us.

We entered another hallway that was spiraling and growing longer. "It's like some kind of funhouse from hell," the soldier shouted.

Dunaway put more distance between us. The hall turned steeply upward. I threw the soldier on my back and Skyclimbed toward the opening that Dunaway had already gone through. We fought our way out of the hall and into a large room where the noise and distortion finally stopped. Six cells lined each side. Three more of the Outin hundred and four were there.

"We've got two men helping Copeland," one of them told me. They, like every member of the military or law enforcement, knew Spencer on sight.

I noticed that one of the solid cell doors was already open. I pointed. They shook their heads. "Open the other doors," I yelled. They did, and Baca, Ampora and Kirby rushed out. The other cells were empty. "Where's Clastier?" I yelled.

"He was in that one," a soldier answered.

"Damn it." I slapped the door. "Kirby, do you know Dunaway?"

She looked confused.

"Come on!" I left through the door opposite the one I had entered; they followed. Immediately the distortion resumed.

This time I tried various powers to temper it but nothing worked. After what seemed like days, we emerged into the night. It was, thankfully, normal again. Spencer, mostly recovered now, stood with two friendly soldiers.

"What happened?" he asked.

"Dunaway got to them first."

Spencer looked at the mystics and back to me. "He has Clastier?"

"Yes."

"Damn him!"

"Why does he want Clastier?"

"Same reason Omnia does. Clastier is the next best thing to having you. And in Dunaway's case, it's even better because he can't kill you but he can kill Clastier."

"And there's something worse . . . Clastier knows what the Jadeo is."

27

Baca came over and hugged me. I hadn't seen him since he saved Dustin and me after we left Outin the first time. He'd been in prison for more than two years because of me and his first act was to embrace me. "You needn't have come," he said in Spanish. "This was too much risk."

"I'm sorry we didn't make it sooner."

"It's not been so long. Time's a funny thing."

I smiled. "Nice tattoo."

"When I was first captured, they put me with other inmates. One was a member of the Movement, an artist from Peru. It's his work." It was fantastic, stars changing into butterflies. "I'm sorry to say he died during my escape attempt." He bowed his head. "That's when Omnia realized I was a mystic. They spent months trying to convert me to their side." He meant torture. "I've been in power-controlled solitary ever since."

"I'm so sorry, Baca."

"No, Nate, it is I who am sorry. I should have escaped to save you this trouble."

I shook my head.

"How's your brother?"

"Baca, you are my brother."

He smiled. "Then your other brother, Dustin."

"He's okay. I don't see him much."

"That's never good. Brothers ought to see each other every day. There are too few brothers in the world."

Kirby shapeshifted into her younger form and kissed me. "I knew you'd come. Dumb thing to do, but I knew you would."

Ampora took my hands and pulled them to her lips. A single tear rolled down her cheek. "Thank you, Niño. You should not have troubled yourself."

"We need to go," one of the soldiers said. "It's almost two clicks to the transport plane. Normally, we'd take a helicopter but . . ." He pointed to the still burning heap of wreckage. The plan was to fly the plane to the nearest portal that would get us to Crater Lake. We'd be in the air for about twenty minutes. The odds were still heavily against us but there might just be time.

As we entered the jungle the first explosion occurred. The soldiers immediately took up defensive positions.

"Use no force," I yelled.

Spencer created a dense blue fog that extended from just above our heads and continued hundreds of feet into the air. But after two more near misses it was clear the bombs were not being dropped from above. And while we were still figuring it out, the fourth one exploded.

"Henderson and Martin are down!" one of the soldiers screamed.

"They're detonating them from satellites," another shouted.

Thick smoke mixed with Spencer's blue fog. Flying dirt and rocks injured Amparo's leg. I did a healing and stopped the blood.

"We have to move!" a soldier yelled. "They'll keep hitting closer and closer until air support can pick us off."

I carried Amparo while doing a low Skyclimb. Henderson and Martin were dead. I read the minds of the remaining four soldiers who were questioning their decision to help me. They would be lifelong fugitives . . . if they lived.

Two more explosions on top of each other. "Dawson is hit," a soldier cried out.

Baca screamed in pain. While racing toward him, the other soldier pulled me to Dawson; his whole left side was burned and bleeding.

"This is a Lusan," I said, handing it to the soldier. "Move it across his injuries." Then I continued in the direction of Baca.

Trees fell as the next explosion rocked the air. Before I could get back on my feet another opened a crater next to me. I'd lost track of everyone and my ears had been damaged by the blasts.

"Spencer," I said over the astral, "we're in trouble."

"I think I've located their satellite."

"Seriously? You can do that?"

"I can only home in on it when they are using the signal to detonate these things. Damn, I need one more."

"I don't think you'll have to wait –"

This one threw Amparo and me into a crater. I rushed to her side; she was hardly breathing. I had enough minor injuries to make doing a full healing difficult, but it would have to do. I left her cradling two Lusans.

"I've sent their satellite out of orbit. They won't be able to correct it," Spencer said on the astral.

I found Baca on the astral maybe eighty feet away and crawled over to him. At least two of our remaining soldiers were now exchanging ground fire with Omnia forces. "No force," I said, but no one could hear.

Baca was dead. I tried to revive him until Spencer found us and stopped me.

"Let him go," he said on the astral.

"Damn Omnia!" I shouted, unable to hear my own words.

Shots whizzed all around us.

"Spencer, do you have a pen and paper?"

He looked at me, puzzled.

"Give it to me," I mouthed.

With bullets flying in all directions, I carefully traced the butterfly and stars tattoo off his arm, then stuffed it in my pocket.

"We'll meet again and before again," I whispered.

Three of our soldiers, Amparo and Kirby were still alive.

We moved Spencer's blue fog into the direction of Omnia's shots and I brought the rain back to that section of the jungle. It gave us enough cover to reach the airfield. None of us could hear, so we communicated over the astral or with hand signals and made it out of the trees. When we got to the hangar, the plane was gone.

"Are there any other portals we could reach?" I asked Spencer.

"No."

"There can't be much time until they get here."

One of the soldiers patted my shoulder. It seemed like he mouthed, "Back. Up. Plan."

We followed him across the field and thirty yards into the trees. There in a tiny clearing and under heavy camouflage was a helicopter. It took less than a minute to clear it with Gogen, and suddenly we were airborne. Spencer gave the pilot the location of the portal as he flew dangerously close to the treetops. He and I took turns keeping us in a Timefold. The chopper was slower; it would take nearly fifty minutes to reach the portal. During the flight we fell out of the Timefold many times and were exposed, but Kirby employed other techniques to help conceal us. We hit the portal without further incident, and any doubts the soldiers had vanished once we were inside. The awe never left their faces, every portal was different, each one unforgettable. It streaked with swirling leaves and in places opened to the dense portions of the outer galaxy.

Back at Booker's lake house we healed our ears and Amparo made a full recovery. Losing Baca was hard on me, but my thoughts were stolen by something much worse than death. Clastier and the Jadeo were now in the hands of Dunaway, which meant that Omnia might no longer be our biggest problem.

In the confusion of getting everyone healed and settled, it was several hours before I realized Linh was gone. Once I found her on the astral, she refused to talk to me.

Spencer and I sat on the deck watching the clouds over Klamath Lake. We'd been searching the astral for Clastier ever since we returned but both he and Dunaway had vanished.

"What is all of this for?" I asked in despair. "I mean, in the end, will any of it matter?"

"Haven't you seen enough to answer that yourself?"

"That's not what I mean. Enlightenment, the shift, awakening - whatever you call it - surely it'll still come whether Omnia kills me or not."

"Perhaps, but when?"

"With all the other dimensions, changes through Outviews, the parallels, I'm not sure what's really happening half the time."

"Nate, don't you see? It's all happening."

"Even with all I've learned, I have a tough time understanding. How are we ever going to convey it to the masses?"

"That's what the Movement is for," he said, life sparkling in his turquoise eyes.

"What if the Movement fails?"

"What if it succeeds?"

"More than two years in and I still don't know exactly what the Movement wants," I said. "So tell me, what does the world look like if we win?"

"Let me ask you something first. Do you like the way things look now? The way we're heading?"

"Of course not," I said. "But that's not enough. Revolutions always start with someone pointing out what's wrong with the status quo. And too often the post-revolution world isn't much better, sometimes even worse."

"This is no ordinary revolution. This change cannot be reversed. Once awakened, a soul cannot deny what it knows. I've seen many people discover their soul, touch just a hint of its power, and become terrified."

"I understand that."

"Yes, you do, and you know what it almost did to you, what it did to Dustin? Most people cannot handle what it is to know their soul. It changes everything they've ever believed about the world. It's a massive cover-up and we're all complicit."

"Yeah, but no one set out to disconnect us all."

"Just because there is no one to blame doesn't mean something didn't go wrong."

"We were talking about the Movement."

"When people see a glimpse of their soul and then try to go back to being 'normal,' their life becomes more difficult. The soul, once awakened, cannot be denied."

"So you're saying that just showing people what is possible will –"

"The numbers will expand exponentially . . . then, the world will move closer to what it should be. There will no longer be crime or war. Hunger and poverty will vanish. Greed and corruption will fall away. It will be the end of division and hatred. Put simply, it will be the beginning of unity and love."

"Can we get there?"

"We must."

"It seems so far away."

"But that's the wonder and beauty of it . . . the future we are speaking of is right here, all around us, easily within our grasp. You have seen it because it is here. All we need to do is open our eyes."

"So the Movement, the revolution, is about opening our eyes to our souls. That sounds simple but how does that get rid of Omnia and all the failed ways of the past?"

"It is simple because hatred and fear cannot exist where there is only love."

We continued to sit, in silence, while I pondered his words, until Spencer excused himself. He was communicating with someone on the astral and although he could do this with many people at once, occasionally he required privacy. His secrets bothered me but not as much as they once had. It was often difficult; I trusted him.

I found Aunt Rose in the kitchen "sneaking" a piece of squash pie with almond topping. It was sweet enough to have been served in my parents' dessert-famous restaurant without anyone missing the sugar. Could it have been almost seven years since Mom, Dad, Dustin and I all ate at the Station together? I missed them all . . . I missed my childhood.

"Well, you and pie in the same room is almost too much sweetness to bear," Rose smiled as she swallowed a bite.

"Linh's gone."

"I know. What are you still doing here?"

"You mean I should go after her?"

"That's why she left, so you'd chase her."

"Seems like a game."

"It's not a game, Nate. She's hurt."

"She doesn't understand."

Rose raised an eyebrow. "And you do?"

"I'm just trying to keep her alive."

"Nate, there's a whole Movement that's trying to keep *you* alive. You don't always like it, do you?"

"That's different."

This time she raised both eyebrows. "Yes, I'm sure you think it is."

I scowled.

"She's with the Old Man."

"I know."

"Then what are you waiting for? Go bring her back. We

don't need any more distractions."

ooooo

Linh and the Old Man were in a hidden valley high in the mountains surrounding Crater Lake. They were carefully planting seeds from a large bag slung over their shoulders. The Old Man saw me as I came down from my Skyclimb but Linh didn't. I watched for a while. The wind played with her long dark hair. Her face had a lovely concentrated look as she tilled the soft earth, then delicate fingers dropped seeds, covered them and lightly patted the dirt. When she glanced my way, I waved, but was ignored.

"What are you planting?" I asked.

"Trying to save the food supply," the Old Man blasted. "Gonna take a long time before all seven billion people on this planet are breatharians. In the meantime, they're gonna need food. Course some crazy corporations are trying to screw that up," he ranted. "The arrogance of man astounds me. Why some folks think they know more about nature than nature knows about nature . . . these same jumbleheads stare into the night sky, behold billions of stars, know there are trillions more they can't see, but they proclaim we're all alone in the universe. Aren't we just so damn lucky to have been born on the only place in all of existence that supports human life? Bah!"

"Omnia knows that whoever controls the food supply controls the people," I said.

"These are original seeds, sown by the ancestors." The Old Man held some out, as if he was showing me nuggets of gold. "They've been maintained and passed down. My people and other indigenous cultures are guarding them and planting them in protected areas around the planet. But Omnia . . ."

"I'm going to stop them."

"It needs to be soon. The bees are disappearing; the GMO-corrupted seeds are cross-pollinating and contaminating the pure ones. They don't know what their meddling will do. And it'll be too late before they figure it out."

"It's on my list."

"Big list. I believe in you, boy, you've come a long way. Now, see that you don't forget about the girl . . . she's important, too." He winked at me.

ooooo

Linh and I walked among the old trees. As always, they calmed me. "Linh, I'm sorry."

"I'm glad you made it back."

"We didn't all make it."

"I know. I saw."

"What else do you see?"

She stared away. When she looked back her eyes were filled with tears. "I need to be able to believe what you say, Nate. All the time."

"Linh, we rescued them. It had to be done that way."

"Just because you know many things doesn't mean you know everything. I know things, too. You're not alone in this."

"It's all so crazy, I feel like the whole world depends on me, and the future is –"

"I've seen things about the future . . . awful things."

"Tell me."

"No." She recoiled. "There are some things about a person's future they shouldn't know."

"About my death? I'm not afraid to die, Linh, you should know that. I've been through so many."

"Not you."

"What then? Yours . . . Amber's?"

"I don't want to talk about it."

"Listen, Linh. You know the future is not set. Whatever you have seen can change. It might not even have been from this dimension."

She was quiet for a minute and then changed the subject. "Do you miss your parents? Kyle?"

"Of course I do. Wandus tells me that missing someone is selfish. He says we must be grateful for each moment we share with someone and that once it has ended, we should only be filled with the joy of what it was."

"Then I'm selfish because I miss Kyle so much."

"But Kyle, my mom and dad, all still live in Outviews and other dimensions. And their souls never die."

"So why did you cry over Baca and Crowd?"

"Because knowing and doing are two very different things and I'm still learning."

She nodded.

"Come back with me, Linh. Please."

"Do you promise not to shut me out anymore?"

"I promise."

29

"Kirby, Amparo, Wandus, Rose, you and me . . . there are too many of us here in one place," Spencer said. "Kirby, Amparo and Wandus will leave this morning."

"To where?" I asked.

"Do you really want to know?"

I shook my head.

"Omnia is furious over our victory," Spencer said. "But of course, the public doesn't have a clue we freed the mystics. We need new recordings of you."

"What good will they do? Omnia controls the media and has the Internet locked down. It's been almost a year and a half since we managed to get our message out to a wide audience."

"There is a way to project them in the sky. Similar to what we used to record the Storch meeting."

"Incredible, and they can't stop us?" I asked.

"There's always a counter to everything, but it will likely take them a long time to figure it out."

"The Storch meeting was a high-level government official trying to recruit me and his sweet quote about people being expendable was even more helpful to us than his admitting to Lightyear's crimes. We need another scandalous scene like that. Let's not waste the impact of broadcasting in the sky on some new-age talk. Let's find Omnia's leader and get some dirt."

"One step at a time," Spencer began, "If we track him down, there'd be many options. In the meantime, let's concentrate on getting the Air-Projection set up first. To do that you'll need to go back to Outin."

"Are you serious?" I asked.

"Dustin is the only one who can teach you Air-Projection."

"You don't know how?" I looked at him puzzled.

"I've only just learned it's possible. It's not a technology that comes with a manual. This is an advanced energy technique that requires using forms from all five great soul powers."

"But Dustin? Hard to believe he's more advanced than you."

"We each have our strengths," Spencer said.

"Okay. I want to talk to Dustin anyway. Since he was also Storch, he'll know where Trevor is being held."

"Nate, I thought you were leaving that alone."

"No, I've never stopped searching for Trevor. Ever since I saw the painting he gave me hanging in Storch's office, I knew Dustin could help."

"There is no trace of Trevor on the astral," Spencer said.

"That doesn't mean he's dead. I have never felt his change."

"Trevor is not a mystic. You cannot waste your time nor risk your life on one ordinary person no matter how good a friend, no matter how many lifetimes you shared."

"I won't let him waste away in another prison."

"Do you know how many are in prison? Millions."

"Spencer, it was Dachau . . ."

"Dachau is not the worst humanity has to offer."

"I don't recall seeing you there." My voice rose. "You can't say, unless you were there."

Spencer closed his eyes and sighed. "There are too many distractions. You've never understood that this is about much more than one life, the lives of a few friends . . . this is everyone's lives at stake."

I took a deep breath. "I need to help the people who have helped me, who have loved me. If I don't do that, then I can't be expected to lead. I'm haunted by enough demons. Let me quiet the ones I still can."

"You could die. Do you think I say these things to frighten you? Look how close we came to dying during our first two attempts at rescuing the mystics. Even our last effort nearly ended in disaster, and we had inside help. Do I need to mention the time when you went to help your friends at the Shakespeare Theatre in Ashland; trying to save Dustin from Fitts; Hawaii, Prague, the Outin incident? Do you think death can't find you?"

"I don't have to worry about my dying, you worry enough about it."

Linh walked in. "What's going on?"

"Now our B-movie hero wants to rescue Trevor," Spencer said, hoping to enlist Linh as an ally to his cause.

"I'm coming with you," Linh said.

"I'm counting on it," I said.

"Argh." Spencer threw his hands up, exasperated.

"I'm sorry, Spencer. You can't control me anymore."

"I never could," Spencer brushed a hand through his hair. "If you insist on this, do it from Outin, it's your best chance."

"Thanks." I smiled. "Do you at least see that this is about loyalty? Fighting the betrayals will never stop the betrayals. Embracing loyalty is the only way."

"Your loyalty should be to the Movement."

"They aren't mutually exclusive. Do you know how you're always telling me to trust the universe? And that you can't just trust the universe when it's convenient?"

"Yes."

"Well now I'm telling that to you."

ooooo

Rose helped Linh and me prepare for the trip to Outin. "I think I'll come along," she said. "At least far enough to see Dustin." Spencer left at the same time but promised to be back at the lake house before us. It would turn out to be his first broken promise.

Omnia continued to search aggressively for an entrance to Outin. Mt. Shasta had become a giant military base, so entering from there would be too dangerous. Linh had the idea for us to return to Pasius, the peaceful dimension where we'd found my parents still alive, and go to Outin from there: Mt. Shasta in that dimension was still a peaceful sanctuary.

As we took our first steps on the starry ground of Outin, both Dustin-two and the one from our world materialized before us.

"Whoa, how did you do that?" I asked.

"Outin is like a microcosm of the universe. There's this basket-weave-pattern of wormholes across the whole dimension," Dustin-two answered.

"And you know where they all are?"

"We've found a bunch of them but Outin is like forever big. I'm not sure we'll ever find the end."

"If it has an end," my-Dustin added.

"How'd you know we were here?" Linh asked.

"Oh, you won't believe it!" Dustin-two said. "We have this viewing power that lets us see everywhere we've ever been, even after we're not there anymore."

"What?" I asked.

"It's as if we had a video camera mounted on our heads ever since we were born and all we have to do is think of a place we've been and it'll show it again," Dustin-two said, waving his hands around. "But what's really cool is we can look at all those places in the current time, too."

"It's part of Foush, but it takes an inordinate amount of energy so I only keep it open to the entrance," my-Dustin answered.

"Incredible. Does it work in the regular world?"

"I don't know but we've been to Pasius twice and couldn't do it," my-Dustin said. "It's like Pasius and especially our world have heavier atmospheres or something. You know, Outin is so pure."

"Speaking of Pasius, why haven't you sealed the entrance from there like we did to the one from our dimension?" I asked.

"They don't know it's here. No one's coming from there."

"They will. Omnia's been to Pasius. They killed Kyle and . . . they killed Dad." I looked at Dustin-two. "I'm sorry."

He zoned out and stared far away. It was a look I knew well from my-Dustin. Then he vanished into an Outin wormhole.

"I didn't mean to just blurt it out like that."

"He'll be okay," my-Dustin said.

"Where do you think he went?"

"Probably the Vines; he's addicted to the Windows."

"What about you?" Linh asked.

"Me too." He smiled at her, his first since we'd arrived. "So Omnia's invading other dimensions now, even a peaceful one like Pasius. Is that why you're here visiting your exiled criminal ex-brother?"

"You decided to stay here. No one forced you."

"It was only a matter of time before you found out about Storch. You might have killed me and God knows we don't need anymore of that kind of karma between us."

"Well, I know who you are, and you're still free and alive, so why do you stay?"

"Only way I'm ever leaving Outin is dead. This place was made for me . . . or vice versa."

"But you went to Pasius," Linh said.

"And you showed up in Russia in 1912," I said.

1885	9781935070221	1885

Location: B3

VOM.KFJ

itle:	Outmove (The Inner Movement)
ond:	Good
ser:	vo_list
tation:	Workstation-01
ate:	2022-02-14 21:26:22 (UTC)
Account:	Veteran-Outsource
Orig Loc:	B3
mSKU:	VOM.KFJ
Seq#:	1885
unit_id:	4190688
width:	0.92 in
rank:	4,242,488

delist unit# 4190688

xxxxx

"A man's gotta travel every now and then." He winked at me. "It's a big world full of time and troubles."

ooooo

We sealed the entrance before heading to the lodge, then took a glorious and healing swim in the Monet-like Floral Lake. Linh looked softer and happier than she had in years. But our relaxation didn't last. I worried that Omnia would soon figure out a way to attack from inside my head. There was too much I didn't understand about the soul powers.

"So you said you need my help with another power," Dustin said, as we walked along the shore.

"Yeah, seems you're the only one who can show me how to project images onto the sky."

He squinted his eyes. "I'm not even sure it's possible but . . . did Spencer tell you I could show you?"

"Yeah. He calls it Air-Projection."

Dustin smiled. "Then, I guess it must be doable. It's just been a theory . . . I spend most of my time practicing. There may be five great powers but there must be a million different ways to use each of them." His voice was excited. "I've been exploring variations and really getting into blending them, you know, seeing what's possible, what I can do."

"It seems Spencer is paying attention."

"I wish I could watch everything and see all the possible futures like he does, but whenever I try anything like that, my head starts to hurt." He slapped my back. "It's kind of cool to know that no one else knows how to do Air-Projection and that I sort of invented it."

"Can you show me?"

"Are you sure you trust me, little brother? What if instead of showing you this power I taught you something that could kill the people in the Movement?"

"I don't think so."

"You don't think I'd do that or you don't think you trust me?"

"Dustin, where is Trevor?"

"Ohhh, now the truth comes out. Are you here to find your old concentration camp buddy or learn the secret of Air-Projection?"

"Both."

"And, by the way, I noticed you didn't answer whether you trusted me or not." He turned to Linh. "Does he talk to you in this double-sided slippery way too, Linh? I don't know how you put up with it."

"Dustin," I said.

"Nate," he moaned.

"What?"

"Straight answer time, anointed one," Dustin grabbed my shoulder.

"I trust you, all right?"

"Look me in the eye and tell me that."

"Oh, come on."

"Do it or the bunny gets it!"

"You've lost it, man."

"No, little brother. I've found it, and you know I have. There is so much you don't know, and it freaks you out that your screwed-up older brother isn't such a screw-up after all. Your great mentor Spencer Copeland has twice sent you to ask my advice . . . and even saving your holocaust pal depends on me."

"Saving Trevor only depends on you because you're the one who locked him up."

"Ahhh, see, you're still confused. It wasn't me, Nate. Storch was a man, he was separate from me."

"Your soul was aware of both incarnations. How do you explain that? Maybe you couldn't do anything about also being the one trying to destroy me, but you could have told me. Dustin, why? Why were you silent?"

"You wouldn't have given me a chance. In your eyes, sharing a soul with Storch has made me guilty of everything."

"Don't you see? It wasn't you being Storch . . . the betrayal was in your silence," I yelled.

"I know." His words trembled and were hardly audible. "I was scared."

The admission surprised me. We stared at each other for a few seconds before he turned away. "Of what?" I finally managed.

He turned back and I read his expression. Dustin was baffled by my question. "What do you mean of what? Of everything!"

"I don't –"

"No you don't because you think your life has been tragic and hard, but you're like the poor little rich kid complaining about having a rough day because his Ferrari is in the shop so he had to drive a Lexus. Your 'tortured' Outviews are baby food, Nate. Your life is so far out of perspective. Did you ever wonder why *I* met Crowd first? How long did you ponder why Dad put *me* on the list? How many mystics have *I* met?"

"Dustin, I know you're important, I know you know things –"

"Important! You say it like the only reason I'm important is because *you* say I am. Is it exhausting thinking you're the king of the world?"

That wasn't a conversation I wanted to have. "Let's get back to where Trevor is."

"No, Nate," Linh said. "You guys need to get back to being brothers."

"Great, the other Dustin is coming back," I said, pointing at Dustin-two heading toward us. "Now I get to argue with two of them."

"Don't worry, he just looks like me; we're surprisingly different," Dustin said.

"What's he pulling?" Linh asked.

"It looks like a Window," I said.

Dustin reeled around and started running toward Dustin-two. "No," he yelled. "Don't bring that here. No!"

We started running, too.

31

After an aggressive brotherly scuffle, Dustin-two and I managed to subdue my-Dustin. But for an instant, when I first looked into the Window, I wished my-Dustin had succeeded in preventing me from seeing it. The world inside the Window was as close to a real life hell as I'd ever seen. The worst Outviews and my scariest nightmares didn't equal the horrors inside that Window.

Tens of thousands of bodies lay rotting, many still breathing and moving, even screaming, while grotesque animals, large insects and oily, deformed birds ate their intestines and fed upon their open sores. A centipede-creature the size of a loaf of bread was eating a man's eyeballs while he tried to swat it off with what was left of his arms. I looked in the other direction and a huge vulture landed to feast on his already gnawed legs.

Stumbling, zombie-like humans caught and ate the same animals, bird and bugs, which were eating the people. Less than half the inhabitants wore filthy rags that barely covered them. The rest were naked, but it was difficult to tell because they were coated in layers of grime, and, oddly, some were even painted. The only water I could see were blackened pools and streams. An old woman cupped her hands and drank from a large pond; a tar-like liquid ran from her fingers. The dark gray-brown sky was filled with green and purple noxious smoke spewed by factories that seemed to produce pollution as their main product. Crews of toothless scarecrow-looking women with hollow faces moved large carts filled with the bodies of babies. It wasn't clear where they came from but they dumped them into waiting trucks. A pile of human limbs burned near a low building; men and women were being raped in the streets. Gangs roamed, beating and killing, but I turned away once the cannibalism became obvious.

Linh screamed and then threw up.

"What is this place?" I asked.

"It's a parallel dimension called Carst," Dustin-two said. "Omnia has sent millions there. All the 'missing' people from 92426 that everyone wonders what happened to . . ." He motioned into the Window.

My brain was slow to comprehend. "92426 is my dimension. What is this place?" I repeated, as if he'd never answered. "How . . ."

"Carst is a place so unevolved that people live worse than animals."

"I can see that but what does Omnia –"

"Omnia has sent close to twenty million people there from 92426 and other dimensions. Anyone they want to get rid of," Dustin-two said.

"Why did you bring this to show me?" I asked.

My-Dustin was still held to the ground by Gogen but yelled at Dustin-two through gritted teeth, "Stop it. Just shut up."

"He has to know," Dustin-two said to my-Dustin.

"Know what? Why did I need to see this nightmare?"

"Because that's where Trevor is."

I choked and coughed, trying to find my breath. I wanted to kill my-Dustin.

"You did this," I screamed at him.

"No," he shouted, fighting Gogen, trying to get up.

"But you knew!"

"I couldn't stop it. I couldn't save him."

"You knew!"

Linh intercepted my charge. She was somehow stronger than me, stronger than my rage. Her grip felt soft like a salve, but a glance back into the Window doubled my fury.

"How could you have allowed this?" I spit my words at him while fighting Linh.

"I didn't, Nate. It wasn't me, it was Storch."

"But you kneeeeeew!"

Linh's strength was incredible, but my power and rage won. I landed on my defenseless brother and raised my fists together in the air. Then, with all the power-enhanced force I had, I brought them down toward his face. Blinding wrath and vengeance controlled me until my locked fists were less than a millimeter from his face. Suddenly, both of us were flung high into the air. We moved at such speed that it was impossible to breathe. My vision blurred but returned as we arched into the skywaves, which changed color and splashed like water as we penetrated them, yet nothing was wet. Our rapid descent slowed to a float. We drifted down into a dense forest of giant silhouettes. We passed though the large gray and black trees that appeared to be only shadows, and hit the ground hard. The stars were obscured by white ground fog and pink mist.

"Where are we?" I asked.

"Beats me, I've never been here before," Dustin said. "Hey, I'm not pinned to the ground anymore, still want to fight me?" he asked, shoving hard, sending me tumbling through two shadow trees.

A person ran between the trees, or rather a shadow did. Two more ran at me from the other direction, then three came out of nowhere. "Dustin!" I yelled. But it was too late. Seven or eight "shadow-people" pulled me deeper into the forest. My powers were empty against these non-people.

"Who are you? Where are you taking me?" I yelled, but it only came out as a whisper.

They talked among themselves, all at the same time – whispering gibberish. It didn't feel like Outin without the star-ground; even the skywaves weren't visible through the shadows and mist. I yelled for Dustin again but he couldn't have heard the faint sound that escaped my lips.

With each movement, the shadow-people grew longer or

shrank in angles as shadows do. I couldn't keep track of where they were. I broke free and ran, then slammed into their solid but translucent bodies. They bent, turned and twisted so that every direction I went ended in a wall of shadow-people. I kicked and pushed but could never get through. Finally, exhausted, I sat in the mist and gave up.

"What. Do. You. Want?" My voice still hushed. I looked up, demanding an answer. They were gone. I was sitting alone in the shadow-forest. After I got up and paced around, it seemed obvious that they weren't coming back. I wasn't sure which direction to go and wished I could Skyclimb and tried. All my powers had returned! Skyclimbing in shadow-tress felt like learning it again. I ran across the treetops and soon found my bearings. A silhouette walking in the distance, heading toward the lakes, had to be Dustin.

"Why aren't you Skyclimbing or taking a wormhole?" I asked, when I landed next to him.

"I just feel like walking." His voice was low, defeated.

I nodded. We walked together in silence for a while.

"Aren't you going to take another swing at me?" Dustin asked.

"No."

"Where did those shadows take you?"

"I don't know, somewhere in the trees."

"I looked for you but that forest is the strangest I've seen here. The slightest breeze shifted everything, even my movements caused the trees to rearrange. I've never felt so lost . . . it's a tragic place."

"Yeah." I stopped and stared back toward the charcoal-gray trees. "The shadow-people reminded me of something I'd forgotten."

"What's that?" He looked at the forest, too.

"The power is in surrender."

Dustin kept watching the trees as if he expected to see something that would answer his questions.

"That's what they showed me. It's hard to remember when we're weak with anger that there is strength in forgiveness," I said.

"So you've forgiven me? I don't feel any stronger."

"That's because you have to forgive yourself."

Dustin nodded slightly and we walked on in silence. Soon after the shadow-forest faded into the distance, Linh saw us and ran to me.

"What happened?" she asked.

After I told her the story, she asked Dustin how come he'd never been to the shadow-forest before.

"I doubt it's really there," was all he said.

"If you go into the Carst Window you'll have to stay twenty-four hours until the portal opens again. Do you want to stay there that long?" Dustin asked.

"Nate, that's crazy," Linh said.

"Trevor has been in there for two years."

"And remember when you come back, your memory will be split, you'll feel brain-damaged," Dustin said.

"What's he talking about?" Linh asked.

"Only half of my life memories will be here; the other half will be filled with stuff from Carst."

"The schizophrenia will give you a glimpse into what it's like to be me," Dustin said.

"You can't go," Linh said.

"It's not permanent."

"How long does it last?" Linh asked.

"Just get me to Floral Lake."

"I may not be able to stop you," Linh said. "But Nate, I swear if you're not back once that portal opens again, I'm coming in after you."

"Linh, if I don't return, then I'm dead." I looked into her eyes. "And I get that you may want to die too; just don't go into Carst."

"But you are."

"I'm going for Trevor, he's still alive. If I die, you'll feel the change, and if you want to join me, run into a hail of Omnia bullets, jump off a bridge, whatever . . . but. Do. Not. Go. In.

There." I pointed into the Window where we could see hundreds of young kids leaving a factory, many missing limbs. They were chained together in groups of twenty.

ooooo

Once inside the Window, Carst's horrors cut through all my senses. The suffocating stench of burning flesh, reeking piles of human waste, death, decay and chemical fumes scorched my lungs. Ditches and puddles overflowed with urine, blood and a toxic stew of poisons. The temperature must have been near a hundred, humid, stifling and absent of any air movement. The moaning sounds of death, cries and screams made it impossible to think.

I stood out like a glowing god - clean, healthy, fully alive. Only Skyclimbing and levitating kept me above the clamoring hands of beggars, hunters and thieves.

Now in the same dimension, it took only a few minutes to find Trevor. He could have been a skeleton, if not for the dried flesh draped on his body. His only clothing was what might have once been a collared dress shirt, stained bloody shades of brown. The buttons were gone, and only pieces of shoelaces knotted together held it closed. Without soul-powers, I wouldn't have recognized him and he had no clue as to who I was. He cowered when I approached.

"Trevor, it's Nate, I've come to get you out of here."

He shook his head, slowly at first but then it changed to a tremble. A tube was attached to his arm, my eyes followed it to a large container, draining his blood. I read the area and discovered they took as much blood as they could from the living. Carst's stronger and more important inhabitants drank it or used it to cover the taste of rotting animals they found to eat. He jumped when I disconnected the tube and healed his arm. Only my use of Gogen kept him calm, but his eyes were wild. In my reading, I saw too many rapes and violations against my friend to count. He refused to look at me. I put us in a dome of healthy air and used various powers to conceal us.

As gently as I could I held his head and stared into his terrified eyes until some recognition began to register. It was a long time before he began to sob. I let him cry until he slipped into sleep. Every few minutes he woke screaming and clawing. Solteer took care of the wakings.

I moved us to a nearby rooftop as darkness set in. There was no real danger to me since I was a superhero compared to the empty shells who populated this horror-world. Still it was the most difficult night of my life.

Slaughters and hunts took place below in such numbers I couldn't believe anyone would be left in the morning. The screams and cries amplified in the darkness, the only light came from fires and eerie green glowing sticks. How had Trevor survived all this time? How did anyone? I did what I could to save any children nearby. They darted around heaps of garbage, scavenging for food pursed by packs of sick empty "people." What was I saving them for? I thought. "Wouldn't they be better off dead? How could I destroy Carst for good?"

I kept Lusans on Trevor all night. At first light, he woke in tears; then, staring into my eyes, he tried to speak, "Ney," he tried. "Na, Na . . ."

"Trevor, no, I'm taking you out of here today."

"Nay, Naay . . . Nay . . . ta."

"You're safe."

"No." He closed his eyes tight.

I did more direct healings around his throat and head.

"It's just a few more hours. I won't leave you," I said.

"No. Can't go."

"Yes. I'm taking you."

Trevor looked at me, his eyes hollow, ringed with purple and black circles, a gaunt, toothless face, pleading. "Kill me." It came out as a strained whisper.

"We'll get you healed," I said. His request shouldn't have surprised me but it did.

"No healing from hell."

I didn't know what to say. "No," I finally managed. "I'm taking you."

"Please, I beg."

"Trevor, let's talk about it at home."

"I would do it for you." He raised his hand and pushed two fingers into my chin. His weakness was devastating . . . everything was.

We didn't talk for a long time.

"Please," he said.

"I can't."

"Please," he was crying again.

It was too hard for him to talk, I communicated with him on the astral.

"I'm taking you home. We can heal you. You will recover."

"No one can recover from this, Nate. Look around. Read my life here. How long have I been here? Twenty years?"

Trevor believed it had been that long and I couldn't get past three days of reading him, it was too gruesome. "Trevor, I'll take you to an island, we'll get you a boat."

"The only peace you can give me is to send me back to my soul. Kill me . . . I would do it for you."

"You can heal."

"I don't have the strength left to recover from this. It's my time and you must do it."

"You'll change your mind once we're out of here."

"Please."

ooooo

A few minutes before the portal opened, I used Gogen to stop his heart, fulfilling his wish to die. "We'll meet again and before again, old friend." I said, kissing his forehead, then draped his body over my shoulder and headed for the portal.

Linh and both Dustins were waiting as I came out of the Window. No one spoke as I carried Trevor to a high bank over Floral Lake. They helped gather flowers. Once his body was completely buried by flowers, I set fire to it. After keeping it burning for hours, all that remained was a small pile of dust and bits of bone. I created a wind to blow it far over the lake. Only then did I speak.

"Someone will answer for this. Without vengeance, I swear

I will find the person responsible." I looked at Dustin. "Do you know who runs Omnia?"

Amber and Yangchen were waiting at Booker's lake house when we returned, but no one knew where Spencer was. Trevor's loss impacted me more than all the other deaths, not because I ended his life and not because we were closer than I'd been to the others, but because his long slow suffering, and the very existence of Carst, showed a level of cruelty that went so far beyond greed or lust for power that it caused my perspective to shift radically, and I no longer recognized anything, least of all myself. The haunting screams of those who remained in Carst, like a tinnitus torture, never left my ears. Instead of hardening me to suffering, it had the opposite effect. To see anyone or anything in any pain at all could cripple me.

Carst had to be destroyed, and if that wasn't possible, I needed to empty it and seal all the entrances forever. There were three people who might be able help: Yangchen, Spencer and the Dark Mystic. Yangchen had no answers, Spencer was missing, and the Dark Mystic was as far away as ever. Linh said I'd been distant since my return from Carst. It was true, but I didn't know if I could shake my frustrated focus until Omnia fell.

Yangchen counseled me on ways to improve my powers. We worked on Air-Projection, being careful to keep our -early experiments small enough to avoid detection by satellites. Booker had installed the very best anti-listening devices in the house and around the property but we also utilized a Time-

View-Cover or TVC, a technique known to only a handful of mystics. It allowed a person to conceal a space that they could travel within while holding their breath. Skyclimbing made it possible to make this area quite large, and it moved along with the initiator. A TVC was similar to a Timefold in that it made the initiator invisible, but it was much more stable and longer lasting.

"Do you think Spencer is using a TVC to avoid detection?" Linh asked Yangchen.

"I hope so."

"You really don't know where he is?" I asked.

"No. I'm puzzled . . . and troubled."

"I think he's gone for the Jadeo," Linh said.

"Kirby told me that Dunaway knows how to use TVCs and she's never known anyone so skilled at moving through Outviews," Amber said. "He could be anywhere."

"I have to find him," I said.

"Ironic that a member of the Movement and one of the seven is a greater threat to the Movement than Omnia," Linh said. "Until we get the Jadeo and Clastier back from Dunaway, it's going to be difficult to go after Omnia."

"Unfortunately, Omnia will not wait for us to get our house in order," Yangchen said. "They have hit squads roaming Outviews, other dimensions and across our current time seeking all incarnations of Nate, the mystics, Kyle, Dustin and you two." She pointed to Amber and Linh.

"Us, too?" Linh was surprised. "I knew they would kill us in this world, but other times and dimensions . . . Why are we that important? And Kyle?"

"Oh, Linh, each of us is important. Some maybe more than others in certain times or specific lives, but the stronger a soul becomes, the greater its role in helping others."

"Nate, what happened to your arm?" Amber asked.

"Nothing, it's a tattoo." I hadn't shown it to anyone, but Amber spotted the bottom of it.

"It's beautiful," Amber said, pushing up my sleeve. "The butterflies from stars are for the Movement but where does the 'ENDURE' come from?"

"It was Baca's tattoo. I added endure –"

"Endure was the painting Trevor gave you," Linh said.

I nodded.

"A good motto for the Movement," Yangchen said. "Come, walk with me, Nate." Her tone made it clear the girls were not invited. I followed her to a cliff overlooking the lake. Several boulders had naturally formed to benches, or, knowing Booker, they'd been carved to appear naturally formed. "I sense great change in you since your night in Carst."

"Have you seen it? It's the most horrible place in existence."

"I've not been there but I assure you, there are worse places."

"How can this beautiful universe contain such terror?"

"Those parts are a reflection of us. Humans are hurt, afraid and lost. That kind of desperate fear gives rise to many horrible things. You want to shut down Carst, you wonder how to stop Omnia . . . you know how to do these things, you only forget."

"Love."

"Yes, love – a small, simple word, but nothing is bigger in its reach, nor more complex in its power."

Yangchen went on to tell me everything she knew about the Dark Mystic. "It's time for you to seek him. I believe you are ready. You must go off alone. He may appear as someone else; he is cautious."

"Does he know me? How will he find me?"

"The Dark Mystic would know you even if he weren't one of your mystics. But remember, he is not like the mystics you are used to. You think the Old Man of the Lake is cranky, you think Spencer holds secrets, that Crowd was tricky and that Amparo is overly entwined in your karma . . . The Dark Mystic will make all that look trite. I think you are ready but I do not know for sure, only he will. So be careful, Nate."

"But mystics are supposed to teach and help me, right? Why do I need to be careful?"

"When you guide-write, it's impossible to channel all the information you're receiving into your fingers fast enough to write the message clearly. That's what it's like to talk to him, and his definition of teach and help is unlike any you've known . . . Nate, he may think killing you is the best way to show you something. A betrayal more brutal than anything Amparo ever did might be how he helps you. He may have been the first mystic. No one knows for sure because he has always existed in the earliest lifetimes anyone has ever found. The Dark Mystic is the greatest test you will face in this lifetime."

The sound of someone singing shattered the tranquility of the forest. It was even more jarring because of the Time-View-Cover I'd used during my weeks of solitude.

Yangchen had warned that the Dark Mystic could appear as anyone, even someone I'd known in a past life.

I Skyclimbed around several trees. The beautiful voice used the acoustics of the redwoods, surpassing any concert hall. As it echoed through the mighty trees, I couldn't place its origin. Circling and climbing, until suddenly, just below me, I saw the singer – a man in his mid-thirties, wearing cowboy boots and a black felt cowboy hat. He walked among the trees singing about the big sky at night. After a few more lines, I recognized the old Steve Earle song, "Me and the Eagle," that my dad had liked so much. But this version was different. He sang it with such perfect emotion that when he got to the part about dying in these mountains, I choked up. I interrupted his next song.

"Hey, what are you doing here?" I called down, still concealed high in the branches.

"Nate, what do you think I'm doing? Looking for you."

"What for?"

"You've gotta listen to this new song I wrote." He was still walking and hadn't even bothered to look up toward me.

"Who are you?"

"You mean today?"

"Yeah, today."

"Name's Flannery. Hasn't your brother mentioned me?"

"You know Dustin?"

"Pretty much kept him alive at Mountain View."

"Are you a doctor?"

He laughed. "A doctor? Ain't that a question!" He shook his head. "Wooo . . . no, can't say I'm a doctor."

"Then you were a patient at Mountain View?"

"Yep."

"So, are you crazy?"

"Is your brother?"

"Depends on what day you're asking."

More laughs. "Are you gonna come down here and have a polite conversation?"

"I don't know yet." Almost before I finished speaking he was next to me in the tree. I fell a few feet.

"Didn't mean to startle you, Nate. Can I still sing you my best song?"

"Uh, first tell me, are you a mystic?"

"Sure, I love music."

"No. I asked if you were a mystic."

"Well, I'd rather you call me a songwriter. Yes, I'm a mystic, but music can teach things a mystic can't."

"That's how you got through?"

"What, your TVC?" He smiled. "That's how I found you."

"How come no one else has?"

"The only people who can spot a TVC aren't looking for you. Well, there'd be old Spencer Copeland and as usual, he knows right where you are, but he's not needing to bother you just yet."

It wasn't terribly surprising Spencer could know my whereabouts but a little disappointing. If he knew where I was, why hadn't he come? He wasn't back at the lake house or anywhere else on the astral. I hadn't felt his change, so he was probably still alive but if he died in another dimension, the change might never catch up to this dimension.

"Are you the Dark Mystic?"

"What's dirt music?"

"Never mind. Why are you here?"

"I want you to hear this song."

"All right, go ahead."

"You're a bit more uptight than your brother."

"I've got a little more to deal with. Not to mention that when you knew Dustin, he was heavily medicated."

"Only his physical body . . . his soul was just as clear as new glass. And that's how we were conversing . . . well, that and music."

"Dustin doesn't sing."

"Maybe not, but he's a damn fine listener." He smiled. "I always liked that about him. Probably the best song listener I've ever known. Now, let's see if it runs in the family."

He reached into the empty air before us and a guitar appeared. "Whoa, where did that come from?" I asked.

"It'll sound better with some strings attached."

"Okay, but how did you do that?"

"You mean this?" He looked at me puzzled and strummed the strings.

"No, how did you make the guitar appear?"

"Oh, this guitar was there all the time."

"You know what I mean," I was getting a little frustrated.

"Yeah," he grinned. "I know just what you mean. Listen to the song. It's time to sing. We can talk afterwards."

I took a deep breath.

I AM CHANGE
I am change, I am smoke and mirror
I am ashes, ashes turning to dust
I am crazy, I am sane
I am desire wrapped in clouds and thunder
hear my call I am small in the midst of it all
I am small hear my call
sadness is heavy in the eyes
deeply searing ancient love lines, the soul moves
across time, turning page after page
once a peasant, then a slave perhaps a king or a
queen, a shaman, a child and all that is wild, I am
dirt I am leaves turning to soil butterflies appear

and disappear it's a fine line hold my hand
feel the tide move inside
I am change, I am smoke and mirror
I am ashes, ashes turning to dust
I am crazy, I am sane
I am desire wrapped in clouds and thunder
hear my call I am small in the midst of it all
I am small hear my call
we are here once, or is it a thousand times
close your eyes, it's life, it's death, change is
what you see, and what you feel, open eyes:
in a sigh in a kiss, in a scream, dream after dream
I am change, I am smoke and mirror
I am ashes, ashes turning to dust
I am crazy, I am sane
I am desire wrapped in clouds and thunder
hear my call I am small in the midst of it all
I am small hear my call
looking down from the trees whose mystery
grows deep, they speak in soft words,
change will change the way you break,
when you wake, that first step
tears brim, love wins, when change makes its
way in, it's not black, or just white,
but when dark turns to light, and hand hold tight fist
and nightmares persist,
the voices will sing or the voices will cry
am I sane or crazy, is it change that I see
and change that I feel is it a dream,
just a dream, dream, just a dream, just a dream
I am change, I am smoke and mirror
I am ashes, ashes turning to dust
I am crazy, I am sane
I am desire wrapped in clouds and thunder
hear my call I am small in the midst of it all
I am small hear my call

"I have to admit those are beautiful lyrics, but Flannery, your voice could make the fine print of a mortgage document sound good. Is that a regular human voice or are you using some sort of soul power?"

"Ah, you should know, all good singing comes straight from the soul."

"True enough. But tell me where beautiful guitars come from," I said, pointing to his.

"Everyone knows beautiful guitars come from the Martin factory."

I gave him my best not-amused look.

He laughed again. "Okay, okay. But let me tell you something. If you're going to convince the world that they have to give up TV, Walmart and McDonalds, then you need to lighten up a little. No one wants to follow a tight-ass."

"I'll try." He was right. But it was hard for me not to be defensive; my childhood hadn't exactly been normal. After my dad died it went from fairytale to twilight zone.

"Choose the right girl and it'll be easier. Choose the wrong one and it won't."

I nodded and managed a laugh.

"Now answer me this. If you could have any physical possession right now, what would it be?"

"A camera."

He looked at me like I was crazy.

"Okay, a camera. Really? Okay, it doesn't matter. Can you visualize it? The lens, the buttons, what color, all that?"

"Yes."

"What you have to understand is that everything is energy. It is so. Whether you understand it or not."

"That much I know."

"I knew you did but I needed you to know where we were starting from. Everything is therefore just an arrangement of energy. Perception, imagination, conceptualization. A guitar can be produced, a solid object," Flannery knocked on the tree trunk, "isn't really." He pushed the guitar into the tree where it seemingly vanished. Then he reached his arm in and pulled the guitar out again. "Now, produce your camera."

My best efforts continually failed. "It's not there."

"Everything is everywhere. Don't be limited by your mind. Your soul can arrange energy in infinite ways."

I was back on Tea Leaf Beach at my first meeting with Spencer when he showed me the basics of Gogen. In spite of the enormous growth of my powers over the prior two years, this seemed too hard.

"Here," he said, producing a baseball bat.

"What's that for?"

"Look." He pointed to the camera I'd been visualizing. It was floating two feet in front of me. I reached for it but withdrew my hand quickly as he smashed the camera with his bat.

"What'd you do that for?"

"I thought it would be easier for you if you had all the pieces."

I looked at him like he was crazy.

"I couldn't just give you the camera." He smiled. "Now go ahead, put it back together."

It took a while, but the pieces reassembled. Next I made a baseball and tossed it at him. "Try the bat on this next time."

"Sure enough. Be sure you practice what I showed you. I'm late for a gig. I never like rushing sound check."

"Thanks, Flannery. I hope to catch one of your shows sometime."

He tipped his hat. "And Nate, it must run in the family. You listen to music like your brother." He smiled, then turned and walked through a giant redwood.

35

Two more weeks alone in the redwoods did not entice the Dark Mystic. If Flannery was him then maybe I'd passed my first test . . . or maybe I'd failed. It was time to return to the lake house. Spencer had been missing for over a month and there'd been no word from Dunaway. Perhaps he had no further interest in trading my life for the Jadeo or Clastier. Even IF had been silent. Something was wrong and I could no longer afford to search or wait for the Dark Mystic.

I Skyclimbed from Crater Lake in the dark. No moon interfered with the dazzling stars. Linh was wrapped in a blanket on the deck watching the sky. It reminded me of the night we sat out together at Amber's beach house.

"Waiting for me?" I asked.

"So it seems." Linh smiled. "Did you see him?"

"No."

"It doesn't matter. Your first priority should be the Jadeo. The Dark Mystic is a distraction. Have you forgotten your oath? How long until Dunaway figures out what he has, if he hasn't already."

"Dunaway could be anywhere and I have no way to trace him."

"But you do. Your dad left you the list of the nine-entrusted. They are all trying to protect the Jadeo. As soon as you lost it and it was no longer safe, each of the other nine had to become engaged in the hunt."

"If they're aware."

"Even if they aren't. I talked to Rose over the astral a lot while you were gone. She thinks the only way the Jadeo has remained secret all these centuries is because the original nine-entrusted didn't swear it as humans, but made their oaths as souls. It's part of your strongest karma in every life. Even unknowingly, the nine will act in ways that protect the Jadeo. And the Jadeo, in danger, will awake any of the nine."

"So you think they are searching for the Jadeo? Maybe that's where Spencer's been."

"Exactly. If we can find the other eight, we may find Dunaway."

"And it's more than nine because we all may have any number of simultaneous incarnations."

"I know and that's even better. More people, more chances."

I rewrote the original list from Dad's desk and noted what we'd learned:

1.Dad
2.Spencer Copeland - mystic
3.Lee Duncan – original whistle-blower against Lightyear
4.Travis Curry – Mayan scholar (also an incarnation of Kyle)
5.Ripley Gaines – famous Archeologist
6.You – Dustin and also Luther Storch
7.Marie Jones – not found
8.Kevin Morrison – not found
9.Helen Hartman – not found

"One of the last three names on the list is another one of your incarnations."

"Something is stopping me from figuring out which one," I said, reviewing the list.

"You've been distracted. But you've got to concentrate on this now. Who are the last three?"

"And who is the traitor? Remember, one of the original

nine-entrusted betrayed the oath and has killed me and the others many times, across countless lifetimes, trying to get the Jadeo for himself." I settled next to her.

"I thought that was Storch," Linh said.

"I did, too, when I first found out about Dustin being Storch, but now I don't believe it. Dustin is distraught over being Storch. He saved me from being killed by Dunaway. Maybe because he's my brother, I think he's better than he is, but I don't believe it's him."

"I'm not convinced but let's look at the others. Likely it's not your dad, Lee or Spencer. We're pretty confident about Curry and Gaines. So you and the betrayer are in the final three names: Kevin Morrison, Marie Jones or Helen Hartman."

"Pretty common names. Hard to track"

"What if you could go back to the original oath? Couldn't you trace them through time?"

"That's a long way back. I've never been able to get anywhere near that far under my own control."

"What about Calyndra? The portal could take you right there."

"Yangchen won't show me."

"What? She thinks you're ready to meet the Darth Vader of mystics but she can't trust you with the location of a portal? What if you just went into the Wizard Island portal and asked to go to the entrance of Calyndra?"

"I've tried it, no luck. Amber must know how to get there. When we met a hundred years ago, they were themselves. I was some cop in that incarnation. It was different going through an Outview, but they'd come through Calyndra."

"So Yangchen trusts Amber with the knowledge but not one of the seven, one of the nine-entrusted, a fellow mystic, the leader of the damned Movement. Who the hell is Amber?"

"I'll go talk to her."

ooooo

Amber answered my knock on her bedroom door by jumping into my arms. After a conspiratorial look at me and up the hall, she dragged me into her room and shut the door, landing on the bed, kissing until we were naked.

Later, as I was dressing, I noticed several boxes of books on quantum physics, mysticism, astronomy and philosophy.

"Did you read those?" I asked, pointing to several boxes of books.

"Yeah, earlier."

"Do you ever miss reading the old-fashioned way?"

"You mean spending hours turning pages instead of absorbing a book in seconds? Uh, no."

"Amber, I need a favor. You remember once upon a time, you and I set out to find Calyndra?"

"Yes."

"Will you take me to the entrance?"

"But I don't know where it is. Yangchen used Solteer on me. One minute we were in the woods and the next thing I knew we're on a New York street in 1914."

"Amber, I can read you and find out what happened, where the entrance is. Will you let me?"

"You can do anything you want to me." She winked.

But it didn't work. It was hard to tell which tree was which. The lighting was strange in the reading. "I think I could figure it out if we were closer. Can you take me to the place you remember in the woods?"

"I can get you near enough."

"Good. I can read you there, I'm sure it'll make sense. Let's go first thing in the morning."

"Okay. Will you stay here tonight?"

"I can't."

"Linh?"

"Yeah."

"You think by not choosing, you can somehow have us both, but don't you see, you aren't having either of us."

"I love you both. Isn't love the most powerful thing in the universe? I'm baffled."

"You sure are." She kissed me.

I thought Amber would be upset to see Linh with me in the morning, but they genuinely liked each other. We were through the Wizard Island portal and in the Santa Cruz Mountains before anyone else at the lake house was awake. The Skyline-to-the-Sea Trail stretched nearly thirty miles from the mountains to the Pacific Ocean. I'd long known Calyndra was there but had never been able to locate it. Over the past couple of years, I'd spent some time between Castle Rock and Big Basin Redwoods, the two California State Parks through which the trail passed. My ability to recognize portal entrances wasn't perfect, but I'd become familiar enough with the area, and, based on reading Amber the night before, I was finally close enough to feel its pull.

"Do you guys feel the energy? It's so strong, I don't know how I missed it before," I said.

"Is it always so windy here?" Linh asked.

Leaves and sticks were suddenly flying through the air, hitting us. "Amber, was it like this when you came through?"

"No, and where is the sun?" The sky was collapsing in on itself. Angry clouds twisted and rolled, black over purple, swallowing the sun. "Read me quickly so we can get in the portal," Amber yelled above the oncoming storm.

The sky exploded in spectacular lightning as a deluge of thick rain unleashed. It tore down in rippling sheets, painful blades of water cut into our skin. The winds of earlier were but gusts compared to the hurricane that now crashed through the forest. In seconds all orientation and the girls were lost.

ooooo

I woke up disorientated, under an old Spanish clock tower, with cars speeding past all around. A young boy was staring at me.

"I'm Tapscott."

"Hi, Tapscott, do you know where we are?" I asked, rubbing my eyes, trying to shake off a headache.

"Santa Cruz, the town clock tower."

"Thanks. I'm a little confused as to how I got here."

The boy smiled, pointed up to the clock, and said, "Time's a funny thing, Nate."

That brought me fully alert. "You know me?" I scanned the area for police and Omnia agents.

"Of course I do, I'm a mystic."

"I'm sure you are." The kid amused me. I was a famous fugitive; maybe the kids play Nate and the mystics like Dustin and I used to play superheroes. Still, I needed to get out of there. How had that storm moved me so far away from the forest and were the girls okay? I stood up and decided my best escape was a small TVC.

"I've always wanted to travel in a TVC," Tapscott said.

"Are you reading my thoughts?"

"You're kind of sloppy with them."

A little kid trying to be serious usually made me laugh but this wasn't a normal kid. I looked closer at his face; his eyes were powerful.

"Are you really a mystic?"

"Truly."

"How old are you?"

"Ten."

"How does a ten-year-old get to be a mystic?"

"I guess I was in the right place at the right time."

I studied him. This boy made me suddenly feel old, yet the wisdom carried in his eyes left me feeling trivial. "May I read you?"

"Have you ever read a mystic before?"

"No."

"Me neither, but I've heard it can be debilitating."

"Then maybe you could tell me more of your journey." I put us in a TVC and could maintain it without holding my breath.

"For the first four months of my life, I slept well but I wasn't fully here yet. Once my soul settled into my new body, normal sleep was lost for the next five years. Then the nightmares invaded."

"Outviews."

"Yes, but of course I didn't know it then. And my parents couldn't imagine what I went through when I slept. By the time I could talk about it, I didn't know what to say. It was a natural part of me like playing with toys and eating candy. I knew that on most nights I would have to go to those places and hope to survive."

"Did you?"

"No. Not until I met my first mystic."

"Who was that?"

"A lady I called Whisper. She appeared at our public library. We went there two or three times a week, but it took a long time before I realized no one else could see her."

"I know that feeling."

"I was six or seven then. She spent the next few years helping me to understand, showing me which books to read with Vising; teaching me not to fear death or anything else for that matter. My parents said the public library was the best thing that ever happened to me, they were right."

"A good book has the power to change a person; a great book can change the world," I said.

"My father died when I was eight."

"Sorry."

Tapscott nodded slightly and stared with understanding eyes. "Then more mystics began showing up."

"When did you learn about the Movement?"

"Almost two years ago. Once you started getting all that coverage, IM went from an obscure fringe group into a . . . a real movement. There are a few million affiliated now."

"I know. Kind of amazing."

"We need more. Omnia is powerful. People are afraid of change."

"You're pretty wise."

"Past lives. Spend enough time in them and you're not your earth age anymore. Once your soul is awakened, this life is but a blink in your existence. But you know all that."

I smiled and nodded. "Yes. So what are you supposed to teach me?"

"We'll teach each other."

"I'd like that."

"Someone doesn't want you to enter the Calyndra."

"Do you know where it is?"

"I wasn't even sure it existed."

"It does."

"I know another way to get to the past."

"Outviews aren't enough?" I asked.

"Not Outviews. Something that allows much more freedom, something that anyone can do if they are of clear mind."

"I'm listening."

"Do you know about Airgon?"

37

Our conversation was interrupted by Linh reaching me on the astral. She and Amber were at a nearby lighthouse. Yangchen was with them and angry. It was a couple of miles away. We headed to them immediately. During the walk, I shapeshifted into a teenage girl so I wouldn't be recognized.

Tapscott explained Airgon. It was truly an awesome power that allowed anyone to view all of Earth's history. Unfortunately, controlling it was as difficult as comprehending it. Airgon was done through air molecules that never changed. The concept was that the air that, say, Thomas Jefferson breathed in, was still on the planet and that each time one of those molecules was present it absorbed a trace of the surrounding energy. Fast-forward to the present and any given molecule can be "read" so that the viewer can see anything that ever happened in the presence of that molecule.

"You've done it?" I asked.

"All the time. It's like the craziest video game imaginable."

"Have you found any way to direct your search?"

"No. I'm only ten, remember? I'd have to be very old to do that. It's an unfathomable amount of molecules dating to the origin of the planet - billions of years. However . . ." He stopped walking and grabbed my elbow until we made eye contact. His were sparkling and his tone changed to an excited hush. "It's not as hard as you might think because each molecule has seen so much and then there are their counterparts in all the parallels."

It was impossible to do while using another power because the concentration required was intense. A person needs to squint until they can see all the surrounding energy. He told me that it would usually take a couple of minutes until a molecule could be isolated. Then through focusing attention, the molecule would glow slightly until it began producing images in the viewer's mind. He called it "cosmic communication."

I showed him Timefold, which had to be learned before undertaking a TVC. He slipped away just prior to reaching the others. "I'll see you again," he said. "I try to avoid confrontations. There's enough of that in the world, I'm looking for peace." Before I could argue, he was gone.

ooooo

As we drifted onto the beach, Linh and Amber both shot me warning looks. Yangchen, clearly angry, seemed older and hard. "Just what did you think you were doing, Nate?" Yangchen blasted.

"I was doing my job," I snapped back.

"Your job? What is that, exactly?"

"Yangchen, what's wrong with you? I'm trying to get the Jadeo back, that's my job."

"That is fulfilling an oath. Your job, the most important part of your every thought, decision and action, should be to stay alive. Has Spencer not explained this to you?"

"Spencer isn't the best explainer. Why don't you tell me why my life is so important when everyone around me is dying and when death isn't anything more than a word that means, 'went to another place'?"

She laughed for a moment, then shook her head. "Nate, the Movement is fragile, you must be strong, you are its leader."

"It feels like you and Spencer are the Movement's leaders."

"We are only here at your request to help you through this. You weren't even supposed to be in this position for another eleven years. And even so, you would have still been unprepared. Spencer and I, along with the other mystics, are trying to remind you of your power . . . Nate, this is your Movement."

"Then why are you so upset about my wanting to go into Calyndra?" A salty breeze was blowing.

"Omnia is waiting for you at the time of the original oath. Do you not recall that one of the original nine entrusted is a betrayer? The traitor is part of Omnia. You would have been slaughtered as you stepped out of the portal. The three of you would have been wiped away and the ripples of that would be inconceivable suffering for a thousand years in the past and ten thousand in the future."

"I didn't know."

"Do not do, unless you know what the doing does."

"Then there's not much I can do, because I know nothing."

Yangchen smiled. "Spencer did well with you."

"Where is he?" I stared off to the lighthouse as if it might have an answer.

"I wish I knew."

"Could Omnia have him?" Linh asked. "I mean someone as powerful as Spencer?"

"Omnia's power is enormous. I'm not just talking about the economic and earthly resources they possess. They have more mystics than the Movement has and unlike our divided Movement, their forces are united, and they are not working in hiding."

"But we have the advantage of being the oppressed. The more they turn the screws against their opposition, the more they fuel the fires against them. Time is on our side."

"If only that were true. For now, they are manipulating time better than we are. We may have passion and a better understanding of the powers as our greatest assets but all of that means nothing if the Dark Mystic sides with Omnia."

"What?" Linh said. "Is that possible?"

"Anyone can choose sides," Yangchen said. "You think Spencer is working to protect the Jadeo. Well, that may be; his actions are always difficult to understand. That man works in complexities that would require anyone else many lives to comprehend. If I had my guess, he's trying to prevent the Dark Mystic from crossing over to Omnia."

"He said the Dark Mystic doesn't like him," I said.

"Maybe not in this life," Yangchen said, "maybe not for a hundred lives, but Spencer can find the point in time when most anything happens and no one is better at changing it than he is."

"Then why –" My question was interrupted as the sky tore open. Special Forces, sent by Omnia from some other dimension, dropped through the ragged portal.

In a blur it was over. Linh was gone.

"What happened?" I yelled, as Yangchen pulled Amber up from the sand.

"We must go now!"

Clouds gathered and swept us into a storm similar to the one that blew us out of Calyndra. Yangchen held my arm like a vise. She gripped Amber with her other hand. A swift force pulled and in a confused mist we landed in the Redwoods. Amber was unconscious and before I could ask Yangchen anything, I blacked out. The next thing I knew, the Old Man was dropping me into the Wizard Island portal. Seconds later Yangchen pushed us into a Booker-brand golf cart. Jurassic-like vegetation seemed to devour the thick humid air as we sped down a "road" not more than a few inches wider than the golf cart. The heat added to my wooziness, making talking or even thinking a chore. When our ride ended, we continued on foot, forcing our way through nearly impenetrable jungle. Finally, we reached a door hidden among large stones. We entered and immediately descended steep, wet, mossy steps. At the bottom there were two doors. Yangchen opened the one on the right. A long hall eventually led into a spacious room. Surprisingly, there was natural light coming in from several small tinted windows on one wall.

"We're in a Movement safe house, about thirty feet below the Amazon jungle. Those windows look out onto a small tributary that leads to the great river. They're on the side of a short cliff and completely camouflaged from the outside."

"Where's Linh?" I asked Yangchen. Amber had a lost look and was obviously still trying to shake off her fog.

"Omnia has her."

"No!" I yelled. All I could think of was Carst.

"They won't send Linh there." Yangchen read my thoughts. "She is far too important a prisoner." There was no doubt in her response. I believed her.

"What happened?" Amber asked faintly.

"I'm sorry to say that we've entered the final phase."

"What's that?" I asked.

"Omnia has found a way to breach the parallels and has begun interdimensional warfare."

"Is that as awful as it sounds?" Amber asked, fearfully.

"Yes, that's why we refer to it as the final phase." She rubbed her eyes and pinched the bridge of her nose. "The bad news is we've never been closer to defeat, but because of duality this means there is equally good news . . . we've never been closer to victory."

Yangchen assured me that the Movement's greatest priority, after protecting me, was to locate Linh. "Our mystics have all been alerted. Not surprisingly, Linh is not on the astral but her change has not been felt. They want her alive."

ooooo

Over the next few days we slept a lot; the soul storms, portals and dimensional-blend were draining. Yangchen explained that dimensional-blend occurs when two or more dimensions are directly open to one another without being buffered by a portal. "Tearing into another one is extremely dangerous," she said. "Fortunately, the initial reports are optimistic and it appears that Omnia's ability to puncture the parallels is still basic; but I must caution, we're still in the final phase and it may be only a matter of time until Omnia's forces are freely roaming in and out of them at will."

"What happens if they keep blending dimensions?" Amber asked.

"No one knows for sure but none of the theories are good. It's a difficult problem to explain but simply put, things would stop making sense."

"Sounds like that's already happened," I said.

"The compromised dimensions," Yangchen ignored me and continued, "would become a drifting mess from which the inhabitants could neither reach their souls nor maintain a 'normal' human existence. And because all dimensions must awaken before any of us finds completeness, the consequences could be dire."

"We have to stop them," Amber said. "How is Omnia able to do this?"

"Omnia's wealth and earthly power has allowed them to create an organization that is so vast and efficient that they can make breakthroughs at a rate far greater than the Movement."

"How long do we have to stay here? I'll go crazy stuck in this cave. I need to do something."

"What would you do, Nate?" Amber asked.

"I'd find Dunaway. Now that we're in the final phase, surely he'll see that joining forces is the only way to win. He's the only other surviving one of the seven; I just know we were meant to join forces. Together we'll find the Dark Mystic, rescue Linh and then stop whoever is running Omnia."

"He's got Clastier and the Jadeo. Dunaway doesn't seem to think he needs the Movement," Amber said.

"He doesn't even know what the Jadeo is."

"Maybe he does now. How hard would it be for him to get that from Clastier?"

That was obviously the great concern. Dunaway had Clastier hidden and I couldn't even communicate with him on the astral.

"I know," I said, defeated. "If he finds out what it is, it's over – not just the Movement, but the world as we know it."

"Whatever that is," Amber said. "Do you recognize much of the world anymore?"

I remained lost in my thoughts.

"Anyway," Amber continued, "when do I get to know what the Jadeo is?"

"Nate, don't let fear take you in," Yangchen said. "Even if Dunaway is able to discover the Jadeo's secrets, he must open it and that is nearly impossible for all but the nine entrusted."

"Yangchen, I can't stay here; there's too much to do."

"It's too risky for you to be out there right now."

"It's riskier not to be."

"I know you want to find Linh." Yangchen took my hand and held it in hers. "You feel responsible for the loss of the Jadeo and Clastier to Dunaway. You must forgive yourself for these things. You will do more good being safe and finding greater power within. It is remarkable that we haven't lost you yet. The entire world is divided and you are how that is defined. If you were captured, the Movement would fall; as long as you are free . . . there is a chance."

"It doesn't feel like I'm free when I'm hiding in some bunker. What good are all my powers if I can't use them?"

"You will get the chance soon enough. And remember, one who is in touch with his soul is always free."

ooooo

That night, sleep came hard, fitful and interspersed with Outviews.

"Dosen," Tesa, appearing just as she had in 1917, said, as I entered the screened porch furnished with antique white wicker furniture. "Yes, as I recall, today is the one when Nate is in your eyes."

"You've mentioned him before," Dosen said.

"Nate, are you seeing this in an Outview?" she asked, staring at Dosen.

I didn't have any way to communicate with her, as much as I tried.

"Don't worry, love," she said. "You'll learn how to access the universal mind in your next life. I know you are there. But I do wish you could join us for tea."

Another old lady joined them. At once her eyes revealed her to be Spencer. "Is he here?" Spencer asked Tesa, while looking at Dosen.

"Yes, he's in the middle of an Outview from the time of the Movement's revolution against Omnia." Tesa picked up a cup and sipped. "Quite exciting." She looked back at Dosen, "In case you are unsure, Nate, we are well beyond your lifetime." Tesa put her cup down and manipulated the air with her hands until a full-color, holographic scene appeared. It showed Clastier speaking in front of a large crowd.

"An Outmove," he began, "is a bold act of faith, when one trusts the universe no matter the situation, and proceeds from the soul rather than the personality one is presently draped in." I hadn't heard or read that before and assumed it was from the missing pages. Stacks of books, clearly titled *The Clastier Papers,* filled the table next to him. While he continued to share his wisdom, I wondered when the speech would happen.

"The date is not important," Tesa said. "It is in the future. At least as of now, it is what the future holds. Clastier must be protected."

Spencer cut in, "There are many events that can change this future."

I wondered if Amber, Linh and I all lived to see that speech when suddenly a gunman came from the crowd and shot Clastier three times. Among the screams and confusion, I saw Linh run to his aid. Her healings came too late; Clastier's blood-soaked body lay limp in her arms. I screamed and within the Outview felt his change. Then I remembered I was Clastier and his death might mean the Outview would end.

"Even your thoughts can alter the future," Spencer said. "You must be careful."

"But Omnia is closing in. How can I be careful about what I think when I'm just trying to keep us all alive and get the Jadeo and Clastier back?"

The hologram display showed an empty stadium, as if Clastier had never been there. I wondered what I had done. Then the area filled with soldiers and buses full of prisoners. Hundreds were shot, countless more were loaded and shipped out to horrible prison camps, many were headed to Carst. Amber boarded one, destination unknown. Outside the entrance, a type of laser guillotine had been set up. Two hooded soldiers pushed me into the contraption. A bank of video cameras focused as the beam cut off my head.

My screams woke Amber and Yangchen.

"Amber, you're alive!" I panted.

"You're alive too, Nate," Yangchen said.

Amber held me until my breathing slowed.

"Where were you?" Yangchen asked.

"Future, not sure when."

"Was I there? Or Spencer?" she asked.

"Spencer. I didn't see you."

"Tell me exactly what you saw."

ooooo

Well into the next day, Yangchen continued to assure me everything possible was being done to find Linh. I couldn't eat and searched the astral constantly. Both Yangchen and Amber used Solteer to calm me. Even so, I remained highly agitated. Yangchen was called away to assist with a dimensional breach, but I suspected it had something to do with the Outview.

The absence of both my guiding mystics, Yangchen and Spencer, left me floundering. The interior of the "bunker" was as posh as such a place could be, but it felt like a prison. Amber and I hadn't been completely alone since the night in San Francisco, years before. But with Linh being held, my guilt ran deeper than normal and I remained distant.

We meditated and I generally tried to catch my breath, but the pause wasn't good for me. As much as I wanted to follow Yangchen's advice, going within was impossible while the outside world was calling in such desperate ways. It wasn't until another Outview forced me once again to face the depths of the conflict that I was reminded there is no separating the two.

39

The Outview showed another concurrent incarnation thirteen months in the future, one that threatened to unravel the delicate threads still holding me together. I was Fred Means, a recently discharged vet of the U.S. Air Force, now working for the National Security Agency. Nineteen months ahead, things had gone from terrible to nightmarish. Not only was every phone and email monitored and recorded but also, through a network of satellites and ground stations, the NSA listened in on conversations inside most buildings including nearly every residence on the planet. They knew everything about everyone. Dissenters were rounded up in huge numbers, then placed into the earth's largest prison system. With the legalization of drugs, there were plenty of empty cells to fill. An estimated two million "revolutionaries" were incarcerated in the U.S. They were the lucky ones. Nineteen million Americans were listed as missing. In my role at NSA, I knew most had been sent to Carst. Approximately sixty-six thousand more were in secret prisons scattered around the globe, people deemed "too valuable to kill," at least until they could be exhaustively interrogated (some called it torture).

If they'd wanted to be humane in their "cleansing," Omnia could have sent their enemies into the portal-of-no-return at Kilauea, the dissidents would never be heard from again and the karma would be minimal, but Yangchen said they didn't even know of the portal's existence.

The number of insect-sized drones spying on citizens topped a million, implanted microchips were mandatory for all persons thirteen or older, and cash had been replaced by digital "money." These steps, along with the earlier bans on guns, free speech and the press, were welcomed by the population in order to preserve safety and the American way of life. It was very successful. Crime and corruption, at least by old definitions, had been virtually eliminated. The new order was mirrored in most of the rest of the world, resulting in a massive decline in terrorism. We secretly allowed the occasional plane to be blown up, school shooting or stadium bombing to keep everyone in fear, but otherwise life was peaceful, unless you were on the watch or wanted lists. That was part of my job at NSA, to compile data profiles - whom to add to the watch list, whom to recommend for arrest, and where to find those in hiding. It was all based on profiling data, utilizing internet browsing histories, conversations, shopping records, TV viewing patterns, books read, associations with people, organizations, even which corporations a person dealt with, or didn't. Another big component was travel: had you ever been somewhere with a high concentration of people on the watch list, or where arrests had been made? And a huge red flag came if you'd been anywhere near one of the Movement's centers, prior to or during its time in operation. And my biggest job? The one that occupied the majority of my working hours? Tracking Nathan Ryder.

It was like Dustin and Storch. Within the Outview I desperately needed to go to Outin and find my brother for some advice. What to do? Was there a way to give Fred Means full memory so he would know what I did? Was that advisable? Which personality was stronger? Were we each obligated to fulfill our own destiny? The paradox was wild in my mind. I wanted to be at the bunker thinking it over, discussing it with Amber, but what if I couldn't get back?

This bastard was helping to send people to Carst. Did he send Trevor? That answer came quickly; he was on a committee that reviewed Trevor's case and recommended his transfer. It was Storch and the slave trader rolled into one. How could my soul be a party to that kind of brutality? Hundreds of years ago in Africa it was disgusting and unbearable enough, but this was within this life. Time's a funny thing. While this tragic, toxic self-betrayal swirled in my mind and threatened to drown me, two new thoughts emerged. Most Outviews I involuntarily entered brought me in at the death, so Fred Means was likely about to die, and secondly, he might know where Linh was being held.

I scanned the area, searching for danger. Fred was at home reading a book on his iPad. Dunaway might send an IF strike-unit in to kill Fred; NSA, CIA, FBI were some of IF's favorite targets, and they usually hit them at home. Omnia had possibly found out that Fred shared my soul. Spencer didn't think they were capable of discovering current incarnations, but now that we'd entered the final phase . . . anything could happen.

I looked around; all appeared calm. Maybe everything was fine, but then a coughing fit quickly turned into gasping. He stood up choking, trying to reach water and nearly made it to the kitchen but fell to his knees in the dining room. Fred crawled a few more feet, wheezing and turning blue. I saw what he was reading on his iPad and knew I'd have to return earlier on the last day of Fred's life.

ooooo

Amber was alarmed. "Where were you?"

"Outview."

"I know, but you were sweating and shaking, that's not normal."

"I do that after a lot of Outviews."

"Yeah, but not during them."

"This one was different." I told Amber what I'd seen.

"Can you get back?"

"I think so. The question is can I stop him from eating those carrots. Carrots, can you believe it? Or, at least heal him before he dies."

I arrived in Fred's life thirty minutes prior to his death. My presence would panic him for many obvious reasons, so I stayed in a Timefold until I could hold him with Gogen.

"Oh my God," he said, more calmly than I expected. "You're a gutsy guy, Ryder, I'll give you that."

He recognized me, of course, but not my soul - our soul. My very presence meant he would not be eating carrots so he wouldn't choke to death. I scooped up the iPad and quickly found what I was looking for. He'd been reading the interrogation reports of Linh.

"Remarkable," he said. "Everyone expected you to rescue her a year ago. Where have you been, Ryder?"

I ignored him. Vising was not a reliable way to read electronic formats, as it tended to skip sections or read out of order. I actually had to read it but there was too much, so I scanned, looking for a location. It was possible to take the iPad back with me but I didn't exactly know how. After almost ten minutes, I still couldn't find a reference to where they had her. "Where is she?"

"I'm not telling you anything."

I raised him up with Gogen and pushed him to the top of the cathedral ceiling and suspended him almost twenty feet above a large glass coffee table. "Where is she?"

"Hey, put me down!"

"I'm going to drop you if you don't tell me where she is. I wonder how sharp the glass will be when your head shatters it."

Fred was sweating. "I don't know where she is."

I didn't want to read him; because we shared a soul it was possible he'd be able to learn too much about me and the Movement. "Then I'm going to drop you through that table on the count of three. Are you ready? One . . ."

"But I don't know!"

"Two . . ." I jostled him a bit.

"Wait, wait . . . please."

I stared up at him impatiently.

"They'll kill me if I tell you."

"That sounds like a personal problem. Three!"

"Okay, she's at Quantico," he screamed.

I let him drop a few feet before stopping. "How long has she been there?"

"Since May," he whimpered.

"Where was she before that?" I didn't want him to later recount what period I'd been interested in.

"She was held in Los Angeles for several days following her capture, then transferred to Petersburg."

"Florida?"

"No, the federal prison in Petersburg, Virginia."

"I see in the reports she has been subjected to torture. Is she okay?"

"It's not torture; it's heightened interrogation methods."

"Don't give me that bureaucratic double-speak. What do you people call murder? Enhanced retirement?" I tossed him back toward the ceiling, then let him plummet to within inches of the glass and rolled him onto the floor. He didn't stop screaming for several seconds.

"What do you call what you just did, Ryder?" He asked through gritted teeth. "That's as much torture as anything."

"You seem fine. But we can try again if you don't answer the question."

My head suddenly felt blisteringly hot. Experience told me to get out now. The glass of the picture window shattered, slicing into my arms and back as I leapt through. The whistle of the incoming missile spurred me to Skyclimb even before I hit the grass in his backyard. The explosion's flash and fire knocked me from the roof of his neighbor's storage shed. Badly burnt, I stood unsteadily.

The sound that had haunted me for years - approaching helicopters - broke through the ringing in my ears. I fled the Outview and landed back in my body in the bunker.

Amber screamed.

"I'm okay," I told her.

"You're a burnt, bloody mess," she said. "You're smoking!"

She helped get me out of my smoldering clothes and into the tiny shower. Everything hurt. Amber pulled shards of glass out of my back and arms, then administered Lusans while I recounted my experience.

"Fred Means is dead, I felt the change," I said. "Just before the explosion, I saw the clock. He died thirty minutes after I got there, it was the same time as when he choked to death on the carrots. Do you realize the power of that? Does that mean he would have died no matter what? Are there a thousand ways we each may die on our given day?"

"I've studied that a lot over the past two years. It is possible to change the date of our death but it isn't easy. It is linked to the time of our birth and every major incident in between," Amber said quietly, as she moved the Lusan over me. "Our death isn't just our destiny, it affects every other person in our life. Changing it is a monumental task; you could spend a lifetime trying to alter your death."

"Death is just waking from the dream," I said, "or the nightmare, if you're in a place like Carst."

"So Linh's at Petersburg right now?"

"Yeah, do you know it?"

"When I was with Yangchen, we worked with the group in the Movement that tries to locate high-level prisoners –

mystics, top Movement officials, Booker's associates, people like that."

"People like Linh."

"Yeah, and I saw research on a bunch of the facilities. They've taken most of the federal prisons near large military bases and turned them into holding interrogation incarceration centers, or HIICs. Petersburg is an important facility because of its proximity to DC, Quantico and the huge bases around Norfolk, but we didn't think they were equipped to hold mystics there."

"Linh's not a mystic."

"Her soul powers are of mystic level. And how long until she actually becomes one?"

"Yeah, I guess you're right."

"You can't go after her."

"Amber, you know me well enough to know I have to." I sat up and moved the Lusan onto my scorched and bruised legs. "I'd come for you."

"But you shouldn't. I wouldn't want you to. Do you think Linh wants you to risk your life to come and save her?"

"No. I don't think she wants me to, but she expects me to . . . she knows I'll come and you would know it too."

She nodded. "I'm coming."

I was ready to argue but there was no room for disagreement in her eyes.

"Okay, we need a plan."

ooooo

The following day, with Rose's help, we were in a rental house owned by an unknown Booker corporation. His property management firm rented twenty-one homes in Virginia Beach, along the oceanfront, between 66th and 75th streets. In addition to having a fabulous ocean view, our house was less than a block from the Association of Research and Enlightenment – the Edgar Cayce Foundation. Cayce, perhaps the most famous prophet since Nostradamus, had lived in the first half of the twentieth century. His foundation accumulated and operated one of the great metaphysical libraries until Omnia shut it down during the first crackdown. Like a grand New England resort, Cayce's original building sat abandoned on the hill overlooking the coast. The more modern structure, located a few hundred yards below, housed the famous library and was occasionally used by Omnia researchers, but was otherwise empty and guarded only by a few soldiers in a checkpoint on Atlantic Avenue. Omnia had not discovered the portal located in the original structure.

Not surprisingly, the Amazon was riddled with portals and Rose was able to communicate over the astral as to the best ones to get Amber and me to Virginia. She cautioned us on the risks, but was partial to Linh and worried less about my death than Spencer and Yangchen did. We arrived in darkness and easily slipped through some old gardens to 68th Street, then cut across a deserted Atlantic Avenue, and were in Booker's house in time to see the sunrise over the ocean. A motorcycle flew over one of the small dunes that separated us from the beach. It nearly crashed in a spray of sand before the rider, dressed in black, righted the bike and swerved into our driveway beneath the deck. The man had a guitar in a soft black case strapped to his back. He lifted the dark helmet off and looked up at me grinning.

"Flannery, Rose said you were in town," I called down.

"Yeah, I'm playing at a music festival not far from here. I've got a new song for you," he said, disappearing from the driveway and reappearing next to us on the deck.

"How did he do that?" Amber asked.

"Amber, this is Flannery; he's a crazy, weird and talented mystic."

"So, he's like all the mystics," Amber said. "Weird and kind of crazy."

"No, he's a special kind of crazy," I said.

"Amber, do you love music?" he asked.

"Yes, of course."

He smiled. "And do you love to dance?"

"Who doesn't?"

Her answer obviously pleased him. Flannery took his

guitar out and began to play. "This is a new song I've been working on, I hope you like it. Don't tell me if you don't. I'll know on account of your not saying how great it is, so if you do like it, don't forget the part about telling me how great it is." He winked.

Amber couldn't take her eyes off him as he sang in a mesmerizing voice of changing times, lost freedoms and nature under the strain of human greed. The lyrics were brilliant and devastating but the upbeat melody created a beautiful song. We were silent when he finished.

"You didn't like it?" Flannery asked, dejected.

"We loved it," we said in unison.

"But you didn't dance. It's better when you dance. I'll play it again. Will you dance this time?"

I held out my hand to Amber and we danced on the deck as warm salty breezes blew away the remaining coolness of the night. It was the type of song that pulled emotions from the deepest parts of you. I swear there were four more instruments playing along with his guitar. For those moments, lost in that music, all the problems and pressures of my life no longer existed. I twirled and spun Amber as my feet caught the rhythm and his lyrics carried me away.

He sensed my bliss as the song ended. "Nate, you might even listen better than Dustin. Music . . . power to change the world."

"I wish it were that simple."

"Never underestimate the power of a song."

ooooo

We discussed the planned jailbreak during breakfast. "I've got quite a few friends locked up at Petersburg," Flannery said. "Sadly, I've got friends in half the prisons in the world – most of them don't deserve to be there."

"We welcome your help, but we're only going in for Linh. I don't want any distractions."

Flannery shook his head. "You've never been in prison, have you, Nate? That's a rhetorical question. I can tell you haven't. Once people have been locked up they acquire a certain look, a kind of distant stare that's barely noticeable unless you recognize it. And there's a constant, yet subtle, tension in how they hold their shoulders."

"Sorry if you're disappointed, I've managed to avoid prison," I said, with a chuckle.

"It's okay, you've got other things going for you, but the reason I brought it up is because if you'd been inside, you would know that distractions are exactly what we want."

"What do you have in mind?" Amber asked.

"Amber, I'm glad you asked. I was thinking maybe you and I could get some dinner this evening. I know this great little vegan place at the end of the boardwalk, then maybe a walk on the beach under the stars and I'll write you a love song."

Amber laughed. I shook my head.

"Where does beauty like yours come from?" Flannery asked. "I became a musician so girls like you would fall in love with me."

"It worked," Amber said, smiling.

"Okay, okay. Can we get back to the plan . . . rescuing Linh? Remember?" I said.

Flannery passed Amber a slip of paper. "Call me."

Amber unfolded it. "It's blank."

He winked. "Just think of me and I'll be there."

"Fine, I'll go alone," I said.

"Nate, relax. Don't be so serious all the time. Life is for living."

"Exactly. I want Linh to be living."

"Let me spell it out for you. I'll talk to a few of my friends, they'll spread the word to the right people, and by late this afternoon the entire prison will be in full riot-mode. We'll drop in as it erupts, use Solteer on every guard we encounter, totally mess with their reality."

"I'm good at Solteer," Amber said. "I'll put some to sleep and have the rest seeing all kinds of terrifying images."

"I'm thinking we can Gogen the entire electronics of the place to open every cell and exterior door," Flannery said.

"So Linh will be swept out with hundreds of others? I like it."

"Right, then we head straight back here and escape into the Cayce portal before they even realize it was about Linh," Flannery snapped his fingers twice. "It'll be legendarily smooth."

It wasn't.

A serious problem arose when we discovered there were no known portals anywhere near the prison. Flannery, in an ostentatious mood for Amber, produced a fancy black Porsche. Normally a two-hour drive to the prison, we made it in under an hour after an impressive display of Timefolds, TVC and his Atomizing which was a combination of manipulations of space with Gogen and energy with Vising.

"You've got to teach me that Atomizing," I said, as we blurred through traffic with pulsating g-forces.

"I showed you at our first meeting. The camera, remember?" Then he looked back at Amber through the rearview mirror. "I asked Nate if he could have any physical object in the world and he chose a camera."

Amber laughed. "Why not the Jadeo?"

"It's not like that," I said. "It's making something new. So I could make a replica of the Jadeo but not the original."

"Is that how you vanish and appear, too?" she asked.

"Same principle," he said.

The prison guard towers were suddenly before us. Sinister razor wire, capping endless fences, glinted in the setting sun. I shivered, thinking of Linh in this place. It had once been an all-male facility housing about four thousand inmates. Omnia had converted it to hold seven thousand people. The sprawling prison surprised me with its size and fortress-like appearance.

"It seems so quiet," Amber said.

"Look," Flannery said, pointing through the windshield at a column of thick black smoke rising from the rear of one of the larger buildings. Two units over, more smoke appeared.

After leaving the car in the visitors' parking lot, we Skyclimbed within a TVC. I strained with Amber on my back since she still couldn't Skyclimb. The extra effort required to maintain a TVC left me a bit unstable and I crash-landed into an old painted-brick building. I took the brunt of the impact but Amber got banged up too. The sirens began wailing.

"We've got to hit the electronics now!" Flannery yelled.

Flames engulfed the side of an administrative wing. At least a hundred guards adorned in storm trooper riot gear marched ten feet away; however, we were still concealed within a TVC. Flannery squatted trance-like as he communicated with his buddies and directed their actions.

"I've got the locks." The deafening roar of a thousand convicts surging free made my announcement unnecessary. Linh still had not surfaced on the astral and our only confirmation of her presence at Petersburg came from Fred Means more than a year in the future.

"Find out what the most secure unit is," I shouted to Flannery. "That's where they'll have her."

"Omnia's mystics have to be blocking her astral view," Amber said. "Does that mean they're here?"

It was something we should have considered before we arrived. If their mystics were on site, then the break might be more challenging than we anticipated.

Boom. Boom. Boom.

I landed hard on my chest at least twenty feet from where I'd been standing. "Amber!" I found her bleeding badly. A twisted piece of metal gashed her leg. It would be impossible to get the shrapnel out without opening an artery. Amber looked from the wound to me. I saw the fear.

Flannery raced over out of the smoke. He somehow dissolved the metal and in the same instant had her leg tightly bandaged. "Lusans!" he yelled, as he dropped back into his trance posture.

Boom. Boom. Boom. Boom.

The second Lusan flew out of my hands. I crashed into a dumpster. Amber bounced off a chain-link fence. Flannery hadn't moved.

"It's not our team," Flannery yelled. "Omnia is detonating the bombs, it's all been wired. They're going to destroy the whole place . . . and everyone in it."

I hadn't felt Linh's change and I believed Fred, which meant I had to find her now. There were too many buildings, too much fire and smoke, and a sea of screaming inmates and battling guards. My only hope was to leave. "You guys have to protect me," I said, diving under a concrete bench. "I'm going into an Outview."

"Nate, no!" was the last thing I heard.

ooooo

Fred's iPad lay on the coffee table. I heard him in the kitchen cutting carrots. Frantically, I searched for Petersburg - sixty-eight results were found. The sound of chopping echoed down the hall. After adding Linh's name, the results narrowed to four. The second one yielded the information I needed - she was held in B-unit.

"Don't move, Ryder." Fred was pointing a gun.

"Fred, listen to me. You and I have something in common. I don't have time to talk about it now, but I'll be back. Just don't eat those carrots."

"We've got nothing in common, Ryder. You're a terrorist and I'm a patriot and you won't be back because you're not leaving." He punched a button on his phone. "Just sit tight, the authorities will be here in a few minutes."

"Fred, look into my eyes."

"Nice try. I've spent the past couple of years studying everything about you and I know you've got an array of skills - hypnotism, telekinesis, ESP, morphing, shapeshifting, et cetera. If I didn't know better, I'd say you were the devil. But I'm not a religious man . . . I think you're some kind of freak, a pitiful, misguided and very dangerous freak. And if you so much as blink wrong, I won't hesitate to kill you. I'd do it now but I'm not much interested in becoming a national hero."

No matter how long I was in the Outview, I would return to Petersburg within a minute of when I had left. It was impossible to separate myself from the urgency of rescuing Linh. Gogen didn't even require me to blink. The gun and the cell phone flew from his hands to mine. Before Fred could react, he was pinned to the wall. I ran over and whispered into his ear.

"I know the NSA can hear everything that happens in this house but I don't know if they can hear my whispers. It doesn't matter, you'll be dead soon anyway and not by my hand. But if you should somehow live through this day, you should join the Movement. You've traveled the world, you particularly liked Monaco and Egypt, you've got a couple of degrees, speak three languages and read constantly. But Fred, your view of the world is extremely limited. There is so much more, but your life has only contributed to holding humanity back. It has nothing to do with your work at the NSA; even if you sold cars, if you deny your own soul, you block the path to enlightenment for all."

Gogen had him paralyzed so when I looked into his eyes for almost ten seconds, he couldn't turn away. I left him in tears with the awareness of our soul connection.

It would be eleven months before I next encountered Fred Means. I felt the change and was sad that Fred had killed himself, unable to cope with the soul knowledge I'd shared with him.

Petersburg had erupted during the forty seconds I was away. Falling back into my current consciousness from the Outview, I looked up at the concrete bench. Amber and Flannery were gone; laser bullets, fire and colored smoke danced a hostile lightshow in the air. At least five hundred yards and two razor wire fences separated my bench and B-unit. Crossing the flat open ground exposed me to the guard towers. Even if the fire and smoke created enough cover, the laser bullet crossfire ruined my chances.

A hand painfully gripped my ankle. I screamed, seeing it coming up out of the ground. Another grabbed my other leg and pulled me down into the earth. My mind and thoughts continued working normally, as if nothing strange was happening, but there was no feeling in my body. Being freed from the physical super-charged my brain. My mental capacity, soul memories and clarity were so magnified that when, moments later, back in my body, I felt limited and clumsy.

"You okay?" Amber asked. We were in some kind of dark, damp storage room.

"Yeah, great. What happened?"

"I Atomized you," Flannery said.

"You can do that?"

"Not normally, but you can do it to yourself; you just don't know how yet, so I kind of helped you."

"Cool. Linh's in B-Unit. Let's Atomize ourselves over to

there."

"B-unit," Flannery said, "that's too far. Atomizing only works in very short distances. Or, I should say, that's all I'm capable of doing. In theory it probably works across the universe but that's beyond me."

"Where are we?"

"The old chow hall. You remember the maps?"

Boom. Boom.

"That's probably the new chow hall getting hit," Flannery said.

Boom.

"Let's get out of here," Amber said.

"What about taking short hops to B-unit? Atomize, come out, Atomize, out again . . ."

"It'll take too long," Flannery said. "I have to do each of you separately. By the time we get there the unit will be blown up."

Boom. Boom. Boom.

The building came down around us. "Get Amber to -B-unit!" I yelled to Flannery as I Atomized myself. Now that I'd experienced it, I could do it.

I emerged in a courtyard littered with burning bodies. Two storm troopers fired but I was gone before their laser bullets reached me. Within my bodiless state, my intuition and timing were perfect. As Flannery said, there were limits - I went as far as possible in each Atomizing jaunt but pressure built to rematerialize. This time I burst onto the roof of a cellblock and was grateful for the smoke blocking the tower's view.

Boom. Boom.

The building went out from under me.

Boom.

I Atomized in the falling fiery debris. There might be injuries to my body on my next emergence, I thought. Atomizing oneself was a power beyond all the others. I made a silent wish that the Movement's enemies would never know this one.

The administration wing that housed the warden's office felt safe, at least from the bombs. B-unit, still intact, was visible from the window and just two buildings over.

Boom. Boom. Boom.

D-unit was gone.

I landed on A-unit's roof. There was a break in the smoke and I could see inmates with laser guns fighting guards. They were going to level this place quick. Shots came from a nearby tower. Pain burned my arm and waist. I Atomized into B-unit.

Incredibly, Amber and Flannery found me on a metal stairway. They were fine, having mostly traveled underground. A minute of healing on my wounds from all three of us was all we had time for but it was enough to keep me going. Flannery used some kind of partial TVC to get us through a battle on the next floor.

Boom. Boom. Boom.

C-unit must have been hit. B-unit vibrated and a portion of its west wall collapsed. We scanned each floor as best we could and found Linh on the top level. She looked emaciated. Her cell was unlocked like all the others but she was chained to her bed. I knocked out the video cameras and then freed her from the restraints.

"I knew all this noise was your doing." Linh said, trying to smile.

"We're getting you out of here," I said.

"The roof, hurry!" Flannery shouted.

Four stories above the prison, we surveyed our options amidst the war zone below. The parking lot was too far away and had been overrun with escaping convicts. The other exits, where employees parked, also had major fighting. Fires blocked most of our other routes.

"The river," Amber yelled.

The Appomattox River waited beyond a ribbon of trees growing up a steep bank. Without hesitation I stepped off the roof and Skyclimbed toward the woods. Linh was light in my arms. Flannery had Amber on his back.

Boom. Boom.

B-Unit disappeared in a pile of rubble.

Boom.

The force of the explosion sent us crashing into a stand of

pines. Somehow, I didn't drop Linh. Flames licked at our heels. Struggling to Skyclimb through the burning woods, sick with smoke, still weak from my laser wounds, my every thought traced the Outviews. The Atomizing had shifted focus and priority from human survival to spiritual understanding. One of the mystics had once explained vibrational frequency to me, but I never really got it until I rearranged the energy that made up the physical Nate. The weight of the human world is felt both physically and mentally. Our body is at the slowest vibration. Once it dissipated, I felt freedom similar to the euphoric release experienced at my Outin death.

"Nate, Nate!" Linh's terror-filled cries brought me back. She was on fire - we both were. Flames leaped and twisted in every direction. We came down in a rolling heap against a glowing, hot, razor-wire fence. Smothering, choking, screams. I was gone again.

Floating black water. The next time I awoke, someone was talking to me. "Nate, are you there?" Brittle skin. Smoke-crusted lungs.

"Linh?"

"No, it's Amber."

"Where's Linh?" My eyes opened; it was dark. My night vision made everything blurry green.

"She's okay."

"Are you?"

"Yes."

"Am I?"

"You need to work on yourself. Flannery and I have done all we can for you. He's still helping Linh and the others."

"What others? Where are we?"

"A few of Flannery's inmate friends were at the river when we got there. They had a couple of rafts brought there by relatives on the outside. Quite a few injuries. We're on the James River now - the Appomattox feeds into it."

"How long has it been?"

"An hour, maybe longer."

"No one's after us?"

"They haven't found us yet."

"Those outboard motors will make it hard to hear helicopters . . . until it's too late."

"You worry too much."

"I hear helicopters in my sleep." I shivered.

I counted six figures in my raft, hard to say how many in the other, its silhouette barely visible, but both were big river rigs like the ones used by rafting companies back home on the Rogue.

"We were over the final fence when Flannery went back for you and Linh. The burns were horrible . . . it's incredible how much the flesh can handle."

"Linh?"

"She's okay. You took the worst of the fire, but she was in rough shape before we got there. She's in the other raft with Flannery."

Lusans and the energy healings helped my vision return to normal and much of the pain to recede. I found Linh on the astral. "Hey, how are you doing?"

"Glad to be out of prison. Thanks for coming."

"I'm sorry it took so long."

"Kyle kept me company."

"Really? I guess that's why I haven't heard his voice in my head for a while."

"He told me about Fred Means, said you'd need help dealing with it."

"Why'd he think you could help?"

"Because I knew Fred Means."

We hit a rough section of water. Flannery interrupted the conversation, also speaking on the astral. "This day's gonna make a helluva song."

"It's not over yet."

"We're not far from the Hampton Roads and then it's a quick push out to the Atlantic. We'll straddle the coast until we're at the beach house. Might have time for a bite before sneaking back to the Cayce portal and safety. Shame to leave that Porsche behind though."

"How come they haven't come after us yet?"

"You saw Petersburg, they've got their hands full. Up until twenty minutes ago we could still see the glow from the fires. They don't know she's gone, yet."

"I've made the mistake of underestimating Omnia too many times . . . they know."

"Think positive, dude."

"Thanks for saving us back in the fire." The first few drops of rain hit my face.

"There can't be a world without a Nate," he said. "Hey, that could be a song."

I returned to my astral conversation with Linh. "When did you meet Fred?"

"He came to question me two days ago. I knew right away he was you and it freaked me out because I thought he was there to help me."

"Did you tell him anything you shouldn't have?"

"I'm smarter than that. If he was a good guy, then he already knew everything I did. If he was bad – I thought of Dustin and Storch – then I wanted to be extra careful because he might have powers."

"What happened?"

"It was strange, especially for him. Remember, you and I have had many past lives together, which means so have Fred and I. And he recognized me. I don't want you to think he was enlightened in any way, but he had that feeling that people get when they meet someone for the first time who is already familiar to them."

"Did he say anything?"

"He didn't have to. His every question about my involvement in the Movement demonstrated his confusion. Fred Means knew it was impossible, knew it was wrong for a hundred reasons but in those hours we spent together, he was overwhelmed with love."

"But he didn't recognize me as sharing his soul?" I said.

"He didn't love you and miss you with the desperation that crosses centuries," Linh said. "He's part of you, sometimes that's harder to see."

"Then why don't I feel that same desperation when I look at you?" I regretted it as soon as the words were out.

Linh was quiet for a moment. "Because Fred could never have me in this life and you already do."

It was my turn to be quiet.

"You just don't realize it yet," she added. "In a cruel test by the universe, you've not witnessed the right Outviews."

"And I love you anyway . . . in *this* life."

"You got yourself out of that one," Linh said.

Amber interrupted, touching my hand and pointing to the lights blinking on the infrared cameras mounted to a bridge we were about to pass under. I broke off the astral and threw us into a TVC.

Pain from maintaining the TVC felt like small shards of broken glass in my stomach. I bit my lip bloody waiting for the choppers to pursue and fire upon our rafts. Kyle, back in my head, said, "Fear is a plague."

"Are they coming?" I asked, relieved my old friend was providing guidance.

"They are here."

A pair of flying gunship engines screamed overhead. Blades cut through the darkness. Whop! Whop! Whop! That sound had terrorized me for years.

"The TVC held," Amber said.

The helicopters banked sharply, heading straight back, bearing down.

"Omnia may have found a way to crack a TVC," I yelled. "For all we know, these choppers flew in from another dimension."

"We'll be okay," Amber said.

"Nothing is sure, there's no safety," I growled.

"Steady," Kyle warned.

"Kyle, you're still there?" I panted. The choppers skimmed the water, their roar torturously loud.

Amber screamed. They missed our heads by inches . . . less.

"They don't see us!" I shouted. "Kyle, are we safe?" He was gone. That made me think we were all right. Maybe he'd only been there for Linh.

Before we reached the ocean there were three more flyovers, the final one's super-bright searchlight blinding Amber and two of the inmates. Flannery handled their healings, while I maintained the TVC. Chesapeake Bay emptied into the Atlantic. Our exposure remained the same but seeing an old brick lighthouse with my night vision brought a sense of déjà vu. The ocean felt safer. Three miles straight down the beach we'd be at Booker's beach house. Before I could warn Amber that the TVC would fall apart, an Outview overtook me.

Two hundred years earlier, I raced through the jungle, afraid I'd be late and the man wouldn't wait. I'd never been to El Castillo, the old lighthouse on the coast. As a young girl, I'd heard tales of the Mayan coastal city of Tulum, and even whispers of the sacred box that came from there. The Jadeo's legend had been known, but not believed, for generations; by the time of my birth it had faded to myth and to those that would come after, it would be nothing at all. The reason Nares had chosen this remote place puzzled me, yet I would not have questioned him. He commanded respect among the greatest of our people, so I, a very young woman, a mere peasant, did what he said.

The narrow trail was hardly a trail at all and I worried I'd be lost in the jungle. Finally, the trees surrendered to the cliffs and what was left of ancient Tulum's white and gray, carved stone buildings appeared. The lighthouse stood, though in ruins.

"You've come, Bola." His arms pulled me up firmly. I knew no one stronger nor gentler. His kiss, containing more passion than my entire village, brought us to our knees and we rolled into the tall grass. It was only then that I looked into his hazel eyes and saw, past the wisdom and courage of Nares, the soul of Linh. "There is little time." We kissed again.

"I'm sorry; it was a long way and twice I lost the path."

"I had to see you before I leave."

"But where are you going?"

"The future."

"I don't understand."

His eyes penetrated mine and I could swear he spoke to me without speaking, but as the young peasant woman, psychic communication made no sense to me. "I would take you if I could," he said.

"Please, Nares, you must take me. We could be together where you are going." Our families forbade our union. "Pleeeeease," I begged.

"Oh, Bola, if it were possible I would, if I could stay and find a place for us . . . but I must go. So much depends on it."

"Someone else can go."

"Others are going. Our efforts affect the past and histories not yet written. I wish I could make you understand but it is beyond my own understanding, and words do not come easy to me, you know this."

"When will you return?"

"I will not."

"Why must this be?" I cried and pulled at him. "Where is the fairness?"

"Life is not fair." He ran his large rough hands through my long black hair, framing my face and kissing me softly, repeatedly. "Leaving you would be impossible if I were not sure we would meet again."

"But you said you were not coming back," I said through tears.

"We will meet again in another lifetime, and others." He held me close and whispered forcefully in my ear.

"Even if that is true, it is far away. It is too much to ask, too long to wait," I said.

"A lifetime is shorter than anyone knows. Don't waste it on what might have been. Everything will be . . ." He gently pushed me back so our eyes could speak again. "Don't you see, Bola? Everything will happen, everyone gets it all, sooner or later. And we will have our time. I promise we'll be together and have more than our share."

Something caught his attention behind me. I turned and saw a circle of yellow light open in the sky above El Castillo.

"I must go."

"No, please don't."

"Bola, be strong." A long kiss. He ran and scaled the lighthouse with an ease that seemed unnatural and leapt from the top higher than was possible. I watched, stunned, as he was pulled into the yellow light and vanished.

Without thinking, I ran to the base of El Castillo and clawed my way up, reaching the top, bloodied and breathless. Using all my remaining strength, I jumped toward where the light had been. Nothing pulled me in. Legs kicking, arms flailing, I plummeted to the ground. Dead.

I surfaced from the Outview screaming.

"Your name is Nathan Ryder, you're nineteen, you're from Ashland, Oregon," Amber said.

"No, No! I'm Bola, where is Nares?"

"Nate, where were you? What happened?"

I searched my memories, they gutted me. "He's gone. We were in Mexico. Where was . . . What future?"

"Nate?"

"Damn it!" I sat up.

"What happened to you?"

"Is living all pain?" I said, softly.

"Attachment brings suffering," Kyle said in my head.

"Kyle? Save me, man!"

"Where's Kyle?" Amber asked.

"Kyle?" I yelled, but he was gone. "Where's Linh?"

"She's inside, asleep. We're back at Booker's lake house. As soon as you slipped into the Outview the TVC crumbled. Before Flannery could get any protection up, they were on us. I pushed you out of the raft and jumped. Flannery Skyclimbed over the water with Linh in his arms and reached us just as the machine gunfire ripped through the first raft. I'm not sure what he did. Some kind of a Timefold or modified TVC combined with Atomizing, hard to say, but we streaked through the waves in a fast-forward blur until we crashed onto the beach right in front of Booker's beach house."

"How did we get here?"

"I think Flannery Atomized you, because you vanished. I kept screaming at him, asking where you were, but some force was pushing me toward the old Cayce building. It was like having the worst headache and my legs felt like rubber. He carried Linh as we raced through the streets; it was dark and deserted."

"You obviously made it to the portal."

"Yeah, that was a trip. All I saw were stars and colors. Flannery held my hand. I wanted to ask about you but I couldn't speak. The portal was a maze, I think we were in several, but it's impossible to recall any details until we reached Wizard Island. There was a car waiting on the road and it brought us here."

"When did I show up?"

"Flannery went inside a few seconds before me. I followed him out to the deck, but when I got here, he was gone and you were lying on the chaise."

"Where's Linh?"

"I told you, she's inside resting."

"Is she okay?"

"She'll be fine. Yangchen is with her." Amber winced as she sat down on the cushioned chair next to me.

"What's wrong?"

"I think I cracked a rib, not sure if it was during the wave-ride - that was intensely painful - or when we hit the sand."

I put my hands on her ribs and did a healing. She looked at me until I returned her stare. My hands roamed her body and pulled her over to the chaise. I stopped before it went too far. "I've got to check on Linh."

"I guess you should," Amber sighed.

ooooo

Yangchen met me in the hall near Linh's room. "She's much stronger now but she's sleeping; don't wake her."

I nodded and thanked her. Linh looked much better than she did at the prison. I watched her for a minute and tried to recall more details from our life together as Bola and Nares, then climbed in with her and fell asleep. In the morning I woke to an empty bed, but soon found Yangchen, Amber and Linh eating breakfast in the dining room. One of Booker's staff saw me come in and brought me a plate of tofu-garlic scramble and blackberry cobbler. I was famished.

After a stilted exchange of "good morning" greetings, Yangchen briefed us. "Omnia has begun sending more of our supporters to Carst. It seems they need additional space in prisons for dissidents as opposition is mounting."

"Omnia is ignoring history. This kind of crackdown is not sustainable," I said.

"They're arresting people now who *might* be subversives. Gay couples, interracial couples, anyone with a past involvement in the new age, those who've read books on the 'dangerous list,' even picking up people at random."

"I've heard door-to-door searches are common and that warrants are no longer required," Amber said.

"That's true and the seizure of books, music, and art that's considered anti-government has become widespread."

"How do they have any support left?"

"It's all being done in the name of fighting terrorism and crime. The majority of the population is still supportive. Many believe and repeat the official mantra, 'If you haven't done anything wrong, you have nothing to worry about.'"

"That's because the population doesn't know Omnia is really in charge," I said.

"Of course not. Anyone who believes Omnia is real has joined the Movement. The rest still believe the government is there to help and protect them," Amber said. "The sheep don't realize the government was taken over years ago."

"That's not fair," Linh said. "It's impossible for average people to find privacy. So discussions are difficult. As soon as anyone says anything in opposition to the government, they're labeled a terrorist and arrested or worse, they simply disappear. The Omnia-controlled media keeps repeating the government line, 'If you aren't hiding anything, you don't need privacy. You only need your right to privacy if you have something to hide.' And it's not getting better."

"No, it's not," Yangchen said. "We've had reports that Omnia is working on micro devices that can be implanted in peoples' heads so their thoughts can be monitored."

"I can't believe people aren't rioting in the streets," Amber said, agitated.

"Omnia keeps the stores stocked with plastic junk made in China, food products filled with sugar, salt and artificial colors, and lots of great TV shows. Most people are happy with that," I said.

"How does Omnia ever expect to return things to normal after these crackdowns?" Amber asked.

"This is the new normal," Yangchen said. "Surely, Omnia never thought it would go this far. Every time there's any trouble, they overreact, which spurs more demonstrations. It's become a vicious circle and now we're left with a world that makes Orwell's 1984 look like the free-love 1960s."

It was so depressing I could hardly think about it. What kind of world were we fighting for? What would be left? They were driving people into the arms of the Movement but the world was becoming more polarized by the day as Omnia increased its standard method of spreading hate and fear.

"Any word on Spencer?" I asked.

"None." Her tone and dismissive expression conveyed her serious concern but also told me the discussion would go no further.

"You've got to go back to Carst and record what you see," Yangchen said. "If you project that into the sky, we'll turn huge numbers of people against Omnia."

"I can't." I started to shake.

Yangchen looked at me like a protective mother and then, like an impatient boss. "Okay, first we'll try the same method you used to record the Storch meeting after it happened. What you witnessed during your night in Carst with Trevor should be more than sufficient."

A lump formed in my throat at the mention of Trevor. Even doing the Storch method in order to record the horrors of Carst for the Air-Projection was going to require me to relive what felt like the worst night of any of my lives. I didn't know if I had the strength to endure that. A twinge of pain at my tattoo caused me to look at the Movement's emblem and the word "ENDURE" under it. Trevor or Baca might be trying to send me a message. They, along with Kyle, Dad, Mom, Crowd and a million more I'd never known, had all died for this cause. It occurred to me that Trevor might have hung onto life and endured Carst so that I would see and feel that gruesome, unspeakable world.

"Nate, are you okay?" Amber asked.

I nodded absently.

"Omnia has made a mistake with Carst. It has given us a chance to go after more than just public opinion. We can hit Omnia's greatest strength," Yangchen said.

"Their control of the economy?" Amber asked.

"Ahh, one would think that," Yangchen said. "Omnia has for so long convinced the world of the importance of money . . . but the money isn't real - pieces of paper, blips on a screen - it is nothing. Their power is in their control of governments and therefore the militaries. Omnia has the guns. They directly or indirectly have influence over the NSA, CIA, FBI, Pentagon and most of their counterparts around the globe."

"How does the existence of Carst help fight that?" I asked.

"The remaining soldiers from the Outin one hundred and four."

"I thought they would all have been discovered and investigated after the mystic rescues," Linh said.

"No, we put out a story that the Movement had them prisoner and we're proposing an exchange with Omnia," I said.

Yangchen smiled. "And there are still ninety-eight on active duty. Many are in secret contact with the Movement and are reporting the beginnings of unrest in certain branches of the military. You can't make twenty million people disappear without a large percentage being connected to members of the service. They've also seen quite a bit of senseless torturing and death. That takes a toll on a person. It doesn't always harden them; sometimes it makes a person softer."

"Of course," Amber said. "Everyone knows people who have disappeared or been charged."

"And if we can show the world where they are . . . imagine the reaction."

We were able to record my earlier visit to Carst using the method Dustin taught me for the Storch meeting. That meant I didn't have to go back, but reliving the final night of Trevor's life took its toll. Severe flu-like symptoms barraged my body for the next few days. Yangchen thought the Atomizing had also weakened me.

"It can have a delayed reaction, especially if you're Atomized through a portal. I didn't even know that was possible," Yangchen said during one of the many healings she gave me.

Amber and Linh visited a few times, but mostly I was out of it. And there were lots of Outviews.

ooooo

It was weeks after the Titanic went down. I sat as Hibbs with my mistress, who was Spencer.

"Do you have full memory?" I asked her, while I finished dressing for a meeting at the White House.

"What are you talking about?"

I sighed. Spencer was missing and there I was sitting with his soul who certainly knew his every movement through all of eternity and yet I couldn't communicate with him. I kissed her.

"I'll see you tonight, then."

"Billy, You've practically lived at the White House for the past fifteen years. Cleveland, McKinley, Roosevelt, even Taft, have all been personal friends. Don't let him push you around on this. He's got no future; he'll never win re-election."

With my full-forward-memory, I knew Taft would lose the election but that didn't help me as Hibbs. At that time, Taft was still President of the United States and, more importantly, he was in Omnia's pocket. "We'll see what he says."

"Do you really think Bill Taft is going to threaten you?"

"We've been through this. I don't see how he can avoid it. He's under a lot of pressure from the kingmakers, he knows the truth about the Titanic, he's behind the new income tax, and he talks peace. But he knows war is needed to enrich his backers and consolidate Omnia's power."

ooooo

Bill Taft and I had known each other for years. He'd occasionally even taken my advice, but this was different. The three-hundred-plus-pound president was agitated even at our greeting. We stood in front of his desk. Two other men were in attendance whom I did not know and to whom I was not introduced. Taft, at six-two, was nearly four inches taller than me, and because of his huge frame, he was giant-like. His chestnut hair, rosy cheeks, handlebar mustache and blue eyes normally gave him a cheerful appearance, but I'd never seen him that cross.

"Billy, I need your backing on the Federal Reserve and the income tax." He spoke in clipped, hushed tones.

"Mr. President, you know full well where I stand on these issues."

"Of course I do. That's why I asked you here so I could change your mind. And Billy, why is it Mr. President all of a sudden? You've always called me Bill."

"Yes, and we were always friends."

"We're still friends, Billy."

"Like your friend Major Butts."

"Damn you, Billy! Damn you." Taft's face reddened, his

fists clenched. He half-charged me like a linebacker. The other men tensed. "I miss him; you have no idea how much I feel his loss."

"You sacrificed him."

"How dare you!" Taft's voice rose.

I don't know if I would have been so brave just as Hibbs, but I had full memory of Nate's life and history. I didn't believe Taft had prior knowledge of the Titanic's intentional sinking, but he sure knew soon after. He and Butts were very close friends but Butts was secretly working to undermine the Federal Reserve, and the introduction of the federal income tax while Taft was, at the least, completely beholden to Omnia and possibly part of its hierarchy.

"I'm sorry, Mr. President, we are no longer friends. Your friendships don't seem to end well."

"Let me tell you something, Mr. Hibbs. The world you imagine - a place of fairness and truth - it only exists in fairytales. The real world is full of compromise, deals and betrayals."

"Maybe your world, Mr. President, but not mine."

"Don't pretend you got rich by following the rules. It's not possible."

"Following the rules is one thing. Murder, war, creating a system of financial slavery is quite another."

"It is time for you to leave."

"I couldn't agree more." I stopped at the door. "And Mr. President, be careful what you trade for re-election, it might not be worth it."

"Are you threatening me, Hibbs? It sounds like you might be threatening the President of the United States."

"I never threaten, Mr. President. I simply advise."

ooooo

On the short drive back to my office, I wondered if my actions had been wise.

"Mr. Hibbs," my secretary began, as I walked in. "This is Mr. Caper. He doesn't have an appointment but he insists you'll want to meet with him."

Mr. Caper rose and extended a slender hand. He was impeccably trimmed and manicured, his suit hand-tailored. But the accoutrements of wealth and gold-wire glasses did little to mask his identity.

"Are you armed, Dunaway?" I asked.

"I am a gentleman." He smiled, slightly.

Trapped in this Outview, I knew there was a chance I was going to die, although, in my prior visits, Hibbs consistently lived until 1937, twenty-five years beyond my meeting with President Taft. Still Dunaway's arrival did not bode well.

"After you." I ushered him into my office.

Once seated at the small conference table, I asked him if he was there to kill me.

"Quite the contrary, Hibbsy, ol' boy, I'm here to save you."

"Hard to believe."

"Ain't it though?" He pulled out a cigarette case and offered me one.

I shook my head and reached for my own. As Nate I was surprised by how much Hibbs' case looked like the Jadeo. It caught Dunaway's eye too, and he must have thought the same thing. Hibbs later told me he'd modeled it after the Jadeo.

"How are you going to save me, or the better question is, why?" I exhaled smoke in his direction.

"The President is about to become compliant in your assassination."

46

"It's a problem. A big one." He inhaled the cigarette slowly. "See, if you die tonight, like they plan, your mistress, played by our very own Spencer, will use every contact, trick and resource to expose the plot. And you know what? It works. A scandal erupts. The President is brought down and a chain of events takes place that actually throws America into a second civil war - communists against capitalists. Omnia, of course, comes out on top and that makes them unstoppable by the time you and I are born a hundred years from now."

"Doesn't Omnia know this as well?" I asked.

"Why yes, I'm sure they do. At least our modern Omnia. Omnia back here in 1912 doesn't know yet."

"I would assume our modern Omnia could get word back to the 1912 group and make sure it goes their way," I said.

"Yes, you'd think that. But these 1912 guys aren't as emboldened as our bloated power-lords. See, back here in simpler days they're just about to make the play for the big time. Up until now, it's all been easy - backroom deals, corruption, a little war here and there. But they're right at the cusp of going for it all - income tax, WWI and II, and the biggest deal of all, the Federal Reserve. They're grabbing it all and they aren't about to risk it for some prophecy delivered from the future. I mean how well did you fare trying to stop people from getting on the God-dammed Titanic?"

"Okay, I'm listening," I said.

"It's amusing. Our modern Omnia is battling the 1912 version because they both want different outcomes. We can use that to our advantage."

"Kind of like the only two surviving members of a generation's seven battling each other because they want to take different paths to the same outcome." I smiled.

"No. Omnia is the enemy; you're just in the way." He crushed out his cigarette.

"Until now, you've been the betrayer, the killer in the crowd, but now you're a co-conspirator who needs me to live," I said, rising out of my seat. "Then, you'll dispose of me at a time of more suitable convenience."

"Okay, Hibbsy. I'm mean, despicable, obnoxious and disliked . . . that cannot be denied," he mimicked. "That's the difference between you and me. I'm just trying to save the world, I'm not trying to make friends. You're trying to save the world, get your picture put on a stamp, and have a national forest named after you or something. Maybe you should study a little more history – that is your subject, right, Nate? The people who change things weren't always sweet and popular."

"I can think of a few – Gandhi, King, Mandela."

"Ha! How much change did they actually achieve? They were smart strategists with good PR but they became martyrs to their causes. They weren't saints."

"Who is a saint? They each changed the world for the better," I said.

"Fine. Whatever. They're all on postage stamps, even have national holidays. I'm sure you'll be studied by schoolchildren one day and maybe even be an excuse for a department store to have a giant sale on bedding. In the meantime, I'm going to do more than get people to be nice to each other. I'm going to wake them up and show them their souls!"

"Then you don't need me at all, Dunaway."

"Probably not. But, my life is complicated enough and if Hibbs lives another twenty-five years, it'll be much easier on me."

"I'll do it if you give me the Jadeo and Clastier."

"No, you'll do it because if Hibbs dies tonight you won't be able to stop Omnia in the future, any more than I will."

"There'll be other ways."

"Really? Then why am I here?" he asked, raising an eyebrow.

We stared at each other.

"Forget it," I said, standing up. "You know the way out." I was bluffing. This might be my best chance to get the Jadeo and Clastier back, but if Dunaway was this worried about Clastier, then I was too. I also considered this to be a chance to show Dunaway that we were more powerful working together.

"Good day, then." Dunaway rose, bowed slightly and headed for the door. He turned, before leaving. "I'll see you at your funeral. It will be quite an affair. Two Presidents, senators, governors, Carnegie, Rockefeller and even J.P. Morgan will be there. Sorry you'll be inside a box. Funny, when those school kids study about Hibbs in the future, it'll be as a footnote to history. His assassination triggered the Second American Civil War. I'll see you back in our age, Nate, but you'll hardly recognize it."

ooooo

I caught up to Dunaway in the street. He crushed out a cigarette. "I thought you might change your mind."

"What's the plan?" I asked.

"You have documents that incriminate Omnia."

"Yes."

"I need them."

"Forget it."

"What, Hibbsy, ol' boy, don't you trust me?"

"Hibbs might trust you, but I don't," I answered him as Nate.

"Come on, Nate. I don't want the originals you have stashed at Graydon in Leesburg, just the carbons and duplicate photos you keep in your office here. I assume you've got a few more sets hidden somewhere else. Your mausoleum?

Your mistress's home in Georgetown? Maybe somewhere in New York? I don't really care, the more the better, but I need a set to keep you alive."

"You think I need you to do that? I've spent the last thirty years cutting deals. I was born poor, and now I'm one of the most powerful men in Washington. You're wasting my time, Dunaway."

"I don't doubt you're a great dealmaker and shrewd broker, Hibbsy, but you miscalculated in this case. The President was your last shot and you misplayed. You've got hours left to live and there isn't time for you to run around town flashing documents when there's a target on your back."

He was telling the truth. Maybe all along Hibbs had lived only until 1937 because of Dunaway's intervention. It would be hard to say . . . time's a funny thing and a hundred other dimensions would play out a hundred different ways.

"Dunaway, I'm trusting you." I looked into his eyes. "Very reluctantly, I'm trusting you. Don't screw me. You may have a strong grasp on the next hundred years but I'm no lightweight and I'll find you in another time and undo you. Understand?"

"Hey, Nate, Hibbs has given you a little backbone. I like that." He patted my back. "No worries, I can beat you fifty legitimate ways, I don't need tricks to do it."

He followed me back into my office. I led him down to a secret wine cellar. Hidden safes were a bit of an obsession for me and there were sixteen concealed in various parts of the building. The floor safe in the wine cellar contained the most important papers, including the Omnia proof.

"Stay out of sight for a few days, Hibbsy," said the man who was Dunaway, as I handed him the roll of documents. "Don't go to any of your usual places."

As soon as Dunaway left with the documents, Hibbs departed Washington and several hours later arrived at the Woodgrove Estate in Round Hill, Virginia. The original stone home had been constructed in the 1700s. During the American Revolutionary War, the local regiment used it as a planning site. Throughout the Civil War, Woodgrove was occupied by troops and became an important meeting place for spies. In the early 1900s, a reclusive friend of Hibbs owned the twenty-room mansion, making it an ideal hiding place.

As Hibbs, I sat on the veranda, enjoying the sun setting over the distant mountains framed by the massive white columns. The scent of boxwood reminded me of the hedge at Graydon, a gift from the Prince of Wales. A red fox darted between grand walnut trees towards the apple orchard. My thoughts drifted to Nate's world. I'd have to find Dunaway once I returned to my time and secure the Jadeo and Clastier. Spencer, also a guardian of the Jadeo, had been missing too long. Hoofbeats brought me back to Hibbs.

A bedraggled man Hibbs and I both knew dismounted from the spent horse. It took only an instant to recognize Dustin in his eyes.

"Billy . . . Nate," Dustin nodded at me. He had for--ward-memory.

"Dustin, what are you doing here?"

"There're men at Graydon, tearing the place up pretty

good. Looking for you . . . and the documents."

"Damn! Dunaway betrayed me again!"

"No, he's good to his word on this. But Omnia's got reach, and help from the future. They're not more than a few minutes behind me."

I/Hibbs yelled for his chauffeur to bring the car.

"Send the chauffeur off without you, Nate." Dustin said, turning to the chauffeur. "Head to Harpers Ferry as fast as you can. Don't stop until they force you. Go, man," Dustin snapped.

The chauffeur turned to me/Hibbs questioningly.

"Nate, he won't be able to outrun them. We have to hide you here."

"Trusting my brother is the most difficult-easiest thing." I inhaled deeply. Hibbs reached for his cigarette case. I stopped him.

"Go!" I yelled to the chauffeur.

The spray of dust from the car hung in the still summer air. "Where will I hide?"

"I came through here during the Civil War. I was a rebel spy in that lifetime. This place was built for secrets. Can you Skyclimb?"

"Not in this life."

"Okay." He pulled a rope from his saddle. "Follow me." We came to a well on one end of the house. "I'm going to lower you; about two-thirds of the way down, you'll see a small tunnel. On one side it goes toward the house, the other goes away from it; take that one."

Descending into blackness, I clutched a small torch. The stone walls narrowed toward the bottom. "This tunnel is dammed small!" I yelled up to Dustin, while wedging myself inside. The low ceiling required me to stoop. The rope pulled away as soon as I untied myself.

"You'll be fine. Follow it as far as it goes."

The torch revealed twenty feet ahead; beyond that, darkness. I didn't move until I heard Dustin ride away. There was no way to climb back up.

I wound my way underneath the Virginia countryside.

Hibbs' body was stiff and sore, ready to give up. I reminded him of Dustin's instructions to follow it to the end. The torch blew out a few minutes later. I missed my night vision as Hibbs panicked. "There's no light!" Air rushed in from up ahead. I trudged forward and soon stumbled out into the night. A thicket of brambles and honeysuckle concealed the entrance. I lay against the slope breathing in fresh air.

ooooo

The Outview came at an awful time. Having one within another was rare and usually left me scattered for days. The stunning fjords of Norway greeted me at the end of the first millennium. I didn't have forward-memory, nor any participation; the Outview simply presented, leaving me only as a viewer. And as the viewer, I recognized Omnia agents but could do nothing to prevent their actions. The Viking longboat headed toward the sea, as a great voyage lay ahead. My lifetime as a Viking sailor seemed too insignificant and long ago for Omnia to bother with.

Night soon fell and the three agents, living as fellow shipmates, came at me while we slept on deck. Even if I woke in time there was no chance against three intent assassins. They approached with swords at the ready. The first raised his weapon . . . a spear landed in his chest. He collapsed, bloody, across my body. A warrior always wakes ready and my sword swung full around as I pushed the attacker off and jumped to my feet. Two others approached from behind. I could see one was Linh, but my Viking incarnation had no such recognition and he backed away from both groups. At Linh's side was a second incarnation of mine. The importance of this lifetime was becoming clearer. If two of my souls had two separate incarnations occurring on the same ship, and Linh was there too, it must be a critical piece of the future. An intense fight ensued. Battle axes, swords, spears and mace clashed and chipped, waking more of the ship. Linh followed her first kill with fatal blows to the other two. I had no way of knowing if she had forward-memory but judging by her killing skills, it was unlikely. With order finally restored, I saw that I had died in the Outview but not the one they had attacked in his sleep; instead, the victim was the one trying to save me with Linh. I wondered what change the outcome of the battle a thousand years in the past would have on our current contest with Omnia.

48

Finally, Yangchen's healings took hold and I woke on the third morning back at the lake house feeling strong and healthy, but confused and desperate to know the outcome of my time as Hibbs and the tunnel escape.

I found Dustin on the astral.

"Did Hibbs live?" I asked him.

"Of course he did. I'm only a screw-up in this lifetime. Throughout history, I've been a warrior-wizard of extraordinary skill."

"And modest."

"Someone has to tell my story."

"So Dunaway didn't betray me?"

"Dunaway betrays us all as he seeks his goals but, because they coincide with ours, mostly he ends up betraying himself."

"What about the Viking ship? Did the right incarnation die?"

"Can't help you there, brother. The only Vikings I know anything about play football in Minnesota."

ooooo

Linh, completely back to her old self, had spent the time during my illness working theories about completing the list of nine. "You had Amber worried," she said, flashing a sly smile.

"What about you?"

"I knew you had things to do which would be more difficult with the weight of your human body." Over the years, Linh had developed the ability to conjure and explore visions. It was part of the Timbal power in which Rose and Spencer excelled. Each had a specialty and Linh's brought wide views of different events across time and dimensions whether they involved her or not. "A useful yet troubling trait," she often said. "Can we talk about the nine?" she asked.

"After we talk about the morning in the fjords." I watched her carefully for any recognition.

"I'd rather not."

"You did have full memory . . . yet you used violence."

"Nate, our non-violence pledge was made in this lifetime."

"But you were acting from *this* lifetime."

"That's not true, I was a Viking. Fighting, raiding, exploring made up my entire existence. I did it with honor, no other person on that ship could match my experience and skill."

"But you acted to save me. Would your Nordic-incarnation have done that had you not intervened?"

"We were friends, it is difficult to say for sure, but I think so."

"Two of my incarnations fought, only one lived . . ."

"We saved the right one. If not, you and I would not have been born."

"You sound like Spencer."

"I discussed it with him."

"Is he back?" I asked excitedly.

"No. We talked about the Vikings months ago."

"How come you didn't tell me?"

"It never occurred to me you'd recognize me."

"I didn't, I saw it through an Outview."

"Oh, that explains why you didn't seem to know, because you didn't. Anyway, it was one of those gray areas and there could be no debate."

"Why?"

"Because, Nate, you sometimes act as if this is a game of principles and absolutes. If it wasn't for Spencer there would have been more mistakes made that we couldn't recover from for thousands of years, even tens of thousands."

"How the hell does anyone know what's real or not? It all seems to be sliding and shifting constantly."

Yangchen walked in. "Back?"

"Yes, thank you for helping to restore my body."

"You may not need it to traipse around time but it does come in rather handy here."

"Any word of Spencer?"

"No, I suspect he's on the hunt for the Jadeo. I think it's time we help him out on that front. As you know, he takes that commitment more seriously than any other. It's the most likely explanation for his absence."

"We need to talk to the three remaining names: Marie Jones, Kevin Morrison and Helen Hartman," Linh said.

"We have to find them first," I said.

"We have to find one of them before Omnia does, or he's dead."

"Omnia already knows where Marie Jones is. They just don't know who she is," Yangchen said.

"You know where she is?"

Yangchen nodded. "She works for the Federal Reserve."

"Oh my God, that means she works for Omnia."

"More than that. She is Nate."

"We've been scouring the universe for incarnations of Nate, hoping to protect them before Omnia destroys your every existence," Yangchen said. "And we got lucky with finding one in this time and then I recognized the name as one of the nine entrusted. The complexities were increased dramatically once we discovered she's high up at the Fed."

"Without the Fed, Omnia could not hold onto power," I said. "Can we use Marie Jones to somehow destroy the Fed?"

"It's not that easy. Look at Dustin and Storch, you and Fred Means, Ren and Fitts. I know of no example of one personality changing another through a common soul," Yangchen said.

"Forget changing her," Linh said. "What if Nate can get inside Jones' head and find out things to help the Movement and take advantage of the situation by having Jones do stuff to harm the Fed from the inside?"

The Federal Reserve Bank was the financial arm of Omnia. It had actually been created by Omnia back in 1913 at the same time they got the federal income tax enacted, only the Fed is a private bank illegally given the right to print the nation's money. Movement historians had shown me how the Fed orchestrated the 1929 stock market crash and the ten-year Depression that followed. It was the greatest shift of wealth in the history of the world, at least until they did it again in 2008, when, over the course of eighteen months, the U.S. Treasury was looted and mortgaged into oblivion. In both panics, and many smaller ones during the intervening years, the Fed and the wealthy bankers who controlled it bought land, companies and other assets at pennies on the dollar and created enormous amounts of debt, all payable back to the Fed with interest. The money they lent, like all currency in the modern central bank system, was created from nothing - simply printed. That system allowed Omnia unlimited power because they controlled the wealth. The masses, meanwhile, were left with endless bills to pay. "Keep them entertained with sports and scandals and they'll never notice that all they do is work to earn enough to pay debt, taxes and inflation," a former Fed Chairman said privately. The discovery that my soul had a part in the scheme really bothered me.

"Deal with it, Nate," Yangchen said. "We all have dark aspects. Duality is a great teacher. But Linh has a good idea. If you can use your incarnation as Marie Jones to harm Omnia or help the Movement, it could be the momentum shifter we need."

ooooo

It took some time, deep meditation and using an Outview but I got into the head of my soul-counterpart. Jones presented me with a different look at Omnia villains. A committee she chaired in 2009 made specific recommendations on policies that would enrich the cartel of bankers who owned the Federal Reserve. Jones knew of the corruption and had trouble sleeping. Through an Outview, I witnessed a conversation with her sister in 2009.

"You wouldn't believe how big this is," Jones said. "They have consolidated their position in banks, buried the U.S. in debt the country can never get out of, insuring they will control things for . . . well, forever."

"You've got to let me write about it," her sister, a well-known author, said.

"They'll kill you . . . and me."

"I'll weave it into the plot of a novel."

"They aren't stupid."

"Neither am I."

"I don't think you get it. They've created almost every crisis and war and then funded them. If a private company gets too big, they take it over, either by friendly overpayment with fake money, or by destroying it and picking up the pieces cheap. When someone figures out how the Fed really works, and makes any noise about it, they're either labeled a quack or . . . they die."

"They aren't going to murder a fantasy author. Although that would make a good plot twist."

"Forget it."

"Then what are you going to do? Keep working for them and let them take over the world?"

"They've already taken over the world."

ooooo

Even with her awareness, I'm ashamed to say that Marie Jones went on working for Omnia for many more years, until I showed up.

Within days, by using time manipulations, Outviews and especially Solteer, I expanded her doubt and helped her decide to gather evidence. She had access to information that made the roll of documents Hibbs had amassed look like a comic book.

"Be careful, Nate," Yangchen cautioned, as I updated her and the girls over dinner.

"I'm being extremely careful. Do you have any idea what this will do to Omnia? We'll Air-Project it the same night we put up the Carst videos!"

"That's not what I mean," Yangchen said, quietly. "It is a dangerous thing to mess with a person's destiny."

"How do you know this isn't her destiny?"

She scowled at me. "If this were her destiny, you would not need Solteer to make her do these things."

"She's doing them because we share a soul."

"That does not give you the right to lead her life. You have

Nate to be."

"I don't know, Yangchen, where is that written? I'm not trying to be a jerk here, but how are you so sure that I don't have the right to manage every incarnation of my soul?"

"If you were acting from your soul, you do have that right. But you are acting from Nate, and denying Marie Jones her free will to complete her optimal destiny."

"You may be right. But you don't know."

"Neither do you, Nate," Amber said.

"Maybe not."

"There is no book of 'spiritual laws;' it's just clear. It should be anyway. Meditate on something and the answer comes . . . eventually. You should be able to feel what is true."

"I can't always," I admitted. "And sometimes when I think I understand, someone comes along with a different take and that makes sense too."

"That's thinking, not feeling," Linh said. "When you know without thinking, then it is true."

"Okay, but isn't our ultimate goal to stop Omnia? What I'm doing with Marie isn't hurting her and it's definitely nonviolent. I mean, Yangchen, I'm using soul powers. And how is Omnia going to recover from Carst and the Fed corruption that'll be delivered to the masses on a single night?"

"You know better than to underestimate Omnia. Their understanding of the universe and soul powers are expanding at a frightening rate. They are far beyond the Movement in many areas. Imagine if we premier our Air-Projections of Carst and Omnia's Fed crimes one night and Omnia has a way to make that night never exist."

A heavy silence took the room.

Linh spoke first. "Is that possible, Yangchen?"

"Anything is possible," she said impatiently.

"I know, but are they close to that . . . that ability to kill time?"

"We believe they have achieved it in a distant dimension. Whether they can duplicate the results here is yet to be seen."

"How can we counter that?" Amber asked in a trembling

voice.

Yangchen searched our faces, clearly regretting sharing her terrifying news. "Even if we find a way to counter it . . . I mean, you have to realize, we may have already countered it and Omnia made it so that our counter never happened."

It was extraordinarily horrible news, the worst we'd ever heard. Then I wondered what else Yangchen knew but dared not share.

The following morning while Linh and I were discussing the final two names on the list - Helen Hartman and Kevin Morrison - an Outview pulled me away.

As soon as I saw Marie Jones sitting on her balcony talking to two men in dark suits, it was clear trouble had come.

"What has your contact been with Nathan Ryder?" one of them asked calmly.

"None. The only thing I know about him is what I've seen in the media."

"Please, Ms. Jones, the truth would be more helpful."

"That is the truth. Look, I'm not comfortable being interrogated here. If I'm being charged with something, I'd like to know what it is and then I'd like to contact an attorney."

The two men looked at each other. Three more were inside. They loaded every piece of computer or electronic equipment onto a large cart. One of the men was a mystic. He scanned the condo with Vising and Foush. He didn't seem to be able to do Timbal or he might have detected my presence. Not that they would have been able to arrest me, since I wasn't there in physical form. I recalled the conversation with Yangchen from the night before and a wave of fear gripped me. They might now be able to apprehend me in a non-physical way.

I snapped back into the Outview at the sound of Jones's scream. The two men were holding her upside down, suspending her from the forty-sixth floor railing.

"Jones, we know you're in communication with Nathan Ryder. Admit it, tell us how you are contacting him and what information you've given him. There will be no charges, no attorneys, no other chances. Now, answer," he snapped.

"I've never met nor spoken to Nathan Ryder. Please, I'm telling you the truth," she screamed.

"Is that your final answer, Ms. Jones?"

"Yes, no, what do you want me to say? I've never talked to him, but I'll say whatever you want."

The two men exchanged a casual glance and dropped her. Within the Outview, I felt her terror as she plunged and the micro-second of incredible, complete pain as "we" hit the pavement.

ooooo

To know I had killed Marie Jones, just as if I had thrown her from the balcony myself, sent me reeling in a devastating shredded view across time. Yangchen had tried to warn me. Marie never had a chance to follow her own destiny. At the very point in her life where she could decide on her own path, I pushed her down a road that led to her murder. More than another ghost I carried, the wound of Marie would be felt in all my future incarnations. I needed Wandus to show me how to make this right. How I wished I could just pursue the powers and mysteries of the universe without having to fight for survival. Without a chance to reconcile my soul to what had just happened, I landed in the Middle East centuries earlier.

The market was teeming with traders, farmers and shoppers. Scents of mustard, incense, raw meats and wool wafted as I made my way through the crowd. I had control of the lifetime and forward-memory but no powers. Still, I sensed danger. This was yet another life to survive the exhausting battles waged by Omnia to prevent my time as Nate. I'd gained enough knowledge of the structure of time, understanding of dimensions within infinite universes, and simultaneous lifetimes, to know this "game" with Omnia had been going on longer than anyone knew and would likely, in some form, last forever. I recognized a man across the bustling square. He'd seen me, too, and there wasn't anyone from any lifetime I would've rather seen at that moment. Spencer came from behind a stall and led me quickly into a deserted alley.

I grabbed him and pulled him into a hug. Tears welled in my eyes. "Where have you been?" I asked.

"Lost."

"What do you mean?" I recalled my second meeting with Spencer on Tea Leaf Beach, where he warned me that it was possible to get stuck in between time, but it never occurred to me that *he* could.

"Omnia has breached the parallels. It's made it impossible for me to get back. They've elevated this contest to something never before seen . . ."

"By using interdimensional warfare."

He nodded. "Then Yangchen knows?"

"Yes," I replied.

"I've been trying to get back to inform the Movement."

"We found out when they took Linh."

He instantly looked concerned.

"We rescued her. She's fine."

"How long have I been gone?"

"Six weeks."

He sighed, relieved. "It's been thirty-eight years for me."

"Dunaway?"

"Still has the Jadeo."

"I've been pursuing it through time, even managed to do a walk-in as one of the conquistadors who killed you in Mexico. I got to the Cenote at the same time as your dad. I met his stone axe and was dead before he recognized me."

"Omnia is beating us badly."

"It appears that way. I believe they have intentionally prevented me from returning to our time."

"How?"

"Piercing dimensions. Depending how advanced their abilities are, they can rearrange almost anything."

"The Movement thinks Omnia is still at a basic level."

"Maybe in our current life. But time's a funny thing, I've been wandering across a hundred or more lifetimes during my exile these thirty-eight years and I've encountered Omnia's agents in almost all of them."

"Am I trapped back here too?"

He looked upset. "Do you have powers?"

"No."

"It's been impossible to escape this lifetime. As soon as I saw you, I realized it's because I needed to be here when you came. So perhaps we shall help each other yet again."

"What can we do?" I asked.

"I haven't been able to communicate with you in our time but I've had some success getting to past incarnations, and I have a pretty good idea who is running Omnia."

"That's the break we've been needing. Is it some—"

Omnia agents appeared at the end of the alley. Spencer pushed me into a run. We darted around the corner. "Don't get separated," he yelled, as we entered an enormous square filled with thousands of people. "This is a dangerous city."

I stayed close to him as we pushed through the sea of soldiers, religious devotees, children and peasants. "What's going on here?" I shouted above the noise.

"A festival to cel—" I couldn't hear the rest of his answer as the crowd swelled and pushed us apart. I looked behind for a second to see if the Omnia agents were near. When I turned back around, Spencer was far ahead. His eyes found mine. I saw agents right behind him and screamed his name.

Amber found me doubled over on the floor. "Spencer!" I shouted.

"You're Nathan Ryder from Ashland, Oregon."

"Damn it. I know who I am. Is Spencer here?" I jumped to my feet intent on searching the house and grounds. He must have made it back, too. My body folded, dropping to the floor.

"Nate, you've been yelling and flailing for hours. After the third time you fell out of bed, we left you on the floor."

"I don't care about that. We've got to save Spencer. Please go look for him."

Linh and Yangchen rushed in at my yelling. I gave them a quick version of the events in the Outviews. Linh and Amber left to search for him while Yangchen asked for every detail I could recall about where I'd seen Spencer and what he said.

ooooo

"He's not here," Linh said breathlessly. "We've looked everywhere." Amber helped me to the kitchen where Yangchen did extensive healing while I devoured a platter of steamed vegetables.

"I'd love a Coke right now," I said.

"He hasn't evolved at all." Amber rolled her eyes.

Yangchen excused herself. In her absence I told them more about my time with Marie Jones and Spencer. After what seemed a long while, Yangchen returned.

"You must go," Yangchen said firmly.

"Where?" Linh asked.

"To meet Booker."

"I can't," I said weakly.

"It is not a short trip, you'll be able to rest on the way. With a few Lusans, you'll be fully recuperated in a couple of hours," Yangchen insisted.

"This is important?" I asked.

"You need to ask that question?" she asked.

"No," I said. "When do we leave?"

"Now." Yangchen hurried us into the helicopter. Booker had summoned us, which had never happened before. Something major was going on.

"Are you coming?" Amber asked Yangchen.

"No, I'm needed elsewhere." She told us it would take more than twenty hours of travel to reach our destination.

"Why can't we get there through the Wizard Island portal?" I asked.

"This island cannot be reached by any portals," Yangchen responded.

"Seriously?" I'd never heard of such a place.

"Then why can't we meet here?"

"You know it's not safe for Booker to come here."

"It doesn't seem safe for us to be traveling for twenty hours by conventional methods. But I guess Booker knows what he's doing."

Yangchen nodded.

"What's it about?" Linh asked.

"He'll explain."

"Yangchen, promise me you'll continue to search for Spencer."

"Of course," she said, shutting the helicopter door.

ooooo

The island held the distinction of being the most isolated in Booker's collection. We didn't need the water to block remote viewers. Recalling that tactic reminded me of simpler times before I knew of Carst, puncturing dimensions, and the war with Omnia had expanded into lifetimes across thousands of years and throughout the parallels. The island was not likely to draw much attention from satellites that monitored nearly everything now.

The final leg of our journey was by seaplane, refueling twice at ships along the way. After a few hours sleep, the pilot left the tiny island in order to pick up Booker and two other guests. Amber, Linh and I would be alone until late the next day.

The "shack" was the main structure on the small patch of land hidden among thousands of miles of open waters. Although a shack by Booker's standards, anyone else would call it quite spacious - six bedrooms, three baths and a large greatroom. The island wasn't big enough to have one of his trademark golf carts but there were bicycles. Solar panels and large water tanks kept everything comfortable. We went for a swim and tried for a half hour to forget the stakes and consequences of our every action.

We relaxed on chaises, letting the late afternoon sun warm us. My physical strength had returned during the trip, but I was mentally exhausted. We hadn't spoken much during the journey as I rested and thought about Marie and Spencer. On the beach, the sun felt like a lover, caressing, soft and penetrating. As the warm breeze brought scents of exotic tropical flowers and Amber and Linh exchanged hushed small talk, I thought of Floral Lake in Outin and wondered about Dustin.

"I read our horoscopes yesterday, and all of us are supposed to have a good month," Amber said.

"We need it," I replied, sipping a smoothie. With no staff on the island, we fended for ourselves. The kitchen was stocked well enough with basics and the pilot had unloaded a crate of fresh fruit and vegetables.

"Every month can be good," Linh said. "Astrology is too limited."

"What are you talking about?" Amber asked, sharply.

"The problem with astrology," Linh began, "is that it's

based on a comically tiny number of planets."

"Hey, everything helps. It's not easy to navigate this world. If everyone studied –"

"The power path, astrology, Chinese year of the rabbit, it's all external, and it's all based on human interpretations of incomplete data and superstition," Linh interrupted.

"How do you explain the accuracy of astrology?"

"There isn't any. People who follow astrology and the like are usually more in tune with their higher selves so they get their guidance that way. Plus, most forecasts and readings are so general that people can easily make them fit their lives and find something in there they want to hear. And finally, if you flip a coin and guess the outcome, you'll be right a bunch of times."

"Whatever," Amber said, annoyed. "You claim every month can be good, so how do you explain the horrible few years we've had."

"Have they been that bad? We're still alive."

"Not all of us," Amber reminded."

Linh's eyes flashed anger. It was a surprisingly insensitive jab from Amber. We all knew how much Linh missed Kyle.

"Anything can be manifested; we just haven't been doing it," Linh said.

"Why not?" I asked.

"It's more difficult than it seems, and all distractions must be minimized."

"Distractions? We've been swimming in nothing but distractions for years."

"That's no accident," Linh said.

"I've known a great astrologer," Amber pressed. "She called stuff about me that was specific and crazy-accurate."

"I'll bet she was psychic," Linh said, "even if she didn't know it. Tarot cards, I-ching, numerology, all those things are just tools to awaken our own intuition. The cards don't tell us any more than the stars."

"That sounds a lot like what Clastier says," I said.

"I know, I've read some of his stuff. He's brilliant. Imagine what's in the missing pages."

"Do you agree with her?" Amber asked me, but Linh answered first.

"Nate is Clastier, Amber; he wrote the papers," Linh said.

"I don't think Clastier is saying astrology, et cetera, is phony," I said. "He's saying they are tools, not answers. The answers come from ourselves."

"That's what I'm saying." Linh said.

"All the time we've spent practicing the soul powers has proven this. No matter how much information we have on what the power is, what it does and how it works, it doesn't come together until we find it from within," I said.

"There's a movement about that," Linh smiled.

"All right, we have the time on this island. Let's manifest something. Let's make some peace," Amber said.

"Manifesting is about knowing," I replied. "As Wandus would say, 'That's a trickier trick than it sounds.' Consciously creating circumstances is a tremendously powerful thing and that's why it's so deceptively difficult."

"It's not just –" I didn't hear Amber's answer because Dustin interrupted over the astral.

"I was just wondering about you," I said.

"Yeah? Well I was just worrying about you. You've got a rough night ahead, brother."

"Why?"

"I saw it in a Window. A storm's coming."

I looked at the cloudless blue sky and calm surf. "Tonight?"

"Yeah, like a massive hurricane. You need to get ready."

"Okay."

"And Nate . . . one of you dies."

When I pressed Dustin for details, his only response was, "I couldn't see through the storm, it was just there. I can't explain it."

I told the girls about his warnings and we discussed our options. There was no way off the island; its location outside the typhoon belt meant steady rains were normally the worst weather. There was no storm shelter, but we did find a few rolls of masking tape and taped the windows with asterisk patterns. Amber said it would reduce the amount of flying glass if the storm came as fierce as Dustin predicted. The only room without windows was a pantry located in the interior of the house. Nothing happened for many hours; the sky remained blue and completely clear. We wondered if Dustin's Window existed or if he'd mistaken ours for a different dimension. Then, just after dinner, the first clouds appeared.

"Do you see that?" Amber said, pointing.

"The clouds are forming right out of the ocean," Linh gasped.

"Damn it! You know what that means?" I shouted, as the sea lifted all around, swirling into thick clouds. "Someone is causing this storm. Omnia must know we're here!"

I attempted to break up the clouds with Gogen but they were too large and pliable. Knowing it wasn't a natural storm, I tried every power within my knowledge to stop it from growing but nothing worked.

It was as if the menacing clouds had devoured the sun whole, like an enormous black, blue and white dragon gobbling up a small child. Thunder rumbled, building to near constant booms. Lightning webbed across the now darkened sky. My final attempt at protection was a weather dome; it collapsed instantly into a puddle. The super-typhoon had been created by someone extremely powerful. Winds shook the house until it whined and creaked. The clouds ripped open like blisters. In a terrifying deluge, the air vanished, overrun by a waterfall dumping with the force of ten Niagaras, flooding the tiny island.

We retreated into the pantry.

"This has to be the worst storm ever," Amber said, raising her voice above howling winds and crashing rain.

"Can this house hold?" Linh shouted. "There goes the power."

Total darkness.

"Everyone use Gogen to keep the house together. I'll concentrate on the roof, Linh, north and west walls. Amber, east and south."

Ever since Dustin signed off, I'd been trying to reach Yangchen on the astral. Now I made futile attempts with the other mystics. Even Dustin was unreachable. But he knew what was happening. Surely, he'd get word to the Movement.

A horrible ripping sound. All my efforts went back to Gogen and the roof.

Kyle's voice came through, "Things are not always as they appear."

"Kyle?" I asked silently.

"Remember, you can't trust the universe just when it's convenient."

"Kyle, what do I do?"

Shattering glass. Linh screamed.

"Kyle?" I begged him to return.

Splintering wood and crashing metal.

I held the roof with all the energy of Gogen until a section slipped.

Crunch. Bang. A wall collapsed somewhere.

"We've got to hold it!" I yelled. Earlier we'd discussed what would happen if the house were destroyed. But at the time, the sky was still blue with only a warm tropical breeze. The island didn't have much contour, mostly flat beach, trees and some small rises. Our backup plan centered around a tight cluster of palms amid a ringed rock outcropping, which might have been the highest point on the island.

Shattering glass. Crashing boards.

"How much longer can the house withstand this?" Amber shouted, as the thunder grew even louder.

"Keep on Gogen!"

Another section of roof went. Boom. Crackle. Thump. Thump. Bam!

"Remember the rock-trees." I yelled. We had tied ropes there.

Shattering glass. Riiiiiip. Crunch.

"Can we even get there?" Linh screamed.

Most of the remaining roof went. It sounded like a freight train plowing through the house. Water flooded in, four or five feet deep, and floating debris knocked me into a beam and tangled my legs. With the collapse of the pantry, and everything else, my night vision nearly blinded me during lightning strikes every few seconds. I lost sight of the girls. The water, freed from the structure's last confines, receded and ran across the land. I found the girls again; we forced ourselves toward the rock-trees with Gogen against two hundred mile per hour winds.

The typhoon swirled. Amber kept getting thrown about. She still couldn't Skyclimb, which Linh and I were using to supplement Gogen. It seemed obvious Amber was the one least likely to survive the storm, but saving them both had been my obsession for so long, I might die trying to save her.

It was as if the ocean turned upside down over the island. "We're going the wrong way!" Linh yelled, grabbing my arm.

Visibility didn't exist, the only light coming from the terrifying lightning. Rain poured in thick sheets that made breathing difficult. I didn't know if Linh was right, nor did I ask how she knew. I just grabbed Amber and swam through the air. The main force of the wind was now at our backs, making progress a bit easier, but side gales continued to knock us to the ground.

Not far from the rock-trees, the torrent increased. A small trail became a raging river. Getting airborne with Skyclimbing was impossible in those conditions.

"We'll never get across that," Amber shouted.

"Where else can we go?" Linh yelled.

I looked around and could only see faint outlines of nearby trees as the wind and rain washed out everything.

"Maybe over there." I pointed toward the bulk of the island's trees.

The "river" pulled Amber and me in. It sucked us downstream and pushed me under the surface, twisting in vines, leaves and mud. I fought back up and miraculously surfaced next to Amber. Linh was running along the bank.

"Get back!" I yelled too late.

The ever-widening river grabbed her legs. She disappeared for a few scary moments before emerging several feet in front of us. Battling the raging current, we worked over to each other, frantic, as we cascaded toward the ocean.

"Never let me go!" Linh screamed as our hands locked. Amber was on my other arm.

We struggled to keep our heads from sinking, in the turmoil of mud and debris, tumbling down the violent river, somehow managing to keep hold of each other. Then the world ended. I saw it too late. The river poured over a cliff. I reached something and gripped with bleeding desperate fingers, just at the edge. Linh slipped and grabbed my ankle. Amber hooked into the bend of my elbow. My hand locked on an exposed root. The rushing water tried to pull us down. Rocks, broken parts of the house and crashing ocean waves waited twenty feet below. Here it is, I thought; Dustin was right, one of us is about to die, maybe all three of us.

"Nate, help! I'm slipping!" Linh screamed.

I tried holding her with Gogen but it weakened my grip on the root. Amber slipped too. I now had her in my other hand. My only choice was to let go of Amber and grab Linh or let

Linh go over.

"Kyle!" I yelled, realizing I could only save one of them.

No response.

"Hold on, Linh."

She kept slipping. The suction from the waterfall pulled hard on her legs. Linh's hands were now gripping just my feet.

"Amber, can you reach the root?"

"I'm trying!"

The force of the river was pulling her, too. I had to decide. If I did nothing; Linh would go over any second. If I saved Linh, I'd have to let Amber go over.

"Nate," Linh cried.

Time suspended. The years and the universe had grown impatient with my inability to choose between Amber and Linh and now there was no time left. I could save only one – even if I loved them both, I could only have one. It had to be Linh.

The decision gave me the strength to do what otherwise would have been impossible. But as I started to release Amber, I remembered Kyle's earlier message. "Things are not always what they appear. You can't trust the universe just when it's convenient."

Instead, I pulled my leg back hard, which broke Linh's grip and she went tumbling backwards over the falls, screaming.

53

Without Linh's weight, I managed to pull us up to the tree. Now on the other side of the river, we clung to each other, pushed with Gogen and battled through unrelenting winds and water until we found the rock-trees. We strained to get the ropes secured around our bodies. It was freezing, my body was drained, and Linh was gone.

"Nate," Amber shouted, pulling herself as close as the ropes would allow, rubbing my arms trying to warm me. "You're in shock. You've got to hold on."

The storm raged in loud fury. My voice hoarse, I yelled above it, "I let Linh die." My breath came in gasps. "I. Let. Her. Die!"

"Don't think about that now. We have to get warm."

"How can I not . . ." My teeth chattered uncontrollably. " . . . think about . . . that? I lost her . . . again."

Several trees had been snapped or uprooted. We'd chosen ours carefully before the storm. Closely surrounded by rock outcroppings and other trees, we were shielded from the brunt of the wind on all sides.

Amber stopped rubbing. My shaking increased. She pushed a Lusan into my lap, then rubbed another around my upper back and neck. I passed out.

I woke with three Lusans in my lap, my body still. "I'm sorry," I said to Amber, while thinking of Linh, then dropped out again. The next time my eyes opened, there was silence.

Glorious silence.

"Is it over?" I asked.

"I don't know, it just stopped a minute ago," Amber said. "It could be the eye of the storm."

Darkness still shrouded the island, but without lightning, my night vision allowed a view of the incredible damage. Aside from the rock-trees and another stand nearby, the landscape had been transformed into a ravaged wasteland. We decided to stay tied to the trees; there was nowhere else to go.

"Thanks for . . . the Lusans," I said.

"You saved me."

"Linh asked me to not let go."

"You did your best."

"Did I? How do you know? I kicked her over the edge. I killed her."

"Did you feel her change?"

The thought had not occurred to me. How could it have? There'd only been a few conscious minutes since we made it to the rock-trees. Feeling through the energy, I discovered her change had not been made. "She's alive!"

"Where?"

I searched for her on the astral, but found nothing. Still, I knew she was alive. "We've got to go find her." I wriggled out of the knots and ropes. My legs were rubbery and gave out when I stood.

"Are you sure you're up to it?"

"Who cares? She's out there and needs help. You stay here."

"No, I'm coming."

"I'm going to Skyclimb."

"I'll follow on the ground."

Returning to my feet, slowly this time, I hugged her. "First sign of rain or wind, get yourself back here."

"You too."

I leapt up to the tops of the few surviving trees, and then took long leaps across piles of uprooted trunks and debris. The waterfall was still draining excess water from the island. I scanned the ocean below.

Suddenly conscious of the sky, I realized the storm had returned to its hellish origins and left the Milky Way and billions of other stars in its wake. "Linh, Linh," I shouted in a raspy voice that didn't sound like my own. I walked along the cliff until it eased into a beach, all the time calling her name, all the time begging the universe to lead me to her, calling on my guides to tell me how to find her. Amber caught up to me just as the sun peeked over the horizon and turned the ocean gold and orange.

"I followed your voice," she said.

"It's not working very well," I said hoarsely.

"We'll find her."

"We have to," I gasped. "If she dies, it'll be because of me and I can't bear that."

"It was an impossible situation."

"Nothing is impossible," I whispered.

"It's true, everything is possible, but there are moments that are impossible."

ooooo

Halfway around the island we found her, partially covered in sand and trash, rolled on her side, just out of the surf. "She's breathing," I said, scooping her up in my arms.

We got her to a clearing. Amber made Lusans while I did hands-on healing. It didn't take long before she opened her eyes.

"You're safe. The storm is over," I said.

"Are you okay? Amber asked.

"Good," she said softly, seemingly answering us both.

Linh had Skyclimbed as she went over the falls and had been able to run along the churning waters until she found a thick chunk of Styrofoam insulation amidst the debris to hold onto. The surge pushed her out to sea but soon the tide pulled her back. As the storm waned, she was able to kick her way to the beach. She collapsed with the waves on the sand not long before we arrived. Linh wasn't talking much. I learned the story only by reading her.

"Shouldn't we think about food and fresh drinking water?" Amber asked.

Before I could respond, the quiet of the post-storm morning was shattered by the sound of approaching planes.

Three seaplanes circled the island twice, one of which I recognized as one we'd flown in the day before. I left Amber with Linh and went to meet the planes a quarter mile up the beach at the same small inlet.

Booker was off the plane by the time I got there. He hugged me. "Looking at this disaster, it's hard to believe anyone survived," Booker said. "We've brought food, water, first aid and blankets."

"How'd you know?" I asked.

"Yangchen watched it on the astral."

"Did Omnia do this?"

"No. Let's talk about the storm later."

One of the pilots wrapped me in a blanket. A couple got off the plane with Booker. The woman's eyes were a shade of blue that existed only in myth. She wore her curly blond hair pulled back in a ponytail. I thought she was a movie star, but I'd never seen her before. The man, however, was as familiar to me as was Spencer. I instantly recognized him as one of the nine entrusted and also as a man from Clastier's time who worked to suppress my papers; his name on the list was Ripley Gaines. I sank to the ground, dizzy.

Amber and Linh reached us.

"Are you okay?" Amber asked. "We didn't want to wait."

"Yeah, but . . ." Before I could tell her about Clastier's enemy being one of the nine, Travis Curry, the author of the Mayan books, emerged from the plane. I looked at Linh as she waved at him. Travis was an incarnation of Kyle's soul but I wasn't sure he had forward-memory. Even so, Travis was another of the nine. Why had Booker assembled one third of the nine entrusted at one of the most remote spots on earth?

"You know these men, don't you?" Booker asked.

"Why are they here?"

"We need to get the Jadeo back," Curry answered before Booker could.

"My dad and Lee are dead, Spencer's lost in time, Dustin's at Outin. That leaves Kevin Morrison and Helen Hartman. And if you aren't the traitor," I said to Ripley Gaines, "then we know for sure it's one of them."

"Why would I be the traitor?" Ripley asked.

Booker, Travis and the woman all turned to me.

"Because you spent a lifetime trying to destroy my work as Clastier," I said bitterly.

"Please, Nate," the woman began. "We've not been properly introduced. I'm Gale. This is Dr. Ripley Gaines, and I assure you, any wrong that may have occurred prior to this lifetime has been made up for this time around."

I was ready to blast her on the lessons of karma, ask if she knew how much harm her boyfriend had done to me during Clastier's time, ask if she'd read the papers or understood that they might have been released a century or more ago if it hadn't been for Ripley, but she stared at me with those eyes. Her eyes told me that she knew all those things and more. They were the eyes of an unmade mystic, teaching at a glance, asking for patience and friendship.

"I'm Nathan Ryder."

Gale smiled. She knew that, too. Everyone knew who I was. They either wanted me dead or protected. I'd learned to see people that way, and I could quickly deduce friend from foe. "There is much to discuss," she said. I somehow knew Gale was good.

Linh walked over to Travis Curry and they shared a long embrace. I would later learn that he didn't have forward-memory but had met enough mystics and heard enough messages from Kyle that his awareness brought him close to it.

"I'd invite you up to the house," I said to Gale, motioning to a swath of natural and manmade debris, "but it's a bit of a mess." I looked back at Booker. "I want to know where this storm came from."

"Let's have that discussion back on the mainland. We brought the extra plane to get you all out of here."

"Where are we going?" Amber asked, wearily. "Nowhere is safe."

"There are places," Booker said.

"You brought us here," Linh said, evenly. "That very plane dropped us on this rock in the middle of nowhere hours before an epic storm. I'm not going anywhere until you answer Nate's question."

"Nate, you know I've always been straight with you," Booker said.

"I believe that's the case," I said.

"I'm avoiding this conversation because you won't like the answer. I know how you are, and you're going to jump to conclusions and condemn our decisions before you think it through, before you remember that everything we do is to protect you."

I was embarrassed to hear his assessment in front of these "strangers," especially Gale; for some reason, I wanted her to have a high opinion of me.

"I'll hear you out Booker, I owe you that."

"For some time it has been critical that the surviving members of the nine entrusted meet. As you stated earlier, it is not currently possible to gather everyone. Circumstances also created an urgent need for Ripley and Gale to hide and it seemed very likely that this would be the only time that Ripley could attend."

"We've been brought through a Time-seam," Gale added.

"Quite fortunately, just prior to our departure to join you here, which we believed was the safest location for this gathering, the Movement got word of a new satellite, and our tracking showed they were going to discover you last night. TVCs and Timefolds were considered but apparently they are perception-dependent, meaning they offer no concealment from orbit. The storm was the only option."

"Wait, you're saying the Movement had something to do with starting that typhoon?" I asked incredulously.

"Yangchen created the storm."

"We almost died!" I looked at Linh. Her steely gaze never left Booker.

"No one could reach you," Booker said.

"Dustin managed to find me, without needing to drown us."

"Nate, calm down. I'm just telling you what I know. None of the mystics could connect with you on the astral. There are no known portals anywhere close to here. Omnia would have annihilated you all with a satellite strike before midnight . . . no survivors."

"She couldn't have just used some heavy cloud cover?"

"I had the same concern. Yangchen told us the only way to hold the clouds in place long enough was a storm. She's an expert on utilizing elements."

"We almost died," I repeated.

"She didn't know it would be so severe."

"We almost died," I whispered this time.

"Nate, do you think for a second that Yangchen would ever try to harm you?"

"You know what, Booker, I don't know what to think half the time. Take Ripley here, he's one of the nine entrusted, we've fought side-by-side over countless lifetimes trying to protect the most sacred object on earth, and yet, he tried to kill me very recently. And we're not talking about one of my ordinary lives. He did everything he could to stop Clastier's work from getting out." I shook off my blanket and walked over to Booker. My voice was hoarse and strained. "One thing I've learned is that in any given life, we're all capable of the most amazing deeds and the most horrendous acts . . . because we're human."

"But it's only a human mask," Gale said.

"Sure. I know. But when that human mask is on, our true identity, our soul, is forgotten."

"The Movement is trying to change that," Gale said.

"*You're* trying to change that."

"I don't seem to be doing a very good job . . . and the Movement tried to kill us last night, so I don't have high hopes for them either." I looked around at the ravaged beach and shivered in the breeze.

Gale had somehow calmed me down without even trying. While we were talking, the pilots put up a large tent and opened canvas camping chairs. Ripley, Travis and Gale watched in awe as we created Lusans to aid in our recovery. One of the pilots brought fresh clothes, water and food. While devouring crackers and bean dip, Booker suggested we move into the tent.

Travis Curry told us things about the Jadeo that I'd never heard. I wasn't sure if Spencer even knew, but its history was much richer than I'd imagined. Like a child, I believed that the high points of the sacred object revolved around me and absently assumed that the rest of the time it sat hidden, unknown to all but eight of the nine entrusted who remained loyal and the betrayer, who sought to exploit it. There had been hundreds of close calls, losses and even a few complete disappearances over the long history of the Jadeo.

"Throughout the centuries, people have lived their lives as if the world was merely what it appeared to be," Curry began. "They believed themselves to be superior to all else in nature and that by building roads, bigger buildings, and inventing dazzling technologies, they were evolving."

"The accumulation of wealth is not the path to enlightenment," Booker added. "I'll say it before anyone else. More stuff does not equal evolution."

"Although it has been invaluable to keeping the Movement alive," Ripley added.

"And me," I said.

Booker winked at me.

"Agreed," Curry continued, "but for the most recent part of human history, we've thought that this material world was all there was. Yet, all through the ages, there have been happenings and activities occurring all around us, unseen by most and unimagined by the vast majority. Visits from other planets, other times and other dimensions are as common as flights from Chicago's O'Hare." He paused. "And the battle for the Jadeo has been part of that."

"I'm glad I'm not the first to have lost it," I said.

"On the contrary," Curry said. "Your friend Dunaway doesn't even know what he has. When the traitor succeeds in locating it, which is only a matter of time, Dunaway will be destroyed."

"That wouldn't hurt my feelings," I said, but then regretted. "Except the traitor would have the Jadeo and . . . I think Dunaway will one day prove to be a powerful ally to the Movement."

We went on to discuss how each of the nine possesses the power to locate the Jadeo but often the process could take years. However, three of us together could amplify that power and hopefully find Dunaway and the Jadeo before the betrayer did.

"There have been indications that the betrayer is in some way connected to Omnia. This is why the Jadeo can't be allowed to float out there any longer. If Omnia were to find the Jadeo and open it, all hope would be lost," Booker said calmly, while looking only at me.

"You'll forgive me," Amber began. "I don't even know exactly what the Jadeo is, and I'm not asking, but why would such a thing that could cause such irreparable damage have been created in the first place?"

"Because of the incomprehensible good it can do," Curry answered. "When it was forged, those involved understood that something so powerful could, in the wrong hands, be misused. That is why the nine entrusted were chosen and charged with its protection."

"It's like the Clastier papers," Gale said. "The world was not yet ready to receive them in Clastier's time, so they have been hidden and guarded until now."

I looked at Gale and then at Ripley. The idea that he fought me so hard during my life as Clastier in order to make sure the papers were not released before the world was ready, well, it seemed an awfully convenient explanation. "Too easy," I said.

"The truth is usually simple," Wandus said in my head. "How does a hummingbird fly so fast? By flapping its wings very fast."

"We're not saying the Clastier papers are anything close to the importance of the Jadeo, just that there is a time for everything," Ripley said.

"Ripley, as you know, is an archaeologist," Booker said. "He knows about timing. He has made a discovery that changes ten thousand years of history. Not surprisingly, there are many powerful groups who want to suppress his finding."

Amber seemed satisfied.

"Is that why you're hiding in time?" I asked Gale.

"We know almost as much about running, hiding and protecting things as you do, Nate." Gale smiled.

Soon the tent was cleared except for Travis, Ripley and me. It took hours of joint meditation, but we found the Jadeo and Dunaway. He was on a large yacht off the east coast of Mexico. Booker would send a team immediately.

"How soon can you get me there?" I asked. "No offense to your people, but Dunaway is one of the seven, and I'm best equipped to handle him."

"No offense, Nate, but your track record with Dunaway indicates you could use some help. My team will be there in less than eight hours. It'll take twenty-four to get you there . . . unless . . ."

"What?"

"We stop and see Wandus first."

Linh, Amber, Booker and I were on one plane, while Travis, Ripley and Gale took another. Assuming we got the Jadeo back, I might not see them again; if we failed, however, a second gathering would have to be risked.

Linh, still pained by what had happened, opted to sleep through the flight instead of talking. Booker, distracted by his laptop, ignored us.

Amber and I had a long conversation over the astral, mostly speculating about what Ripley might have found that could have so changed history, but we also recounted the saga that had brought us to this point. Then Amber's mood shifted and she asked a question I hoped would never come up.

"Last night, just before Linh went over the falls, I felt you about to let go of me. What changed your mind?" Amber asked.

"Kyle had come to me before the storm and told me that things aren't always what they appear. If I let you go, you'd die for sure, but Linh could Skyclimb and had a chance."

"But you chose Linh?"

"I saved you both."

"But you chose Linh."

"I kicked Linh over the falls. She isn't even speaking to me."

"You did that thinking it was the only chance to save us both, but before that, you chose Linh; when you thought only one of us could live, you chose Linh. You were going to let me die."

"How can anyone make that choice? There was only a second or two . . ."

"Yet, you decided."

"Death is only a door."

"Nate, don't get caught up in denials and what ifs. Take the good out of that storm. You found clarity in something that has hung over the three of us for years. Who does Nate want? You couldn't answer, until you *had* to. And you chose Linh."

"Amber, it's not that simple."

"Yangchen taught me that the most complicated things are usually the simplest."

"Spencer taught me just the opposite."

"You need to tell Linh what really happened," she said, suddenly crying.

"Are you okay?"

"Wrong question, Nate! I'm anything but okay . . . I'm destroyed. I wanted you to want me and only me."

"I do –"

"Don't say anything, Nate. Life isn't fair and this isn't our time."

"Amber . . ."

"We'll be together again. I know that."

"Amber, I love you."

"I know that, too."

ooooo

Booker chose that moment to begin the most comprehensive update on the Movement I'd ever received. Amber retreated into herself. Booker had to call me back to the present several times.

"Nate, this is important. It is likely to be a long time before we see each other again."

"Sorry. Do you think I could just read you and get the information that way?"

"No. Part of my problem with Omnia is the way our privacy has been disappearing. Having someone inside my head seems to be the biggest invasion of my privacy I can imagine. Plus, it kind of creeps me out. Sorry, we're going to have to do this the old-fashioned way."

The information fascinated and scared me at the same time, but also gave me hope. The Movement had infiltrated *every* government agency, and more importantly, we had operatives inside all major corporations. IM members or sympathizers were part of most militaries and law enforcement agencies. At the same time, IM centers had all been discovered and destroyed. Meetings were extremely rare and more members were in prison or Carst than free. "We're so close, yet so far," Booker said. "We need to get the Air-Projection up and we need to find out who is running Omnia. The success of those two things could turn this all back in our favor."

"If we find out who's in charge, what are we going to do?" I asked, worried about the Movement using violence.

"Let's hope we find him before Dunaway does."

"My question still stands; what if we do?"

"That'll be your decision, Nate. You should start thinking about what you would do with a person who has caused so much suffering."

ooooo

Linh could not be talked into going to see Wandus. She returned to the States with Booker.

"I'll make sure she gets back to the lake house," he said. Linh didn't even hug me goodbye, saying only that we'd talk when I returned.

Amber and I waded through the surf and stood on the beach watching the seaplane take off. I lingered until it was a dot in the distant sky.

"Come on," Amber said impatiently. "It's not safe for us to be standing around." We climbed the rocky cliff and halfway up I spotted the portal Booker had assured us would be there.

Once inside, the light sound of a soft spring rain and the strong aroma of pine and carnations overwhelmed us. We floated in what could only be described as orange pixie dust. "This is my favorite portal ever," Amber laughed.

When first emerging from the portal, it felt as if we were stepping into another portal, or a kind of fairy world. Among the normal green trees and ferns were hundreds of shimmering orange ones. Then, all at once, the trees evaporated into the sky, turning it from blue to orange.

"They're butterflies," Amber squealed. "Like your tattoo!"

It took a minute for the truth of her words to sink in as the swirling and fluttering grew, until millions of monarch butterflies left the trees and danced above us. Their collective flapping wings reminded me of the rain sound from the portal but louder.

Wandus laughed as he floated down from the treetops. "They tickle, you know?"

"Wandus, where are we?"

"I do this each day. When it gets warm enough they take off. You try this tomorrow and you'll see, they tickle . . . from the inside out." He settled a foot off the ground between Amber and me.

"Where are we?" I repeated.

"I think you are here. Are you not?" He smiled at Amber.

"Where is here?"

"Who knows? One thing I do know is that here is not there, unless it is."

"Is this place real?" I tried again.

"No place is real by the definition implied in your question."

I was getting frustrated. Amber tried. "How do the butterflies get here?"

Instead of answering as I expected, "By flapping their wings," he said, "a billion butterflies come here every year from all over North America. They come to this one forest in the middle of Central Mexico for love."

"Incredible," Amber said.

"Yes, it is. Scientists don't know how they do it but

scientists also say I can't levitate. Scientists don't know as much as they think. Given all there is to know, they know nothing at all."

"I don't either," I said.

"You know the most important thing to know . . . your soul is part of everything; it is the butterfly, and your body is the caterpillar. Once this is understood, then all the power of the soul can be touched."

"Why is it so easy to forget?" I asked.

"The human world is afraid. I forget, too. This is why I stay away from the human world, so I don't forget."

"Not everyone can do that," Amber said.

"I hope they have better memories than mine." Wandus smiled, but his yellow teeth quickly vanished and his leathery face turned sad. "Omnia is keeping the world distracted. Time is running out for the Movement."

"It can all change in an instant," I said.

"An instant can last ten thousand years."

"Why did you send for us?" Amber asked.

"I am old; I worry. There has been too much energy used on chase and strategy. These have their place, perhaps, but this is not a war to be won on human terms . . . this is a spiritual quest for every soul residing on this planet. It must be seen that way or you will not succeed."

"But, Wandus, I need to get the Jadeo back. Clastier is being held by Dunaway. Spencer is lost in time, there are still two names unaccounted for on the list of the nine entrusted, and Omnia is sending thousands of people to prison every day. I have to deal with all those things."

"You will think apple and I will think pear," Wandus' eyes left mine and gazed at the ground littered with thousands of butterfly bodies like fallen autumn leaves.

"Are they dead?" Amber asked.

"Many freeze in the cold night." He swept his arm in a long slow arch; all the "dead" butterflies came to life and took to the skies. "It is always a spiritual solution."

"I don't know how."

"Yes, you do."

"How can I do all these things?"

"Look at this. What do you see?"

"An old rotting log."

"That is what your eyes see; look with your soul."

I stared. I kept expecting it to change to a beautiful healthy tree. Nothing. I turned back to Wandus.

"Your soul is not your brain, not your thoughts, it is nothing connected to the physical energy you are so accustomed to navigating with." He walked away.

"Where are you going?"

"Away."

"Why?"

"You're not trying."

"I am." I looked at Amber for help.

"This is not your first day of school, Nate. This is the final week," Wandus said. "Your soul is the cosmos – the stars, the oceans, a comet, those butterflies. You have been there, over and over, yet you keep returning to your personality. If you want the wisdom of your soul, let go of *yourself*."

I stared at the log, thinking about how I felt in all the different portals, about those moments of entering different lifetimes, of how each death always felt exactly the same in the final instant. Then I was meditating. My eyes opened. Instead of the log, I saw a glittering puddle of tiny stars quickly transform into butterflies of every color. They flew in a confetti explosion all around me, lifting my body with their soaring energy. Wandus and Amber were gone but as the stars and butterflies filled the forest, I could feel Amber as if she were standing there, as if I were inside her. All the mystical and spiritual happenings of the past few years could not have prepared me for the euphoric sensation of communicating with Amber in that way.

The soul-sensation lasted forever but ended suddenly. Amber and Wandus had not moved. "You see," Wandus said, smiling.

"Yes," I said, looking from him to Amber. "I had no idea. It's beyond imagining."

"This is what must be seen by everyone. This changes everything, does it not?"

"Everything," I repeated, still in awe of the experience. I could not take my eyes off Amber; she was so much more radiant and magnetic. There were butterflies and stardust filling the air and for a moment I wasn't sure if I was back with my soul or just Nate.

"Why did it take this long for me to see this?" I asked.

"Understanding must be accumulated before one is ready."

"Do you live this close to your soul?"

"It comes and goes. But as I age, it comes more."

"Can I see it?" Amber asked.

"Oh, Amber, you were there," I said softly.

"But all I saw was the log."

"Amber," said Wandus, "you will soon know this understanding, too. Yours will come in a different way." They stared at each other a long time. "You know this."

She nodded and brushed away a tear, stoic and sad.

"Are you okay?" I asked.

She turned away. "I'm fine."

I looked to Wandus for clarification.

"All the answers eventually come. Do not worry now." The cloud of butterflies thickened as they began returning to the trees.

"They're the symbol of the Movement," I said absently.

"They are the symbol of transformation . . . reincarnation, change. Everything changes. They remind us that no matter what hardships we face and what obstacles may appear to be, they become something beautiful, free . . . magnificent."

"It's hard to see that in the world today. Soldiers seem to be everywhere, freedoms are vanishing, and Omnia has stolen anything of value."

"Soldiers are pawns to the masters of war; it has always been this way. Soldiers will never end war. Their very existence makes it impossible; even drones must be flown by someone."

"How do we stop them?" I asked, desperate to remove any block so that everyone would be able to feel what I had just felt.

"They will stop only when fear is gone. Fear will end only when people sit and observe their fear in mindfulness and see it for what it really is . . . nothing. Love allows no room for fear."

"That's not an easy thing for any of us to do," Amber said.

"No, it is not," Wandus replied. "Fear and suffering are strangely comforting to people. We think it makes us feel, we think we understand it; the absence of fear is an unknown and the unknown is scarier to us than the fear."

"How can I teach people to get to where I just was? How do I tell them to let go of their fear?"

"It is a long road. People must let go of possessions; then much fear and suffering will be removed. When they see that all they need is internal and not external, they will find that place."

"That's the secret, isn't it?" Amber asked. "Everything is within us."

"Yes." Wandus smiled. "We've been mistakenly living in an external world."

"Is that why you are a breatharian and have no possessions?

"Thich Nhat Hanh said, 'My actions are my only true belongings,' and that is how we should all be," Wandus said.

"But I can't bring the whole world to this forest to speak with you. How can I show them?" I asked.

"You can bring them all here, you can take them to all the mystics, you can show them what you've seen, and tell them what you know. You can do all this with your words. Once people realize there is something more, they will want to know what it is and they will discover that in order to see what they've never seen, they will have to surrender what they've always seen."

ooooo

Amber and I strolled through the magical forest. There wasn't much time before I had to meet Booker's team on Dunaway's yacht. There was a portal nearby that could get me to Wizard Island at Crater Lake and from there, straight to the yacht. Wandus had explained that the butterfly forest benefited from a slight time wrinkle when the butterflies were present, so my time there didn't actually count against the clocks.

"I wanted to float with the butterflies in the morning, but now it looks like we won't be here. The time wrinkle here fluctuates with the winds and we have to go soon."

"The time stuff is confusing," Amber said.

"Just remember, tomorrow has already happened somewhere, and yesterday is still going on someplace else."

"Thanks, that clears it up," Amber said sarcastically, giving me a gentle push.

"Have you noticed those little stars are gone?"

"What happened to them?"

"I think they're around only when Wandus is."

"But they're on your tattoo."

"It was Baca's tattoo. His farm wasn't far from here. While you were off looking around, Wandus told me Baca used to come here often and actually showed it to Wandus."

"Is that how it got to be the symbol for the Movement?" she asked, pointing to my tattoo.

"Yeah, Wandus brought Booker and Spencer here." The wisdom Wandus possessed and shared was incredible, but I felt untethered without Spencer. I'd lost so many people, yet it was impossible to think of defeating Omnia without him.

"You miss Spencer, don't you?" Amber could read me better than almost anyone other than Spencer or Yangchen, unless it was about her. There she was blind. I wished she could have felt our souls uniting like I did; then she'd understand I loved her more than my own life. "I think I should go and spend some time with Linh," Amber said, taking my hand and then letting it go. "You don't need me getting in the way between you and Dunaway."

"What? No. Stay with me."

"Linh and I need to talk about things without you being around."

"I'm not comfortable with that."

"I'm sure you're not." She laughed, but only for a moment. "And I need to see Yangchen."

I studied her. "Stay."

"I can't."

"Why?"

"There are things we don't control, even when they are about our deepest desires."

"Amber, we can control everything. Don't you see? That's what the Movement is about, putting our souls in charge."

"For everything you've learned, Nate, you still don't get it. When our souls are in charge, selfishness will be gone. And most of the passion you feel will go with it."

"I don't think so."

We looked at each other a long, long time. Silently talking, remembering and loving, until little stars once again streamed in like confetti and Wandus appeared.

"Time to go, my friend."

57

The portal dumped me onto the deck of an elaborate multi-million-dollar yacht. Grender, the leader of Booker's team, helped me up.

"No one's on board, Nate."

"What? He was here!"

"Not anymore."

"When did you all arrive?"

Grender checked his watch. I remembered him from reviewing Booker's vast collection of employee profiles. They were all committed to memory. "Twelve minutes ago."

"Let me look."

"Suit yourself but we've searched everywhere."

"This guy is not normal. I mean if he's really gone, where the hell did he go? We're in the middle of the ocean. Fifteen minutes ago he was still onboard." I'd checked on the astral.

"All due respect, Nate. Time's a funny thing."

I chuckled, annoyed, and went below. Dunaway must be into something lucrative to afford a boat like this, I thought. A cup of tea sat on a table, still warm. He was right, no sign of Dunaway. I ran into Grender again in the back bedroom, which had been Dunaway's.

"Dunaway left you a note," he said.

"Why didn't you tell me that before?"

"Before what?"

"Up on deck."

"What are you talking about, Nate?"

I looked at him and back at the door. There was only one way into that room and I hadn't passed Grender in the hall. "Oh, you're kidding me!" I ran.

I was out of breath when I reached the upper deck. Dunaway was waiting in the portal I'd come through. "Couldn't leave without saying goodbye, Nate. Might not see you for a long time . . . but time's a funny thing." He laughed, morphed into Grender and back to himself, and laughed even harder. I dove for him but the portal closed and I crashed on the deck.

He'd taken my portal. How did Dunaway continue to best me? I picked myself up as the real Grender jogged up.

"What'd I miss?"

"Dunaway shapeshifted into you. He waited so he could take my portal and escape."

"Clever bastard. I'd like to have seen that. Shapeshifting, portals, all kind of sci-fi, isn't it?"

"Where's the note?"

Grender pulled it out of his shirt pocket. It was addressed to me and still sealed. I ripped it open and read it:

Dear Nate,

You amuse me . . . thinking you could find me and what? Capture me? Ha! You're not smart enough to see it, but I should be the least of your worries. And I say that even though I now know what your precious Jadeo really is. Now you're scared, aren't you? Good. Next time we meet, you'll be terrified.

Love, Dunaway

I crumpled the note and threw it on the deck. I reached Yangchen on the astral and found out the closest known portal was on Curaçao. Grender told me it would take twenty minutes to fly there on one of his seaplanes.

The island of Curaçao floated in the scents of oranges and exotic flowers. Colorful Dutch houses and fruit traders from Venezuela on one side gave way to cacti and crashing waves. There were two portals there, one at the old Fort Nassau located on the island's high ground, the other in a stone arch sculpted by long-attacking tides. Yangchen didn't know which one led to Crater Lake, only that one of them did.

"It's a great place," Grender said, as we walked the dock. A couple of his team were securing the seaplane in its slip. "A big, little island. One hundred seventy-one square miles, former Dutch colony. A favorite of cruise ships."

I was about to ask Grender if he could get me to Fort Nassau when I heard a familiar voice call my name. Tapscott, the young mystic, rode up the beach on a horse, handed me the reins to another, and smiled.

"Tapscott, what are you doing here?" I asked, puzzled.

"Waiting for you."

"How long have you been waiting?"

"I don't know, a couple of weeks. It's been fun, kind of hoped you'd be a few more days."

"Come on," he said, motioning to the empty saddle.

"Never been on one before," I said.

"Good thing he's gentle, probably won't mind you much. If he refuses your guiding, try Gogen."

I leaped up and steadied myself in the saddle. The horse didn't seem to notice. "Thanks, Grender, for all your help, I'm good."

"Booker told me to stay with you until you were heading back to the states."

"And I'm on my way."

He looked dubiously at the kid and me sitting on horses like a carnival photo op, scratched his chin, then looked back towards the marina.

"Look, Grender, you're welcome to come if you can round up a few horses."

"Hell, we'll be at the Santa Barbara Resort if you need us," he said. I was almost surprised Booker didn't have a house on the island.

ooooo

"Do you know where the portals are?" I asked Tapscott as we rode down the beach.

"Sure. But there's something else to do before you go."

"I hope it involves food." I hadn't eaten since the last

island.

"I've got you covered." Up the beach a little way, perched awkwardly on a low craggy cliff, was a corrugated metal shack. A faded sign advertised a carrot, an onion and some kind of green leaf. Turns out they served the tastiest grilled vegetable dishes in the southern Caribbean, and there was a tropical fruit cobbler that reminded me of my mom's desserts.

While we ate, Tapscott told me why he was there. "You have not been practicing Airgon."

"I've been too busy. Do you have any idea what my life's been like?"

"I do because I have experienced parts of it through Airgon," he said. "I'm only ten, but I don't know why you let someone as pretty as Amber leave you."

"What do you know about Amber?"

"A few minutes ago, I captured an air molecule from you. It was inhaled and exhaled during your time in the butterfly forest with her. It showed me everything around it. And since you breathed that same molecule several times, I saw a lot." He laughed. "But you want to know the best part? Amber inhaled the same molecule. So I saw the same scene from her perspective."

"Really? Tell me what she was thinking."

"It's not always about thoughts.

58

Tapscott explained that Airgon's best application centered around its way of showing and understanding the energy present in each moment. It took me a while to get my head around that but, when he talked about the time between Amber and me in the butterfly forest, it made sense.

"Amber has three great desires in this life. The first is to align her personality with her soul; second is to be with you; third is seeing the Movement succeed," the ten-year-old mystic said in a manner which belied his youth.

"I could have guessed that without Airgon."

"Yes, but you also would have guessed that it is those same three desires which motivate her. Instead it is her awareness that she will not obtain any of them that determines her actions and reactions."

"Why won't she obtain those desires?"

"They contradict her destiny."

"But we can change our destiny."

He raised an eyebrow. "Have you ever tried? It's crazy-wild hard."

"What is her destiny?"

"I don't know, Airgon only shows so much. But if you want to know, you could always just ask her."

"Does she know?"

"Oh, yes, she knows; it has weighed on her for some time."

"She won't tell me."

"You won't know unless you ask."

He made sense. I would ask her and if she didn't answer, Yangchen might tell me.

"You got all that from Airgon?"

"And more. For instance, your inability to decide whether you want most to be with Amber or Linh, your turmoil over wanting to lead the Movement and wanting to run and hide, needing to make Dustin proud of you while at the same time trying to show you don't care what he thinks, missing your mother and being angry with her . . . you're a huge jumble of conflict and contradiction."

"Aren't we all?"

"Some more than others."

ooooo

After eating, we continued our ride and were soon in a rural area. He showed me how to inhale deliberately and with a clear mind. Hundreds of thousands of simultaneous images appeared, overloading me until a kind of circuit breaker switched and my subconscious cranked into action. Tapscott said they were called Airgon trips. The images came charged with energy and surrounded by feelings. It was mind-blowing.

"You can do Airgon anywhere but the islands in the Caribbean are particularly good," Tapscott said. "The trade winds, proximity to other cultures and clean air help make it more productive. A lot of places can be stagnant and sometimes you'll wind up getting a whole bunch of results from the Industrial Revolution or Europe's Dark Ages, not fun stuff. California is usually difficult for some reason."

"What about Washington, DC?"

"Never tried it there."

ooooo

It would be fair to say that during the next hour I learned more from Airgon than I had in my entire life up to that day.

Instead of using Vising to absorb a book in seconds, Airgon allowed me to absorb billions of fragments from millions of lifetimes – most unrelated to my soul. Conversations, emotions, thoughts, knowledge, and information of every type filtered through me at an absolutely stunning speed.

Complex business deals from forty years earlier, lovers' intimate moments two weeks ago, a feud between neighbors, a child playing, farmers in their fields, soldiers dying . . . every kind of thing, across human history and from all over the world. The molecules traveled and circulated with each occurrence imprinting its energy pattern.

Another two hours of Airgon trips left me mentally exhausted. The process would eventually become invigorating, Tapscott said, but the first few times were tiring. In the billions of fragments I absorbed, dozens contained the Jadeo. I came across the betrayer and believed he would be recognizable when encountered in this lifetime. One thing that struck me was how many wars littered the timeline of humanity's existence on earth. Probably three-fourths of the fifteen billion fragments involved war, violent crime or some other heavy conflict. Seeing it that way seemed to prove that we were doing something wrong, even the so-called "good guys" must accept part of the responsibility for this abysmal record.

When we reached the portal on a deserted section of coast, Tapscott asked if I had any other questions.

"Now I understand how important Airgon is, and I'll practice more, but what is it going to show me?"

"Everything."

The trip had been easy and, after a lecture from the Old Man on Wizard Island, I took the portal-to-anywhere to the lake house, then stumbled into Amber in the foyer. She hugged me, long and warm, then stood back and said, "Linh's out back."

Linh sat on a bench near the lavender labyrinth as if expecting me. Her expression was stern.

"We need to talk about the island," I began.

"What is there to talk about? You kicked me over the falls to my death."

"You didn't die."

"I should have."

"No. Kyle came to me and told me that things weren't what they seemed. There was only a second to decide and I decided to let Amber go, but in that instant, I recalled Kyle's warning and I let you go instead. If I'd let Amber go she would have died, but by letting you go, you both lived."

"How do you know that's what Kyle's message meant?"

"I don't, but that's how I took it."

"You got lucky." She glared at me. "And who do you want now?"

"Linh, I've been confused about so much."

"Damn it, Nate! You're nineteen years old, one of the entrusted nine, one of two surviving members of your generation's seven, dozens of people have died for you . . . died! You don't get to be confused."

"I'm trying."

"Not hard enough. Not even close."

"You didn't let me finish."

"Finish, then."

"I'd rather talk about this when you aren't so upset."

"If we had that luxury that might be a good idea. Unfortunately, there are more than a few powers conspiring against us." Her eyes suddenly overflowed with tears.

"I know, I'm sorry." I reached for her.

"Sorry is just a word!" She pushed me away.

"Linh, it's you . . . I may not deserve you, you may not want me any more but through the fires, prison and all the deaths, through battles, killings, floods and all the confusion, it's always been you . . . even when I didn't know it."

Her face softened a bit, then she turned away and started walking toward the lake.

"Where are you going?"

"I need to meditate; there's too much stuff in my head right now."

I watched her walk away, not knowing if I should follow. She vanished into the mist coming off the lake. A few seconds later, she screamed my name. I Skyclimbed.

Linh knelt over Spencer's still body. I dropped to my knees and laid my hand on his chest. Linh already had a Lusan moving. His pale gaunt face made him appear twenty years older than when I had last seen him, but he was breathing. Linh made a fifth Lusan. I tried desperately to reach him on the astral. And, suddenly, with his body still not responding, Spencer answered from the astral.

"I'm trying," he said. "My body is failing." The astral allowed him to speak, free from physical burdens.

"What can I do to help?"

"Lusans and healing are about all you can try."

"Are you going to make it?"

"The odds are good."

"What happened?"

"Too much."

"How did you escape the men in the square? How did you

get back?"

"Yangchen, she . . . it was quite something. Omnia agents actually had their hands on me. It was over, so I thought, and then, the sky split open just over my head and I was pulled up through a dimensional split."

"Then the Movement can pierce dimensions, too?"

"It seems so."

"We're back in it!"

"I'm not sure it's a cause for celebration."

"Why not?"

"It's akin to MAD during the Cold War."

"Mutually Assured Destruction."

"Yes. Neither the Soviets nor the Americans could escalate the war because to do so would mean both sides would be destroyed."

"I know the history, but you think this is the same thing?"

"Worse. They only had the ability to blow up earth a few times over. Omnia and the Movement could destroy all of existence."

"You mean our universe?"

"The multiverse, everything."

"How is that possible?"

"We don't know what is possible. But it's clear that dimension-blending can make whatever does occur so unrecognizable that we all might as well be amoebas floating in a constantly changing ocean."

"Then what do we do?"

"Same as always: protect the Jadeo and stop Omnia."

He opened his eyes and looked at Linh. "Hello, Linh," he said, weakly. His attempt at a smile quickly turned to a grimace.

"I've missed you." She said, blinking tears, unwilling to take her hands from the Lusans to wipe her cheeks.

"The thing is, Linh, I've loved him too," he said, reading her. "It's not always worth it during the lifetime, but in the long run, you'll be glad you did."

"It's not the time for advice on love," I said.

"There's always time for love." Spencer coughed. "I

wanted her to know in case I don't make it."

"You'll make it. Let's try to get you to the house?" I used Gogen to hold him on my back and Skyclimbed as gently as possible. Linh followed closely. Spencer wanted to be put on the big leather couch in the grand living room.

"If the Omnia agents didn't injure you before Yangchen pulled you out, what happened to leave you in such bad shape?" I asked.

"She pulled me out some time ago, but we were separated somewhere in the split." He paused and closed his eyes. "I've been battling my way back for months - stuck in some awful places." He didn't talk again for several minutes, and I thought he might be asleep.

"As I said, in case I don't make it, there are things we must discuss now."

"You should rest, it'll wait."

"It will not. I know who is running Omnia."

"Devin Moore controls Omnia," Spencer said.

I knew his name only because most people did; he had more money than Booker.

"Are you sure?"

"Yes, absolutely. I came across a lifetime that confirmed it. Devin Moore is the most powerful man on earth."

"If you were to take all the powerful people alive and put their power together, it still wouldn't equal his," Yangchen said gravely, as she walked in. "We've suspected him for a while." She went to Spencer. "I'm sorry I lost you."

"No, on the contrary, Yangchen, you found me, you saved me."

"How are you?"

He didn't answer; they just stared at one another.

"How do we stop the most powerful man on earth?" Linh asked.

"Because the key words are 'man on earth,' there are awakened souls who possess enough soul powers to topple Devin Moore," Spencer said.

"The mystics?" Linh asked.

"A few of them. The Dark Mystic, Nate . . ."

"You, Yangchen," Linh said.

Spencer nodded. "You have to remember that Omnia has access to soul powers as well, and not just the basics. They travel through Outviews, pierce dimensions, and other things yet to surprise us, I am sure."

"Devin Moore was among a handful of people we believed might be running Omnia. Now that Spencer has confirmed this, I will tell you what we know," Yangchen said. "Moore was born so rich that even if he was a drug addict with a gambling problem, his great grandchildren would never have to work a day in their lives. However, Moore has neither of these afflictions. His only known vice is working. His inheritance, shared between two siblings, was greater than the gross domestic product of many countries." Yangchen stopped as if absorbing for the first time the power that Devin Moore wielded. "Booker, usually one of the top five billionaires on the planet, always trails Moore, who has held the number one spot for two decades. Even with Moore's massive holdings, if the assets he controls as head of Omnia were calculated, Devin Moore would hold the distinction of being the world's first trillionaire."

"If he already has everything, why does he want more?" Linh asked.

"Greed," I said.

"Too easy," Spencer said. "It's something else, but I don't know what it is . . . yet."

"Moore, like Booker, shunned publicity so we don't know much about him personally," Yangchen continued. "He has staff to deal with everything. There's an entire company employed to kill stories about him or topics not to his liking, as well as additional ones to kill other things not to his liking."

"Since he controls Omnia and Omnia controls banks, governments and the media, I wouldn't think much happens in the world that isn't to his liking," I said.

"It's a big world and controlling seven billion people is not entirely possible," Yangchen said. "Plenty happens that he doesn't like. The Movement is the biggest example of this but not the only one. Now that we know for sure it's Moore, we'll see what else we can find out. We already know that there don't seem to be many ex-employees around. Working for Devin Moore appears to be a lifetime appointment where loyalty is prized above everything."

Later, while walking alone above the lake, I found a poem

from Linh in my pocket.

LOVE IS FALLING
Love is falling, swift, like rain
love is cold, disappears, in shadow
touched, quickly and gone
on my tongue I swallow
oh love, I swallow and cry
and I, a red and bruised petal upon petal,
curls in and breaks to pieces falling
into no one's hand, into no one's hand.
Tears so hot against my cheek,
throat swells chokes and disparages
concern, that which I have neglected
and warned unto, dissolute passage
where dream and diamond talk clear.
Crushed, forever forgotten
to a world where black and mirth
chant, syncopated, disturbed.
Cold water embraced
my boneless body in moments silent –
the sun that warmed my opening, my
awakening cut off cruel, and sudden and sure –
love turned inside through to release
loud and long,
where frog and cricket and
nighttime sounds silence.
My lost and scattered dream relinquished
violently into dark and light, this abyss.
Like a bat I pushed from rock and weight
to surface, alive. Alive! To what?
My mouth tore ragged sky into thousands,
breath that burned, such pain I fell backward,
floated as shards and debris splintering ugly openings . . .
my eyes stung, lungs tightened,
this landscape where thought and emotion
Escher strange and beatific, became
just that, an epoch, an eternity unknown lifetimes

discarded like clothes, dirty, ragged, wet, and old.
I let them go and escaped,
like a bird, whose wings silently
soared on rhythms of wind –
listen, I am wind, and trees
safe and true
it is here, I step forward
into clean skies.
I am willing to be that light,
that abandonment, oh this is new,
this is life, distilled as radical
buoyant butterflies,
reckless in thought
and object of change.
Fresh and quaint, my hardship
unravels with you, strangely close.
I am the depth to where we went,
and it is there, I have risen.

I read the poem three times. There were aspects of Linh that even she didn't understand and certainly many that eluded me. One day, the discovery of those parts through some tender demand would fill my hours. With tear-blurred eyes, I headed off to find her.

Along the way, I stopped to check on Spencer. He held me in urgent conversation. We talked about Moore and I recounted the meeting with the scholar Travis Curry and the archaeologist Ripley Gaines, and about my last encounter with Dunaway. He listened without comment.

"What if we don't get the Jadeo back?" I asked.

"It's troubling not to possess something that one wants so desperately." He reached for a cup of tea, letting it warm his hands. "In the case of the Jadeo, it is important to see the good . . . In Dunaway's hands it appears to be as far away from Devin Moore as it could be."

"Yes, it *appears* that way, but for all we know Dunaway is Devin Moore."

"That thought brings back my headache . . . yes, that is

possible, as we've seen with Storch and Dustin –"

"And me and Marie Jones and Fred Means . . . Geez, I could even be Devin Moore."

"Yes, Yangchen told me about Means and Jones. Hardly surprising, given the stakes of this war, that souls are showing up all over the board. Yet, for you or Dunaway to share a soul with Devin Moore would be highly unlikely. That's an old karma, and much larger than one soul."

"So you think I've encountered Moore in other lives?"

"Undoubtedly." A concerned look came over him. "And it's safe to assume that Devin Moore knows which past lives you have in common."

"You think he's waiting for me to go back to them?"

"Count on it." He drank his remaining tea. "Now, Linh will be joining us in a moment, and I'd like to explore the time of your death at the Mayan Lighthouse, when you were known as Bola, and Linh was called Nares."

As if on cue, Linh walked in. I never knew if he asked her to come or if he knew she was on her way. In either case, before she even sat down, he asked. "Tell me about Nares."

Linh looked at me, wondering what the name meant to me. "What do you want to know?"

"It's not what I want; I *need* to know where and when he went after he left the Mayan Lighthouse."

"Do you think Nares caused something to go wrong in the present?" she asked.

He studied her, surprised by her defensive response. Then he looked at me. I could tell Spencer attributed her attitude to the tension between her and me. "Nate, perhaps you should tell us about what happened after Nares left your incarnation as Bola," he said.

"There isn't much to tell," I watched Linh, realizing she probably didn't know. "I was desperately in love with Nares and could not imagine a life without him, so I tried to follow him into the portal."

Linh's face flooded with sadness.

"But when I attempted to jump into the portal, it had already closed and I plummeted to my death."

Linh's expression contorted to a pained look, as if she were watching a puppy get beaten. "Oh, no," she whispered, before dropping her face into her hands. Spencer and I remained silent. Finally, Linh looked up at me. "I'm so sorry."

The sincerity and emotion in her voice caused a lump in my throat and although centuries had passed, the apology seemed to come from Nares and the relief it brought shocked me. Tears flowed from my eyes. Linh left her seat and kneeled in front of me, her head resting in my lap. "I'm so sorry," she repeated through sobs.

At the same time a calmer Linh reached me on the astral. "I didn't know you knew of Bola and Nares. It means you understand, don't you?"

"Yes," I answered on the astral. "I loved you so much, wanted only to be with you . . . I waited and hoped but it was not to be."

"And you lost me to the same cause we are struggling for today."

"It is all the same, isn't it?" Spencer said out loud. "The names and faces change, we change roles, but we play out the same stories again and again."

Linh, as Nares, had travelled into many lifetimes working to defeat Omnia. He worked, when necessary, using mostly violent methods; however, there were several lives influenced by Linh's current life in which Nares refrained from using force. Linh told us of dramatic battles and intrigue used to circumvent Omnia's purposes. But Spencer didn't want the details of the losses and triumphs.

"Who sent you to those lives?" he finally interrupted her.

"I thought you wanted to know where I went."

"Yes, and you've told me enough. Now I need to know who you were working for."

"It is not important," she said, rising from her chair.

Spencer looked as if he'd been slapped. Her abrupt response also caught me by surprise.

"Linh, it's a fair question," I said.

"Yes, I suppose it is . . . but it will go unanswered."

"Why? What are you hiding?" I asked. "We're all on the

same side; we don't need secrets." As soon as the words left my lips, I knew they'd been the wrong choice.

"Secrets?" She blasted. "You are the 'prince of secrets' and only because the title, 'king of secrets,' is already taken by Spencer. Neither one of you is in a position to condemn me for keeping secrets."

Spencer shot me a disappointed look, no doubt thinking he would have handled it more diplomatically. "Linh, please think about this," he said. "You don't need to answer now, but it's important for me to know who sent Nares into the future."

It had never occurred to me to wonder who sent her, but if it had, I would have assumed Spencer or Yangchen were calling the shots. Spencer would have known if it were Yangchen so that left only one other possibility, me. But if I sent Nares/Linh anywhere, it hadn't happened yet. The more I thought about it, the more I saw why Spencer needed to know, why the answer could change so much. I also became more astonished that Linh would not tell us. Who did she trust more than Spencer and me? What possible harm could come from telling us?

61

The following morning Spencer called another meeting. This time Yangchen and Amber were there in addition to Linh and me. Spencer looked worse than he had the prior night and I guessed he hadn't slept much. There was a flash of concern on Yangchen's face when she first saw him, but she masked it quickly. I stood in the corner, near two platters of fruit. I'm sure Linh expected the same topic as I did – who sent her to the future – but instead, Spencer launched into the list of the nine entrusted.

"We've got two names left, Kevin Morrison and Helen Hartman. How come we can't find them?"

"When I first found the list there were only three names we knew for certain. We've found four, we'll get the other two," I said. "Where did my dad get the names, anyway?"

"From a future incarnation of Dustin," Spencer said.

"And where did Dustin get them?" Linh asked before I could.

"He's fuzzy about it. He says he hasn't been able to find that future life, but speculates that Nate told him from this life."

"Sounds like one of Dustin's theories," I said. "Dad taught us young that most things were theories and theories were just someone's best guess."

"Maybe we should go see him," Yangchen said.

"Not sure I'm up to another family reunion . . . the last one didn't go so well."

"Is Outin still safe?" Spencer asked Yangchen.

"For now," she answered.

"We're running out of time to get those names," Spencer said. "We have to get the Jadeo."

"Last night you said it might be just as safe with Dunaway."

"There's been chatter," Yangchen said.

"What's that mean?" Amber asked.

"It means Omnia is looking for it, too," Spencer said.

"All right, I'll go back to Outin," I said. "Nothing is more important than the Jadeo, but remember, Dunaway also has Clastier and he's one of the seven. If we find him, we need a way to hold him."

"He's shown his powers are strong," Yangchen said.

"Getting the Jadeo and Clastier should be sufficient," Spencer added. "If we're lucky enough to secure the Jadeo, we can no longer indulge in the idea of converting Dunaway."

"I disagree," I said.

"Shouldn't we try to stop him?" Amber asked. "He's destroying the Movement's core message of non-violence. There's no telling how many members he's cost us."

"That damage is done. We're beyond image and PR now. Let him do what he will and Omnia will continue to waste resources on Dunaway and Inner Force."

"No," I said. "I'm going to pursue him. I know I can convert him to our side."

"This isn't a contest," Yangchen said.

"Then you won't mind when I win," I said.

"Nate, Dunaway and you are too evenly matched," Yangchen said. "And, surely you've seen that his skills, while maybe not superior to yours, are more dangerous because of his ruthlessness."

"I'm not afraid of him."

"I didn't say you were but you'll need help. Because he is one of the seven, there are only three mystics who can aid you in this."

"You and Spencer, right? But you're not willing."

"That's correct. Even if we wanted to, our hands are quite

full just now."

"I'm assuming the third is the Dark Mystic."

"Yes."

"A long time ago you promised to help me find him."

"Perhaps it is time. We can discuss it this evening."

ooooo

While Yangchen and Linh went for a walk, Amber and I went to the kitchen in search of more food. I told her Linh refused to tell us who sent Nares.

"Linh told me about your lifetime together as Nares and Bola," Amber said.

"Really? Did she happen to say who she was working for?"

"She was working for the Movement, but didn't say who was in charge."

"Yangchen's probably trying to get it out of her right now."

"Maybe. But you should trust Linh. You know Nares and Bola wasn't your only time together."

"I know."

"Linh and I discussed what happened at the waterfall. I told her you were letting me go first."

"Amber, it's not that simple."

"We talked about the different lives in which we'd loved you," she said, ignoring my attempt to explain again. "We all have crisscrossing destinies. Linh and I have been together in many lives, too. We were married once, father and son, brothers, sisters, lovers. Our souls are imprinted on each other and destinies are a complicated thing."

"You know I love you."

"I do, but you made the right choice on the island."

"It wasn't like I chose one of you . . . are you warm?"

She shook her head.

"It's too hot in here," I started moving toward the door.

"Nate, they're coming!" Spencer yelled.

We all knew what to do. We'd been through raids, practiced and prepared, but we'd come to feel safe at the lake house. The golden rule was not to try and save anyone else. It had been drummed into us all repeatedly. It's safest to get yourself out. "We've got to find Linh!" I yelled, grabbing Amber's hand, pulling her towards the deck.

"You know the rules," Amber shouted back as she tried to lead me back to the hidden stairs.

"I've never been a fan of rules. I'm not abandoning Linh again."

Spencer appeared on the deck. Which power he used to get there was in question but his purpose was not. "Nate, please. Linh is with Yangchen."

"You know I have to go," I said.

"I know." He stepped aside.

"I'm going with Spencer," Amber said. "I'll see you in the forest."

There was only time for a glance, and it hurt.

The bright morning sun was extinguished as I hit the back lawn. I hoped it was Spencer's doing and not an Omnia tactic. Helicopters, too numerous to count, were hovering and landing everywhere. Lasers sliced the air so close, I felt the heat. No doubt their night vision could see me easily. I reached Linh on the astral. They'd been on the cliff overlooking Klamath Lake when they felt the warnings.

Yangchen had one of Booker's planes in a TVC and they were taking off.

"Nate, get out of there."

"I was coming for you."

"I don't want you to die for me, Nate. I want you to live for me."

"Ask Yangchen to give me a class five hurricane."

"She can't until we're clear. Nightfall and the TVC are already taxing her."

I was tucked in a Timefold, watching lasers rip apart the lavender labyrinth. Hundreds of troops were suddenly converging on the house. I knew what was coming next and had to break the Timefold to Skyclimb. They locked in on me again but I made it over the cliff. At the same time, the house blew up in a series of rapid explosions. Almost every Booker property had self-detonating defensive measures deployed. I ran along the surface of the lake. Gunships flew across the water, firing lasers. Troops scaled the cliff, shooting machine guns. Then Yangchen's storm hit.

It was the island all over again. The helicopters were swept into the winds and dumped into the lake like toys in a bathtub. Soldiers vanished into the abyss. My prior experiences in supernatural storms allowed me to fight through them but pain burned my chest. The cliff was sheer, the water deep, to stop would be suicide. After a few more minutes, the pain overtook my senses. I couldn't last much longer. A narrow ledge opened just in time and I collapsed onto it. Staying there took enormous energy and my chest was bleeding heavily.

"Yangchen," I said on the astral. "Stop the storm. I can't get through it."

She didn't answer. If anything, the hurricane intensified.

"Nate, where are you?" Spencer asked across the astral.

"Can't you see me? I'm on the cliff over Klamath Lake a mile or so from the house."

"Nate, where are you?" Spencer asked again.

"Spencer do you hear me?"

"Nate," Linh said.

"I'm here on the lake," I answered, scratching the dirt and rocks trying to hold on.

"Any luck?" Linh asked Spencer.

"No, he's not coming through."

"I'm here," I screamed out loud and on the astral. Soaked clothes weighed a thousand pounds in my agony.

"Nate, this isn't good," Kyle said.

"Kyle, can you hear me?" Stinging rain cut my face.

"You should not have done this. You are too scattered. A leader cannot lack focus."

"Kyle!" Pain stole my breath.

"Meditate."

"Screw meditating!" Finally the winds pushed too hard. Clawing, gasping, I slipped from the ledge and tumbled into the churning waters.

63

All I saw were trees and I decided in that moment there could be nothing better than to wake in a warm forest shaded by a million trees.

"He's awake," a familiar voice shouted. Gibi smiled at me. "Close one, Nate."

"But I can't move."

"You're okay, it's early yet in the healing. You had three bullets lodged in your chest, one of those 'millimeters away from the heart things.'"

"I remember the water."

"Not sure how long you were in the lake . . . a while. Spencer bent time and Yangchen split a dimension." She sighed. Gibi, too, looked older and gone were her giggles and sparkle.

Spencer had performed psychic surgery and removed the three conventional bullets. Constant healings for several days helped my body recover from the extensive loss of blood.

Amber and Linh were there now. They both smiled, on their best behavior for the injured warrior. They told me we'd been there at least a week but maybe a month. Between Spencer's time-bend and Yangchen's dimension-split, things got very confused. No one needed to tell me where we were. I knew when I left the lake house that there was only one stop left, "the final command."

Gibi's presence confirmed it; although far from the redwoods, she remained exclusively in the forests. The harshness of the human world weakened her. Losing the lake house, and sixteen other properties at the same time, meant no safe place remained and the Movement had retreated into the forests. In the days to come, I healed nicely but the desperation of our situation became frighteningly clear.

Omnia's ability to find us increased hourly. There, even in the middle of the Gila, one of the largest national forests, I still didn't feel safe. The flow of information from the Movement became more fragmented and we relied more and more on interdimensional dispatches.

Spencer warned, "This is a dangerous road we're on."

"There is little choice," Yangchen said.

Whenever there was a drone flyover, we slipped into the Verde Portal, which led to at least seventeen forested areas around the world. In the month since I regained consciousness, we'd evacuated ten times. Twice we became lost in the portal; the last time it took us three days to find our way out.

"All these forests look the same," I said.

"Only because you aren't really looking at them. Each forest has its own magic and is as unique as books in a library," Gibi said.

On a brisk morning, as the first sunlight filtered through the trees, a drone-warning sounded. We rushed into the Verde Portal and emerged in an open conifer forest. After encountering a nomadic tribe of Native Americans, it was clear we'd traveled through time as well as space.

They were a beautiful people who knew of soul powers. We mingled and taught each other for days. Communicating over the astral removed all language barriers. The break from the stress of our world did us good.

After what might have been four days, we could no longer ignore the battles of our own time. Yangchen went back first. As the rest of us prepared to return, a tear opened in the sky.

"Run," I yelled, without waiting to see who came through the dimensional seam. We dove behind boulders. The laser bullets sang past.

"What the hell do we do now?" I asked, while scanning for

other portals. They usually weren't difficult to find in forests, but none appeared nearby.

Florescent red and yellow lasers hit the rocks above, raining down rubble which sliced my arm and banged up Amber's leg. More laser bullets impacted nearby. We were hemmed in and Omnia's agents could close at will. Spencer tossed an Air-swirl, causing the lasers to bounce away in haphazard angles.

I worked a Lusan up Amber's leg, concentrating on her knee. Spencer sent two more air-swirls out.

"Maybe we should do a storm," I said.

"Nate, look!" Amber screamed.

On our side of the boulders, between two large beech trees, a seam opened. I grabbed Amber and Skyclimbed. Spencer dropped into a Timefold. Linh tumbled behind an old oak, then joined us in the canopy. Eight black-clad agents came through. Four jetted skyward. At first they appeared to be Skyclimbing, but Linh spotted slim propulsion-packs on their backs. It was a technology Omnia had no doubt stolen from another time. Flying agents now neutralized one of our great advantages. We sprinted across the treetops, dodging laser fire, when suddenly three of our pursuers plunged screaming to the ground. I had no idea what happened to them until I saw an arrow hit one in the heart. Our native friends were hiding in the upper branches.

"Are they invisible?" Amber asked in awe. "Or just masters of camouflage?"

There wasn't time to figure it out. The agents on the other side of the boulders had joined the four still on the ground. We glided across the trees until they ended, a wide river on one side and open meadows on the other. Agents broke out of the trees just after we landed in a wide marshy field. I produced a thick fog behind us which slowed them but laser bullets still sliced out of the mist. The war cries of our friends and the screams of the Omnia agents told us we'd been rescued again, and then Spencer appeared.

"We should get back to the Gila before more agents show up," Spencer said.

"Do you think it's any safer there?" Amber asked.

"It has been so far."

This time the seam opened from the ground. Omnia agents poured out like ants. We ran back toward the forest, hoping our friends would offer another round of protection. Suddenly I slammed into a yellow cab! The driver didn't seem to notice as I rolled over his hood, dodged an old blue sedan and plowed my way through pedestrians on a crowded sidewalk. Somehow we'd slipped into a dimension and were running through the concrete canyons of Manhattan.

"Omnia has made a mess of the dimensions," Spencer yelled. "Nate, we're a year in the past."

We ran into a hotel lobby. I knew no one could see us because a mystic had once told me that people from other dimensions can occupy the same space without knowing it. Omnia unleashed a barrage of lasers as we dashed into a restaurant. I knocked over a stack of serving trays, tripped a waiter, and sailed into a line cook bringing us both to the floor. Yet, to all but us, these happenings were odd accidents. We were there but the inhabitants of New York were oblivious. Amber, Linh and Spencer had similar mishaps and I'm certain a man in the dining room had a heart attack caused by a stray Omnia laser bullet passing through his chest.

"We need to get to Central Park," Spencer told me over the astral.

I didn't know if that was one block away or a hundred. We stumbled out to a back alley and Skyclimbed up the sides of the buildings. I started a torrential rain below us as we leapt from skyscraper to skyscraper. I was able to hold the rain to a mile radius and once we got high enough, I could see the park.

"Maybe twenty blocks," I said to Amber, who clung to my back.

"What are we going to do when we get there?" Linh asked.

"There's a portal," Spencer shouted, as he Skyclimbed two hundred feet down to a lower building top. "At Belvedere Castle."

Occasional lasers cut through the storm and from our vantage point, I could see they were spread out, not knowing which way we were heading. There were hundreds of them. I widened the storm. Holding onto Amber with Gogen, Skyclimbing high above the city, and maintaining a large rainstorm normally wouldn't have strained so much, but I'd taken a laser in my shoulder, so my fall surprised no one. Fortunately, Linh caught both Amber and me, then got us safely to another roof. After being convinced I could continue, I went solo while Linh carried Amber.

We landed in the park near the Pond. It was another twenty blocks to Belvedere Castle, but Skyclimbing over trees was much easier and safer. I kept expanding the rain behind us, just in case.

"The portal is directly above the turret," Spencer said. "We can get to Wizard Island from there." Once again, I realized that whoever decided to place the castle at that spot in the late 1860s knew the portal was there. Portals, as it turns out, are not rare. What's rare is the absence of them.

As we dove through, Omnia forces stormed into the park from the side of the Metropolitan Museum of Art between 84th and 85th Streets.

64

Getting to Wizard Island was more complicated than I'd imagined and once there, a frantic conversation ensued.

"Where to? The final command is lost," I said.

"The final command has one move left . . . we can scatter across time, which is why I must know who sent Linh as Nares." He turned to Linh.

"You do not need to know," she said.

"Omnia agents are all over time; they can find us anywhere," Amber said.

"There are places . . . there are times," Spencer said.

"No," I said. "We should stay in this dimension, in the present. The Movement is about awakening the world *now*."

"We can win nothing if we are dead or in prison," Spencer said.

"We've survived this long."

"Can't you feel the noose tightening?" Spencer asked.

"It's been choking me for ages," I said. "But we know it's Devin Moore. Let's find him."

"We need time to regroup," Spencer said. "We should get safely into the past of one of the parallels."

"What about the butterfly forest?" Amber asked.

"Good idea," I said.

"Where's Yangchen?" Amber asked.

"Outin," Spencer said. He looked at me. "She's trying to reach Dustin about the list."

"Let's go," I said.

"Fine, we'll make a plan once we meet up with her," Spencer said firmly.

ooooo

There were now three Dustins at Outin. They were waiting for us at the lodge with Yangchen. Spencer had alerted her we would be coming.

It took me a second to pick out my-Dustin, the one from my life.

"Three against one, little brother." He laughed. "Hey, nasty wound; you should get the shoulder into Floral Lake."

"My leg, too," Amber said.

Everyone followed us there. Amber and I disappeared separately into the tall flowers by the banks to undress. We floated to a spot along the shore where several smooth boulders would allow the others to sit while we healed.

"I saw on the news that you blew up another mall," Dustin said. "Strangely, they say I helped but I've been here at Outin the whole time."

"If it's on the news, it's not true," Spencer said.

"How do you see the news?" Amber asked.

"Oh, it's really cool," Dustin-two answered. "We can see just about anything on TV; it's just finding the right Window."

"If it's on the news, it's not true," Linh echoed. "But there are three of you, maybe one of you snuck out."

I laughed but Linh still laid a little blame on my-Dustin for Kyle's death, and the whole Storch episode wasn't helping.

"I agree you can't trust the media but there's this alternative newscaster. I'm amazed Omnia allows her to broadcast. I really like her."

"The newscasters you like the best are the most corrupt," Spencer said. "Reliable information is scarce."

The Movement had been severely restricted since Omnia shut down the Internet. Years ago, in the earliest days of the Movement, the Internet was a great rallying point for our side, as well as an abundant source of intelligence for Omnia. Then the NSA's monitoring scandal broke and complex encryption software became so common that even the supercomputers used by Omnia couldn't keep up. Eventually they shut it down to curtail the sharing and planning of demonstrations and other Movement activities.

"Now we're limited to communicating over the astral and there are still only a few thousand who have that ability," Yangchen said. "We're training more all the time but it's slowing us down. We've begun recruiting from other dimensions."

"Where are we going to go?" Linh asked.

"How is Dunaway avoiding detection for his Inner Force?" I asked.

"He's got that deal going with Omnia," Dustin-three said.

Everyone looked at him.

"I thought you knew," he said.

"Knew what? Where are you from?" I asked. "What deal?"

"I'm from a parallel almost two years ahead," Dustin-three said, "And, well, word is that Dunaway gave Omnia the Jadeo and Clastier for protection."

"What? Protection? He's fighting them," I said.

"It doesn't have to happen," Spencer said.

"Omnia overwhelmed his people, caught him in another time or something, and he cut a deal to save himself," Dustin-three said.

"We have to find him now," I said, leaving the lake to retrieve my clothes. "Come on, Yangchen, Spencer, how do we find this guy?"

"The only way to track someone like Dunaway is to locate the Jadeo," Yangchen reminded me. "I've been talking to Dustin about the list of the nine entrusted he gave your father from a future life. That's why we have Dustin-three here."

"But the names just came to me," Dustin-three began. "A woman claiming to be Helen Hartman told me the names and said to tell them to my dad."

"What did she look like?" I asked.

"It's the strangest thing; I can't recall anything about her."

"Incredible!" I said. "Spencer, Travis Curry, Ripley Gaines

and I were able to locate the Jadeo by combining our power. You, Dustin and I should be able to do the same."

"I would imagine it'll take more than three this time," Spencer said. "Dunaway isn't likely to leave himself open to that again."

"Okay, but you just told us that Dunaway's deal with Omnia doesn't have to happen. What can we do?" I asked.

"Like Yangchen said, we use the Jadeo to find him fast, but we need help."

"We need to keep Omnia busy," I said. "Do we have any kind of organization left?"

"There are certain areas where the underground is flourishing: Taos, New Mexico, Asheville, North Carolina, Flagstaff, Arizona, parts of Colorado, Montana and Idaho." Yangchen said. "But the numbers are small. In Taos, the solar village of Greater World has been occupied; the scrappy off-the-map community of shipping containers and old school buses, where we hid for a while, has actually been wiped off the map. Nelson County, Virginia is one of our secret strongholds. There was a big center in Sarasota, Florida and our presence is still good there."

"We need to get messages out. Let's make as much noise as we can to divert Omnia resources. Get in touch with Booker," I said to Spencer. "Bring Travis Curry and Ripley Gaines here. We've got you and Dustin. That's five of the nine. Let's grab Dad and Lee Duncan from Pasius and that'll make seven. Surely seven of the nine can find the Jadeo."

"Your dad died in Pasius," Linh said softly.

"I know . . . we'll have to go earlier."

"It's a good plan," Spencer said, "but it'll take some time."

"Then it's good that time's such a damn funny thing . . . and that it moves in reverse at Outin."

Hard to say how long it took, but it didn't matter; Dad, Lee, Travis, Ripley, Spencer, the original Dustin, and I sat around in a circle focusing on the Jadeo. Seeing my dad again brought on a new wave of guilt, but it also strengthened me. I could see his pride and approval in what I'd become. I'd made many mistakes, but they had forged me into a leader with a cause. Spencer and Yangchen were able to pull him from Outin where he was with Spencer after we all went to San Francisco in Pasius, so he knew me. He pulled me aside, "Nate, I see such courage and purpose in you, I'm overwhelmed."

"Dad, something is going to happen once you go back to Pasius."

"I know, Spencer told me. It's okay, part of the destiny we can't change, not your fault." He put his hands on my shoulders. "Do you understand? I didn't die because of you."

I closed my eyes tight to hold back tears. "You don't have to go back."

"I do. But you know it's not the end."

"I know."

ooooo

Yangchen was back in Pasius, the other two Dustins took Amber on a tour of the Windows in the Vines, Linh went to meditate at Clarity Lake, and Gale, who'd come with Ripley, was enjoying Floral and Dreams Lakes. It must have been hours before Spencer broke our silent session.

"It's just out of my reach. Is anyone else getting any closer to it?"

"Same for me," Travis said. "I can almost see it but it's not quite there."

"I don't understand," Ripley said, "Nate, Travis and I had a much easier time back on the island. Who the hell is this Dunaway?"

"Are we sure he's not the traitor?" Dad asked. "What if he's already traded it to Omnia?"

"Or opened it," Lee said."

"I know it can change," Dustin said, "But Dustin-three told us it happened a few months from now."

"Your earlier attempt," Spencer began, "tipped Dunaway to the fact that we could find him through the Jadeo. I'm not sure what measures he's taken but he's done something. We've all searched for the Jadeo countless times over the centuries and it's never been this hard. He must have it in some kind of fog."

"Dad, we're not sure of anything about Dunaway. He's one of my generation's seven but we don't believe he is one of the nine. He sincerely doesn't seem to have a clue about what the Jadeo is."

"But he knows it's important to you, that you are desperate for its return, and he could have gotten information from Clastier."

"Rose has been working with Clastier in another dimension," Spencer said. "And while they have not had any luck finding Dunaway or the Jadeo, she is confident that they've been able to block Clastier's memory of it for now."

"There's so much to understand," I said.

"Don't worry about it, Nate," Dad said. "Pasius is an entire dimension devoted to studying what is possible, and we are just at the tip of the iceberg."

"You're way ahead of most," Spencer added.

"Omnia seems way ahead of all of us," I said.

"Their soul powers are awesome and so is Devin Moore's

lust for total power," Spencer said. Earlier, he'd told everyone about Moore's control over Omnia. The bigger concern now centered on a recent report that in the very near future, Moore would somehow learn of the Jadeo and obtain if from Dunaway. "Let's get back to our search. I can't even discuss the inconceivable consequences should Moore get the Jadeo."

My frustration grew each time it felt like we were about to locate the Jadeo, only to have it slip farther away. As the skywaves turned orange, signaling Outin's evening had arrived, Linh and Gale returned. I was about to suggest we give up, when Spencer called out. "There it is!"

We all saw it but couldn't quite catch it. "It's in a portal," Lee said. "Damn clever. Dunaway has the Jadeo in a portal within a portal, no wonder it's so hard to find." In Pasius, Lee was a renowned professor of portals. "And do you notice, Dunaway isn't there with it?"

"Neither is Clastier," I said.

We all pulsed with energy from being together and so close to the Jadeo. Like a man lost in a desert for days, spotting a mirage, I could taste water, but could not reach it. The Jadeo faded and surfaced, teased and tortured. Finally, in the end we surrendered. Dunaway had it too well concealed. The only way to get it would be to find him.

"Meditate," Linh said to me as the group broke up.

"You sound like Kyle. How did yours go?"

"Miraculous."

Lee Duncan walked over and interrupted us. "Nate, I know of a way that you may be able to find Dunaway. There is a portal similar to Wizard Island, but instead of taking you anywhere you want to go, it will take you to *anyone* you want to see."

"Wow."

"Yes, its existence has not ever been verified but there are references to it in other portals."

"What do you mean references?" Linh asked.

"Portal is a generic term. Wormholes, passages, dimensional doorways, time tunnels, they are essentially the same thing. But portals are more than links; they are each their own dimension. In fact some portals only link back to where they began." He scratched his head as if this were an entirely new thought to him. "Anyway, the point . . . no, what was I saying?"

"References in other portals," Linh said, smiling.

"Ah, yes, thank you. Well, most portals contain information. Perhaps all of them do; we just haven't uncovered it in certain ones. Anyway, they record, for lack of a better word, each passing, meaning everything that has ever happened in a portal is recorded within it, but more than that, a trace of every other dimension that an entity using the portal has encountered is also left. This is how we have discovered so many portals."

"They really are alive," I said.

"Oh, yes. Wizard Island, as you might imagine, would require lifetimes to fully study. But back to my original reason for bringing this up. There have been several small traces of this portal in other portals. As if just one person had used it in the past few thousand years. But it's hard to say for sure if it is real. There are so many variables with portals; extraordinary, really."

"Where is it?"

"Taos, New Mexico."

"A portal like this, in Taos of all places, how come you are only now bringing this up?"

"As I said, it may not exist. Even if it once did exist, portals can move or slip into another dimension and vanish forever. We don't know where most of the portals are. Even in Pasius, it's a very new science."

"But even a chance that it's real . . ." Linh said.

"I didn't know until this morning that you were so desperate to find this person," Lee said. "Really, although I do research for the Movement at Yangchen's direction, I didn't know Dunaway even existed before today."

"Either way, I'm happy to have something to try. Please, tell me everything you know about it."

As I told Spencer what I'd learned from Lee, Amber ran up. "Omnia is coming! We saw it in a Window. All of us, the same ones who are here now, were here, and they killed us all!"

"How much time is there?" Spencer asked.

"Impossible to say," Dustin-two answered.

"I'm going to Taos," I said.

"I'm going with you," Amber said.

"I'm going with Spencer," Linh said. Amber and I looked at her. Spencer seemed as surprised as we were. Yangchen would take care of getting Ripley, Gale and Travis back to where they would be safe. She said something about one of the parallels. Lee, Dustin-two and Dad were heading back to Pasius.

"I love you, Dad. I'll see you again, and before again."

"I'm counting on that." He hugged me tight. "I love you. We've known each other many times, but it's impossible for me to imagine loving you more than I do as my son."

Linh and Amber embraced in a tearful exchange. Then Linh came and looked deep into my eyes. "Be strong, Nate. I'll see you very soon."

"Why aren't you coming?"

"I have to convince Spencer I'm one of the good guys," she said, smiling.

ooooo

My-Dustin and Dustin-three were refusing to leave. "I've got places they'll never find me. If they think taking Outin is going to be easy, they don't know Dustin Ryder," my-Dustin said.

"Ditto," Dustin-three said.

All efforts by Spencer, Dad and me to talk him out of staying failed.

"Good luck, brother," I said.

"Keep that luck, Nate. You're going to need it. And you may have just enough."

"There's a portal over Taos Mountain that can take you to anyone alive," I said.

"Which are we going to first?" Amber asked.

"There is no first. A person can enter it only once. I want to find Dunaway."

"What about the leader of Omnia, Devin Moore? Or the Dark Mystic?"

"I figure the Dark Mystic will find me soon enough and I'm on a collision course with Devin Moore, but Dunaway has the Jadeo and Clastier."

"And you want his help?"

"I need his help."

"He doesn't want to help you."

"I can change his mind."

"How?"

"I don't know yet but I'm sure I can."

ooooo

The portal was more than two hundred feet above the mountain so Skyclimbing wasn't an option. Fortunately, there were several hot air balloon excursion companies in Taos and one of them was operated by a member of the Movement.

We met Cedars, our pilot, at first light near the John Dunn Bridge. It was one of a few bridges that crossed the Rio Grande at the bottom of the gorge. Normally, they took tourists on a breathtaking ride through the seven hundred foot deep rip in the earth. We'd be in the gorge for the first part of our ride but then headed toward Taos Mountain. Balloons couldn't really be steered, except by ascending or descending into air currents, but Cedars agreed to let me steer with Gogen.

"Depending on the wind, we'll be over Taos Mountain in about thirty minutes," he said.

Initially, we enjoyed the dramatic beauty of the sheer walls, huge blocks of brown and black lava stacked, carved and torn open, the land revealing a scar of the violent geological past. The river found the gorge and took advantage, spending the first portion of its 1800-mile run to the Gulf of Mexico protected by the deep walls. We floated up until we crested and could see the endless surrounding mesa and Taos Mountain in the distance. Amber spotted the Earthships as we dropped back into the gorge. There were two tanks and a dozen military trucks there.

Two more balloons had taken off behind us and a purple one was drifting menacingly close. A few small pieces of rock suddenly flew into the basket.

"What the hell?" Cedars said. "Where did that come from?"

More fragments zipped past.

"I think they're throwing them," Cedars said, motioning to the purple balloon. "That's Bark's outfit. He knows better than to be this close." He leaned out of the basket. "Bark, clear off!"

More rocks.

"Damn it, if they puncture us . . ." Cedars adjusted the temperature to make the balloon climb higher.

"Nate, Look! It's Clastier!" Amber yelled.

I spun around and saw Clastier in the basket of the purple balloon and right next to him Dunaway stood smiling.

"Nate," Dunaway yelled. "Let's see who can pop whose balloon first." He sent a big jagged rock zinging toward us. I intercepted it with Gogen and forced it down into the gorge. We both knew I couldn't crash his balloon with an innocent pilot and Clastier aboard.

"Who is that maniac?" Cedars asked.

Another bigger rock came at us.

"Nate, look out!" Amber screamed. At the same time, two more rocks rained in from the other side. I broke them up just in time.

"Dunaway, stop," I yelled. "It's going to take both of us to stop Omnia."

"That guy's on our side?" Cedars asked.

"Just get us out of the gorge," I snapped.

"I've been trying, but I can't get any lift!"

"Nate, I don't need your help with Omnia. Don't need your past, don't want your future, your death is all I ask!" Dunaway sang. A shower of rocks poured down on us.

"He's pulling us down!" Cedars yelled.

I fought off the rocks with a weather dome.

"If you kill me, you lose your powers!" I shouted. Had he forgotten one of the seven can't kill another one of the seven?

"Oh, Nate, I'm not going to kill you. You're going to die trying to save Amber."

"This might buy us some time," I whispered to Amber. I leapt from the basket and Skyclimbed up the side of his purple balloon. As expected, Dunaway joined me. We danced on the top of the balloon floating six hundred feet above the rapids. At the same time, I used Gogen to push our balloon further ahead.

"Nate, save your girlfriend . . . jump," Dunaway taunted.

"No one is going to die here today. IM and IF, you and I, we all want Omnia stopped. Let's do that together and once we've won, you and I can argue about the best way to move forward."

"I think you've suffered brain damage in one of your near death experiences." He laughed. "Why is it you keep nearly dying, when I've hardly had a scratch? Because my methods are superior to yours . . . Of course, I'm smarter than you, too, but that goes without saying."

"I'm still alive."

"For the moment. In fact, you did die once, didn't you? I think that makes you some kind of 'living-dead.' I think I'll call you Zombie from now on."

"What is your problem? Why are you so angry?"

"Easy answers . . . you, Zombie, are my problem and you make me very angry because instead of kicking Omnia's ass, I have to deal with you."

He Skyclimbed down and jumped across to my balloon. It zoomed forward, too far for me to catch in a Skyclimb. I tried to pull it back but his Gogen, or whatever he was using, was stronger. I dropped in on Clastier.

"Nate, you must stop him," Clastier began. "He is reckless and powerful, not a good combination."

"I'm trying."

"You are not. You are trying to convince him to join your cause. Dunaway will not listen to reason. Your only chance is to overpower him. Show him you are stronger."

"Am I?"

"Strength is not about how much power you have. It is about how you use the power you have."

Gogen pushed the two balloons zooming through the narrow gorge at a dizzying speed, still too far apart for Skyclimbing. I reached Amber on the astral.

"I'm scared," she said. "Dunaway keeps telling me that I'm too pretty to die."

"The bridge is just ahead. I think I can get you out."

"What about Clastier?"

"I don't think they'll be time for both."

"He's more important."

"No one is more important."

The steel bridge spans more than 1200 feet across the canyon, which narrows like a funnel as it drops 600 feet to the river. The balloons were going to travel under it. There would be one chance to get Amber out. Using Gogen, I brought two large slabs of rock spinning out into the air between the balloons and Skyclimbed across them to Cedars' balloon. Dunaway had Amber pinned to the floor of the basket and chased me up the side of the balloon. We reached the top at the same time. I leaped to the crisscrossing steel cantilever truss that supported the road above, running and leaping from beam to beam while Amber's balloon passed under us. I

Atomized up through the pavement onto the roadway. A truck sailed into me before I completely rematerialized; the force of the collision threw me out the backside and into one of the low steel railings. No permanent damage. Dunaway had gotten out of the balloon and ran toward me as I regained my feet.

Amber's balloon emerged from under the bridge. Cedars escaped but she had stayed in the basket. I Skyclimbed to avoid Dunaway, while calling Amber over the astral.

"Why didn't you get out?"

"There wasn't time," she said.

"But there was. How did Cedars get out?"

"I helped him."

"Amber, Dunaway will kill you!"

"He only wants *you* dead," she shot back.

Dunaway and I continued our Skyclimbing duel on the bridge as he artfully attempted to make me land in front of a speeding vehicle, which might have happened if they weren't all slowing down for the view. When the purple balloon came out from underneath the bridge, I jumped onto the top of it, then Skyclimbed down into the basket with Clastier and Bark.

"Bark, keep us on the same level with the other balloon. I'll steer," I said, "We need to keep up with Amber's balloon."

"Why can't she jump out of there?" Clastier asked.

"Amber can't Skyclimb."

67

Dunaway Skyclimbed along the east rim of the gorge. It was impossible to know if he was looking for an opportunity to jump into a balloon, waiting to attack, or just keeping tabs.

"I wouldn't worry too much about your crazy friend over there," Bark said. "I think we need to be more concerned with them." He pointed to the parking lot on the west side of the gorge, where several truckloads of soldiers had arrived from the off-grid community of Greater World. I tried a TVC but it wouldn't come together, even a regular Timefold wasn't happening. I searched the east rim for Dunaway. Although he was invisible, I could sense his presence. He knew powers I didn't. Somehow, he'd anticipated my moves and weakened those abilities.

"Amber," I yelled. The balloons were nearly touching. "We've got to push faster."

"Aren't you getting resistance with Gogen?" she asked. "A balloon can only move so fast."

"Bark, can you go higher?"

"Sure, but can she?"

"Amber, we're going to –"

"Something's holding us down," Bark said.

It had to be Dunaway. He'd led me into a trap. The balloon could only be pushed to a certain point, even with Gogen; then it met resistance and now he had us under some kind of ceiling. The soldiers would be able to pick us off as if we were in a carnival shooting gallery.

"We can always do the old splash and dash," Bark said.

"What's that?"

"Down to the river."

We'd still be in range but at least, if we made it to the water, we could get out and hide in the rocks or even float downstream in the rapids.

"We'll have to do it quickly."

"Tell the girl to open her vents to let the hot air out," Bark said, as he did the same.

My heat-warning had been high ever since Dunaway first showed up but suddenly the temperature increased ten-fold. I looked toward the west rim and saw the soldiers setting up to fire a shoulder-mounted missile. I turned back to Amber; she'd seen it, too. We absorbed the desperation in each other's eyes. Even if I maneuvered our balloon out of the way, they'd hit Amber's. We dropped thirty feet. Amber suddenly pushed her balloon over mine.

"Amber, no!" I screamed. She positioned her balloon between mine and the soldiers. The missile came hissing toward us and in the final second, Amber dropped her balloon to make sure to take the impact.

The horror of seeing her basket explode into flames lasted only a second. We were all knocked down, then our balloon spiraled and dropped, stabilizing forty feet down. Amber's burning body plummeted past us before smashing onto the rocks five hundred feet below.

Clastier threw himself on me. "She's gone, she's gone," he said firmly, as he held me.

In my breathless shock, I couldn't muster Gogen to push him off. "I can bring her back."

"No. She was dead before the fall. The missile killed her."

"No."

"She died saving us, Nate. Amber died saving you, don't let that be a waste."

"They're ready to launch another one," Bark said in a shaky voice.

"Drop this thing," Clastier yelled.

Bark opened the vents all the way. I pushed down and out with Gogen. An open ravine joined the gorge ahead on Dunaway's side. I pushed with everything I had. The balloon hit the wall and burst; the basket plummeted thirty feet, hitting the edge of a ledge. I pulled Clastier out and Skyclimbed up into the ravine. Bark remained trapped on the ledge, but held on as the basket and balloon slipped off and disappeared into the gorge.

Clastier and I now had cover from the soldiers. The pause gave me the first real chance to assimilate Amber's death. I felt her change, more than just the difference in the energy, an aching absence tore at my heart.

Clastier took over. "It won't be long until they find us, Nate. Fortunately this area has not changed since my lifetime. Hurry, this way!"

I followed him, like a dying man running from gravediggers. Nothing made sense. My eyes trained on his legs and shoes, the blur of sagebrush and black volcanic rocks hinted at a world beyond Clastier's path. He spoke occasionally as we ran but it might as well have been a new language invented that day. We climbed, ran, stumbled and jumped until suddenly he pushed me into a portal. I floated, lost for an indeterminate time, until he joined me again and we quickly exited into a similar landscape.

"Where are we?"

"Ghost Ranch."

"Is Amber here?"

"There is a vortex here. That's Chimney Rock; in the distance is the sacred Padernal, a volcanic mesa of some importance. Amber is here as much as she is everywhere."

"Why are we here?"

"Sometimes the universe provides just what we need in many layers." Clastier looked at me. I considered my soul in his eyes. There could be no one more soothing to be with at this tragic, gutting time than Clastier. The universe had done at least that much right. "We needed to escape," he continued. "This portal was the closest . . . a happy coincidence, for as I said, there is a strong vortex here at Ghost Ranch and you need this energy."

"Where's Dunaway," I said, gritting my teeth.

"Forget about Dunaway and the soldiers. They are not here. I hid the entrance to the portal. We may have time, we may not, but you need to let go of the idea of vengeance. Amber died knowingly because she believed in the Movement and your ability to lead it. She did not believe in vengeance. You know these things, they are true . . . and you have always known them."

The sunlight caught my attention. I'd never seen the light play just that way. The red rocks seemed to pulse, chamisa and other desert plants whispered almost-words. I could feel the vortex. It brought me in touch with myself. Ghost Ranch was a healing place. My strength surfaced, and Amber's death, although horrible and sad, suddenly seemed to be just another event that happened in this experience. I was stronger than before; each loss or triumph prepared me for the next.

Amber knew what she was doing; that brought a new wave of anger but also, love, and soon the love won out. There were things to do, and I could mourn and miss her later. I'd see her again, one way or another, anyway. Even if the soldiers didn't find the portal, a tear could open any second and I'd be alone against an Omnia army. Clastier was safe but the Jadeo was still at risk and Dunaway may have been captured by the soldiers at the bridge. I'd done nothing to prevent the deal between him and Omnia, I might have even hastened it.

Not surprisingly, Clastier had no knowledge of where Dunaway might have hidden the Jadeo. I'd have to go back to Taos and try for the mountain portal again but first I needed to get Clastier to safety. He and Rose had been in touch and suggested a small dimension which so far had not been breached. It offered almost complete invisibility to 92426 and most other known dimensions and, as luck would have it, was only accessible from Pasius.

The dimension, named Star Sea Island, looked like the Big Island in Hawaii, except an ocean of stars surrounded it instead of water. Clastier planned to work on recreating the pages from his papers that had been lost. Before I left, he warned me against my intentions, but he knew me well enough to know I would not be swayed.

ooooo

I walked across the campus, but before reaching her dorm, I saw her standing next to a tree talking to friends. I watched for a few moments. Seeing her laugh, looking so alive, it was wonderful . . . a wonderful torture. I thought back to when Amber picked me up in her VW convertible, that day she saved my sanity and first opened my eyes to the power of the soul. My memories took hold as I stared. She must have felt my presence because she turned and caught me looking at her. After excusing herself from the group, Amber-two walked over.

"Hi, Nate," Amber-two said quietly, looking intently into my eyes. "She's dead, isn't she?"

I half-nodded. "How did you know?"

"She came, after you and Linh were here that time, and told me that if I saw you again, it would be because she had died."

"I'm sorry."

"It's weird, I didn't know her for more than a couple of hours but she was me . . . I knew her, just not everything about her life. So much of it was the same but most of it, like you, was slightly different."

"Amber was the brightest person I've ever known. I don't mean smart, even though she was smart. I mean she illuminated a dark room."

"She loved you."

"I loved her, too."

"She said you loved Linh."

"Yeah. But one thing I've learned through this is that there is nothing more powerful than love – it's everything; it's who we are. Love can't be limited to one person any more than the universe could only have one star. Love is constantly expanding; there is plenty for everyone."

"Why did you come here? To tell me she died?" Her face showed she knew the answer.

"I want you to come back with me."

"To the land of fast food, fossil fuel, money and the military?"

"Is this dimension so perfect?"

"Perfect doesn't exist in the human world but I think we're a lot closer in Pasius."

"The Movement needs you."

Her skeptical look reminded me of Amber.

"I need you, I can't do this without you. Please, Amber, come back with me. Help us change the world."

"You want your Amber, Nate. I'm not really her. I know I look and sound like her but . . ."

"You are her! Don't you see? You're her soul."

"Maybe so, but we're a long way from dealing with each other on a soul level. Even if you defeat Omnia and the awakening begins in your dimension, it will be long after your lifetime that people are able to see soul to soul."

"We don't know that. And it doesn't matter what the rest of the world is doing. I'm talking about you and me. Our souls can communicate. I can show you everything about her life. If you could feel her feelings you would want to come, I know it. Amber, please." I grabbed her, hugged her and sobbed. She held me. It was Amber, her smell, the way her hands felt on my back. "Please," I repeated.

"Nate, you have to know that our personalities are strangers. It's not like you and Amber. If you understand that, then I will come, not for you, but for her, and because I understand that everyone in every dimension must find awareness and grow toward enlightenment . . . As Amber told me, 'no one gets out of this alone.' But I have another question. Does Linh know you're here?"

"No."

"Nate, when she sees us together, it'll crush her."

"Linh's tougher than that."

"Before we go, let's talk to Yangchen."

"Great idea."

ooooo

Yangchen's office was incredibly sparse with blond wood floors, pale blue shelfless walls, and one large painting showing a field with thousands of flowers, each a different kind. Her desk had a holographic keypad and a shimmering air monitor - nothing else.

"Nate, is Spencer alive?" she asked alarmed.

"Yes. As far as I know. You recognize me."

"Of course, I do, we've spent considerable time together."

"But I died in this dimension when I was ten."

"Oh yes, you do not know. I am the same Yangchen in both 92426 and Pasius. There is only one of me."

"So you live and work in two different dimensions at the

same time?"

"Rather a few more than that."

"Wow. Does Spencer know?"

"Certainly. But if you are not here because of his death, then I am to presume we lost Amber."

"Yes."

"She saved you. Good girl."

"I wish she hadn't," I said.

"Nonsense. She made the right choice; she's known for a long time it would end this way. And you asked her to do it prior to this life, so don't be silly. It was planned and agreed."

"I'm so tired of the guilt I feel all the time," I involuntarily inhaled deeply. "There's so much of it."

"Nate, listen to me. Guilt is fear. Don't allow it. You are in charge of who you are. If you accept guilt you are simply inviting fear into your life. You don't have time for fear."

"I know."

"Don't know. Understand. Live your understanding."

"He wants me to go back with him," Amber said.

"Of course he does. Don't you think that anyone who lost a loved one would go get a carbon copy of the person if they could?"

"It's not just that," I protested.

"It's mostly that," Yangchen said. "But the Movement would benefit, as long as it doesn't break Linh's heart. We need her, too."

"I'll talk to her," I said.

"Dear Nate, please remember when you do to use your spiritual knowledge. Don't rely merely on your emotions as a teenager, that'll just make a mess of things."

"I love Linh. I'll do anything not to hurt her."

Yangchen stared at me. "Yes, you love them both. But remember where you've been. The choice has been made. Your soul made it a long time ago and, if you are present and consider your emotions in a mindful manner, you will know with certainty what that choice is. Only your personality gets confused. And remember one more thing . . . you loved Amber from 92426. This beautiful young woman in front of us is someone entirely different."

Amber-two and I set a time to meet at the butterfly forest. First, I'd go back to New Mexico and make another attempt at the Taos Mountain portal. Before I left Pasius, I contacted Spencer on the astral; Booker would arrange for a helicopter to take me over the mountain. It had its own risks but it was the only avenue open at this point. Then I reached Linh.

"I felt her change," Linh said before I could tell her. "Are you okay?"

"Yes. What about you?"

"I'll miss her, but she knew this was coming."

"Did she tell you?"

"Amber's known for years, not the exact circumstances, just that it would happen. But she only told me at Outin. Then when we hugged goodbye, she told me I'd never see her again in this life."

"Why didn't you tell me?"

"You know I couldn't," she said, almost daring me to bring up her keeping secrets again. I decided against it.

"Linh, I went back to Pasius."

"To find Amber?"

"Yes, but –"

"I'm not stupid. I knew you would."

"The Movement needs her."

"Didn't you hear me? I'm not stupid. Nate, you need her, or rather you want her. You always have."

"Linh, this isn't the same Amber. Our Amber is dead."

"I know that, Nate, but do you?"

"Linh, don't you understand how I feel?"

"How can I, when *you* don't even get it?"

"Please, Linh, I'm trying to pull myself together. Give me some time."

"Time's a funny thing, Nate!" She closed our connection.

ooooo

The helicopter flew in restricted airspace over the Taos Pueblo, but any other route would have alerted Omnia and brought choppers, now stationed at Taos Airport. I should have been thinking about the drop I'd be making into the portal. Instead, I tried to script the conversation Linh and I would have when we next met.

Then I saw the portal, which was nearly impossible to see from either above or below. Only a slight ripple could be seen from the side. When we'd stayed in Taos, I'd often seen strange clouds over the mountain. There were rumors of UFOs concealing themselves, which might have been, or maybe it had something to do with the portal.

I contemplated just what I would do to Dunaway. I knew he needed to be found and stopped, but the method eluded me. Clastier's words had finally gotten through: Dunaway could not be converted, he needed to be surpassed, and only I could do it.

The pilot circled. Greater World came into view. Omnia was crushing all resistance. The Movement's infrastructure had been completely gutted. We clung to the hope of our revolution on the outer fringes of time and dimension. Spencer would never agree, but I now saw the Jadeo as not just something to protect, but something to use. For too long it had been out of the hands of the nine entrusted. It had been a distraction . . . find it, hide it. No, it was time for an Outmove. I was one of the nine, and one of the seven, and darkness was on the verge of overtaking the light. The future was up to me; the Outmove was to use the Jadeo. The pilot gave me a hand signal and hovered as close as safety allowed.

I jumped from the helicopter, unable to see the portal. The mountain rose fast. Could I have missed it? Maybe it was a false portal. My rapid descent sent me into a dizzying spin. The rocks on the peak were less than fifty feet below. The portal was gone! Forty feet, my skin burned, thirty, twenty. In a split second I would explode onto the rocks, ten, five, two, one . . . suddenly, less than an inch from impact, like a bungee jumper, my body recoiled and snapped back toward the sky. Like a rocket, I soared into the portal from beneath.

Perhaps that is why Taos Mountain is sacred. The Native American tribe which controls the mountain allows no one on the peak. The portal stretched beyond my vision in all directions. Turquoise became deep blue and finally indigo until bright sunlight burned through and all was white. The promise of this portal to take me to anyone might be a myth. I wondered how Lee Duncan and his fellow portalogists could ever learn anything within a portal. They were mostly disorientating places and capturing data seemed as unlikely as remembering the details of a dream.

Floating in the midst of light, looking for any direction, I began to feel sick. Was there a way out? A way anywhere? It could be just over my shoulder, just out of reach; it could require a run or a dive, something I didn't know. All I wanted was to reach Dunaway. Everything went black.

My eyes began to adjust. At my back, a massive window, maybe eighty feet by thirty feet, afforded a near-Hubble view of the stars. Inside the warm room, I was cold. A gigantic round fireplace, crafted from black and gray marble, burning trunk-sized logs, warmed me. More of the room came into view – smooth stone floors, two tables of irregular shape, one ten feet long, the other twice that, several comfortable looking chairs. I saw no doors and the ceiling, incredibly high, seemed to be the sky, with a number of skylights revealing more stars.

"Nate, for a very long time, I've been certain we would meet tonight." I did not recognize the voice. It was not Dunaway, but even before I turned to see who owned such a deep and ancient voice, I knew I'd somehow found the Dark Mystic.

He sat in an overstuffed, black leather chair, drink in hand, smiling. The dark brown skin on his smooth-shaved head seemed to glow, gold-mirrored sunglasses matched a shiny shirt, and smoky ebony pants moved as if in a breeze when he stood. "Nathan Ryder," he said, towering over me by at least six inches. "I am your final mystic."

"You're the Dark Mystic."

"People call me that. I've never liked that name, but, in this confusion, it will suffice."

"What confusion?" I looked around the large and nearly empty space, which had the feel of a meeting room at an upscale mountain lodge somewhere in Europe, or perhaps, a spaceship floating in the Milky Way.

"The times we find ourselves in, many find confusing, confounding, counter and complicated."

"Where are we?"

"I call it Slice. It's a dimension of my own making. I've sliced it off of 92426."

"You created a new dimension?" The stories of his powers were understated rather than exaggerated. "How do you do that?"

"Ha, you are young . . ." He laughed a rich laugh. "That you think a question like that could be answered in anything less than a hundred years . . . that you think you deserve to know the answer . . . that you asked it of me, all these things would astonish me if I were capable of being astonished."

"I'm sorry if I offended you." His reputation for being as much good as bad suddenly worried me.

"Yes. They say many things about me, don't they? Some think I am a myth, and I suppose parts of each of us are myths. I can teach you a great number of things, Nathan Ryder, but some lessons will be painful. Death is a teacher like no other in life." He stood close. I saw my reflection, framed by stars, in his gold glasses.

"Are you going to kill me?"

"Do you fear death?"

"No."

"No?"

"I've died too many times, lost too many loved ones . . . seen dimensions, past and future times, and beyond . . . No, I don't fear death."

"Brilliant. How do you feel about it then?"

"Like I do about a door."

"Really? So you're interested in the other side? Please, follow me." He walked to the glass wall. We looked out. The "building" sat on top of an impossibly high cliff. A dark ocean with gigantic waves wrestled a rocky coast a thousand feet below. Stars, close enough to touch, burned through the fabric of sky in such numbers they rendered it translucent.

"It's like the edge of the world," I said.

"Yes, I carved it out of just that. It's the work of a millennium, still incomplete, of course."

"I've never seen a more beautiful view."

"Certainly you have, everyone has, you just forget . . . like everyone."

"That's part of the problem."

"It is the problem. This lack of memory has created the fear which has formed the faults which have made the mistakes which . . . well, you get the idea, disaster ensues."

I nodded.

"Now back to our little discussion of death, you called it a door. That's correct, isn't it, Nathan Ryder? A door?"

"Yes." I didn't like his tone.

He opened a door in the glass wall where none had been before, then motioned to me to step through.

"After you," I said.

His baritone laugh rolled into one long tone before abruptly stopping. "I insist." His voice firm and clipped.

I jerked back, but instantly my heels were teetering on the edge. The wind unsteadied me, my palms turned clammy, I couldn't get any footing.

"There is much to learn from walking through this death you call a door," he whispered. Using the same power that put me there, he spun me around so that my back was to the opening and only my toes remained on the black marble floor. "Are you afraid of death?"

"No. But I'm not ready to die."

"Why is that, Nathan Ryder?"

"I have things to do."

"Thank you for that very specific answer. Enjoy the view." He spun me around again.

"You know why I'm here," I yelled.

"Yet we've just met."

"I'm one of the seven, I have an open channel to the universe, to my soul, in order to help everyone find their own soul, so that the awakening can happen. I am trying to do that," I rambled, unsure if he'd let me fall at any moment.

"Seems you're a rather important fellow, then. Maybe you should live?"

"I think that's the plan."

"Really, who makes the plan?"

"I made it."

"Have you seen it?"

"No."

"Sounds rather unreliable. Why didn't you decide to live forever, then?"

"I wouldn't want to."

"Hmm, but you want to live now? A little longer? Perhaps an hour? Four months? Fifty-eight years?"

"Just longer."

"But there is that plan. May I see a copy . . . what does it say?"

"I just know that my work is not done."

"Well, Nathan Ryder, that seems rather obvious, doesn't it? I mean, take a look around. Not here, speaking figuratively. The world is a mess. One could argue it's in much worse shape than when you came on the scene. So, I'd say your work appears to have hardly begun, much less being done. It seems unlikely you'd be missed at all."

"Why did I make it to the fifteenth mystic if I'm doing everything wrong?"

"Was that the game? You're on some kind of spiritual scavenger hunt?"

"No."

"What you don't realize is that the next generation's seven are already on earth. The little toddlers are all in good shape and they've got a shot at making a difference. If they don't, nothing to worry about, another crop will come behind them. You're in a long line of sevens, and do you know what? They have all failed . . . even the famous ones. Do you know why? Because any time mankind hears a message of love and peace, anything that comes close to the spiritual truth, do you know what they do? They kill the messenger. Your death then is a tradition."

He left me on that ledge for a day. I watched as the sun crept around the horizon. The coast faced due north because the sun rose and set on the water. The spectacle might have explained the Dark Mystic's choice of locations for his dimension, but it wasn't clear if any of what I saw was real. He returned the following night.

"Are you ready to die?"

"No. My life is not complete yet."

"Who says?"

"I do. The life of Nathan Ryder is not complete because I still can make a difference."

"Omnia appears unstoppable."

"They will collapse once I open the Jadeo and show the world –"

"Open the Jadeo? Is that your role? Do you even have the Jadeo?"

"Let me off this ledge and tell me where to find Dunaway."

"Are you telling me what to do?"

My feet slipped and I fell at a forty-five degree angle. The waves, foamy in the starlight, loud in the stillness, pulled me toward them. "No," I yelled.

"My questions have not been answered."

"No, I –"

"I do *not* require you to tell me what I already know. *You* are trying to see even a glimpse of what *I* know. Everything you know or ever will know was known to me prior to your birth a thousand lifetimes ago," the Dark Mystic said.

He left again, and I hung there, fighting fear, on the verge of falling, for another day. The following night he returned.

"Are you ready to die?"

"Yes."

"Really? Why?"

"I have lived so that I am always ready to die."

Suddenly I was sitting across from the Dark Mystic, in a comfortable chair by the fireplace.

"Perhaps your life has not been wasted."

I sighed. The warmth of the fire slipped into my skin and brought my bones back to an acceptable feeling of living. "I want to know all you will teach me."

"All I will teach you is more than all you have learned."

"It'll take forever," I said.

"Remember, forever has already happened; it took an instant."

I did not speak. Instead I thought about everything he'd said since we met. When the sun rose, he offered me a drink. I hadn't eaten since my arrival, but until he offered, the thought of food or water never occurred to me. The velvety black potion tasted like the smell of flowers in the mountains. A single round ice cube floated in my glass in spite of the warm liquid. As much as I drank, the glass remained half full and the ice never melted.

"There are all kinds of powers. They are positive, yet each power has a block which is neutral and, equally important, every power also has an opposite which is negative."

I nodded, afraid to say the wrong thing. The statement was new to me, and the simple symmetry of it brought a clarity that had been lacking in my understanding of the five great soul powers. Yet, if I admitted that, he might push me back onto the ledge, might drop me this time, or subject me to some new torture.

He swirled his own glass. "You must know, Nathan Ryder, I can read your every thought, even the ones you don't know about. So, please do not insult me with fear. If you are not beyond that, then we will have to begin another time."

"These samurai teaching techniques are a bit unnerving. If you want to kill me, then do it."

"In the end it isn't death that kills us; something killed us long ago."

The sun suddenly dimmed, the room falling into complete darkness. I cannot recall how long we sat there unable to see anything but my thoughts; certainly days passed. When the light returned, the Dark Mystic removed his sunglasses and stared into my eyes.

A week before, what I saw would have left me unhinged, maybe even terrified. Now, something had changed. I continued looking past his multicolored irises and pondered whether or not what I was seeing was real or another test. It was not surprising that the Dark Mystic would also be another person I knew, but then I saw many others I had known. I stopped at the slave.

"Your eyes were brown then," I said.

"Yes, the color changes come as one gets closer to their soul."

"Surely you've died since then; it's been almost four hundred years."

He stood and turned away from me, unbuttoned his shirt, then lowered it. I gasped. His back was crisscrossed with long horrible scars from whippings. "Some of those are from me?"

He turned back to face me. "Only the first few."

"But they are all because of me."

He didn't say anything.

"I'm sorry."

"I know."

This time I was quiet.

"The karma from brutality such as slavery, the holocaust, betrayals of the Native Americans, and other acts of genocide, is very strong. It takes a hundred lifetimes or more to clear such things."

"I am still paying," I said.

"We are *all* still paying."

"Why have you remained in that incarnation? *How* have

you remained?"

"I have been a mystic for a very long time."

"We've known each other many times, haven't we?"

"One is not born accidentally as one of his generation's seven. Countless lifetimes are required to prepare to be one of the seven. I have been your mystic dozens of times. During your time as a slave trader, you were also a slave, you were married to Gibi. I was her brother. It was a complex time that ended tragically. I hid in the mountains and became a breatharian. I learned things. Nature and solitude are life's greatest teachers. Stars, Outviews and signs will show a person almost anything. But I encountered mystics, too. Wandus and Spencer have helped me grow; the Old Man of the Lake and Yangchen have given me much."

"If you know all of them, why didn't they just tell me where you were?"

"Do you really have to ask?"

I stopped long enough to think, still distracted by who I'd seen in his eyes, my adrenaline running wild. "Because . . . I was not ready. Because I needed to find you myself."

"Your question should have been, why am I the last mystic. And that is because I am no longer a mystic of the earth. Few mystics have ever created their own dimension. In those mountains, soon I knew how not to die."

I knew better than to ask how. "But you have other incarnations that live and die."

"Yes." He smiled. "Once you connect to your soul, not just for soul powers and Outviews, not just seeing it but to unify with it, you can live all your lives from any one of them."

"I don't really understand that."

"I know you don't; one day you will."

While trying to figure out how to ask him about the other incarnation I'd seen in him, the total blackness returned.

"Is this why they call you the Dark Mystic?" I asked, but no answer came. More days in the abyss.

When he returned we talked again but I did not ask him what I most wanted to know. The cycle continued for a very, very long time – questions, answers, and great periods of solitude. He showed me things but mostly made me find them.

"Today, you should return to 92426."

"Am I ready?"

"I cannot answer that, Nathan Ryder. Only you can if you are ready, and you will only know once you are ready, or . . . once it's too late."

"How long have I been here?"

"Eleven years."

No answer would have shocked me. Still, I wondered what had happened in my world during my absence. Would I recognize it? Who would still be alive?

"Don't worry about such things. My dimension is a friend of time. Only eleven minutes will have passed in 92426."

"That's a relief."

"Maybe."

"Can I ask one last question?"

He studied me.

"I believe the information will be helpful to my purpose," I added.

"Very well."

"During those first few days, I saw something in your eyes and need to know if it's true. Do you share a soul with Dunaway?"

72

The Dark Mystic looked at me, smiling. "Don't worry, Nate. Dunaway doesn't know yet. I have been alive for a very long time. He is still young. Many mystics prepared my soul to be one of the seven. Most of the mystics you know were once one of their generation's seven. It was not meant to be this way with Dunaway and you. Or with Dunaway and me, for that matter."

"Why does he hate me?"

"Dunaway carries the abuse from our lifetime as a slave. It is partially my fault; if I had let that life die, he would have been able to see the completeness in his soul. Instead, he doesn't know what he can't let go of."

"Can't you help him?"

"I was not to be a mystic yet, so I'm limited in what I can do with my own incarnations."

"Who limits you? I thought you've been a mystic for a long time."

"I did not become a mystic until I escaped from slavery into the mountains. Then I began to explore time and dimension. It can be bent and changed . . . large changes are extremely difficult, small ones are but small things. Like a figure eight, journeying the infinite course, I relived many lives as a mystic, returning to the beginning of human history and repeating lifetimes. They are easier as a mystic, and, well . . . we must do something while we wait for the others to figure it all out."

"And Dunaway insists on using force against Omnia because . . . he is lashing out at the plantation owners and slave traders."

"Something like that. Remember, you found me only because you were looking for him. Dunaway is not your problem, he never has been. Often, in life, we fail because we do not realize that our biggest problem is the solution. Dunaway is your solution."

"Thank you." I understood.

He walked me to the glass wall. "One last thing before you go. There are many great truths, and most of them you know. However, remembering this will help you at times of great hardship: we are all each other in one form or another."

Then the Dark Mystic opened a glass door where there had been none, put his hands together and bowed slightly. I bowed in return, looked down at the swirling ocean far below, and stepped out into the open air without hesitation.

ooooo

I found myself walking on a beach. The stars were close. I looked up to see if I could find the Dark Mystic's house. Nothing but stars. "Where am I?" I asked myself, knowing the answer would come – just south of Puerto Vallarta on the Mexican Coast. Before I could ask the location of the nearest portal, a harder question, a light in the distance caught my eye. It approached fast, maybe a motorcycle. Without a heat warning, I decided to wait.

Flannery took off his helmet. "Need a lift?"

"How'd you find me?"

"The Dark Mystic. He helped me quite a bit in the institution, helps a lot of folks locked up. Anyway, I do errands for him every now and then. He suggested I pick you up. Plus, I've got a new song I want you to hear." He motioned his head back to the black guitar case strapped to his back.

"And where are we going?"

"See if we can't catch up with Dunaway."

"I thought he'd be back in Prague after killing my girlfriend," I said.

"The Faust House in Prague got raided; it's now controlled by Omnia."

"Damn."

"I'm sorry to hear about Linh," he said, sadly.

A knot formed in my stomach. "What happened to Linh?"

"I don't know, you just said Dunaway killed her."

"No, you're confused," I said. "He killed Amber, not Linh."

"Oh, sorry about Amber, then. But, you're the one who seems confused."

"Never mind." I took the guitar off his back, slung it over mine and climbed on. "How far is he?"

"Just up the road. There's a series of overlapping portals between here and Baja. Quite incredible, like a cosmic maze. Anyway, he's got a base on this side."

ooooo

The Dark Mystic had obviously arranged where I would reenter 92426. I wondered if it was an endorsement. The knowledge and powers I'd gained during my eleven years with him were going to finally allow me to best Dunaway.

Flannery navigated a narrow trail through Playa Majahuitas, protected lands leading up to the coast. Over the motorcycle's whine, he explained that the Cañon Submarino, an underwater canyon, contained many of the portal entrances. He also sang his newest song, something about earth's music reaching the Pleiades star system through our radio waves.

"You're losing me, Flannery."

He kept singing.

Suddenly we entered a group of buildings.

"How does he hide this in the middle of a government wildlife sanctuary?"

Flannery sang louder, but I had already answered my own question. Dunaway employed a form of semi-permanent TVC to shield the base – no one could see it.

Flannery stopped when we spotted Dunaway standing on the balcony of a two-story, sheet metal building.

"Nate, I'm kind of busy trying to save the world. Can we do this another time?" he yelled down.

I Skyclimbed up to him. "Now is better for me," I said.

"Fine," he sighed. "If this is about your girlfriend, I'm sorry; I thought you'd die saving her, not the other way around."

"This isn't about her."

"Oh, good. Then about the Jadeo, possession is nine-tenths of the law."

"You don't really know what it is, do you?"

"I know it's important enough for you to get your girlfriend killed."

I stayed calm and continued to concentrate on weakening his powers while blocking him from doing the same.

"I'm not giving it to you."

"I think you will."

"Oh yeah, tough guy, why's that?"

"Because I know where it is." I vanished into a Timefold. His panicked expression told me three things: he believed I knew, he thought I was heading there now, and he would try to reach it before I did.

I followed him to a portal entrance above a rock outcropping. The advantage I'd gained from my time with the Dark Mystic was lost as the portal maze twisted before me like a thousand passages inside a hall of mirrors lit by multi-colored strobe lights. Dunaway had been here many times before. If I lost him, I might never find my way out.

I memorized every turn he took, but everything continued to move, with the portals colliding, overlapping and changing constantly. Once I had the Jadeo, how would I get out? He must have a way to know the transformations; he never hesitated in his choice of direction. We were underwater now; I could see it all around like a giant aquarium pulsing with neon. Suddenly he pulled the Jadeo out of a wall, then headed in a different direction.

Because Dunaway remained oblivious to my presence, I used the relatively simple power of Solteer to make him see changes in the portals that were not there. Using Solteer on another mystic caused me blinding pain, but it gave me enough time to employ a technique I learned from the Dark Mystic. Through mental projection, I showed Dunaway the future view of what would happen if he traded the Jadeo to Omnia. Definitely a risky move because it would also show him the Jadeo's true power.

As soon as the vision completed, he looked around. "Nate?"

I appeared. "Do you understand why I must have it back?"

"I do. But do you understand why I can't give it to you?" he replied.

"No."

"If I give it to you, then you will win."

"If you don't, then Omnia wins. Which is worse?" I asked.

"For you it's Omnia; for me, it's not so clear."

"How can you say that after what I just showed you?"

"I don't know." It was the first time I'd heard anything but confidence, arrogance or bravado in his voice. He looked at me questioningly. "Because I hate you."

I showed him the lifetime when I sold him into slavery and beat him.

"Why haven't I seen this past life before?"

"Because you're still alive," I said firmly.

"Impossible."

I raised an eyebrow and cocked my head.

"You're telling me that alive today, a four-hundred-year-old black man, an escaped slave no less, is running around and I share a soul with him?"

"Yes," I replied.

"I would know."

"Yet you don't."

He paced a figure eight. "If what you're saying is true, where is he?"

"He is the Dark Mystic and he resides in a dimension of his own making," I explained.

"You're making this up. Get out of my way!" He shoved me.

I stepped aside. The portal had returned to the form familiar to him. "Nate, if I keep the Jadeo, I can win."

"Not in the stars, Dunaway. Look for yourself. You don't know how to open it. And even if you did, you'd be killed before you could and Omnia would wind up with it."

"Nothing is so sure."

"Dunaway, I'm sorry about our past. You know enough about karma to know that I have paid for that crime."

"Show me!"

"In karma, the debt is seldom paid to the one to whom it is owed, but it will always be paid somehow."

"Show me the payment, Nate."

So I did. I showed him my parents being dragged away by the same slave trader, and later my life in slavery. I showed him Dachau, and fifty other deaths, Lightyear killing my father, him killing my mother. I showed him suffering until he put his arms around me and we both dropped to our knees in tears. Forgiveness is far easier than one might imagine. "I'm sorry," I cried.

"Apologies are meaningless. I cannot begin to make up for the pain *I've* caused . . ."

"But that is the only place where we can begin," I said.

"How many lifetimes am I going to have to pay for this one?"

"Many."

"I don't think I can bear that kind of cruel suffering."

"You can, you have. We all have."

"All the Omnia agents I've killed or had killed . . . they're as good as me . . . as you."

"Yeah, that's the problem with violence; no matter how much we think we're using it against others, it's really always against ourselves." I looked him in the eye. "You see what violence has wrought. It damages the soul. You have taken the wrong road with IF. We must defeat Omnia with non-violence or any victory will not be lasting."

Flannery ran toward us. "Omnia found IF's compound. They've blown it to smithereens!"

"Damn them!" Dunaway shouted. "I have attacks ready to retaliate at seven key military bases, including the Pentagon!"

"We've probably got about twenty seconds before they find the entrance to the portals," Flannery said, breathlessly.

They both looked at me. "Twenty seconds is an eternity," I said. "Dunaway, you must decide . . . return the Jadeo and join the Movement."

He hesitated. "Damn you, Nate, I've lost people up there. Good friends . . ."

"I know."

He thrust the Jadeo into my hand. Feeling the small gold box jolted me; much had changed since I last held it, mostly me.

"Thank you, Dunaway."

"Nate!" Flannery yelled. "We gotta go."

I caught an Airgon particle from Flannery and detected the commandos' next target.

"Dunaway, how do we get to the butterfly forest?" I shouted.

We arrived too late. Amber-two and Wandus were dead. Their bloody bodies, along with twenty-eight other Movement members, lay among millions of butterflies, torn, ravaged and lifeless.

"Sorry, Nate," Dunaway said.

I closed my eyes, and finding no support to lean upon, sank to the ground. "He was a being of pure love . . . and I brought her from the safety of an advanced dimension into this . . . this . . . barbaric society."

Flannery put a hand on my shoulder. I looked up at Dunaway. He had strikes at the ready, we could inflict thousands of deaths in retaliation and weaken Omnia's ability to repeat this kind of massacre. And I wanted to do that, my rage rising within me, smothering out my spiritual impulses.

I could almost hear what Dunaway was thinking. "Kind of tough to turn the other cheek."

Flannery was visibly shaken by the sight. "Wandus didn't even eat food!" he said.

I knelt down beside Amber's body; in a cruel karmic twist, I'd lost her twice in one lifetime. "I will see you again and before again." I kissed her forehead and then Wandus'. As brutal as it was to see them that way, I knew if they had been there with me, retaliation was the last thing they would want. And it was the first thing Omnia would want. We used Gogen to dig graves and bury the bodies.

I found Spencer on the astral. The surviving hierarchy of

the Movement, including Yangchen and Linh, were in hiding. Constantly moving among dimensions, he told me where to meet them but said to hurry as they were considering retreating to another time until they could regroup.

"I've got the Jadeo," I said.

"I know. I felt it happen."

"We can still win this."

"Wait until you hear the full reports of the crackdown."

"Omnia's only doing this because Devin Moore is scared his control is slipping."

"Whatever his motives, the crackdown is working."

"What do we know of Outin?"

"Last report said it was still safe but we've not been able to reach Dustin."

"Me neither," I said. "We'll go through there on the way to you."

"Be careful."

ooooo

Dustin and Dustin-three met us as we entered Outin. They explained that they were not communicating on the astral because, although Omnia didn't have the ability to intercept astral-talks yet, they had found a way to use the energy of them to trace people. It was how the crackdown had been so effective. They had figured it out through the Windows but couldn't figure out how to get word out to us without jeopardizing Outin.

"Is Outin really worth all the lives we lost?" I asked Dustin.

"Nate, believe me, it's been a tough call, but if Omnia had Outin, it would already be over. I knew I'd made the right decision when I felt you get the Jadeo back." He looked at Dunaway. "Cool of you, man."

"Maybe we should use Outin as a base for the Movement," I said.

"Nate, the Movement has nothing left to make a base with. It's down to you and Devin Moore," Dustin said.

"I need to go to Clarity Lake."

Dunaway and Flannery got the grand tour of the four lakes from the Dustins while I went to the fifth lake seeking answers. And what I found there was so monumental, it was astonishing that we'd missed it.

When I told the others, Dustin-three verified it in a Window. If we'd known it sooner, would it have changed anything, I wondered. Spencer, Yangchen and Linh needed to know immediately but we couldn't risk Outin by breaking our astral silence.

"Dunaway, I need to talk to the Dark Mystic."

"You think you can do it through me? Won't that risk Omnia picking up our energy?"

"Not if we do it through an Outview. If you and I both go back to that time, we might be able to talk to him."

"It doesn't sound like fun to me."

"It may not be," I said.

"Try to resist the urge to kill me."

"That won't be easy with you giving me fifty lashes," I replied.

"I'm hoping to avoid that this time."

ooooo

Instead of reaching the slave life with Dunaway, I wound up in a future time. The Dark Mystic smiled, looking the same. I, however, was a woman in her mid-forties with a young son, but I also had full memory. "I was trying to reach you with Dunaway."

"Yes, I know. He would have killed you," the Dark Mystic said. "Dunaway is too new to the world of non-violence and you thought going back into the lifetime that created his penchant for violence and revenge with the one who did it to him was a good idea?" He shook his head. "Apparently eleven years wasn't long enough."

"I wasn't thinking. Is he okay?" I asked.

"He isn't making it back to that life. He's in a different future right now, seeing a lifetime surrounded by loved ones, teaching all that he has learned. It's a good place."

"Nice to know there is a future like that."

"There is a future like just about anything you can imagine."

"You know why I'm here?"

"The mix-up?"

"Yes, how does that happen?"

"There are no accidents. Had you known in the beginning who he was, Dunaway would have killed him and then . . . well, you don't have the years it would take me to explain to you what would have happened."

"So now, what am I supposed to do?"

"Omnia is on the verge of victory. They are using overwhelming, unprecedented force. Therefore, we know their victory will not be lasting. Yet you must stop them because, as you know, time is a funny thing and a victory that doesn't last may still last ten thousand years."

"You aren't going to tell me how, are you?"

"I could only tell you what I would do, and that would not do any good, since you are not me. I can see into the future and tell you what you did, but that would not do any good, since in order to do that thing you must do it first." He nodded and I knew it was time to leave.

75

"Didn't make it back to the slave times." Dunaway said.

"Me neither, but I know what to do." I rounded up the Dustins and Flannery and told them we needed to get the news to the others so that a plan could be agreed upon. Not surprisingly, both Dustins decided to stay.

"Love you, man." Dustin said, hugging me.

"Every time we say goodbye, I wonder if I'll see you again."

He stood back, left his hands on my shoulders, stared at me for a minute. "Me too." He looked down for a moment and then back into my eyes. "This time feels worse."

I nodded.

He made a funny face and laughed, pushing me away. "I'll see you again and before again," he said.

ooooo

Linh ran to me as soon as we came through the portal. "It feels like a hundred years," she said, throwing her arms around me.

"You're not still mad?"

"Life's too short. And you've changed anyway."

"So have you."

"Yeah, hard roads."

"Hard to believe how hard," I said, as Spencer and

Yangchen caught up to us.

"Dunaway." Spencer nodded. "Decided to come over to the dark side?"

"Giving it a shot."

"Thank you," Yangchen said. "We need you."

"You have no idea how much," I said. "We've come from Outin. It's still safe. But I made a discovery in Clarity Lake that changes things."

Lee Duncan ran up. "Nate, you've got to get out of here!"

"Lee, what are you talking about?" Spencer asked.

"We've just received word that Omnia is nearing complete extermination of Nate."

"What does that mean?" Linh asked.

"Omnia has wiped out his past lives."

"That would take forever," Spencer said, "it can't be done."

"Actually, if they knock out the right few hundred," Yangchen said. "The odds of finding that exact formula is off the charts but . . ."

"They may not have it completely figured out, it may be part luck, they seem to be hitting every life he's had with multiple mystic encounters."

"Come on, Lee, you know we all encounter mystics in our lives, whether we know it or not," Spencer said.

"Sure, but I'm talking about mystics connected to this life."

"Look, Lee, what are you saying?"

"They have a way to track you. If you stay here any longer they'll find us all and finish off what's left of the Movement."

Hundreds of Movement members were there seeking refuge. They were the final hope of our cause could all be wiped out because of my presence. If I was a real leader, I could not stay.

"Even if he runs," Yangchen said, "if they complete the formula, they will erase Nate's entire lifetime even before it happens."

"There's a bigger problem," I said.

Everyone looked at me.

"Devin Moore, the leader of Omnia and Kevin Morrison,

the last name on the list of the entrusted nine . . . are the same person."

Spencer went white. Linh closed her eyes.

"How?" Yangchen gasped.

"Somewhere in the translation, a mix-up occurred. It's impossible to know if it was from the woman who gave Dustin the message or from Dustin to my dad or how my dad received it, maybe even before all of that. The point is that the message should have been the eight loyal names and then the betrayer, 'Devin Moore's the one' not 'Kevin Morr-i-son,' so –"

"So all of this has been about the Jadeo," Spencer finished.

"My god," Lee said, "That bastard has killed all those people, and . . . and ruined the world all to get his hands on –"

"This," I said, holding up the tiny jade-encrusted gold box.

"Open it," Yangchen said.

"No!" Spencer, Lee and even Linh yelled in unison.

"He'll know if you destroy it," Yangchen said. "We can end this."

"But it won't end," I said. "In his efforts to find the Jadeo, he has accumulated all the material powers of earth and a huge amount of soul powers. He won't give that up if the Jadeo is destroyed."

"We can't just take it all from him," Lee said.

"I think we can," I said. "I'm going to see him."

After much discussion, everyone agreed it might be our last hope. The final hours before my departure were spent -using our remaining resources and considerable powers to locate Devin Moore. The search quickly narrowed to Manhattan, but we needed specifics.

I fell into an Outview, or rather felt pushed into one. The sensation was new and I suspected it had something to do with the Dark Mystic. The Outview showed me a future in which I discussed this lifetime with a group of students. It was optimistic but provided chilling details about this life that I decided not to share with anyone.

Dunaway would be the only person going with me to meet Devin Moore. There were long debates about whether Lee and Spencer should also go, or if Linh, with her considerable powers, could help; but in the end those options were deemed too risky, and I won the argument. It would obviously be insane to take the Jadeo with me. Instead I found a place to hide it which I believed would ensure its protection in any event.

Linh and I walked alone in the woods while we were waiting word, and we stopped at a clearing where a million stars illustrated my feelings.

"The sky is dazzling here," she said.

"Have you ever astral-traveled to the stars?"

"No. Have you?"

"Yeah, it's pretty incredible. There are planets out there of such beauty it's almost too much to take . . . We should meet out there sometime."

"I'd like that," she said. "What about past lifetimes on other planets?"

"There are billions of earthlike planets within the Milky Way alone." I said. "We obviously don't just have lifetimes on earth."

"How many other planets have you been to?"

"Dozens that I can recall."

"All through Outviews?"

"Outviews and the astral."

"I wish everyone could see beyond this one lifetime . . . it's not even a blink."

"The Dark Mystic said there's a portal on earth that leads to a wormhole in space which allows you to physically visit millions of inhabited planets."

"Will he show it to you?"

"He doesn't know where it is."

"Then how does he know it exists?"

"He went through it once but it is constantly moving depending on the ripples of the multiverse. It took him almost twenty years to return to earth. What happened on the journey home is the reason he is more advanced than all the other mystics combined."

"What happened?"

"He's only told me a few things." I gently took Linh's hand. "There are places in space, like the lakes of Outin, only they are whole vast regions that depict every conceivable alternate reality. The Dark Mystic says 'Everything is real somewhere.' In those psychedelic areas of the universe he experimented with powers and within that solitude actually touched his soul."

"Wow."

"Once he made it back, he realized how limiting earth could be. That was maybe eighty years ago. He has searched for the Milky Way portal ever since."

"How?"

"Much of his time has been traveling through Outviews and other dimensions trying to coordinate and return to the exact place and time when he discovered it the first time. He also said there are portals leading to other galaxies."

"Portals on earth?"

"Yes. He believes there are hundreds, but he didn't say anything else about them."

"Isn't he powerful enough to travel anywhere on the astral?'

"Yes, but not physically . . . yet."

"You've changed."

"I was there eleven years. He took me beyond everything I knew. That's how I could finally get through to Dunaway."

"Will it be enough for you to beat Devin Moore?"

"Yes."

"And then what?"

"Rebuild the Movement."

"Do you really believe that ridding the world of Devin Moore will change anything?"

"Everything can change in an instant." A deer wandered on the edge of the clearing, nibbling leaves.

"Nate, I've seen it." She looked at me closely.

I understood that she understood. Linh meant the future. We both knew it was too soon to talk about it.

"Linh, if I succeed with Devin Moore, I'll admit the aftermath is going to be a very difficult time. I've seen it, too . . . The Movement will have to walk a tightrope," I said gazing off into the silhouetted trees.

"The Clastier papers must be published," she said.

I nodded. They were being prepared at that very moment. The Air-Projection would also happen the night after my meeting with Devin Moore. Carst and Omnia documents would be revealed to the world. If all went according to plan, we would avoid the mistake that we made when we revealed Lightyear's crimes. This time there would be no cover-up and the Movement would fill the void. Clastier's understanding of, and easy way of explaining, our connection to the universe and our souls would be key in educating the population.

I told Linh that the Old Man of the Lake once said, "Half the energy is moving toward awakening and the other half is moving toward GMO, fast food, TV and plastic." And then he asked the question we're all still unsure of, "Which half will win?"

I knew from the Dark Mystic that all sides of one's self, all the factions of the Movement, all the labels we've lived under, the identities of mankind - borders, religions, races, etc. - would have to melt into one before we could see real change. And that time had never been closer. The foundation of the old way was Omnia. If Dunaway and I could remove that foundation, then the remaining pillars would soon fall.

Spencer found us. "They're ready."

"What are our odds of success?" I asked.

"With Devin Moore? The odds are in your favor."

"And with the rest of it?"

"That will depend on how good the leadership of the Movement is in the days and weeks that follow."

Everyone knew that Dunaway and I might not make it back, but goodbyes had been too frequent and we were short on time, so we kept the farewells light and easy.

Still, I lingered with Linh as long as possible, whispered into her ear, then kissed her.

ooooo

Devin Moore dressed like a banker but looked like a leading man, ruggedly handsome, confident, steely-eyed. He stepped onto the sidewalk on Fifth Avenue. His chauffeur attentively opened the back door to his limousine. I Atomized into the back seat next to Moore while the chauffeur walked around and got in the front. Dunaway appeared and pushed the chauffeur across the seat, holding him down with Gogen.

"You're a dead man, Ryder," were Moore's first words, but a hint of fear in his face belied the bravado. He could feel me weakening his powers but his strength was greater than I'd anticipated.

"We don't need to duel," I said. "I have something you've been looking for."

"Where is it?"

Dunaway held up the replica I'd formed using Airgon and other techniques learned from Flannery and the Dark Mystic. Then Dunaway pushed a button and the screen closed between us and the driver.

"You're a fool." His jaw clenched. "Where are we going?"

"Just over to the park. I thought we could take a walk."

"Perfect."

Dunaway turned off Fifth Avenue onto East 68th, then took a left onto Madison Avenue.

"I never imagined you would actually bring it to me." A movie-star smile lit his face. "Our little surge has completely decimated your silly Movement, so it's a little late to surrender. Still, in exchange for the Jadeo, I might allow you to live . . . in prison, of course, but, maybe not Carst. We might be able to arrange a comfortable maximum security cell for you here in this dimension."

"Thank you for being so reasonable."

"I'm not an idiot, Ryder. You had something else in mind, didn't you? Amnesty for Linh? My agreement not to execute Spencer and Yangchen? You must know those are not easy things for me to grant. Oh, wait, you want even more. Safe passage for you and your friends to a distant dimension . . ."

"What are you going to do with the Jadeo?"

"Are you serious? I've spent the better part of a millennium and hundreds of lifetimes trying to wrestle it from you and the others in order to open it."

Dunaway turned left onto 79th Street; we'd be in the park in a few minutes.

"I assumed you weren't just going to stick it in a glass case. I mean once you open it . . ."

"I'll rule the world, Ryder. What did you think?"

"Don't you already rule the world?"

"You know it's not the same."

"I don't understand greed like yours. You have everything . . . *everything* and yet you want more."

"Of course you don't understand, Ryder. None of you do. It's one thing to have everything in the material world, but that was never my goal. It was a simple by-product of my quest to obtain the Jadeo . . . I want everything in the spiritual world and only one thing can give me that . . . the Jadeo."

Dunaway stopped the limousine in front of Belvedere Castle. The entire time we'd been talking, I'd been collecting

Airgon from him and now understood that the mix-up in names had not been our fault. Moore had used powers to conceal his identity from the eight loyal entrusted. Once the Movement formed, he had even more reason to hide. All his filters confused the information and messengers. Airgon also showed the extent of his powers. I had the advantage, but just barely.

Dunaway got out and ran toward the castle. Moore jerked around swinging a laser pistol. Before he could connect or fire, I Atomized out of the car and locked him in with Gogen, so he wouldn't think we wanted him to follow us. It didn't take him long to escape and as soon as he and the chauffeur were clear, I blew up the limo so he would think assassination had been my purpose all along.

He Skyclimbed behind us and flew into the portal with only one thing on his mind, getting the Jadeo, which was finally within his reach. In no time we were at Wizard Island and into another portal. Catching someone in a portal was nearly impossible. He'd have to wait until we were out. And that came fast as we emerged atop the dried lava of Kilauea. Everything hinged on the fact that he'd never been there before.

"Where are you going to run now?" he asked, conjuring a whirling, strangling wind around Dunaway. There was less than a minute before this duel would get out of hand. I used Airgon from Moore to infuse Solteer visions. Dunaway simultaneously weakened Moore's powers enough to slip from the spiral. Moore brought sheets of ice down, possibly to block what he expected might be our next move with the lava. Instead, I pushed all my energy into sending the Airgon-Solteer at him.

It worked. He Skyclimbed after what appeared to be Dunaway diving into a portal. Moore flew after in pursuit of the Jadeo and vanished.

"Are we safe?" the real Dunaway asked, coming out of the Timefold.

"That's a tough question to answer, isn't it?" I said. "But since Devin Moore, leader of Omnia, aka Kevin Morrison, betrayer of the nine entrusted just entered the portal-of-no-return, I'd say the Movement's prospects have improved considerably."

I'd used Airgon from when Dunaway had actually possessed the Jadeo to make the Solteer that fooled Moore into seeing the gold box he'd sought for centuries. Even if Moore hadn't been fanatically obsessed, he could not have discerned reality from the vision.

"We cut the head off the snake," Spencer said. With Moore gone, the force behind Omnia was limited to material power. The chaos that ensued within its ranks, muddled with egos, yes-men and conflicting agendas, played perfectly into the ready hands of the Movement.

The Air-Projection went flawlessly, the world could finally see just what Omnia had done, with their repressive systems, economic models, cycles of wars and horrific prisons. Their mystics saw the horrific errors they had made. Within days the Movement used our members inside the government, law enforcement and military to begin the long process of rooting out and arresting Omnia loyalists. Carst was liberated, but millions had perished and millions more would never recover mentally. Reform would take years. True change could happen in an instant, but in this case, an instant might be decades.

On the fourth day we received word of a counter-revolution. The military had fallen back into the hands of former Omnia allies, members of the wealthy elite who feared the Movement's radical proposals.

"This could get messy awfully fast," Spencer said. "They

still have mystics and worse, they have nuclear weapons."

"They won't use them," Linh said.

"Anything is possible."

"Our sources say they have a hit list. You, Linh, Yangchen, Dunaway, Lee, Dustin and me."

"I think we should split up for a few days until we can get this back under control."

"Is the Jadeo safe?" Spencer asked.

"Very." I patted my jacket over my heart.

ooooo

We made contingency plans, meeting places and contact codes. Omnia rolled tanks into many cities, at the same time shutting down Internet and electrical service in most areas.

"I want to go with you," Linh said at our farewell.

"You know that's not a good idea," I touched her face softly. "We already agreed that everyone separates. It won't be long."

"I don't care." Over the years she'd perfected the ability to hold back tears, but not now.

"It's going to be fine," I said.

"What does that even mean anymore?"

"I love you . . . that means everything to me."

"Me too." We embraced until our souls connected, both knowing unspoken things that the other knew.

As was typical, no one saw or heard the drone. And in spite of all precautions, physical and otherwise, the payload hit its target. There were six of us in the house; fortunately Linh and Spencer were thousands of miles away. The homes on either side were also blown apart, killing eight innocents, five of whom were children. It was an impossible thing to experience – the simultaneous roar of the missile hitting, then detonating, screams, glass shattering, wood shredding, bricks and debris flying, the blinding flash, my ripped and shrieking face, sudden darkness – all in a prolonged, never-ending instant . . . and then there was my dad, glowing in the golden light.

"This time it's time, isn't it?" I asked.

He nodded, somber, but then smiled broadly, like he used to when I did something to make him proud. "You did well."

Epilogue

"My name is Linh, I'm nineteen years old, although I could be older . . . time's a funny thing." I said, speaking to the assembled group of mystics and passionate seekers.

"By now, you know the story of Nathan Ryder and what he sacrificed for the Movement, what he gave to us." I self-consciously pushed my long dark hair from my face. "Nate knew he was going to die that day and with all his powers, he knew it couldn't be avoided. His knowledge had reached the point where he could do more for our cause on the other side of the veil."

Booker, standing in the back, looked up from his texting and nodded. Those first moments after feeling Nate's change, when I begged death to take me too, Rose reached across the astral and insisted I wait. Within hours, Booker arrived, scooped me up, and we flew to Cervantes. Yangchen and Rose were there ready to . . . save me. I too had known Nate would die, but thought I'd learned enough and seen too much that death didn't matter. Reality had other ideas; the loss even now is unbearable.

Those women showed me much on Cervantes, but until I heard Wandus in the waves I didn't fully comprehend what had happened. "Nate led the Movement through the revolution," the ethereal voice said in that wonderful Indian accent. "He fulfilled his destiny and now he will help you fulfill yours."

Someone in the audience cleared his throat and brought me back to the present. "Many of you have heard the legend of the Jadeo and are asking if it was real." I looked into the front row at Spencer and Yangchen; she smiled radiantly, but Spencer's health had not been good, and we didn't expect him to live much longer. "That such a thing could exist was mindboggling, but it was very real. I remember when Nate first showed me the little gold box and we didn't know what it was. We tried to open it, obviously unaware of what was inside."

I sipped from a glass of water. Nate had been dead for three months and I still got shaky talking about him. "When I later learned that the Jadeo contained the last breath of the last shaman who possessed every soul-power and full knowledge of his soul, I didn't understand that through Airgon, it could be passed to whoever inhaled that breath. Once I understood that, I was left with fear *and* hope for the future. If the right person took that breath, he or she could teach the rest of us how to return, and instead of it taking millennia, we might do it in a generation – that was Nate's hope. But if the wrong person got hold of it . . . well, Nate made sure that didn't happen. The Jadeo ended the day Nate died. But we have it within us to make the changes needed to bring our world from dystopian to utopian." I looked up and saw Rose beaming; she had helped me every day since Nate's death. I'd also worked a lot with Clastier, but it wasn't the same as being with Nate.

I'd been voted leader of the Movement a month earlier and needed to update everyone on our efforts at reforms. Nothing would be the same; plans to end poverty, hunger, disease, hate and fear were well underway. Obtaining power from fossil fuels was banned, even wind and solar were only going to be transitional as Lusans would provide all we needed for free. I was in the middle of explaining the complete removal of the old financial system when Spencer interrupted me on the astral.

"I know who Helen Hartman is," he said. Spencer had been devastated by Nate's death, not because of the loss of his friend – he knew he'd see him again – but because of the loss of the Jadeo, so I wasn't surprised he brought up the only name on the list of the nine that had never been identified.

"I'm sure you do," I said. Dunaway was also in the audience. I looked over to see if he was listening in, but he seemed to be only hearing my talk on dismantling the current healthcare system.

"You, my dear Linh, are Helen Hartman."

"When did you figure it out?" I asked, falling for his trick and confirming what, until then, had only been his suspicion.

"The question, Linh, is how long have *you* known?"

"I discovered Helen and I shared a soul through the

Outviews that Nate and I had about Nares and Bola. But the Movement could never find her because years ago, she fought against Omnia's corruption, changed her name and went into hiding. Eventually they found and murdered her."

"So you, Linh, as the leader of the Movement, are the one who sent Nares from the past to fight Omnia in the future?"

"Yes."

"But why couldn't you tell us?" He coughed.

"Because to reveal the future at that point would have prevented it and the Movement would have lost."

"I understand," Spencer said. "There were millions of courses the future could have taken and only one which allowed the Movement to defeat Omnia."

"Yes," I said to Spencer, and at the same time, I explained to the gathering how borders had been eliminated. "The battles we've won are still being waged . . . the past is never completed."

"You know I am dying," he said. "And Lee was killed the morning after Nate, so that leaves you as the final survivor of the nine entrusted."

"Yes," I agreed, knowing where he was going.

"The Jadeo survived, didn't it?"

I looked toward Dunaway again, as the only living member of our generation's seven. He should have led the Movement but stepped aside and nominated me instead. I was sure Nate had told him who I was, but he never wanted to talk about it. Dunaway and I were planning a trip to the Taos Mountain portal, after the gathering, to seek our own eleven years with the Dark Mystic.

I stared directly into Spencer's eyes and let him see the answer to his question, then concluded my speech with a quote from Nate, "Everyone exists only in your imagination. And you exist only in theirs. Therefore, you are all other people whom you encounter, and they are you. Does that knowledge change how you think, feel and act toward others? It should . . . it should change everything."

END OF BOOK THREE

A Note from the Author

Thank you so much for reading my book!

Please help - If you enjoyed it, please consider leaving a quick review (even a few words) on Amazon.com. Reviews are the greatest way to help an author. And, please tell your friends!

I'd love to hear from you – Questions, comments, whatever. Email me through my website (www.BrandtLegg.com) I'll definitely respond (within a few days).

Join my Inner Circle - If you want to be the first to hear about my new releases, advance reads, occasional news and more, please join my Inner Circle at BrandtLegg.com

About the Author

Brandt Legg is a former child prodigy who turned a hobby into a multi-million dollar empire. At eight, Legg's father died suddenly, plunging his family into poverty. Two years later, while suffering from crippling migraines, he started in business. National media dubbed him the "Teen Tycoon," but by the time he reached his twenties, the high-flying Legg became ensnarled in the financial whirlwind of the junk bond eighties, lost his entire fortune... and ended up serving time in federal prison for financial improprieties. Legg emerged, chastened and wiser, one year later and began anew in retail and real estate. In the more than two decades since, his life adventures have led him through magazine publishing, a newspaper column, photography, FM radio, CD production and concert promotion. His books have excited hundreds of thousands of readers around the world (see below for a list of titles available). For more information, or to contact him, please visit his BrandtLegg.com He loves to hear from readers and always responds!

Books by Brandt Legg

Outview
Outin
Outmove
The complete Inner Movement trilogy

Cosega Search
Cosega Storm
Cosega Shift
The complete Cosega Sequence

The Last Librarian
The Lost TreeRunner
The List Keepers
The complete Justar Journal

Acknowledgements

Writing the Inner Movement trilogy has been a dream-come-true. Hearing from so many readers goes beyond my dreams – Thank you. And to those who read prior to publication; Roanne Legg, Barbara Blair, Harriet Greene and Marty Goldman, I appreciate the edits, corrections and "working under deadline," especially Bonnie Brown Koeln and Kate Black. Thanks to Mike Sager for believing. And finally to Teakki, who patiently waited, sometimes singing Go Speed Racer, Go, until I finished writing each day.

Glossary

92426 – Name of Nate's original dimension, where he grew up.

Air-Projection – A method to project a "video" image of soul memory into the sky.

Air-swirl – A concentrated spiraling burst of air – part of the Gogen.

Airgon – By reading an air molecule that has absorbed traces of the surrounding energy, it is possible to view all of earth's history.

Astral – A non-physical plane where spiritual travel and communication is possible.

Atomizing – a combination of manipulations of space with Gogen, and energy with Vising, that causes a person or object to dematerialize and rematerialize.

Beyond-Memory – Awareness of all lifetimes, past, current and future.

Breatharian – A person who survives only on air (no food or water).

Calyndra – A portal, which can transport you to any specific time and place in the past.

Carst – Hellish dimension of torture, suffering and agonizing death.

Clarity Lake – The fifth lake of Outin – swimming causes one to see revelations and receive understanding.

Clastier Papers – The written philosophy and ideas of Clastier (a prior incarnation of Nathan Ryder).

Dimensional-blend – The dangerous result of piercing dimensions.

Dreams Lake – Smallest of the four lakes of Outin (but still quite large). A sea of bubbles. It shows our dreams and fantasies.

Entrusted Nine – The nine original people who swore an oath to protect the Jadeo for all time.

Fifth Lake of Outin – Clarity Lake is tiny but very deep.

Swimming causes one to see revelations and receive understanding.

Five great soul powers - All the soul powers fit into one of the following five classifications:

1.*Gogen* — (many forms) used in manipulating space and moving objects.

2.*Foush* – for enhancing the senses, including Skyclimbing and Lusans (healing light orb).

3.*Solteer* — controls consciousness, such as putting people to sleep and making them see things.

4.*Timbal* — deals with time, Outviews and prophecy.

5.*Vising* — to transform energy and read people.

Floral Lake - One of the four lakes of Outin. This huge lake got its name because the surface is covered with millions of wildflowers. Its waters provide nourishment and healing.

Four Lakes of Outin - Dreams, Floral, Rainbow, Star Falls.

Foush - One of the five great soul powers for enhancing the senses, including Skyclimbing and Lusans (healing light orb).

Full-Forward Memory - Aware of all lifetimes up to current times.

Gogen - One of the five great soul powers, its many forms are used in manipulating space and moving objects.

Guide-write - Transcribing messages from spiritual guides.

Heat warning - The rapid and severe rise in body temperature when danger is near.

IF - Inner Force. A faction of the Inner Movement whose members believe in using any means necessary to defeat enemies of the Movement.

IM - The Inner Movement. A worldwide movement of people seeking to create a world in which all beings live in harmony with each other and work together to return to their souls.

Inner Force (IF) – A faction of the Inner Movement whose members believe in using any means necessary to defeat enemies of the Movement.

Inner Movement (IM) – A worldwide movement of people seeking to create a world in which all beings live in harmony with each other and work together to return to their souls.

Jadeo – A jade encrusted, gold sacred box. Its importance is immeasurable. The original nine entrusted swore an oath to protect it for all time.

Kellaring – A form of Vising, used to block and conceal remote viewers.

Lightyear – A clandestine government agency within the CIA who use psychic and soul powers.

Lusan – Healing, light orb.

Mystics – Enlighten, highly evolved individuals who teach Nate.

Nine Entrusted – The nine original people who swore an oath to protect the Jadeo for all time.

Omnia – An old and powerful group who for several centuries has begun wars, controlled the money supply and been puppet master to political leaders.

One of the seven – Each generation seven people are born who have an open channel to the universe and all the powers it contains in order to help bring about the great awakening.

Outin – A dimension usually entered from Mount Shasta.

Outmove – A bold act of faith, when one trusts the universe, no matter the situation, and proceeds from their soul rather than the personality.

Outview – A vision into other incarnations.

Parallels – The confusing colliding, coexisting half-dimensions all around us.

Pasius – Parallel more advanced dimension where they study soul powers and portals.

Portal – An opening to another time or dimension.

Portal-to-anywhere – A portal that will take you to any one place you choose.

Portal-to-everywhere – A portal that will take you wherever you wish to go.

Portal-to-nowhere – A self enclosed portal which returns you back from where you started.

Rainbow Lake – One of the four lakes of Outin. Its brightly colored waters offer a glimpse of the ever-changing future.

Shapeshifting – The ability to transform physical objects, including people into something different.

Skyclimbing – The ability to run through the sky.

Skywaves – A term used to describe the Outin sky.

Slice – A created dimension.

Solteer – One of the five great soul powers. It controls consciousness, such as putting people to sleep and making them see things.

Soul powers – See Five great soul powers.

Soul storms – Like extreme headaches, Soul storms are the result of exposure to too many Outviews, dimensions and times. Confusion and memory loss result.

Star Falls Lake – One of the four lakes of Outin. The beautiful lake shows us our terrors and fears.

Timbal – One of the five great soul powers. It deals with time, Outviews and prophecy.

Time-View-Cover (TVC) – Allows a person to conceal a space that they could travel in (similar to a Timefold in that it made the initiator invisible, but it was much more stable and long lasting).

Timefold – By adjusting time, relative to the dimension you're in, you can become invisible for short periods.

Timefreeze – A variation of a Timefold, it can temporarily stop time.

Time-seam – A portal created near a vortex that allows a move through short distances of time.

TVC – Allows a person to conceal a space that they could travel in (similar to a Timefold in that it made the initiator invisible, but it was much more stable and long lasting).

Verde Portal – to forests around the world.

Vines, the – A section of Outin where Windows are hidden.

Vising – One of the five great soul powers. Used to

transform energy and read people.

Vortex – Spots where the concentrated energy from the planet and the universe are extremely present, which aids in healing, transformation, awareness, great and positive things.

Walkin – A soul occupying another person's body.

Windows – Moveable portholes (only known to exist at Outin) that allow the viewer to see into other dimensions and times.

Wizard Island Portal – A major crossroads of portals from which many other portals can be reached.

Wormhole – A shortcut through space (and time).